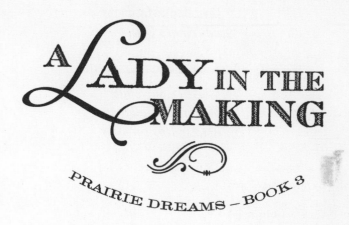

# A Lady IN THE MAKING

## PRAIRIE DREAMS – BOOK 3

# SUSAN PAGE DAVIS

BARBOUR
PUBLISHING

Other books by
## Susan Page Davis

### Prairie Dreams

*The Lady's Maid*
*Lady Anne's Quest*

### The Ladies' Shooting Club

*The Sheriff's Surrender*
*The Gunsmith's Gallantry*
*The Blacksmith's Bravery*

Print ISBN 978-1-61626-441-3

eBook Editions:
Adobe Digital Edition (.epub) 978-1-62029-040-8
Kindle and MobiPocket Edition (.prc) 978-1-62029-041-5

Cover design: Müllerhaus Publishing Arts, Inc., www.Mullerhaus.net

Published by Barbour Publishing, Inc., P.O. Box 719, Uhrichsville, Ohio 44683, www.barbourbooks.com

*Our mission is to publish and distribute inspirational products offering exceptional value and biblical encouragement to the masses.*

 Member of the
Evangelical Christian
Publishers Association

Printed in the United States of America.

# CHAPTER 1

## 1857 The Dalles, Oregon Territory

**Y**ou lied to me, Sam." Millie Evans peeked out the window from behind the half yard of muslin that served as a curtain. Outside the shanty they rented behind the feed store, a tall man with thick, dark hair and a week's growth of beard stood smoking a cigarette.

Millie turned back toward Sam and glared at him. "You said you were looking for a job, but you went and found that despicable man and brought him back here."

"I was looking for a job," Sam sputtered. "But I couldn't find one, and then Lucky turned up."

"Oh, sure he did. Like a bad penny. I suppose you just happened to be in the saloon when he dropped out of the sky."

Sam cringed, and she shook her head in disgust. "I came to The Dalles because you told me we could make an honest living together. Big laugh that turned out to be. And now you've brought *him* here. I told you before, I will *not* go live with a pack of outlaws."

She stalked to the wall and pulled her apron, extra dress, and shawl down from where they hung on nails and threw them on her bed. She stooped and felt underneath the end of the bed frame for the handle of her worn valise. Listening to her half-brother was the biggest mistake she'd ever made.

"Aw, come on, Millie. I just want to make things better."

"Better?" She pulled out the traveling bag and plunked it on the bed. "How is going into crime better?"

"You can have better things. You know. Clothes and—and jewelry, maybe. Lip rouge, stuff like that. It'd be better than scraping by like we are now."

3

"Is that what you thought when you went with Lucky last year?"

"Well, no."

"Exactly. But then two months ago, you wrote to me and said you were leaving the gang and you were ready to settle down in a nice little house somewhere with me."

Sam hung his head, and his face colored. "I'm sorry, Millie." Neither of them had to speak of the money he'd earmarked to buy that little house. He'd lost it all gambling by the time Millie had traveled up here from Elkton. A woman who'd lived thirty years and more ought to know better than to trust a gambling man, even if he was kin.

"We got by," she said. "Between my baking and laundry, we've been eating."

"But I don't want you to have to work so hard, Mil. I know I haven't helped much." That was an understatement. Sam's contributions to their funds had consisted of money he'd pilfered or won at cards. She suspected he only got the latter by cheating.

"If you want to go back to the gang, go ahead, Sam. I'm not going with you, and that's final."

"But—"

"No." Millie folded her best dress. She'd stolen it from a proper lady's luggage more than a year ago, and it was getting threadbare now, but she still loved it. She placed it in the valise and added the apron, her extra stockings, and her few cosmetics. Last of all she put in a brown, leather-bound book and a small wooden box. She walked to the shelf near the stove. "I'll leave you ten dollars. I'll need the rest."

"Where are you going?" Sam's plaintive expression almost made her relent. Though he was past thirty, his boyish face and memories of their knockabout childhood together kept her from despising him. But she'd had enough.

"I haven't decided yet." She opened the coffee tin she kept money in, peeled off the amount she was leaving him, and shoved the rest into her pocket. She'd been saving every penny she could, and had hoped that soon they could move to a real house, even though they'd have to rent one and not own it as they'd planned.

4

Good thing she'd saved most of what she had left when she got here, and hidden it where Sam wouldn't likely look.

"I'll send Lucky away," Sam said.

"For good?" Millie went to the window and pushed back the edge of the curtain with one finger. Lucky still stood there. He tossed his cigarette butt to the ground and crushed it with the heel of his scuffed boot.

"Well, I don't—see, I—Lucky needs me, Mil."

She dropped the curtain and placed her hands on her hips. "He needs you? Oh, that's rich." She'd known the man slightly when her husband was alive. Lucky was bad news then, and she had no doubt he'd grown worse over time.

"No, he does. See, one of his men died, and another's hurt."

"Ha. Killed during a robbery, no doubt."

Sam ignored that. "He really needs me, and he says I'm a good man and he wants me to come back. And if you'd come and help us out—"

"What, nursing wounded thieves and cooking for them? No, thank you." She went to the dish cupboard and scanned the contents. She couldn't take all of their meager belongings. She chose her best paring and chopping knives and an enameled tin cup. She tucked them into her valise and closed it.

She put on her shawl and best bonnet.

"Good-bye, Sam. I'm sorry it turned out this way. Be careful."

"No, wait!"

He followed her out the door.

Millie didn't so much as glance Lucky's way. She strode across the yard between their hovel and the feed store, aiming for the back door of the store. Better to go where other people would see her.

Sam trotted up behind her. "Millie, please."

"Go back, Sam."

He grabbed her elbow and spun her around. "What's happened to you? You're different than you used to be. Did you get soft, Mil?"

"I wouldn't call it that. But I *have* been thinking about right and wrong."

Sam lifted his battered felt hat, scratched his head, and settled the hat again. "We didn't used to think about that much. Just about what we'd eat next."

"Well, those days are over. For me, anyway. Now I know there are things we shouldn't do—things I *won't* do ever again. And stealing is one of them."

"You can just cook if you want to. We wouldn't make you steal. It's too bad though—you were good at it."

"That's enough." She glanced quickly about to be sure no one else was near enough to hear. At the feed store's back door, she left him and entered the shadowy building. Not for the first time, she felt somewhat relieved at leaving her half-brother behind. She cared about him, yet Sam didn't seem to want to change. He didn't like to work, and he seemed to prefer living on the shady side of the law. Well, she'd walked away from that once, and she liked the glimpses she'd had of a better life.

Sacks of feed and fertilizer were stacked to the ceiling in the dimly lit feed store. She wound her way toward the front, where light shone in through two dusty windows.

The store owner nodded at her. "Miz Evans."

Millie paused. "My brother and I will be giving up the rooms out back. I believe our rent is paid through the end of the month."

"What? Oh. Well, I'm sorry to see you go."

She said no more but hurried out and turned toward the stagecoach station. There should have been a stage leaving town that afternoon. She didn't really care what direction it was pointed, though she didn't want to go back to Elkton. The traffic to the gold mines had slowed to a trickle along that route. Trade was so slim her boss at the old restaurant had closed up shop and retired. There wouldn't be a job for her there.

When she reached the stage office, the coach was nowhere to be seen. She went inside and walked to the ticket counter.

"Where to, ma'am?" the clerk asked.

"Where can I go for less than eighty dollars?"

The clerk laughed and quickly sobered. "Well, let's see now." He

6

consulted a book on the counter before him. "Boise, Salt Lake...you might connect from there for someplace farther east, but there's no direct line, ma'am. If you want to go west, you could get to Portland, Vancouver, Oregon City, Eugene—"

"There's a stage going out soon, isn't there?"

"Yes ma'am. They're around back, switching the team. They'll leave in"—he pulled out his pocket watch as he spoke and opened it—"ten minutes."

"East or west?"

"Eastbound."

The door opened, and Sam came in, panting. "Come on, Millie." He walked over to the counter and tugged at the handle of her satchel.

"I am not going with you." She glared at her brother. At least he hadn't brought Lucky inside, but the outlaw was probably lounging outside by the hitching rail.

"So, are you going to buy a ticket?" the man behind the counter asked.

Millie glanced at him. "Please excuse me a moment." She grabbed her brother's sleeve and pulled him aside. "I'm serious about this, Sam."

"But you said you'd stay with me."

"That was when you said it would be just the two of us—like in the old days, when we were at Mr. Stone's farm in Eugene."

A man wearing a woolen suit came in and walked to the counter. Millie edged Sam farther away from them.

"Mr. Stone is gone now, Millie," Sam said. "And I tried to get a job. You know that."

She tossed her head. "You didn't try very hard." Lowering her voice, she added, "And running with a gang of road agents is *not* a job."

His face fell. "Aw, come on. You didn't used to mind lifting things here and there. You had a real knack for it. You didn't do so bad convincing fellas to give you money either."

She pulled back and glared at him. "What are you implying?"

"Nothin'. I'm just saying, you worked for that Andrew fella, and you got chummy with Mr. Stone—"

"David Stone never gave me a cent." She clenched her teeth and pushed back the memory of picking up ten dollars off the gentleman's dresser. "Andrew Willis, on the other hand, was my employer. I cooked in his restaurant, and he paid me a fair wage."

"A pretty good wage, if you ask me."

"I *didn't* ask you. But good cooks are at a premium out here." Although that hadn't helped much in this town. She baked bread for a restaurant and a boardinghouse and sold a few pies to the officers at Fort Dalles, but she knew she could do better in a bigger town.

"Well, if you come cook for us, we'll pay you. Lucky says so."

"With what? Your loot?" She glanced toward the ticket window. The man now purchasing a ticket was watching them with apparent interest. She set down her valise, seized Sam's sleeve, and hauled him outside and down into the dusty street. Lucky stood several yards away, near their horses. She turned her back to him. "Sam Hastings, you listen to me. I don't want to live on the wrong side of the law." She didn't say *again*, but she didn't have to.

"Might be in your best interest to come along with us, Miz Evans," Lucky drawled.

Millie whirled and found him not two feet behind her. He moved quietly for a rugged man. He stood with his thumbs tucked into his gun belt, watching her with a self-satisfied smirk, as though he knew her type and how phony she was. Well, she wouldn't give him the satisfaction of having her cook so much as a cup of coffee for him.

"I'm not interested."

"Sam and I have an extra horse for you to ride. He's tied up yonder with our nags." Lucky pointed down the street with his bearded chin.

Millie looked and saw the horses tied up in front of a saloon. So he'd come expecting to take her along. He and Sam must have planned it all out this afternoon while they shared a bottle of whiskey.

"Just come on along with us nice like, and take a look at our place. You can maybe fix supper tonight."

8

"And if you don't want to stay, I'll bring you back to town in the morning," Sam said.

"After breakfast," Lucky added.

"Yeah. After breakfast." Sam grinned at her.

"No thank you." Millie gathered handfuls of her skirt and prepared to mount the steps to the stagecoach station and buy her ticket. The agent had said she could afford one to Salt Lake and go east from there. That's what she'd do. Her cousin Polly lived at Fort Laramie. She had married a preacher. Maybe Polly and her respectable husband could help her find honest employment. And she'd put as much ground as she could between herself and Sam's outlaw cronies.

Strong fingers clamped around her upper arm. "I said it's in your best interest to go with us." Lucky's cold tone sent a jolt of fear through Millie.

She turned around swiftly, swinging her other arm as she whirled. She struck him hard on his fuzzy cheek and lunged away from him, stumbling over the bottom step.

"You little—"

"Hey!" A stern-faced man strode up the street from the direction opposite the saloon. "What's going on here?"

Millie righted herself, wincing at the pang in her ankle where it had connected with the step. "It's all right. I was just going in to buy my ticket, and I fell."

Lucky's eyes narrowed. Sam stood a couple of steps behind him, staring, his lower lip trembling.

"Are you sure you're all right, ma'am?" the newcomer asked.

"Yes, thank you." She gave him a delicate smile. He wore work clothes, and he was youthful and big enough to give Lucky pause. A farmer, most likely. "I bumped my ankle when I stumbled. Would you mind, sir, if I took your arm while I get up these steps?"

"My pleasure, ma'am." The young man crooked his elbow, and she placed her hand in the bend, leaning on him just a little as they maneuvered the steps. She didn't look back.

As soon as they were inside and the door closed, she turned to him and whispered, "I cannot thank you enough. You must be careful when you leave here, lest those thugs lurk about to harm you."

His eyebrows shot up, and he pulled off his hat. "Indeed. Then they *were* ill-treating you. I thought so at first, but you were so cool, I'd changed my mind."

"That big fellow is one to watch," she said.

The customer who had come in to buy a ticket earlier turned away from the counter, tucking his wallet away. He touched his hat brim as he passed them and went out.

"Well, now," the clerk said. "Made up your mind, have you?"

"Yes." Millie stepped up to his station. "I'd like a ticket to Salt Lake, please, unless you can get me through to Fort Laramie."

"Can't do that, ma'am, but I hear the Mormons are setting up for a mail route from Independence to Salt Lake. Most likely they'll take you through in one of their wagons." He named the price to Salt Lake City. Millie winced but took out her purse.

"They lowered the prices this week," the clerk said, as if hoping to console her. "Trying to break the competition."

She gulped, thinking of the few dollars left in her purse after she'd paid out the price of the ticket. If not for the reduction in fares, she couldn't have bought passage to Salt Lake, and she wasn't sure she could afford to get to Cousin Polly's home. She hated the thought of getting stranded along the way.

"Ma'am," said the young man who had rescued her, "it would be my pleasure to buy you dinner at the boardinghouse down the street. And to bring you back here to make sure you board safely."

Millie smiled at him. "Thank you so much, but there's not time, I'm afraid."

"That's right," the clerk said. "Stage is comin' around now." He nodded toward the window. Millie turned and saw the coach, with the driver and shotgun messenger perched high on the box, pulling up outside.

"Then I must board right away." She hoped the young man would stay close. With him, the driver, and the shotgun rider handy, she ought to be able to get into the stagecoach without interference from Sam and Lucky.

The young man flushed and looked down with a sad smile playing at his lips. "Then it's my loss. I do wish you a good trip."

"Thank you." Millie judged him to be six or eight years her junior—perhaps four and twenty. Just the age when young men tend to think older women are intriguing. Especially attractive older women, and Millie would never be so self-deprecating as to think she didn't fit the bill.

The clerk cleared his throat. "Your ticket, ma'am."

"Oh yes. Thank you so much." Millie put the bit of pasteboard into her purse. "May I leave my valise here?"

"You may. I'll see that it's loaded."

She retrieved it from the corner, where she'd left it to converse with Sam fifteen minutes earlier, and passed it to the clerk.

"Best get aboard," he said. "The driver won't wait."

The young man smiled down at her and again offered his arm. "Let me see you off, ma'am." He didn't ask her name, and Millie didn't give it. She'd be just as glad not to have her name associated with the two rather scruffy men watching from a few yards away. The clerk followed her out and passed her valise up to the shotgun rider on top of the coach. Her gallant young escort stepped up and opened the door for her. She threw a sidelong glance toward her brother. Sam and Lucky stood near their horses, watching them, but didn't approach.

David Stone leaned back against the leather seat and closed his eyes. Not for the first time, he wished he'd ridden horseback instead of taking the stagecoach. But he couldn't take a horse with him on the ship to England, so it was no doubt better to have left it behind. The fact that he owned a small stagecoach line in western Oregon didn't make this journey any less tedious.

The Stone line that he'd run for the last year had two coaches more comfortable than this one. David rode them himself at least once a month, when he went to see his niece, Anne, and her husband, Dan. Daniel Adams was his partner in the business, and he'd proven himself an apt driver and a good businessman. If only David could ride his own line all the way East.

The one bad thing about the Stone line was its length, or lack of it. The route only ran from Eugene to Corvallis, though he and Dan had discussed pushing it through to Oregon City and Portland in the near future. But it hadn't happened yet, so he had to sample other stage lines on his journey. He anticipated several weeks of this tiring travel. Why hadn't he just boarded a ship in Newport? While the thought of rounding the Horn didn't scare him, his niece, Anne, had pleaded with him not to risk it.

"They need you in one piece in England," were her exact words. Well, the way they'd rattled over the road toward The Dalles, he might not get out of Oregon intact.

The stage had dropped into a rut as they approached the town, throwing him against the side wall. The wound he'd received eighteen months ago still ached sometimes when he was tired or racketed around the way he was now, and the jolting sent a deep pain through him. As they waited for the new team to be hitched properly, he rubbed his right shoulder. He quit when the man opposite took notice.

The stop near Fort Dalles would be brief. At least they'd gotten a passable dinner earlier, at the home station. The tenders at the swing station changed the teams swiftly, and the driver soon guided the coach around to the front of the building. David sighed as the door opened to admit another passenger.

"Watch your step, ma'am," said a young man outside.

David turned his head to peer at the new arrival. Sure enough, a woman placed a dainty foot on the coach step. The rancher sitting beside David scooted across to the seat on the opposite side, where a tool salesman was sitting. Great. Now David would have to share a seat with the woman, and he'd have to put up with a big hat, skirts, and no doubt a parasol and a bundle or two.

She paused in the doorway, took stock of the situation, and eased onto the seat next to him. David nodded without making eye contact. Oh well—the other men would have to watch their language and refrain from smoking, but that wouldn't bother him any.

"Good day," she said pleasantly.

He stared at her. The broad brim of her hat shaded her face, but the voice. . .

The two men opposite murmured a greeting. She settled back in her seat and turned to look at him. The smile on her lips froze.

She blinked at him and narrowed her gaze. "Why—Mr. Stone?"

David gulped and stared into the beguiling green eyes of Charlotte Evans—the woman who had tried a mere eighteen months past to cheat him out of his fortune.

# CHAPTER 2

Millie sat rigid on the seat for the first hour, trying not to let any part of her person or her clothing touch the elegant Englishman beside her. With two other passengers in the small enclosure of the stagecoach, they could hardly discuss their last meeting or their mutual acquaintances. David Stone seemed just as indisposed to converse as she was. He'd developed a deep interest, it seemed, in the scenery they flew past as the stagecoach rolled eastward along the Columbia River.

She couldn't maintain that posture forever, especially in a vehicle that lurched and swayed in a manner that made her stomach roil. Her gloved hands, clenched in her lap, at last relaxed, and she allowed her aching back to curve a bit against the seat back. She longed to remove her large hat, but there was no place to lay it, and her valise had disappeared into the boot at the back of the coach. She cursed her own vanity. Why hadn't she worn her plain calico bonnet and not this fancy hat? She'd bought it last year, with money ill-gotten when she betrayed the man beside her. Just thinking about it made her ill.

They must be halfway to the next stop. As soon as they arrived, she would speak to Mr. Stone in private. She must make him understand that she had changed.

The two men across from her watched her, the one dressed as a farmer surreptitiously, and the businesslike one with open admiration. Millie concentrated on keeping her expression neutral. A lady mustn't betray her inner thoughts any more than she should reveal her inner layers of clothing. She avoided looking at either of them, and in consequence her gaze collided once with David Stone's.

That flicker of a moment—coupled with the brief appraisal she'd made on entering the coach—told her that he was as handsome as ever. The tall, blond man was about forty, very fit and good-looking. She knew from experience how charming he could be. But now his blue eyes held a clear dislike bordering on contempt. She looked away and shivered.

If only she'd changed her ways before they met—what might have happened then? But at that time, she'd been godless and without scruples. The way things had gone, she doubted she could ever regain his respect and admiration. But she might be able to partially right the wrong she had done him.

By the time they'd crossed the John Day River at McDonald's Ferry and reached the station on the other side, she feared her spine was jostled beyond repair and she might not be able to climb down from the coach.

"Twenty-minute stop to change the teams," the station agent announced as he opened the door. "The necessary is out back."

The men hung back, waiting for her to disembark, so Millie pushed herself forward off the seat. Her lower back muscles screamed as she emerged through the doorway and groped for the step. The agent offered his hand to assist her, and Millie clutched it.

"Thank you," she gasped as she reached terra firma and inhaled as deeply as her corset would allow.

She made the requisite trip "out back" and returned to the yard, grateful that the men had waited there until she was finished. The driver was applying grease to the wheel bearings while the tenders swapped the team for four fresh horses. The shotgun rider stood by, chatting with the station agent.

Millie approached them with a smile, and they immediately broke off their conversation. The shotgun rider whipped off his hat, and both men returned her smile. Once again, Millie had proven to herself that if a woman acted self-assured and at ease, other people would respond in like manner. At least, decent men did.

"Help you, ma'am?" the station agent asked.

"Yes, thank you. I wondered if there's a way for me to send a message ahead to Fort Laramie and have it get there before I do."

"Not much goes faster'n this stage, ma'am," the agent said.

The shotgun messenger frowned. "Well now, Billy, that ain't the strictest truth. You know, if she was to hit it just right, she might get a military messenger to carry a letter for her."

"I s'pose that's true." His companion nodded. "Sometimes the army will send dispatches and such, and they travel pretty fast. Could be someone will pass you heading out from Fort Dalles or one of the other posts along the way. Might beat the mail coach. Not by much though."

"Oh. Is this a mail coach?" Millie asked.

"No ma'am. This line doesn't have the contract for that." The station agent's face was so sour she feared she'd touched on a sore spot. His competitor must have reeled in the lucrative contract.

Her hopes to inform Polly of her impending arrival dashed, Millie broached her next question.

"Would it be possible for me to retrieve something from my valise?" she asked the shotgun rider.

"Surely, ma'am."

He had her bag down in an instant, and Millie quickly removed the small items she wanted. She thanked the man and stepped away.

She hoped for a word with Mr. Stone before she boarded, and so she waited a few yards away from the coach, watching the men complete their work.

She'd written to Polly last fall, when the restaurant in Elkton closed, about the possibility of visiting her. But once she'd decided to stop at The Dalles with Sam, she'd sent a note saying she guessed she would postpone the trip. She hadn't wanted to cut off the option, but she'd really hoped things would work out with Sam this time. What had she been thinking?

To her relief, David Stone soon appeared around the corner of the building, and she stepped briskly toward him.

He glanced about as though hoping to spot an avenue of escape, then stopped and waited for her to reach him.

"Mrs. Evans."

"Mr. Stone. I wondered if I could have a private word with you, sir."

"I see no need for it."

"Oh, but I do. Great need."

"I've nothing to say to you, Charlotte." He blinked and looked away.

She realized he'd slipped, not intending to use her given name. She'd be flattered that he remembered it, except that was the assumed name she'd used when she tried to lure him into a hasty marriage. His cheeks colored, and she looked down at her hands.

"It's Millie actually."

"Indeed." He strode past her and opened the door to the coach.

His accent still thrilled her, though she understood he'd been in America more than twenty years. Whether he'd been farming or mining since she last saw him, she didn't know, but the clothes he wore gave him an aura of success. A well-cut suit of good cloth, pearl buttons on the figured satin vest, and a hint of subdued luxury—a plain gold watch chain peeking out near his belt. If he was still farming, it was for the entertainment of it.

She walked over to him, afraid for a moment that he'd climb into the coach and shut the door in her face. But he stood there with a resigned air, holding it for her. She might have known he would retain his manners, even though he obviously despised her.

Once in the stage, she hesitated then turned to address him. "Would you like to sit on this side, or do you prefer your former seat?"

"It doesn't matter."

She moved over to the farther side of the seat and settled her skirts about her. For an instant, she wished she'd worn her finest gown. Then she recalled that David's niece had told him Millie had stolen it from her, so that would never do. Her cheeks heated at the memory. He had every right to think ill of her. But she might not get another chance to speak to him in private, so she turned to him as he sat down next to her.

"Forgive me, but I must have a word with you."

"I really see no advantage to that, Mrs. Evans."

He'd left the door open, and at that moment the farmer and the man in the suit climbed in, followed by another man, this one wearing a plaid flannel shirt and worn whipcord trousers. The three eyed her and David, and lined up across from them on the opposite seat. Between them, a bench seat would accommodate more passengers, but no one wanted to sit on that without a backrest unless it was absolutely unavoidable. So now she had one man beside her avoiding her gaze and three across the way ogling her. Millie resigned herself to endure the next twenty-five miles with nothing resolved between her and the man she might, under other circumstances, have truly loved.

David crossed his arms and leaned his head back as the stage began to roll toward the mountain crossing. Charlotte Evans, of all people. Or Millie, as she now claimed. It figured that she'd deceived him in that, too. Could there be another person on earth he would less like to have met up with? And to be forced to sit beside her for—how long?

Why, oh why hadn't he simply declined to get back in the coach? He might have had to wait a couple of days to catch another stage, but a quiet interlude in the Oregon wilderness would be preferable to several hours locked in a box with Charlotte.

"Good day, ma'am," the newcomer on the seat opposite David said, staring at Charlotte.

"Good day," she replied.

"Going to Boise?" he asked.

"And beyond."

He nodded.

"I'm going to Boise myself," said the farmer. "I hope you have a pleasant journey."

"The same to you, sir."

Charlotte knew how to speak prettily without encouraging a fellow; David had to hand her that. She was so good at the role, he'd thought her a true lady.

"I'm going to Boise as well," said the man in the suit. "Henry McCloskey's the name."

"How do you do," Charlotte said.

"What's your line?" the man next to him asked.

"I represent the hardware trade."

"Aha, a drummer," said the farmer.

"A sales representative, sir."

The man chuckled. "Well, I've got a hunnerd and twenty acres in the Owhyee Valley—I run sheep mostly. Name's Stoddard."

The three men chatted among themselves, occasionally throwing a question Charlotte's way. After a half hour, the newest man, who had declared himself a miner, eyed David keenly.

"And you, sir? What do you do?"

"I'm half owner in a stagecoach line," David replied.

McCloskey's eyebrows shot up. "Not this one?"

"No, thank heaven."

The three men chuckled. David couldn't resist a sidelong glance at Charlotte. Her lips curved in a genteel smile.

"Not from these parts," the miner said.

"No, sir, though I've been in Oregon six years."

"He's a Britisher," Stoddard said with an emphatic nod that crumpled his beard.

David said nothing, which he supposed some might consider rude, but he didn't want to talk about himself. Already he'd given out more information than he wanted Charlotte to know. The fact that he'd made a success of the stage line since he'd last seen her might be enough to set her scheming. What would happen if she knew he was on his way to England to claim a large estate?

At last they reached another way station and stopped to change teams. They all got out to stretch their legs, and Charlotte let the other passengers drift by and then grabbed David's sleeve.

"Please, Mr. Stone. I really must speak to you. Forgive me for being such a pest."

He gazed pointedly at her fingers, clutching his broadcloth sleeve. Charlotte pulled her hand away as if it had burned her.

"I'm sorry. But you must believe me when I say that I've changed since last we met. I do hope you'll find it in your heart to forgive me for the wrongs I committed then."

David observed her through slits of eyes. He didn't believe a word she said. If her urgent news was that she no longer took part in swindling innocent people, or that she wouldn't conspire to have him murdered this time, she could save her breath. He'd had a few hours to think about it, and he suspected she'd been keeping track of him.

"Tell me," he said, "did you take the same stagecoach as I did by design?"

"Oh no, sir," she cried. "That was purely coincidence, I assure you, though if I may be so bold, I'd call it a providential one. I've repented of my wrongdoing. I'm grateful that God allowed me a chance to tell you so."

David scowled. Now she was bringing the Almighty into it. If she thought that would convince him, she was wrong. It only made him more suspicious.

"So where *are* you traveling to?" he asked at last. "You said beyond Boise."

"That's correct. I'm heading to Fort Laramie. I hope to live with my cousin, who is married to a minister there."

He nodded, thinking about the length of that journey. They'd be confined in the coach together for several days. He shuddered.

Charlotte—or rather, Millie—had turned her attention to her rather bulky handbag. Perhaps this would be a good time to disengage himself.

"Excuse me," he said.

"No, wait!" Her bewitching green eyes held dismay, almost panic. "I have something of yours. I need to give it to you."

"Something of mine?" He frowned but waited. She drew out a small, leather-covered book and handed it to him. "Your Bible, sir. Please forgive me for taking it."

David took the familiar book and held it tenderly, stroking the soft leather. He'd wondered how it had disappeared from his hotel room in Scottsburg a year and a half ago. He should have known. But even given Charlotte's character, he never suspected she'd steal a Bible. Money, yes, but God's Word? Hardly.

"And this." She held out a small wooden box, and David frowned.

"What's that?"

"Why, your cuff links, sir." She glanced off to the side, as though to be sure no one else could overhear. "I'm truly sorry."

David tucked the Bible under his arm and took the little carved box. He lifted the cover and stared down at the onyx cuff links his grandfather, the fifth Earl of Stoneford, had given him on his twelfth birthday. He'd known they were missing, but he'd suspected one of the hotel staff had pilfered them from his room while he was recovering from a wound. He'd never had an inkling that Charlotte had been in his room, much less ransacked it.

"Thank you." He tucked the box in his coat pocket, and his fingers wrapped around it for a moment. How close he'd come to losing his heart to her—but all she'd made off with was his cuff links. He'd been blinded by her charms. The knowledge left him feeling witless and old.

She looked up at him with a pained expression. "I took ten dollars, too, from your dresser. You'd left it there with a note to the hotel owner, saying it would cover your room."

"Indeed?" He stared at her, unable to think of anything more trenchant.

She nodded. "I burned the note. And I spent the money, I'm afraid. I promise I'll pay it back though, as soon as I'm able. If you'll give me an address—"

"Forget it," David said. He was touched that she'd returned his keepsakes—the onyx cuff links were actually worth more than the money she'd stolen. But there was no way he'd tell her how to reach him in the future. He never wanted to see her again.

Her stricken face reminded him of how much he'd cared for her. Charlotte could be so charming. . .pity she'd gone so wretchedly wrong.

"I read some in your Bible. The truth is, that's partly what brought me to change my ways. And so I thank you for that."

David hated the way her guileless manner played on his sympathies. She was a fake and a fraud. He knew that. But she was very good at it. "Look, I have a new Bible now. Keep this one if you like."

She gasped, and her face lit with surprise and joy. "Oh, thank you, sir. If you're sure—I'd love to keep it, above all things." She took it from him with trembling hands that appeared almost reverent.

"Yes, well, let's say no more about this. The past is the past." He touched his hat brim and turned away. If he made a beeline for the outhouse, she could hardly chase after him and press further conversation on him. But he wondered—was even a tenth of what she'd said the truth?

# CHAPTER 3

**M**illie was not completely surprised that David Stone shunned her. After all, she had stolen from him and tried to lure him into marrying her so she could live in style. Without meaning to, she'd endangered his life.

If only he'd give her the chance to show him that she had transformed into a new Millie Evans.

She almost laughed aloud at the thought. He hadn't even known her real name. She'd introduced herself to him as Charlotte Evans in Scottsburg, because it sounded more elegant than Millie, and he'd still thought the name belonged to her.

The stagecoach jostled and swayed. She was very careful not to move too close to David. More than anything right now, she wanted to avoid giving him any new reason for displeasure.

She was pleased to see that he'd recovered from his mishap. He looked as handsome as ever—tall, fair-haired, with compelling blue eyes—and if anything, more prosperous. The stagecoach line was news to her. So he'd given up farming and prospecting and invested in a real business. She was certain it would thrive under his guidance.

Where was he going? He hadn't chimed in when the others had discussed their destinations. Maybe he was thinking of expanding his stage line and had come to check out some of the roads. Perhaps he contemplated adding this very line to his own. Hadn't the ticket agent in The Dalles said prices were lowered to break the competition? Wouldn't that be ironic, if he was riding this coach to see if he wanted to annex the entire line? She'd ascertained long ago that he was shrewder with financial matters than he was with women. If only certain people hadn't interfered, she'd have reeled him in and had a fine husband.

She turned her face toward the window and silently scolded herself. She must stop thinking that way. God certainly didn't want her to go on viewing David Stone as a potential husband, rich or otherwise. If she wanted to please the Lord—and she did now—she had to get those thoughts right out of her head. But it was hard to do when he was sitting right smack beside her.

The stage kept rolling, day and night. They stopped only to change teams. At swing stations, they had twenty minutes to tend nature's needs and perhaps grab a quick bite of something. Home stations served full meals, and they had a half hour at those. Of course, they had to pay for every bite they ate, and Millie's funds dwindled quickly.

On the second day, they climbed out at a home station and the men hurried inside.

"Taking dinner, Mrs. Evans?" McCloskey, the drummer, asked.

"Oh no, thank you." She'd bought one full meal the day before and had decided she'd have to limit herself to one per day and perhaps a biscuit and a cup of tea in the mornings. If she could hold off and buy her full meal in the evening, she'd feel as though she'd accomplished something and deserved her supper.

"You hardly ate any breakfast," McCloskey protested. He hadn't shaved for at least two days, and a grayish stubble speckled his chin. "Come on, lass. I'll treat you."

Millie was tempted to accept, but David lingered near the door to the station, conversing in low tones with the shotgun rider. Was he listening to see what she would say? Even if he wasn't, he'd see her eating with McCloskey.

Besides, Millie would feel beholden to the drummer for the rest of their journey. Was that what he wanted? Would he expect something in return? Most men did expect a profit on their investment.

"No thank you," she said. "I'm really not very hungry. I'll have something this evening."

McCloskey frowned. "Coach make you queasy, does it? I don't think this one's as well sprung as some. Sure you won't join me?"

"Quite sure." She gave him a cool smile.

"All right then." He lumbered inside.

Her stomach growled, and Millie hurried around the corner of the building, out of sight and sound of David and the shotgun rider.

As they journeyed over the Blue Mountains, David asked himself many times why he was doing this. The air dropped below freezing at night in the upper altitudes, and he wasn't about to cuddle up to any of the other passengers. They huddled under the buffalo robes the driver distributed. Millie Evans kept to her corner, thank heaven. The male passengers took turns on the backless bench seat in the middle. McCloskey, Stoddard, and the miner—whom he'd learned was named Tuttle—stayed with them. Other men came and went, from one stop to another.

By the time they wound down out of the mountains and approached the Grande Ronde River, they had eight men and Millie, all bound at least as far as Boise. They sat three to a seat, unless one or two ventured up to the roof, where some claimed they could sleep.

All of the others tried to engage Millie in conversation. She answered them politely but did not encourage them. David ignored her.

He felt an occasional twinge of guilt that he hadn't offered her a modicum of protection by continuing to sit next to her, but he couldn't bear to be any closer to the woman. As soon as it became necessary to admit a third person to their seat, he retreated into the other corner. After that, they had to put up with whomever chance—or Providence—placed between them. For one stage, a matter of a couple of hours, it was a slightly inebriated farmer who reeked of manure and cheap ale. Poor Millie-Charlotte spent most of that time with her handkerchief close to her nose. Everyone concerned breathed easier when he got out at the next station and did not return.

They headed down a rather steep portion of the trail, pushing David back into his seat corner and making the men opposite brace themselves. Those on the middle seat clung to the leather straps that hung from the ceiling. David took his watch out for a quick look, though he didn't like to show it often among strangers. They'd make Brown's Town by sunset, he hoped.

A sudden jarring sent the drummer completely out of his seat and crashing into a rotund traveler sitting in the middle. The coach listed to one side—David's—and the driver erupted in coaxing "Ho's" and "Whoa now's" designed to convince the team to stop.

As soon as the coach halted, the driver hopped down and could be heard breaking the no-cussing rule as he examined the vehicle. A moment later, the door swung open.

"Sorry, folks," the shotgun rider said almost cheerfully. "Got to have you all step out. We seem to have busted a wheel."

Millie accepted his hand and climbed out first.

"Do you have a spare?" Stoddard asked.

"Nope, but we're only three miles from Brown's. I'll take one of the horses and ride in to tell the station agent. He'll send out a wagon with an extra wheel and a man to help change it."

"How long will that take?" McCloskey asked as he squeezed out the door.

The shotgun messenger frowned for a moment, sending his droopy mustache askew. "Couple of hours, maybe."

"But we'll go on tonight?" McCloskey apparently was in a hurry to get to Boise with his sample cases.

"I expect so, if we get it fixed in time. They don't run the ferry after dark here."

The driver, meanwhile, was unhitching one of the leaders for him. He clipped on shorter reins that they carried for emergencies, and the shotgun rider trotted off toward the river.

David strolled around and eyed the broken wheel with misgiving. Unless he was mistaken, when they'd hit that rock, they'd also cracked the axle.

"I say, if it's only three miles, I might set out and walk for a bit."

The driver pulled a twist of tobacco from his shirt pocket. "Well now, I make it to be about that far. You armed, mister?"

"Yes, actually. Am I apt to need a weapon?"

The driver shrugged and leaned on the unharmed wheel. "This road's been hit before. Been awhile, but I figure that means it's about time I got held up again. Bein' stranded out here ain't good."

David surmised that he'd have as good a chance of keeping his wallet if he walked. The broken-down coach might draw in road agents the way a carcass drew vultures.

"I guess I'll chance it then." It would put him out of range of Millie's piteous gaze, if nothing else. He certainly didn't want to give her the opportunity to seek him out again.

"If we get goin' before you're to Brown's, I'll pick you up." The driver took a big chaw of tobacco. Apparently the halt gave him license to break the spitting rule as well as the cussing one.

David patted his pockets. Wallet and pistol were in place, along with the box from Millie and a few coins. If he was ambushed, he'd lose the cuff links again. But he didn't like the odds any better if he stuck them in his luggage and left them with the disabled coach, so he set off with them in his coat pocket. He deliberately didn't look back. If Millie watched him walk away, he didn't care, and he didn't want to make eye contact and give her hope that he'd stop and talk to her—or worse yet, let her walk with him.

It wasn't Millie, but the sheep farmer, Stoddard, who tagged after him.

"Hey! Mr. Stone!"

David kept walking but looked over his shoulder, only as far as Stoddard's jogging figure, not back to where the others clustered.

"Walking in to Brown's Town?"

"That was my plan," David said. "Thought I'd stretch my legs."

"Mind if I join you?"

He seemed a stout enough fellow, not overly talkative, and he wore a Colt revolver strapped about his waist.

"Fine by me," David said.

They walked along companionably for ten minutes before Stoddard said, "Is that Mrs. Evans an acquaintance of yours?"

David grunted, wondering what he really wanted to know. "I met her once before."

"She a widder woman? I didn't see no weddin' ring."

"I believe so," David said.

They walked in silence for another ten minutes before Stoddard said, "I don't reckon she'd take to a sheep farmer."

David smiled grimly. "I cannot speak for her, but from what little I know, I don't think you can afford her taste."

"Ah."

They'd walked about two miles when a wagon passed them bearing their shotgun rider and another man, with the replacement wheel. The men waved and drove on. David and Stoddard finished their journey in silence and without sign of highwaymen. In less than an hour, they sat together in Mr. Brown's dining room, making up the first supper sitting of the stagecoach passengers and thus getting the best portions of the fried chicken and having the leisure to enjoy it. The driver who would take them onward also ate when they did, grumbling between bites about the delay.

The stagecoach didn't arrive until nearly two hours later, as the sun slid behind the mountains. The passengers went inside to eat hastily, while the coach and horses were ferried across the river. David noted that this time Millie headed inside. She must be purchasing the meal this evening.

"Hey," Stoddard called to him, "we can ride over with the coach if we want. We'll get there afore the rest and can get good seats."

David boarded the ferry with Stoddard. It was hard to feel smug about it though, when they couldn't travel on without the people they'd left behind. He felt a bit sorry for them all—they hadn't gotten the exercise that he and Stoddard had. At least he felt more prepared to get back in the stagecoach and on the road again.

On the other side, David was the first on the coach, and he claimed his comfortable corner again. Stoddard took the one across from him. The other passengers came across the river as twilight descended. Millie, unfortunately, was one of the last to board and lost her usual spot. She settled demurely on the middle seat with two rough-looking fellows. The one nearest her appeared to keep inching closer to her, until Millie looked in a fair way to tumble to the floor.

"I beg your pardon, sir," she said when the coach had been underway for ten minutes. "Could you possibly give me a little more room?"

"Hmpf. Bit of a thang like you?" the man said. He scooted over, but not very far. The first time they rounded a corner, he slid back toward her.

It was dark now, with only a sliver of light shining in from the lanterns on the front of the stage, and David couldn't see much of what else was going on, but suddenly Millie leaped up and whacked the man with her handbag. Since it held David's Bible, he imagined it packed a wallop.

"How dare you?" Millie said in tones that would have frozen the river if they'd still been on the ferry.

David couldn't sit by any longer. "Here, ma'am. Take my seat."

Though he couldn't read her expression, he sensed her hesitation. "Why. . .thank you, sir!"

With some awkward shifting as the stage rolled on, they managed to exchange places without landing in anyone else's lap. David held his ground against the encroaching fellow to his left—though he suspected the offender was less eager to claim more territory when an alluring woman was not involved. But David found it necessary to cling to one of the hanging straps, and his right arm was soon aching dreadfully. This was the shoulder in which he'd been wounded, and after five minutes, he turned around on the seat and faced the other way so that he could reach the strap with his left hand. The next two hours were torture.

*Charlotte*, he thought. *No, Millie. If she hadn't boarded this stage, I'd be sitting in comparative comfort.* He was glad his back was to her now. He didn't want to see her, even in the scanty light they had.

Even so, in his mind he saw her lovely dark red hair, piled high as it had been in Scottsburg when they'd dined together. Her skin was as white and smooth as ever, her eyes as vibrantly green. He gritted his teeth and tried to think instead of Stoneford. Once there, he'd be thousands of miles from the woman he disliked more than anyone else on earth.

# CHAPTER 4

At midmorning of the following day, they reached the verge of the Snake River. At long last, Millie was putting Oregon behind her. What a pity that part of her past traveled with her. She tried to avoid looking at David, since he so obviously shrank from contact with her.

"All out," the station agent called as they pulled up in his barnyard. As she descended from the coach, he droned, "Dinner inside, two bits. The ferry will take you across in thirty minutes. All luggage will be ferried with you."

"Are the horses going across as well?" she asked, looking about for a fresh team and seeing none.

"Nay, madam. This coach and team will stay on this side and head back for Fort Dalles tomorrow. You'll board a new stage once you're over the water."

Millie gulped and looked toward the river. She didn't like water, and the Snake looked rather treacherous. She remembered that fateful night in Scottsburg when David had plunged into the Umpqua. That river had been much calmer. This one, high with snow melt from the mountains, twisted and writhed its way through the wilderness.

Three of the passengers had left them, and Stoddard and McCloskey would part company with them across the river. Perhaps they'd be less uncomfortable now. Millie had pitied David after he took her spot on the center bench, but she'd been more grateful than she could express. She'd tried to express her gratitude at the next stop, but David had brushed her aside. Embarrassed? What gentleman would be ashamed of his gallantry? More likely he was still angry with her.

A married couple joined them at the station on the western bank of the river. Though Millie was glad to have another feminine presence—the men had grown weary of not swearing or smoking, and the miner had taken to chewing tobacco and spitting frequently out the window, though the rules forbade it. She hoped that with Mrs. Caudle's arrival, this would stop.

They were all ferried across with their bags. The water swirled and tugged at their low, flat craft, but strong cables and ropes held it from being swept downstream. Millie clung to one of the railings and stared at the pile of luggage, which was secured to the deck with ropes. Mrs. Caudle looked a bit green-faced, and Millie imagined she presented an equally distressed picture.

At last they landed, with only one of the passengers being ill, and that one of the men. The new coach was waiting for them on the eastern shore and carried the eight of them to the station yard a short distance away, where the luggage was put down for those who had finished their journey.

"Good-bye, Mrs. Evans," McCloskey said before disembarking.

"Farewell, sir. I wish you Godspeed."

The salesman tipped his hat and left them to claim his valise and sample cases.

"We'll have to make up some time," the new driver said.

"Aye, see if you can make up half an hour on this stage," the station agent told him. "But whatever you do, don't have another wreck."

"Don't you worry," the driver told him. "I know this road like I know the back end of my wheel horses. We're all rarin' to go."

Mr. Caudle paused before entering the stage. "What about Indians, sir? Have they bothered the traffic along the trail this year?"

"Not yet, and please God they won't," the driver replied.

"I admit I'm a little nervous, since that massacre—"

"That was nigh three years ago, sir." The driver seemed a bit disgruntled at having the safety of his bit of trail cast in doubt.

"But they shut down Fort Boise—"

"True, but there be troopers back and forth. They man the

31

cantonment near Fort Hall every summer, and they've set up for the season, to make sure wagon trains get through safely. Now, let's get aboard and head out, shall we?"

Geography wasn't Millie's long suit, but she knew they were still many miles from the vicinity of the old Fort Hall. She hadn't given much thought to the Indian troubles in Idaho when she'd bought her ticket. She was in Idaho now, and she'd have to trust God and the cavalry to see her through.

They set out again with only six aboard, and the miner made no secret of his plans to leave them at the next stop. Millie sighed and leaned back against the leather-covered headrest. She'd hardly slept a wink last night. Perhaps she could catch a nap now. Though she could barely imagine sleeping with the intriguing David Stone so close, her exhaustion would surely come to her aid in that matter.

Her hope of slumber soon drifted out the open window. Although the party had become smaller, the atmosphere in the coach had not improved. Mrs. Caudle sat between Millie and her husband, and the most notable thing about her was her heavily applied scent. Millie barely had time to recognize it before her nostrils were overcome and it became a stench.

Mrs. Caudle plunged into conversation at once, introducing herself and insisting the others give their names and home towns.

Millie pasted on a smile. "I am Mrs. Evans, and I'm lately of The Dalles, but I'm traveling to Fort Laramie to visit my cousin."

"Oh, how lovely for you, my dear," Mrs. Caudle said, laying a moist hand on Millie's wrist. Her cloying perfume caused Millie to swallow hard and avoid inhaling deeply. "And has Mr. Evans remained at home?"

Millie hesitated and shot a quick glance at David, but he was staring out the window.

"Mr. Evans met his demise several years ago," Millie murmured.

"Ah, what a shame."

*Not really,* Millie thought. If he hadn't gotten himself killed when he did, he probably would have beaten her to death. Of course, she would never say such a thing to anyone. Sam knew she'd been unhappy, and he'd seen her once or twice with bruises on her face, but even her half-brother had no idea the extent of her suffering under James Evans's hands.

"So he is at home after all," Mrs. Caudle said sweetly. "At home with the Lord."

Millie couldn't respond to that. She took out her handkerchief and put it to her nose, not to cover her sorrow, but to filter the overbold perfume of her seatmate.

David said merely, "David Stone, of Eugene." His words were few enough that his accent was not obtrusive, and no one commented on it. The others gave a bit of their background.

When the turn came to Mr. Caudle, he gave his name—Robert Caudle—and said, "I'll let Agnes tell it."

Mrs. Caudle chuckled. "Ah, my husband is too modest."

Millie got the feeling this was the moment she'd waited for, and sure enough the lady continued with relish.

"Mr. Caudle is headed to Washington to help lobby for statehood. He'll be attached to our new senator's office. Isn't that delightful?"

Millie and a couple of others murmured their assent.

No one seemed desperate to hear more of Mr. Caudle's official duties or how he came by this position, but his wife held forth anyway.

David sat across from Millie, in the same corner he'd started out in at The Dalles. After a few minutes, his eyes closed, but she couldn't tell whether or not he was sleeping. He was too genteel to snore or let his head loll to the side.

Millie leaned toward the window, hoping to catch more of the breeze. After a while, she rested her arm on the window ledge, her handkerchief clasped lightly in her fingers.

"Don't you think that's true?" Mrs. Caudle leaned closer and elbowed her sharply.

Millie jumped, a bit startled at the woman's audacity. Her handkerchief flew from her fingers.

"Oh!" She tried to look out and behind the coach, but the bit of white muslin was gone on the perpetual breeze.

"What is it?" Mrs. Caudle asked, louder than necessary.

"It's nothing," Millie said. "Just my handkerchief."

"What? You lost your handkerchief? Robert, quickly! Pound on the ceiling and tell the driver to stop."

"Oh no," Millie said quickly. "Please don't. There's no need."

"But madam, if you lost a piece of your property," Mr. Caudle said, leaning forward to peer at her with all the ostentation of his position, "of course we can ask the driver to stop."

"Yes indeed," his wife added. "Those men work for us, after all."

By this time the three men opposite were all paying attention, though none of them spoke. David hadn't moved, other than to open his eyes in narrow slits. As soon as Millie glanced his way, he closed them again.

"Please don't," she said, leaning past Mrs. Caudle to appeal to her husband, and thus getting a strong whiff of the by-now nauseating perfume. "I should be excessively embarrassed if you asked them to do that. It was nothing but a scrap of muslin, and we're running late already. I shouldn't like to cause another delay. Indeed, that handkerchief is not worth the trouble."

"Hmpf." Mr. Caudle sat back and folded his arms. "Very well then."

Millie exhaled and closed her eyes for a moment, relieved to have averted the halt. The other men would no doubt have resented her for the rest of the journey if she'd demanded the driver and shotgun rider stop and look for her handkerchief or wait while she did so. She already knew how the driver would feel—he was bound to make up lost time and would see her as a troublemaker. And Mr. Stone? David appeared to have drifted back into slumber, but she wondered if he wasn't very busy thinking behind those closed eyelids. Thinking bad thoughts about her.

David tried to ignore the conversation on the other side of the coach. The Caudles, while attempting to be pleasant, were anything but.

He had to give Millie credit—she maintained a gracious demeanor but did not prompt the loquacious Mrs. Caudle to ramble. Alas, the woman needed no encouragement from others; she achieved it under her own steam. If only Millie were a little less polite and would tell her to be quiet.

The handkerchief episode surprised him mildly. Millie was determined not to delay them all. Her attitude reminded him of the Charlotte he'd liked so well in Scottsburg—before she started hounding him to take her out walking every evening and led him into chaos. She seemed a modest, somewhat self-effacing, and, yes, charming lady. Of course, he knew too well now that she was not what she seemed.

Because of Charlotte, David had become much more cautious where women were concerned. He'd left England a bit spoiled for romance by a crush on his older brother Richard's wife. Elizabeth Stone would never, ever so much as hint at impropriety, but David adored her. His niece, Anne, didn't know—she was only an infant then, and David would never admit to anyone how much he'd admired Anne's mother. But his wanderlust, combined with the pain of knowing he would never be able to openly love Elizabeth, had driven him from Stoneford and England. That and the fact that he'd had no responsibilities to live up to. Richard inherited the earldom, and there was John between them in age. David was certain he'd never inherit the title, and so he was free to follow adventure wherever it led him.

That turned out to be America. He'd recovered from his heartache after a while and had become enamored of a young woman in Independence, but that had gone nowhere. He'd moved to Oregon, undergoing a few flirtations over the years, but had never come close to thinking he'd found the right woman.

Charlotte had interested him far more than the wide-eyed girls on the wagon trail or the jaded women in the western towns. Quite striking, she was, with that rich red hair and those startling green eyes—rare coloring, and she wore it well.

He realized with a start that he was staring at her. He closed his eyes again. Best not to look at the woman. She was lovely on the outside, but her heart would drag a man to destruction.

A sudden bang outside the coach brought him upright.

"What was that?" Mrs. Caudle screeched, clutching her husband's arm.

Before Mr. Caudle could answer, two more pops and a blast from directly over David's head confirmed what he already knew. Those were gunshots, and they were under attack.

# CHAPTER 5

**G**et down," David called to the ladies, reaching inside his coat for his pistol. The two other men on his side of the stage also produced weapons, but Mr. Caudle, it seemed, was not so well prepared.

Millie gazed at him, her green eyes huge in her white face.

"I advise you ladies to sit on the floor. You too, Mr. Caudle, if you've no pistol." David moved to the middle seat and maneuvered to see out the window and forward, but only trees met his view.

Another shot fired from above him. He hoped the shotgun rider's aim was true.

The coach continued to roll, and the driver's whip cracked several times.

"Up, there, boys! Go!" The driver's yells seemed ineffective because a moment later the coach stopped so suddenly that David was thrown forward onto his previous seat. Mr. Caudle catapulted to the floor, where his wife and Millie had taken hasty refuge.

David could imagine only two things that would stop the coach so suddenly without any noise of breakage—one of the horses must have fallen in harness, or the outlaws had felled a tree across the road and they'd plowed into it. An unearthly shriek came from one of the team, and he pitied the poor animals.

"Hands in the air!"

"All right, all right," the driver said grumpily.

"Throw down the box."

A moment later a thud evidenced the driver's compliance.

"You got mail sacks?" the gruff voice demanded.

"Nope, nary a one."

"Awright, git down. Both of you."

In an odd way, this conversation bolstered David. It meant both the driver and his shotgun messenger were still alive.

A shadow fell over the passengers, and the door flew open.

"Don't shoot, fellas," the driver cried.

The masked robber held him around the neck, a pistol aimed at his temple. "Come on out, folks."

David hesitated and eased his pistol into his coat pocket.

"Throw yer guns out." The outlaw was bigger than the driver and easily kept him under control. "Come on, gents. I know some of you have revolvers. Let's see 'em."

The other two passengers, who were nearer the door, tossed their guns out the window. David wondered if he was foolish not to follow their lead.

"Only two?" The robber asked.

A second outlaw scooped up the revolvers and tossed them forward of the coach, then came to the doorway.

"Well now, what have we here? Ladies!"

Mrs. Caudle raised her head and held out a beseeching hand. "Oh please! Don't hurt us. I'll give you my pearl necklace."

"That's right nice of you, ma'am."

David eyed the second robber carefully. That voice seemed somehow familiar. He wore a cloth tied over his face, but his straw-colored hair showed beneath a battered felt hat. His blocky build and dull gray eyes were all David needed to identify his former farmhand, Sam Hastings.

"Everybody out," the man said, standing back. "And no funny business. Ladies first."

Millie rose shakily, looking decidedly ill.

Mrs. Caudle almost tumbled out, talking the whole while. "You mustn't hurt anyone. I'm sure we'll all cooperate. Just take what you want and be on your way."

"Hush, you!" The robber prodded her with the barrel of his rifle, and she squealed and jumped aside.

Millie held up her skirt, exposing a shapely ankle, and followed Mrs. Caudle outside.

The outlaw gave a little gasp as she poked her head out the door.

"Mil—er, watch your step, ma'am."

David held back and climbed down last. He pulled his hat low over his eyes, but there was no way he wouldn't be recognized. Of course, the man he feared would know him had never been the brightest penny in the cashbox.

The passengers lined up, with David at the end nearest the stagecoach. One man trained his gun on them while the stockier robber collected the valuables. He began with the Caudles, relieving the lady of her necklace, her earbobs, and a handful of coins from her purse. Mr. Caudle contributed a watch, his wallet, and two cigars. David resigned himself to giving up his watch—he'd bought it during his storekeeping days at wholesale, so he wasn't overly attached to it—and rejoiced that he wasn't wearing the onyx cuff links. If they didn't search him, perhaps he'd keep those and a reserve of bills tucked into a tiny pocket Anne had sewn inside his boot top.

He had no intention of opening fire. It wasn't worth the risk with two women present and several unarmed men. Besides, now that he was out of the stage, he realized there were at least five outlaws, maybe six. As he'd feared, one of the team's horses was down—a big, brown wheeler. The other five stood uneasily in harness, shifting and snuffling. If the robbers left with their loot, the driver and shotgun rider would have to cut the traces and reconfigure the rest of the team.

Two of the outlaws had climbed to the roof of the coach and were going through the luggage. A fifth gang member was packing the contents of the treasure box into a sack for easier transport.

A shot—too loud and too close—spun David around. Mr. Caudle apparently wasn't unarmed after all. He'd brought out a small pistol and let the man with the rifle have it.

The one holding the bag of the passengers' belongings stood uncertainly for a moment. That was Sam for you, always a half-second behind. The thought flashed through David's mind as he whipped his own revolver from his pocket.

By the time he had the gun out, Sam had moved, and quickly.

He fired in Mr. Caudle's direction and jumped behind the stage-coach. Mrs. Caudle screamed as her husband went down.

David whirled and let off a shot at the robber drawing a bead on him from the top of the stage. The man jumped back and dropped his revolver over the edge of the roof. David didn't think he'd hit him, unless in the hand, but he swooped on the brigand's revolver and backed toward the woods with a gun in each hand.

"Run! All of you take cover," he said without looking around at the others.

The passengers scattered, and he heard branches breaking and brush rustling as they obeyed—all but Mrs. Caudle, who sank to her knees beside her husband's inert body, still screaming. The stage driver snatched up her husband's pistol and joined David in keeping up a stream of fire toward the robbers while the other passengers retreated, and the shotgun rider managed to grab the rifle dropped by the outlaw Mr. Caudle had shot. The three of them backed into the woods, keeping up their fire.

"How much ammo you got?" the driver yelled to David from his refuge behind a big fir tree.

David patted his vest pocket. "Six more rounds and whatever's left in this gun I picked up." He fumbled to reload his own.

"I think this is empty," the shotgun rider said hefting the muzzle-loading rifle he'd picked up. He'd fired its single shot during their retreat. "Wish I coulda got one of them revolvers they took. Jay?"

The driver peered at them from behind his tree and waved Mr. Caudle's revolver. "I fired two shots. Don't know how many are in this thing."

The road agents seemed to be conferring. David hoped they weren't cooking up a plan.

"Here. I think there's a couple of rounds left in there." He passed the outlaw's gun he'd confiscated to the shotgun rider. The three of them might have a dozen rounds. If used well, that might be enough.

He turned and squinted into the dim woods behind them. Millie was peeking from between a couple of smaller trees, her wide-brimmed hat easy to see. David waved them back, hoping she'd read his signal to get farther into the forest.

A sudden thought chilled him. Had she signaled the robbers by letting her handkerchief fly out the window? Maybe she had a gun in that bag with his Bible.

Millie knew she ought to forge farther into the woods, but she couldn't tear herself away. Did David know that was her brother out there?

Mrs. Caudle's screams tapered off into wrenching sobs. All else was quiet, except for the snorting of the horses and occasional shrieks from the felled wheeler. Millie glanced at the other two male passengers, who huddled behind trees. She edged out from her cover and flitted up to where she could hear David and the other men talking.

"Think they'll leave now?" the shotgun rider asked David.

"I don't know. If Caudle hadn't brought that pistol out, they'd no doubt have left us alone."

The driver dashed between the trees to where they stood. "I have another gun in the driver's boot. I wonder if they're still up there by the coach. Maybe we could get it."

"Is there anything I could do?" Millie asked.

The three men turned their rather disdainful gazes on her.

"You'd best get back with the others, ma'am," the driver said.

"Hey," a man shouted from up near the stagecoach, "You done shot Lucky."

The shotgun rider let out a grim chuckle and said softly, "Not so lucky today, was he?"

"You can't git away with that," the robber yelled.

"Sounds like they want more trouble," the driver said.

"We don't have the ammunition to hold them off for long," David said calmly.

Millie gulped. "Listen, they probably wouldn't shoot me. I could go out there and try to calm Mrs. Caudle down. Maybe I could pick up one of the passengers' pistols. Or cause a diversion so that one of you could get them."

"Too dangerous," the driver said.

"I wouldn't hide behind no woman's skirts, anyhow," the shotgun rider muttered.

David turned his head and trained his eyes on her—glacial blue in shadow of the trees. "They wouldn't shoot you because one of them's your brother. Isn't that so, Mrs. Evans?"

"What?" The driver stared at Millie.

Her throat tightened. She wanted to deny it, but she couldn't.

"Yes. It was Sam who held the bag."

David nodded. "As I thought. Did you signal them to attack?"

"What? No!"

David looked at the other two men. "She lost a handkerchief out the window just minutes before the road agents stopped the stage."

The driver and the shotgun rider stared at her, and their gazes weren't kindly.

"I didn't know," she cried, but their faces held patent disbelief. "You must believe me. I left The Dalles to get away from my brother. I refused to—" She shook her head. What did it matter? Now that David had spoken against her, they would never believe her.

David seethed inside as Millie shuddered and wilted. Did she expect him to protect her in this nefarious game? Sam Hastings had impersonated him once and tried to claim David's belongings. Did he know about the estate in England? Maybe he and Millie had come up with this plan to finally get rid of David and go claim his wealth and position.

"Millie!" Sam stayed hidden, but his voice came loud and clear. "Come on, Millie. You come with us."

Millie raised her chin. "No! Go away!"

"Come on, Mil!"

"I told you, no!"

David edged over to another tree, wondering where the other robbers were. Why should they hang around now, other than to attempt to get Millie to join them? Was she really a confederate of theirs?

He caught his breath. Through the trees, he'd spotted a saddled horse. At least one of the road agents had left his mount unattended.

He was about to move toward it when Millie cried, "David! Look out!"

Rather than turn toward her, he swung toward the flicker of movement he'd caught from the corner of his eye and fired two rapid shots. The outlaw went crashing through the brush toward the horses.

Behind him, more gunfire erupted. David hoped the unarmed folks were keeping low, but he didn't have time to look. He stumbled toward the road, conscious of the three meager shots he had left. When he came to the tree line, he looked up the road, forward of the stagecoach, where the harnessed horses plunged, neighed, and kicked at each other in their frenzy to escape. Sam was helping an outlaw mount his horse. So, Caudle hadn't killed Lucky after all. The big man lay low over his horse's neck and headed away from the altercation. Three more horsemen appeared out of the woods to the side. David raised his revolver but doubted he could make the shot from this distance. Still, he couldn't bring himself to fire at Sam when Millie stood nearby.

The driver ran up beside David and let off a shot, then his revolver clicked as Sam Hastings swayed, clutched his chest, and fell to the dusty road.

The driver swore. "At least I got one of 'em."

The other outlaws were out of range now, galloping away eastward, leaving Sam behind, lying in the dirt as a cloud of dust swirled in the air and the stagecoach team thrashed and screamed.

Before David could catch his breath, Millie dashed past him, holding up bunches of her skirt and gasping for breath. She ran to the outlaw lying in the road and knelt beside him.

"Sam! You big old oaf! Why did you do this, Sam?"

David tucked his pistol inside his coat and walked heavily toward her. He patted his pockets for his handkerchief and found it crumpled beneath the cuff link box.

Millie had torn off the cloth that had masked her brother's face. Sam's eyes were shut tight, and his mouth twisted as he pressed both hands to his chest. Blood oozed between his fingers, and his labored breathing set David's teeth on edge. He knelt in the dirt across from Millie. She tossed him a glance. David could see that the wound was beyond what little help a handkerchief could offer, and he tucked it back in his pocket to keep it clean. Millie would need one later.

An odd feeling seized David, as though he was watching this tableau from outside the frame. Millie had saved his life back there when she'd warned him. Offering a clean handkerchief seemed poor recompense.

"Sam, I'm so sorry," she choked. "Hold on now. We'll take you to a doctor."

Sam coughed, and blood splatted from the corner of his mouth. "I'm past doctorin', Millie. You get Old Blue, huh? Take care of him."

"Old Blue?" Millie looked around in distraction.

"Is he there?" Sam asked.

"Yes, I see him." The roan had run a little way after the band of outlaws but had stopped and was nervously snatching mouthfuls of grass at the edge of the road, keeping an eye on the activity near the coach.

Sam pulled in a shuddering breath. "He's a...good hoss."

"Yes." Millie sounded as though she were the one strangling.

The driver went to his team, but after he and the shotgun rider had somewhat calmed them, he came over and stood gazing down at Sam. "Is that the one? Her brother?"

"Yes." David stood and brushed off his knees. "I'm afraid there's nothing we can do."

The driver inhaled deeply through his nose. "Caudle's dead, but the fella he shot got away. Hal and I will see about getting the team set to go. We need to get these passengers to the swing station. It's about five miles. As soon as I pass the stage to another driver, I'll come back with some men and all the horses we can harness to once, and we'll drag ol' Star off the road." He nodded to the downed coach horse.

David nodded. "If it will help you, that blue roan the outlaw was riding can pull in harness."

"You sure?" The driver eyed him with speculation.

"Yes." David didn't bother to explain that Old Blue had belonged to him, once upon a more-trusting time.

Millie burst into tears and flung herself on Sam's body. David guessed her brother had breathed his last. He stood in confusion. He ought to offer his comfort or at least some show of sympathy, but how could he? Her brother was an outlaw and had brought him nothing but trouble. So far as he could see, she was in on the robbery plot. The best thing he could do would be to distance himself from her.

"Best let her have a few minutes," he said to the driver. "Let's see about the harness."

The three of them—David, the driver, and the shotgun messenger, Hal, managed to get the straps off the dead horse without cutting any of them. It was an awful job, and they had to call upon the other two men to help roll the dead animal partway over, but at last they freed all the leather. David's clothes were bloody when they finished. Old Blue sidled and snorted a bit when buckled in next to the remaining wheel horse, but he didn't protest too violently, which encouraged David. Maybe they'd get to the next stage stop without further incident.

Two horsemen rode up from the direction of the river as the passengers were preparing to enter the coach again. After a brief explanation of what had happened, the two farmers on horseback decided to finish their journey with the stagecoach for safety. The shotgun rider tossed Blue's saddle and bridle into the boot, and they set off with Sam's body on the roof and Mr. Caudle inside with the sober passengers.

Millie and Mrs. Caudle sat together in the front, and David joined the two other male passengers on the rear seat, with Mr. Caudle lying on the bench in the middle. The two women wept incessantly—Mrs. Caudle with a loud keening and Millie in stoic silence. The tears streamed down her cheeks, and she swiped at them periodically with David's handkerchief.

The next forty minutes dragged on and on. No chatter relieved the tension. The only interruption to Mrs. Caudle's crying was when they started up a steep incline and her husband's body slid off the seat, landing on the boots of the three gentlemen at the rear. She let out a scream, but David held out a hand toward her.

"Please, madam, control yourself. I believe your husband will rest easier on the floor until we reach the station. It's not far."

Millie put an arm around Mrs. Caudle and drew her back against the leather cushion. "There now, my dear. The Lord is welcoming him into glory. You must think of that and calm yourself."

"But what of his trip to Washington?" Mrs. Caudle wailed. "Oh dear, I haven't any black. I wonder, can I get dress goods in Boise?" She began her keening again, and Millie sat beside her with tear tracks glistening on her cheeks, patting the older woman's hand and murmuring her sympathy.

Thoughts of glory would give Millie no comfort. David eyed her with new respect. Heaven's gates would not open for Sam Hastings, he had no doubt about that. Millie must know it, too, and yet she offered sympathy without bitterness to Mrs. Caudle.

# CHAPTER 6

They arrived at the swing station, and all tumbled out. The bodies were removed from the stage, and Mrs. Caudle sat down with the station agent to make arrangements for transporting her husband's remains back to Oregon. Millie could see no alternative to having Sam buried there at the station. A small graveyard on the hill above the road was the resting place of two previously departed travelers, and the tenders, who took care of the teams, offered to dig a grave.

She had no money to pay them nor to hire a room for the night at the stage station. The few coins she'd had left were in the outlaws' sack. Sam must have passed it to one of the others, as it wasn't found at the scene of the robbery after they fled. That fact also left Mrs. Caudle destitute. The two male passengers grumbled about their losses as well, though each had planned for such an event and concealed some money about their persons. Sam had never reached David and the shotgun rider with his sack, and so the driver and the two women were the only ones who lost all their valuables.

The agent, a Mr. Kimball, remarkable for his fiery-red hair and beard, refused to make the driver wait. To Millie's surprise, David let the stage go on without him. She'd figured he'd want to get as far from her as he could. Instead, he got a cup of coffee from Kimball's wife and took it outside. Millie and Mrs. Caudle sat down in the dining room.

"We don't normally serve meals," Mrs. Kimball told them, "but sometimes it's a plain necessity."

She served the ladies tea and biscuits.

"I can't eat a bite," Mrs. Caudle said, so Millie felt justified in eating all four biscuits. No telling when she would get another meal.

Mrs. Caudle had arranged for one of the men to build a coffin for her husband.

Mr. Kimball brought her some money, saying, "I've changed your ticket for you, madam, so that you can head back to Oregon on tomorrow's westbound."

"And they'll carry Mr. Caudle, too?" the widow asked in a quavery tone.

"Aye, they should be able to put the box on the roof." Mr. Kimball refunded most of her money for her husband's ticket, since he would travel for less as freight, and so the lady had enough money to see her home. He'd kept back enough to pay for the materials for the coffin and to pay the man who built it fair wages.

Two hours after they arrived, he came back into the house and approached the table where they still sat. "The grave is ready, Mrs. Evans."

Millie rose, feeling stiff and empty. Sam wouldn't even have a rough coffin, as Mr. Caudle would. But Sam had grown up poor, and she didn't think he'd mind.

David Stone and Mrs. Caudle joined her. Mr. Kimball drove the ladies in his wagon to the burial plot among the weeds, and David walked along behind, with the two tenders. The four men lifted the body out of the wagon bed and lowered it into the ground, wrapped in a blanket Kimball had given for the purpose—saying he would add it to Mrs. Evans's bill.

She didn't know how she'd pay for that, and she supposed she'd be charged for the night's lodging as well, but she wasn't about to reveal her penury to the host now.

Her tears welled up as the men settled the body in the hole. Poor Sam. He'd had no idea how to go about living, and so he'd done it badly. Some people learned from their mistakes, but Sam wasn't that kind. The fact that Millie hadn't been able to help him— had in fact, up until the last few months, encouraged him to live in crime—saddened her.

God had grabbed hold of her and changed her. Even if she looked the same on the outside, she was different in her heart. She ought to have done a better job explaining that to Sam.

The tenders climbed out of the grave and stood back, leaving the passengers and the station agent near the edge. Mr. Kimball opened his Bible, and Millie sobbed.

David should have left with the stagecoach, but he felt so guilty, he couldn't go on and leave Millie to bury her brother alone. He told himself repeatedly he had no reason to feel remorse. Sam had brought this on himself. And David owed him no loyalty. Still, he stayed.

As they stood by the grave, Kimball read a psalm from his battered Bible. The sun set behind the mountains, and David's mind roamed.

Kimball startled him by saying, at the end of the psalm, "Mr. Stone, would you say a few words?"

David nearly choked but managed to turn the reflex into a cough while he did some quick thinking. He couldn't say what a fine man Sam was or that he was in a better place.

"I was sorry to see Sam Hastings come to this end," he said. "He chose his path, and this is where it led him. May we all learn from this and seek to do what's right. Shall we all recite the Lord's Prayer together?"

That ensured everyone closed their eyes and didn't stare at him. They repeated the words together, with even Millie joining in, her voice faltering toward the end as she wept. David passed her another clean handkerchief—the last until he managed to have some laundry done. She accepted it meekly and pressed it to her eyes.

The two hired men stayed behind to fill in the grave, and David walked back to the station house. He let the wagon outdistance him. When he came to the barn, Kimball was unharnessing his horses, and the ladies were nowhere to be seen.

The blue roan nickered from a nearby corral, and David walked over to stroke Old Blue's nose. They would have to pay for overnight accommodations, and he doubted Millie's purse could stand the strain. He walked into the barn.

"Mr. Kimball."

"Yes?" The host hung a set of harness on a peg and turned toward him.

"That roan horse that belonged to Mrs. Evans's brother— perhaps you might consider buying it from her."

Kimball's eyes narrowed. "Don't need another saddle horse."

"No? He's a good mount, and if nothing else, you could resell him."

Kimball scratched his chin through his red beard. "Maybe so."

David took that for what it was worth and strolled to the house. They spent a bleak evening there. Mrs. Kimball prepared a room for Mrs. Caudle and Millie, but David had to bunk in with the tenders in a small room partitioned off in the barn. One of them stayed up late, constructing a casket by lamplight for Mr. Caudle's remains, and his sawing and pounding kept David awake.

The next morning a westbound stage went through and took Mrs. Caudle and the corpse of her husband. Everyone around the station seemed to breathe easier after that. A couple of troopers came by, bound for the Green River, and Millie prevailed on them to take a letter for her.

Another eastbound stage would not pass through until the next day. David borrowed fishing gear from their host, paid twenty-five cents to Mrs. Kimball to pack him a lunch, and set out for a leisurely ramble along a stream. Anything to avoid seeing Millie's tear-reddened eyes all day.

He found a place to sit in the shade and half-heartedly cast his line. If he'd claimed Old Blue, he might have ridden him on eastward. David began to wish he'd forsaken the stagecoach line and gone on alone, despite the risks of facing Indians and robbers. But it was too late for that, and if Mr. Kimball bought the horse, Millie would have enough to allow her to eat between here and Fort Laramie. He leaned back and settled his hat lower, prepared to catch a nap.

He was almost put out when he started getting nibbles, but after he pulled in his first fish—a foot-long trout—he began to feel a little more enthusiastic. As the sun began to lower, he ambled back to the station with four good-sized fish. Mrs. Kimball accepted them with thanks and told him he wouldn't have to pay for his supper or breakfast, since he'd earned his keep. She also informed him that a small wagon train of freighters had passed through heading west, the first of the season.

After supper, Kimball approached David as he lounged in a rocking chair on the porch.

"The lady said that one of the outlaws stole the roan from you, and I should bargain with you for it, sir."

David eyed the fellow in surprise. Millie obviously needed money, yet she'd passed up an easy deal? "No, he didn't steal it. The horse belonged to her brother. Give her the money."

Kimball hesitated. "All right, then. He's not much of a coach horse though. I suppose I could sell him as a saddle horse."

Remembering the dead horse at the scene of the robbery, David arched his eyebrows. "Did our driver yesterday speak to you about removing the dead horse from the road?"

"Yes sir. My men went out this morning with a team and cleared it before the westbound got there."

David nodded. "Good. And don't forget, Mrs. Evans has a saddle and bridle to sell you with that roan."

Kimball left him, and David rocked and watched the stars grow brighter.

"Mr. Stone?"

"Yes?" He turned at the soft, feminine voice.

Millie left the doorway and came over close to him.

"The station agent has offered me thirty-five dollars for the horse and saddle. I know he's worth more than that, but I haven't time to stop and find another buyer."

"Do as you wish," David said.

"But Old Blue is yours, sir."

David stood, shaking his head. "No, I gave him to your brother. And I told Kimball to deal with you."

"I thought you might like to keep him or try yourself to drive a better bargain. Sometimes a man can do better than a woman at this type of business transaction."

David felt his face flush. He wanted only to end this embarrassing conversation. "Char—Mrs. Evans, your brother had that horse for nearly two years. I gave him Old Blue to use while he was in my employ, and once we'd parted ways—well, I never expected to see the horse again. Please consider it your brother's gift to you, as he wished."

"I can't do that. Please!" Tears streaked her cheeks.

David sighed. He'd run out of handkerchiefs, an untenable situation for a gentleman. "If there had been time before Sam died, I'd have told him to consider the horse his, to do with as he pleased. Since there was no such opportunity—I felt the time was better left for you to say your good-byes—I didn't make it a formal gift to him. But I'm telling you now: That is how I looked upon it. I never thought to reclaim the horse."

"You're very good, sir, considering how Sam and I treated you."

"That is neither here nor there. If you wish, you may tell Mr. Kimball I said that horse and his saddle are worth at least fifty dollars, and he ought to give you that much. He has to resell it, and of course he wants to profit by the transaction. But I think fifty would be fair in this case."

"Thank you. I'll tell him." She smiled ruefully. "I considered keeping him and riding on by myself, but they say it isn't safe in these parts."

"So I've heard. Despite the fact that stagecoaches seem to draw outlaws, I believe you're safer with the stage than you would be alone in this wilderness."

"Yes, my conclusion as well." She drew in a breath, and for a moment David saw again the beauty he'd squired in Scottsburg. "I'll bring you the money—"

David held up his hand to silence her. "Let us say no more about this."

Millie ducked her head and turned away.

David knew he couldn't sit opposite—or worse yet, beside—her tragic figure for days or even weeks as they journeyed east across the Oregon Trail. Before retiring to the barn for the night, he sought out Mr. Kimball. He'd have to wait another two days for the next stage, but in David's mind, it would be worth it. He had no deadline, and he would be much more at ease if he didn't have to board the same stagecoach as Millie.

The next day, an hour before noon, the stage approached from the Snake River. The tenders had the fresh team ready, and Millie came out of the house dressed as she had been the whole trip, in a plain but serviceable dress. She'd replaced the wide-brimmed hat with a cloth bonnet.

Mr. Kimball walked to the coach and opened the door. The four passengers inside got out to stretch their legs. Mr. Kimball handed Millie inside. She peered out the window. David could tell the moment she spotted him on the porch. Her brow furrowed. She was wondering, no doubt, if he was going to board. He turned and went into the house. Mrs. Kimball was pouring coffee for one of the eastbound passengers, and David got a cup from her.

Ten minutes later, the stagecoach left with a blast of a horn and a drumming of hooves.

Mr. Kimball came inside a moment later and walked to where David sat. "Mrs. Evans asked me to give you this."

David unfolded the paper. Two five-dollar bills fell out on the table. She must have written the note earlier and planned to give it to him in the stagecoach, where he couldn't escape. He shouldn't feel guilty that he'd forsaken her company. The woman was relentless. Still, he felt a pang as he read her words:

*Mr. Stone—*

*I don't presume to call you David now, though you once asked me to. Thank you for your assistance at this difficult time. This money replaces what I took from you in Scottsburg. I beg you to believe me, that I am not the same woman you knew then, and I am very sorry. I had no part in the holdup, and I had no inkling Sam and his cohorts were planning it. God has forgiven my sins, and I hope someday you will, too.*

*Mildred Evans*

# CHAPTER 7

Millie huddled in her corner of the seat, avoiding conversation. The stage headed across the Idaho Territory and would dip south when they neared the old Fort Hall. They would follow the wagon train route most of the way, though it was too early in the season to meet many emigrant trains. Freighters were another story. Many mule trains were heading west with supplies for merchants in the Oregon Territory.

Millie's spirits sank to an all-time low as she contemplated Sam's death and David's final insult—he'd refused to travel on with her. She had no doubt that his reason for not boarding the coach was her presence. He would rather stall in the wilderness an extra two days than share the same space with her. When she'd first realized they were fellow travelers, her heart had leaped. She'd had her chance to apologize and return his property. If only he would believe in her once more—but perhaps that was too much to expect.

Tears sprang into her eyes, and she reached for her handkerchief. Her hand came out with David's crumpled one. She'd intended to wash it at the Kimballs' and return it, but she'd forgotten. If she ever got his address again, maybe she could send him a dozen nice handkerchiefs.

Immediately she knew that would be foolish. David couldn't bear to be with her. He certainly wouldn't want to receive another reminder of her wickedness. He might even think she was mocking him—after all, he'd gotten that ridiculous notion that she'd signaled Sam and Lucky by dropping her handkerchief out the window. If she didn't care so much for his good will, she would find that amusing.

The driver yelled, and his whip cracked. Millie gasped and clutched the handkerchief to her breast. Not another holdup. If Lucky's men had found their way over here and gotten ahead of them again, she'd give them a piece of her mind.

The recollection that Lucky had been shot—Mr. Caudle had fired his pistol point blank into the man's abdomen—set her head whirling as the stage leaped forward and the team's hooves pounded on the trail. Sam's death was probably due to his kindheartedness in helping Lucky get on a horse and escape. She seriously doubted that the outlaw was in any condition today to ambush stagecoaches.

Nothing halted their progress now, and the horses ran on for what seemed an age. The passengers held on to whatever they could grab to brace themselves. No one spoke, but all had strained faces. The driver continued to urge the horses on, but no percussions of gunfire came, and no shouts to halt and deliver their money.

At last they pulled into a farmyard and stopped between a large barn and a snug log house. A moment later, the door opened, and the shotgun rider said cheerfully, "All snug and sound, folks."

Millie accepted his hand and stepped down into the chilly twilight air of a mountain valley.

"What happened?" demanded the passenger who disembarked behind her.

"Saw a few Injuns," the man replied. "There's been some trouble through here lately, and we didn't want to take any chances. Hard on the horses, but here we are."

A man came from the house and shouted, "You boys are early."

The driver went over to talk to him. Millie assumed he was the station agent. She made her way around the house in search of the "necessary." When she came back, the driver met her near the steps.

"Not going on tonight, ma'am. You might as well get some supper and see if they've got a bed for you."

Merrileigh Stone sat in the tiny chamber she optimistically referred as the morning room, working on her needlepoint. This house, set in an unfashionable quarter of London, wasn't large enough or grand enough to hold too many rooms for the master and mistress to lounge about in, but one needed a place to carry out the humdrum business of life without worry about mussing the rooms visitors might see.

Smaller and less formal than the drawing room, this parlor took the abuse of the family and saved the more elegant furnishings of the other room for company. Merrileigh preferred to conduct most of her daily business here. Another advantage of the morning room—it allowed her a view of the hall if she positioned her chair just so and left the door open. Through the aperture, she could see anyone going in or out of her husband's study across the passageway.

This morning the objects of her attention were her husband, Randolph Stone, and a young man of slight build and plain mien, his only remarkable feature a shock of wavy blond hair that many a maiden would envy.

He was dressed nearly as well as Randolph. His suit might not be of as nice material, or as flawlessly tailored, but it was fashioned of sturdy fabric and quite stylish. The young man would pass as suitably dressed in nearly any group of London men, though he obviously didn't belong to the class known as "gentlemen." A professional man with a good position.

After a scant twenty minutes closeted with the young man in his study, Randolph saw the visitor out and then came to the morning room. As happened too often these days, Randolph was unable to keep a scowl from his face. Sometimes Merrileigh didn't think he even tried, though she found it most unattractive.

She looked up from her needlepoint. "What is it, my dear?"

"Nothing of consequence."

"Wasn't that Mr. Conrad's man?"

"Yes. Iverson. I don't like him."

"That is neither here nor there. What did he say?" Merrileigh set her needlework aside, rose, and gave the bell pull a tug.

Randolph sighed and slouched into a chair. "My cousin David is returning to England."

Merrileigh clenched her teeth. They'd feared this turn of events for some time. "Rather brazen of him, after all this time."

"I couldn't say," Randolph drawled. He stifled a yawn, as though bored to death with the topic, but his wife knew better.

"Why shouldn't you say?" She rounded on him and glowered at

his lazy form. "If you only cared a bit more, Randolph, we might be living at Stoneford this very minute."

"I don't see how. So long as David's alive, we shall never have that estate." He squinted at her with a bitter air. "You must let go of the bone, Merry. There was a short time when we thought we might have a chance, but I know now I shall never be Earl of Stoneford."

"And why shouldn't you? For years we thought the man was dead. If that were true, you'd have stepped in when Richard died. You were ready to do that. You were *here*. And where was your cousin?"

"Off shooting buffalo and chasing Indians, I expect. Something like that."

"Yes, and I say—"

Merrileigh broke off as the maid entered, bearing a tea tray. She resumed her seat and waited until the maid had unloaded the tray and left them. The mistress lifted the teapot—a charming porcelain pot decorated with violets, but she wished she could replace it with a Doulton tea set. Perhaps one day. She poured two cups full and doctored one to Randolph's taste.

"Here you are." She held out the cup, and he came to get it from her, then resumed his seat.

Merrileigh reached for the second teacup. "As I was about to say, David has done nothing—absolutely nothing—to entitle him to claim his father's title and fortune."

"Other than be born the earl's son," Randolph said drily.

Merrileigh ignored that. "You, on the other hand, have remained close at hand, ready to serve at an instant's notice."

Randolph gave her a wry smile. "Unfortunately, that instant never came, and I was never called to do my duty."

Her lip curled, and she took up the sugar scissors. She needed *something* to sweeten her day.

"I had resigned myself to never knowing one way or the other whether David was alive," Randolph mused. "The sting was fading."

"Yes, and you were set to live out your days a tragic figure." She stirred the sugar into her tea. "Mr. Stone, you know my feelings on the subject."

He frowned at her. "Really, my dear, your suggestion that we take some action—well, it was out of the question. You knew we had no money to search for David, and to what end? To confirm that I would never be earl?"

"Or to confirm his death, in which case you would be. To me, that is worth risking a lot."

"But we didn't have a lot. You knew the limits of my income when we married."

Indeed, she had, but her parents had encouraged the match anyway.

"And when Anne so gallantly decided to brave the frontier, the savages, the bison, and all the rest of it. . ." He shrugged and sipped his tea.

"Yes, you were content to let the late earl's daughter do the work."

"Why not?" Randolph sat straighter and eyed the tea table critically. "I say, do we have any biscuits?"

"Only these shortbread wafers."

"I detest those bland things."

"Then find a way to increase the household budget."

He scowled at her, and Merrileigh scowled back. Both knew they were fortunate to have a cook, a parlor maid, a house maid, and a footman. Merrileigh had hoped that by now they would have increased their income and Randolph would have loosened the purse strings a bit. Unfortunately, that hadn't happened. The few timid investments he'd tried had lost value.

"Perhaps if Albert's school wasn't so costly. . ."

Randolph let out what sounded like a snarl. "You know we can't afford a live-in tutor. We've been all around that several times. There's not room in the house for one, anyway, let alone enough money for his salary."

Merrileigh said quickly, "Yes, I know, my dear. I was merely wishing."

Albert would, in a few short years, be ready for university if they decided to send him. Merrileigh didn't think they'd be able to afford that either, but Randolph was adamant that the boy needed to be prepared to earn a living. She wouldn't bring it up now—she was in no mood for another argument. But personally, she thought the money would be better spent to buy him a commission in the Royal Navy. Once he became a ship's officer, the Queen would pay for his upkeep. And now that the war in the Crimea was over, even an army commission might not be too bad.

Randolph shrugged. "Maybe by autumn we'll be invited to a house party at Stoneford. It will be good to see the old house opened again. I wonder how the shooting will be."

Merrileigh's hand trembled as she raised her cup to her lips. How could he be so accepting and unambitious? Randolph seemed to have given up all hopes of having prospects. So long as friends invited him to house parties in the country now and then and received him at their card parties and balls in town, he didn't care. But she cared.

One of Merrileigh's greatest humiliations was the inability to reciprocate the invitations they received. How long would their friends keep hosting them when she and Randolph had no country house to invite them to visit? Even a simple dinner party was difficult in the cramped, unfashionable townhouse.

If she'd only known when she married him how little prestige she would have, she might have refused Randolph's suit. Of course, she'd been on the upper edge of what was called "the marriageable age" at the time, and her father had bade her consider that Randolph Stone might be her last chance. She was not homely—some considered her fairly pretty, she knew. But without a fortune, she was low on the list for suitors. Randolph's proposal had perhaps saved her from disgrace and ridicule. As Mrs. Stone, she could secure her place in society.

But she'd soon found that Randolph, though received in polite society, had little of the popularity David and his brothers had enjoyed. It seemed the Stone name carried little cachet without money. Time to have another talk with her brother.

# CHAPTER 8

Millie's journey to Fort Laramie took weeks longer than she'd expected. Stalled in Idaho while the cavalry dealt with the Shoshone and Bannock, she eventually met a small band of civilians heading eastward. With a small military escort, they traveled to the Loring Cantonment, from where a lieutenant was about to embark for Fort Laramie with an escort for emigrant trains.

"We'll need to travel fast," Lieutenant Fenley told the men of the party. "We have to get through the Shoshone territory quick, and the Sioux aren't happy either. We've had word of them gathering and letting off steam."

"There'll be a lot of wagon trains coming through," said John Collins, whose family had had enough of the West.

"It will be our job to see that they make it safely through to Oregon," Fenley replied. "Our company will join the first westbound emigrant train we meet and escort them through Indian country. Then we'll go back for the next one."

"You won't go all the way to Fort Laramie, then?" asked another of the drivers, a freighter heading for Missouri to purchase supplies for merchants on the Columbia.

"Only if we don't meet a wagon train coming through," Fenley said. "It's early yet, but you never know."

Millie negotiated a place for her valise in Collins's wagon, and they set out the next day. Millie helped Collins's wife cook, much to the lady's relief. The couple had three young children, and it was all Mrs. Collins could do to keep them away from the fire, let alone cook over it.

Millie's skill was soon rumored throughout the company, and since most of those traveling were men—only one other woman besides Millie and Mrs. Collins had joined them—she was soon able to make an arrangement with several gentlemen. They provided the supplies, and Millie cooked for them whenever the wagons stopped. The Collins family gave her their protection and a place to sleep at night near their wagon. Her other clients paid cash.

Rather than going to Salt Lake, as Millie had originally expected to do, they headed more directly to Fort Laramie and took the Sublette Road, bypassing Fort Bridger as well. Millie had turned down two marriage proposals by the time they reached the Platte River. She didn't want to marry a soldier she barely knew, who'd be off most of the year guarding settlers and dodging Indian arrows.

They found that stagecoaches were traveling regularly along the Platte, with mail for the Mormon settlements. Millie had enough money to procure passage on one of their eastbound coaches. At last she left the Collins family and the military escort behind and ventured on in the stagecoach, which would travel day and night until they arrived at Fort Laramie.

This was hard, Millie thought. She hadn't planned to spend the whole of the spring traveling and then begin a new life. But she needed this. Needed to forget the past—her life with Sam, and before that her short and stormy marriage to James Evans. And she needed to let go of her memories of David Stone and the hopes he'd inspired in her. She'd almost succeeded in quelling her unfulfilled dreams until she met him again on the stagecoach.

She'd have to focus on the future. Find a new place for herself. Because David was out of the picture and out of her life.

David surveyed the small enclave at Schwartzburg, thankful to have gotten this far. He remembered the place from his westward journey. It was run by a shrewd German at the time, but Anne and her friend Elise had told how the men on their wagon train had exposed Schwartz's criminal activity and handed him over to the cavalry. They'd left a young man in charge of the station. Anne and the wagon master had asked him to check on the fellow and send them a note telling them how things were going at Schwartzburg.

Pretty well, from what David could see. The corrals were full of healthy-looking livestock. An emigrant train was camped a mile west of the trading post, and a dozen or more travelers had ridden or walked back to deal with the trader.

Inside the post, a tall, handsome young man stood behind the counter.

"Help you, sir?" he called as David walked in.

David ambled over to the counter. "Are you Georg Heinz?"

"*Ja.*"

David smiled and held out his hand. "Greetings from Mr. Rob Whistler, the wagon master who set you up here."

The young man frowned for a moment. His eyes narrowed as though he was putting together what David had said, and then a smile broke over his face. "Ja. Herr Whistler."

Another man, older and a bit stooped, with gray-sprinkled hair, lumbered over carrying a burlap sack. He set it on the counter and looked up at David.

"Georg's English is getting better, sir, but if there's anything you need help with. . ."

"You're working here with him?" David asked.

"That's right. My name's John Kelly." The storekeeper shook David's hand. "Georg took me on a couple of years back. My wife and I thought we'd stay a few months while we got over the grippe and got our strength back, but we like it here, and Georg asked us to stay on."

David nodded. "I'm glad it worked out for all of you."

"You're an Englisher?" Kelly asked.

"That's right."

Georg's eyes widened. "You are the one?"

"What one?" David asked.

"The one Herr Schwartz said was buried out back?"

David laughed. "I've heard that story from my niece. I'm him all right. But as you can see, I'm still alive."

"That is good, sir."

"Yes," David said. "Very good. Can I write a note and send it on the next westbound? Mr. Whistler and my niece wish to know how you're faring, young man."

"I do well," Georg said.

Kelly nodded. "He's a good lad. A good businessman, too, and an honest one. He's put by a good nest egg and hopes to get himself a wife one day."

David just had time to write his letter and post it before the stage driver blew a blast on his horn. Although the stage was uncomfortable and crowded, it rolled steadily eastward, carrying David closer to England with each revolution of the wheels. He had even met a few interesting people during the last two weeks. One, a man with an interest in a New York rail line, had visions of taking the railroads west. Another fellow traveler was a government man who'd been sent to Utah to try to negotiate with Brigham Young over the accommodation of federal troops there. He gave the opinion that there would be a war with Young's followers before the year was out, which set all the passengers on edge and sparked a debate that lasted nearly three hundred miles.

But the best thing about the stagecoach, in David's opinion, was simple: It was now free of Millie Evans.

Merrileigh hated to part with even four pence to go out visiting, but the cost of an occasional hackney to bear her across town was far less than keeping a horse and carriage—even if she and Randolph had had ample room at their modest establishment, which they didn't.

She must have a serious conversation with her brother, Peregrin Walmore. Rather than wait for him to come around to the house, she decided to descend on him. Peregrin hadn't the means to maintain his own house in London, but he shared a rented house with two other young men. His annual income was enough for a minor gentleman to live frugally, but Peregrin shared Merrileigh's tastes, and therefore could not live frugally.

An amiable fellow of one and thirty, he supplemented his

income by gambling and trading horses. Unfortunately, sometimes his trades and his card games went sour, leaving him frequently out of pocket. If his modest fortune had not been tightly tied up, she had no doubt he'd have blown through it long ago. As it was, he lived large each time he received his allowance and cadged off his friends for the rest of the quarter.

Though Peregrin's interest in the Stone family's fortune was peripheral at best, Merrileigh hoped she could convince him to become her ally. This investment might be more lucrative for him in the long run than the faro table at Tattersall's.

Peregrin knew how much his sister had hoped the death of Richard Stone, the seventh Earl of Stoneford, would bring the title to Randolph. None of that would have been possible if Richard had fathered a son. Or for that matter, if either of his brothers, John and David, had had sons. The three brothers had flagrantly shirked their duty, so far as Merrileigh was concerned. Richard had one girl, Anne, but neither of the other brothers had married or produced an heir, to her knowledge.

Their cousin Randolph, however, had outdone them all, producing Albert as well as a daughter, Francine. Merrileigh considered she'd done her duty well—though a second boy wouldn't have been unwelcome. Still, her husband had a sturdy heir. If only Albert were old enough to help her now.

But Peregrin would have to do. Even though the young man was perhaps not the paragon of virtue and fine character that one could wish for, her brother was certainly capable when he was sober.

She descended from the hackney before his house. Much to her chagrin, Peregrin and his two comrades lived on a better street than she did. She bade the driver to wait, realizing it might cost her an extra twopence. But that was preferable to chasing down another hack later.

Sweeping up to the front door, she lifted the knocker and gave it three peremptory raps. A moment later, a footman opened the door—a gawky boy whose pale hair stuck up in odd lumps and pinnacles.

"Is Mr. Walmore in?"

"Yes marm. This way, please."

The boy held the door while she entered, then awkwardly sidled past her to lead her to the drawing room. Merrileigh hated this room—the dark paneling and high, narrow windows reminded her of a solicitor's office. The three young men sharing this house really should hire someone to overhaul the decorations. She didn't suppose they had the funds between them though, and if they did, they probably wouldn't care to spend them on household niceties. Single gentlemen weren't prone to do a lot of entertaining in their homes.

She settled in on the worn horsehair sofa and rehearsed how she would tell her tale to Peregrin. He was already aware of her husband's situation, which should make it quite simple to understand.

Since Richard and his next brother, John, had died, only David stood between Randolph and the earldom—and the grand estate at Stoneford. How Merrileigh had hoped that David had also met an early end. It seemed so likely. He'd left England twenty years before Richard's death, and after the first ten years of his absence, the family hadn't heard a word from him. So why couldn't he have conveniently died in the American wilderness—leaving behind proof of his demise of course?

Alas, that cheeky girl Anne—Richard's only daughter—had traipsed across the ocean and found her uncle David alive and well, presumably panning gold and guzzling whiskey in the Oregon Territory. If Merrileigh had had anything to say about it, the unworthy churl would have died then and there. But Merrileigh didn't get everything she wished for. Not without hard work, anyway.

Peregrin arrived five minutes later, disheveled and wearing his dressing gown. Merrileigh frowned but refrained from expressing her displeasure. At least he was home and willing to speak to his sister before noon.

"Good morning." She turned her cheek for the expected kiss.

"Ho, Merry. What brings you out so early?"

"My husband's cousin David."

"Oh? What's the word now?" Peregrin lowered his voice and

glanced toward the door. "Hold fast." He walked over and closed it, then returned to settle in beside her on the sofa.

"Randolph received word from the solicitor's office that David is on his way home."

"Oh. That rots."

"Well, Randolph can only think of delightful fall weekends at Stoneford with his cousin, but I tend to share your opinion."

"If David comes home, it pretty well means your Albert will never have a chance at the title." Peregrin stood and walked to the fireplace. He leaned with his elbow on the mantel, his brow furrowed. "What's to do? I suppose you can't break the entailment, now that David has turned up."

"We couldn't anyway. Believe me, I made sure Randolph pursued an inquiry in that direction. No, the only way he can come into the earldom and install our family at Stoneford permanently is in the tragic event that David dies."

"Mmm. No kiddies, what?"

"No. That's one good thing. Mr. Conrad showed Randolph a letter he received from Anne last year, shortly after she'd located David. She stated straight out that he hadn't married, and so had no male heirs." She let that sink in. Her brother generally saw the lay of the land if you let him look it over at his own pace.

"So." Peregrin's face brightened. "If old David doesn't get him a bride, Randolph is still in line."

"Exactly." She smiled at him, feeling they were halfway to understanding each other.

A discreet knock came on the door panel. Peregrin strode over and opened it. "Hope you don't mind—I asked for coffee."

Merrileigh's mouth curled. She couldn't stand the stuff. She declined a cup and waited patiently while the footman served Peregrin. Once the servant was out of the room, she cleared her throat, ready to approach the topic again.

"Now Perry, I didn't tell you this before, and perhaps I should have, but the fewer people who know, the less likely it will get back to those we don't wish to know it."

"Oh? What's that?" He took a sip from his cup.

"Two years ago, when Anne Stone first took it into her head to go to America and find David, I felt it was in our best interest—Randolph's and mine, and of course Albert's—to try to find out quickly whether or not David was still alive."

Peregrin's sandy eyebrows arched. "Oh? Well yes, I can see that it might be an advantage to know, but surely Anne—"

"To know before Anne knew," Merrileigh said deliberately.

He set his cup down on the saucer. "Go on."

"Randolph wouldn't hear of spending any money on it—he couldn't see the need. He was content to sit back and let Anne spend her funds to do the job."

"But you weren't."

"No. It was my opinion that our interests would be better served if we were one step ahead of Anne. If we *knew*."

Peregrin's eyes opened wide, and he pulled his head back. "Why, Merrileigh, you shock me."

# CHAPTER 9

**D**avid stepped down from the cramped stagecoach and looked around. Fort Laramie had sprawled since he'd passed through nearly seven years ago. It looked almost a proper town now, and the walls of the old stockade—Fort John—were left in disrepair. The main buildings of the present, garrisoned Fort Laramie weren't fenced in. The large barracks dominated the other structures, and the Indian encampments seemed smaller than he recalled. The place had looked overrun with tipi villages last time he was here. One of the passengers had said something about the army making the Indian bands move several miles away to protect the grazing for their animals and those of the emigrant trains. Probably a good decision.

"One hour," the station agent bellowed. "Dinner available next door. They've got fried chicken today."

David arched his back to stretch out the kinks and turned toward the station house. It was a bit past noon and quite warm for early June. An hour's reprieve sounded good. He'd ridden the last fifteen miles squeezed in between mail sacks in a covered farm wagon the Mormon fellows called a stagecoach. At least they were getting through.

"Mr. Stone!"

A dreadful feeling hit him, like a pebble plinking off his head. He'd told himself he'd be safe from Millie Evans if he only ate supper and got back on the stage, without strolling down the street or even glancing about the fort's parade ground.

Slowly, he turned toward the voice. Sure enough, Millie was hurrying across the street toward him, her feet raising a small cloud of dust that accompanied her wherever she walked. She wore a dainty hat, and beneath it her hair glinted red in the sun. He was surprised that she had on the same faded traveling dress she'd worn two weeks ago. Had she completely lost her wardrobe and her sense of fashion?

"Thank heaven! I was afraid you'd take the Salt Lake line and I'd miss you entirely." Her smile seemed a bit strained.

"Oh?" David did not see any point in telling her how he'd had to piece together tickets on one local line after another to get this far. She had no doubt done the same thing. The overland mail contract to California had gone to John Butterfield, but he was setting up a southern line. The man was probably wise to go through Texas and New Mexico Territory, as the stages wouldn't have to deal with winter weather, but it certainly didn't make travel any easier in the North.

"If I'd had any idea what the route was like. . ." Millie shook her head. "That doesn't matter though, does it? We've both come this far. I've been meeting every stage for the last week, hoping I'd find you."

"Indeed?" David normally spoke more than one word at a time—in fact, his family and friends would say he was an adept conversationalist—but Millie's effusive welcome tied his tongue. Apparently his efforts to disconnect from her had failed. He cleared his throat. "Might I ask why you were so eager to see me again?"

She put a hand to her brow. "Of course. How uncivil of me. But you see, I'm near desperate. Might we find a place to sit down, and I will tell you my predicament?"

"Well. . ." David couldn't truthfully think of a reason to refuse. "I suppose so, but I need to be ready to board the stage again soon."

She nodded. "I hope to find a way to travel on it myself."

"Oh? I, er, understood you were planning to make this place your new home."

"I was, but—" Millie glanced toward the stage driver, who was throwing luggage down willy-nilly in the dusty street. "Oh sir, your bags. You'll want to watch them here."

"What? I say!" He strode to the edge of the street. "Sir, I plan to go on with you."

"You'll have to wait," the driver said. "The colonel has several

69

sacks we need to add to the load. Unless you want to ride on the roof, but we're tying some freight on there."

The station agent came to David's side.

"I'm sorry, sir. I only just got the word. Most likely the tavern next door can put you up for the night."

Dazed, David looked from his discarded valise to the station house and back. "All right, yes. Thank you." He glanced at Millie, who hadn't budged an inch. "Uh. . .Mrs. Evans, perhaps you will be my guest for dinner?"

She smiled, not the winsome smile meant to charm a man, but a beatific expression of gratitude. David got the uneasy feeling he had restored her faith in mankind, and he didn't like meaning that to Millie.

He found himself sitting opposite her ten minutes later in what looked to be a perfectly respectable dining room.

"It transforms into a wicked saloon after sundown," Millie confided, "but during the day it's not so bad."

He couldn't help wondering if she'd seen the inside of the place after dark. They both fell to their dinner, and he noted that Millie ate as much as he did. Had she gone hungry these last few weeks? He couldn't help a pang of remorse.

When David had finished the main course, he stirred the coffee placed before him. It seemed the proprietor had no tea. "Now, Mrs. Evans, could you please tell me what this is about? And let's be direct, shall we?"

"Yes, indeed." She brought a fan from her handbag and fluttered it before her face, sending a little backhand of a breeze David's way, for which he was thankful. The heat had nearly driven him to strip off his coat, which he would rather not do in public.

"It's my cousin, Polly."

David lifted his cup. "She being the relation who lives here?"

"Did live, sir. She's gone on."

David paused with the cup nearly to his lips. "Gone on to. . . ?"

"To glory, sir. She and her husband both. Her husband was the fort's chaplain this last year and a half, but now they are without one—until the army sends another, that is. Polly and her Jeremiah are buried in the graveyard."

"I'm sorry." David set his cup down. It seemed somehow disrespectful to slurp his coffee when speaking of the deceased. "What will you do now?"

"That's just the thing. I don't know. I've had to spend the money you so graciously let me keep from the sale of Old Blue just to get this far and survive here. Lodgings and food. I earned a bit on the way, cooking for the people I traveled with. But that's run out, and now I've not got enough to go on. I fear I'm stuck here."

David winced. At least she was telling him straight out instead of hovering around and pilfering from him. But how did he even know she was telling the truth? Maybe she knew she couldn't charm him again, so she had switched to a different tactic. But how did one convey such a delicate thought? He didn't wish to insult her if she was truly destitute. Coming on the heels of her bereavement for her brother, even David felt the cruelty of the situation.

"So you've spoken to some of your cousin's acquaintances?" he asked.

"Yes, several. They've been quite kind, especially the colonel's wife. The colonel even gave me five dollars, but he said that he couldn't do anything officially."

"And your cousin's belongings?" David picked up his coffee cup then, to give him something to do besides look across the table at Millie. She did look rather fetching in that hat, though the dress was as drab as dishwater.

"Oh, they're to go to Polly and Jeremiah's daughter. She's married and has five children, but her husband is coming, or so I'm told, to settle the estate and auction their things."

"Ah. Perhaps if you waited for him. . ."

"No, I can't ask them to take me in."

"What will you do then?"

She let out a big sigh and clasped her hands on the table. "I have a plan."

David raised his cup slightly in a sham salute. "Always a good idea."

She smiled then, and his stomach flipped. She really was lovely, even now when she was poor as a church mouse.

"Yes, I always thought so." Millie sipped her coffee.

"And your plan is. . . ?"

"Well, if you hadn't come along, I'd have continued as I have the last several days, walking about town and seeking work. But employment seems hard to come by here." She raised her fan before her face and waved it, hiding her expression as she added, "Oh, there are jobs, of a sort, but I don't want that sort."

"Ah yes."

Millie wouldn't engage herself as a barmaid or worse, of that he was sure. Better to latch on to a well-heeled gentleman passing through. Like himself.

She surprised him by saying, "I'm known as quite a good cook, and I'm willing to do housework or laundry if I must, but they have plenty of laundresses for the fort, and the officers hire enlisted men very cheaply to do for them. I had no luck at all seeking a domestic position. At least, not without other requirements, which I refuse to meet."

Her face flushed, and she fanned herself again.

"Yes, well, a military post is no place for a decent single woman."

"Thank you, sir."

So. He'd designated her a decent woman. Now he would probably have to help her out of this scrape or forever bear the guilt of depriving her of the chance to live an upright life.

"I have friends near Philadelphia. I grew up outside the city. I feel sure I could find an old acquaintance who could give me a reference for work."

He cleared his throat. "Perhaps I could have a word with the colonel."

"Thank you, but I doubt it would do any good."

"Well, since we'll be here until tomorrow, I might walk over to his office." A sudden thought struck him. "And where are you lodging?"

She looked away. "They've let me use a little room in the officers' building, but I fear I've displaced a young lieutenant, and they will

72

all be glad when I've left."

At least she hadn't needed to resort to a tavern. "Have the officers' wives been courteous to you?"

"To some extent. There are only three ladies at the fort now. I am told they expect more this summer, but it's clear I can't receive their charity much longer."

With a sigh, David set his coffee cup down. "Well, since I have the afternoon free, I suppose I'll stroll over to the fort." She wanted him to promise more than that, he could see it in those tragic green eyes. But he couldn't. Not yet. First he wanted to verify her story. He wouldn't wish any woman to be forced into her situation, but he wasn't about to be duped again.

He pushed back his chair. "Perhaps we shall meet again later."

She opened her mouth and closed it.

David paid for the food and walked out into the bright sunlight. The wind over the prairie made the air bearable. He'd left his luggage in the tavern owner's keeping, and now he took his time getting over to the fort. A sliver of conscience chided him—he ought to have escorted Millie to some safer place, but where would that be?

It took only minutes and a confident attitude to admit him to an audience with the colonel. He explained his circumstances and quickly told the officer he'd taken a room at the tavern and planned to take the next day's stage eastward. He didn't want the man to think he was here to ask a favor for himself.

"I ran into Mrs. Evans at the stage stop," he said, watching the colonel's face. "She's an old acquaintance of mine."

"Oh yes. Charming lady. Such a pity." The colonel shook his head.

"Yes," David said. "She told me of her cousin's passing."

"And her husband as well. He was an excellent chaplain, but he insisted on doing a lot of mission work among the Indians. I fear it killed him."

"Oh?" David frowned. "I thought illness took them."

"So it did. Diphtheria, if our surgeon is correct. There was a small outbreak among the Brule Sioux. Mr. Morton wouldn't stay out of their camp. He did great kindness to the Indians of course, but his job was to see to our men's spiritual needs. Because he tended to the savages, he's no longer with us."

"Ah. But Mr. and Mrs. Morton were Mrs. Evans's relatives?"

"So I understand. My wife was very friendly with Polly Morton. She informed me that on her deathbed Polly was fretting. She'd just received a letter saying her cousin was coming for a visit, and she wanted everything neat and clean. My wife assured her we'd get a striker—that is, an enlisted man—to redd up the house for her. Unfortunately, I ended up hiring a couple of men to pack up their belongings instead."

David left the colonel's office vaguely ill at ease. Millie's story seemed to be true, and the cousin had indeed expected her arrival. That was comforting. The part that bothered him was his perceived responsibility. What did Millie expect him to do?

He supposed he could pay her way back to civilization. He hated to have her further indebted to him. But he couldn't drive off and leave her here. No gentleman would do such a thing—even to a woman of questionable character.

"And how did your venture turn out?" Peregrin took a sip of his coffee and waited for his sister to continue.

She grimaced. "I sank all I had into it. All I could lay hands on without arousing Randolph's suspicion, that is. If he ever learned that I'd gone ahead without his knowledge. . ." She shook her head. Perhaps it was best not to give her brother the details. Peregrin would probably not scruple to hire thugs to get in the way of someone he didn't like, but she couldn't bring herself to admit she'd done just that. "Anyway, nothing came of it, and I used up all my year's income as well as a bit I'd tucked away, and loans from several friends."

"I seem to remember you touching me for some cash about that time."

"Yes, well. . .I'm afraid I wasn't forthcoming in my reason for needing it."

"You told me you'd lost heavily at cards, and you didn't want Randolph to know."

Merrileigh waved her hand in dismissal. "I paid you back eventually, and all the rest, but I went without the least luxuries for months on end."

"I know what that's like," Peregrin said. "Seems like I'm never flush more than a week after I get my quarter's allowance."

"That's because you keep gambling when your luck runs black. You just don't know when to hold off on betting."

Her brother smiled impishly at her and ran a hand through his hair, which disarranged his golden locks even more, putting her in remembrance of the footman who'd let her in. Did none of these young men care about their appearance anymore?

"Still, if I hadn't given you a round sum back then, I could have covered most everything in '55, and I surely would have come even last year. Here I am still out five hundred pounds."

"Good heavens." Merrileigh winced, knowing she had little chance of convincing her brother to risk more of his income. Her own annual pittance, which her grandmother had left her, was spent during the first three months of the year to pay off her dressmaker for last year's expenditures and for food and wine served at two dinner parties which she absolutely *had* to host to avoid letting herself and Randolph look like cheap hangers-on. Oh, and two new dresses and a few trifles her husband would doubtless refer to as "fripperies." But they were necessary, every one. A lady couldn't appear at an assembly wearing last year's gown, or take a promenade in Hyde Park sporting an outdated chapeau. It simply wasn't done.

"Does that crestfallen demeanor tell me that you'd hoped I could stand you another sum so that you could try to—oh, I don't know. What is it you think you can do about all this, Merry? Do you hope to hinder David from coming home and laying claim to the title?"

"Well. . .would that be so unreasonable?"

Peregrin laughed. "Not to my way of thinking. Why, if I had one half-wild cousin blocking me from a huge fortune, I'd—well, never mind what I'd do. But I think it's safe to say you must be careful to whom you present this idea."

"I'm well aware of that." She scowled. "It was such a blow when

I learned my first attempt had failed."

He straightened and eyed her with new realization. "Don't tell me you hired someone to go over there and—"

She smiled sheepishly. "Perhaps you also recall me asking if you had any contacts in America. Specifically in New York."

"Why, yes. I thought it odd at the time. I suppose I thought maybe you would pass a name on to Anne if she wanted to hire a private detective."

"Not Anne. Me. I sent word ahead—by a ship that sailed just days before Anne's." Merrileigh laughed. "She didn't tell us her plans. We wouldn't have known if Conrad hadn't told my husband. He was awfully embarrassed about it—said he shouldn't have let it slip. But I seized the opportunity and set someone up to watch her and see if he could find David before Anne did."

Peregrin shook his head. "I'm speechless. You ought to have told me, Merry. I could at least have helped you set things up."

"You're right, I should have. I'm sure now that he bilked me out of far more than his services were worth. But toward the end—ah, toward the end, I was so excited. It was all I could do not to tell Randolph. I'd had word from the fellow I hired. He was close, he said. It was to be over within a matter of days. And then the next thing I know. . ." She sighed. "It was all for naught, and we heard from Anne that David was safe."

"That's bad luck."

"Yes. I haven't had the heart or the means to try again, but now it's becoming urgent. In David's latest letter, he told the solicitors he planned to leave Oregon this spring—a month ago, in fact, as soon as the mountain roads were open."

"What, he's going it overland?"

"Apparently. He could be nearly to New York by now."

"Surely not."

"That is my hope, that it will take him much longer than it took the ship that brought us the news. But when Conrad's man came around to see Randolph the other day, he said we could look for David by fall."

"And you still don't feel you can bring Randolph around to where he'll commiserate and try to do something?"

Merrileigh shook her head. "I brought it up once, way back before Anne left, and he was scandalized at the thought. I daren't suggest that we might have the power to change things."

"Haven't we, though?" Peregrin met her gaze with anxious blue eyes.

Merrileigh smiled. She had not misjudged her brother. His wit might be even keener than she'd thought. "I should have put it all before you the first time."

"Yes. Perhaps we could have worked together to a happy outcome. But you have to understand, Merry. I haven't any money I could lend you now—none."

"What about your friends?"

"Heavens, no. I can't ask them for anything right now."

She sighed. "I wonder if I could borrow enough to send someone to New York."

"Have you any jewelry—"

Merrileigh gritted her teeth and shook her head. "I'm afraid not. Nothing that would bring enough." Again, it was probably best not to tell everything she knew.

"Well, maybe you could go around to the solicitor and see if they've heard any more from David."

"That might help," she said. "Though I think we need to have someone on the spot. I mean, if we wait until he sets foot in England, the danger would be much increased."

"Yes. It would be better to send someone over there—someone you trust. You know David's sailing from New York?"

"I believe so. Perhaps Mr. Conrad's office can say for sure." Merrileigh rose. "Thank you, Perry. Talking to you has been a great comfort, even if you can't help me in other ways. I needn't remind you to keep this to yourself."

"Of course. I hope you find someone to help you—and the means to underwrite the venture. And be assured I'll support you in any way I can."

She had no doubt of that—after all, this venture was in Peregrin's best interest, too. If his sister rose in fortunes, he would go up a notch in society's stock. Of course, he'd probably come around more often for help with his debts, but Merrileigh wouldn't let that bother her if he helped her and Randolph get discreetly into the position of largesse.

He saw her to the door. She had forgotten all about the hackney until she saw it sitting there in the street.

"Oh dear, I didn't expect to be so long. . . ."

"Now, that I can cover." Peregrin hurried away for a minute and returned with a few coins in his hand. "There you go, Merry. I wish I could invest in your adventure, but this will have to do."

# CHAPTER 10

**M**illie sat as long as she felt comfortable in the dining room, lingering over a second cup of coffee and a slice of cake that the owner said came with the meal. When men began to come in and line up at the bar for drinks, she felt their eyes on her and decided it was time to leave.

She thought about asking for the piece of cake David didn't eat but gave up on it when a trooper came to her table and said, "Share a drink with me, ma'am?"

"No, thank you." She scurried out into the sunshine and walked toward the parade ground.

What would she do if David wouldn't help her? She'd never felt so powerless. She didn't even have a horse. If she stole one from the military enclave, no doubt she'd be tracked down and hanged.

Why hadn't Polly and Jeremiah settled in a nice, quiet town? Most places she could find work. She'd offered her cooking skills at the tavern, but the owner wasn't interested in a cook. He wanted saloon girls, and Millie was determined not to sink to that level.

She could go back to her old ways of stealing, but where would that land her? The only alternative she could think of was to marry one of the cavalrymen—which would take time and would likely lead to a miserable existence. Or she could wait for a wagon train to come through and see if she could attach herself to it. She didn't want to go westward again though, and nobody was apt to take her along when she couldn't pay for her own supplies.

Tears flooded her eyes, and she wiped them impatiently with her sleeve. *God, I've begged You to help me find a way to support myself. You're supposed to be with me. Why do I feel so alone?*

She smiled wryly. At least now she'd have a chance to return

David's handkerchief. She'd washed it several times after soaking it with her tears—tears for Sam, for Polly and Jeremiah, and for remorse over the past. If she were honest, she had also shed tears for David and what might have been.

He came around the corner of the men's barracks thirty yards away. Should she approach him? She stood still, gazing at him. He cut such a dashing figure, even after weeks of rough travel. His carriage did that, she supposed, even more than the well-cut clothing. But now she was more interested in his mindset.

*Lord, You say in the Bible You'll help Your children. I need that help now.*

How could she bear it if David rejected her pleas and left the fort without giving his aid?

He looked up and saw her. His steps faltered for an instant, then he came on. Millie inhaled and raised her chin. She had always prided herself in being able to command a serene expression in any circumstances, but now she didn't know how to compose her face. The grieving sister? The gracious fellow traveler? The desperate pilgrim?

Without thinking about it, she mirrored David's countenance—brows lowered, lips slightly parted, eyes somber.

*Dear Lord,* she prayed, *please soften his heart so he can help me this once.*

He walked across the open parade ground and stopped a yard from her. Millie waited for him to speak.

"I am sorry about your cousin."

"Thank you." She clenched her teeth, determined not to cry. Even if he refused to help her, she would not let him see her weep again.

"And you feel that if you got to Philadelphia you could find proper employment?"

"I'm sure of it. There are many opportunities there, and I do have skills." She couldn't stop herself from taking a step toward him. "Mr. Stone, if you help me, I promise to repay—"

"Please." He held up a hand, and his expression told her she'd crossed the line with him. David had enjoyed her company when he could think of her as a genteel lady. When she sank to the level of an impoverished widow begging for aid, his whole attitude toward her had changed. "I shall not expect any repayment. Just. . .get to where you can establish yourself in a respectable manner." He took some money from his pocket. "Here is ten dollars. I shall purchase your tickets, but I would appreciate it if you use this to buy your own meals and necessities. If you need more, tell me."

"Oh, sir." The tears spilled over, to Millie's dismay, but these were tears of relief. Even though he didn't want to be seen paying for her meals—he probably would rather she didn't acknowledge him at all when other travelers were about—she would be grateful to him for the rest of her life. God had used him to answer her pleas, and the Almighty, at least, would not be embarrassed when she expressed her gratitude.

Her cheeks flushed as she accepted the money. "Thank you. I shall endeavor not to embarrass you on this journey." That seemed paramount to sustaining their relationship for the next thousand miles.

He nodded. "I shall arrange the tickets. Be at the stage stop in the morning."

The hack pulled up in Chancery Lane, one of London's stodgiest business streets. Merrileigh gathered her skirts in preparation to climb out. It wouldn't do to trip over her wide crinoline and fall on her face. The footman opened the door and held out a hand to steady her. She stepped down without mishap and eyed the discreet sign beside the modest, half-timbered building: JONATHAN CONRAD, ESQ.

Conrad's firm had been the Stone family's solicitors forever, so far as Merrileigh knew. Probably since the first earl. She had never had occasion to visit them personally before today.

She hesitated. It was risky. She mustn't spill any of her intent. But still, if she hoped for any sort of a chance for Randolph to become the new earl, she needed information. Already her mind raced ahead to what she would do with that knowledge. She would need an emissary. Perhaps she could ask Peregrin to find a man she could trust among his acquaintances. But could she have confidence in one of his friends? Letting too many people in on the plan was dangerous. No more blunders! She squared her shoulders and walked to the door.

In the office, a clerk took her calling card and bade her sit in the antechamber while Mr. Iverson finished with another client. A moment later, a door to an inner room opened, and a gray-haired gentleman with luxuriant whiskers emerged. He turned and spoke to the man behind him.

"Pastiche. That's the one you want to back on Saturday."

Iverson, the junior partner, appeared in the doorway, and over the older man's shoulder, Merrileigh glimpsed his regretful smile.

"I'm not a gambling man, sir, but I wish you well."

"Ha! You'll wish you were. Pastiche. He's the horse to be beat, I'm telling you. You won't get a better bit of advice than that."

Iverson continued to smile as the gentleman limped toward the outer door, but shook his head. The clerk, meanwhile, had risen and handed Mr. Iverson Merrileigh's card and then hurried to open the door for the departing client.

Iverson stood for a moment, fingering the cream-colored card. It ought to impart to him Merrileigh's station in life, imprinted as it was with a nosegay of geraniums and white violets, signifying gentility and modesty. After a moment, he looked up and smiled uncertainly.

"Mrs. Randolph Stone. How do you do, ma'am?"

Merrileigh rose and gave him a slight curtsey. "I do fine, sir."

"I'm afraid Mr. Conrad is not in the office today. He only comes in two days a week now. Perhaps you would like to come back on Monday."

"On the contrary," she said, looking him up and down, "it is you I wish to see, Mr. Iverson."

"Ah. Then come through, please." He stepped aside to let her pass and said to the clerk, "Tea in my chamber."

The inner office had only one window, rendering it quite dark. Iverson's desk was positioned before it, no doubt so that he had the advantage of the light while he went about his tedious duties. Shelves on two sides of the room held leather-bound books—legal tomes, she assumed—and pasteboard file boxes. No doubt the Stones' lives and her chances of living in luxury, as opposed to threadbare gentility, lay in one of those files, gathering dust.

Iverson sat down behind the desk, eyeing her warily. "Well then, Mrs. Stone, what may I help you with?"

Merrileigh leaned forward with what she hoped was an engaging smile. "I was wondering. . .is there any new word from Mr. David Stone? The family is quite anxious to welcome him home."

"No, nothing since what I shared with your husband a few days past."

Merrileigh smiled regretfully. "Pity. I hope to host a dinner party for him shortly after his arrival. You will give us word if you hear anything, won't you?"

"Surely. I shall communicate anything of that sort to Mr. Stone. Your husband, that is."

She nodded. "I suppose I'm too eager to move forward with my plans. You know, it helps the hostess to think ahead when it comes to staging a social event."

"Of course."

Still, she wasn't sure he wouldn't mention this call to Randolph on their next meeting, and that could cause some friction. Merrileigh settled back in her chair and cleared her throat. "Mr. Iverson, I'd like to be sure you understand that I am not here on behalf of my husband. In fact, Mr. Stone has no idea that I've come to see you."

He gazed at her blankly. "All right."

"Don't misunderstand me. We're all delighted that my husband's cousin is coming home."

"Yes," Iverson said. "It will be good to have an earl in residence at Stoneford once again."

"Yes." Merrileigh decided to advance a bit further and see if she could determine where the man's loyalty lay. "My husband and his cousin have always got along very well. When they were lads, that is. As you know, they've not seen each other for more than twenty years."

"Yes, so Mr. Stone told me. Mr. Randolph Stone, that is." Iverson nodded happily.

"To be sure. But you must understand, that though they are quite amiable toward each other, they are, in a sense, adversaries."

"Adversaries?" Iverson sobered. "I'm not sure I understand you, ma'am."

"Why, David Stone, and only David Stone, stands between my husband and the earldom. You must see that."

The young man picked up some papers from the desktop and tapped the edges on the desk, straightening them. "I suppose, in a sense. . ."

A quiet knock in the door drew his attention, and Merrileigh felt his relief that the conversation had been interrupted.

"Come in," Iverson called.

The clerk brought in a tray with a teapot, two cups and saucers, a pitcher of hot milk, and a cone of sugar.

"Ah, here we are," Iverson said with a smile. "May I pour for you, Mrs. Stone?"

"Yes, please."

When they were settled with their tea and the clerk had backed out of the room and closed the door, Iverson said carefully, "Now, Mrs. Stone, I must tell you that if your husband has a notion of—"

"I told you, my husband doesn't know I am here."

"You did say that, but even so, I must say that if he hopes to break the entailment—"

Merrileigh laughed, and Iverson stared at her, his face flushing.

"Sir, as to my husband and his notions, well, truthfully, he hasn't any. It is I who make the inquiry. Not for my husband—he is content to let his cousin resume his place at Stoneford. Not for myself—for I know my place, and I am satisfied with my position in life." It was a lie, but she hoped the color it brought to her cheeks would be interpreted as modesty. "I am asking on behalf of my children, sir.

For it is they who will suffer."

"Suffer?"

"If David Stone were to die this instant, my husband would become Earl of Stoneford."

"Well, yes," Iverson said cautiously. "That is, if Mr. David Stone has no direct heirs."

"But he hasn't. Mr. Conrad told my husband last winter, when your office first heard from David, that he was living in the Oregon Territory, unmarried. Without issue, as the law says—no children. And that means that if my husband did ever inherit the title, our eldest, Albert, would follow him."

"Well. . .he would certainly be the next in line if that were the case." Iverson frowned at her. "But madam, as I was going to tell you before, if you have any idea of the title bypassing Mr. David Stone and coming to your husband—or your son—without going through proper channels, well, that would be quite impossible. However, if you did want to pursue such a notion, it would be best for you to seek out an attorney not connected to the Stone family. You see, whatever happens, we here at Conrad and Iverson are committed to serving the earl. And right now the heir apparent to the title is David Stone."

"Oh please." Merrileigh touched a hand to her lips. "I hadn't a whisper of an idea that we would try to break the entailment. No, that belongs to David, if he is able to claim it."

"Then I fail to see the purpose of this conversation."

Merrileigh studied him thoughtfully. The junior solicitor did not seem at all inclined to favor the idea of Randolph or Albert being in a position to inherit the earldom. She must tread carefully.

She shrugged and gave him a smile. "I expect you'll think me silly, Mr. Iverson, but I thought perhaps it would be in the family's interest to send someone across to—to ensure David Stone's safety. We all know he was attacked in Oregon."

"Yes." Iverson rubbed his jawbone absently. "Odd thing that. We never did find out what was behind it."

"I suppose it was a random incident," Merrileigh said quickly.

"Some Yankee thug out to rob him. But really, I think it might be wise to send a. . .a sort of bodyguard to meet him in New York and accompany him here."

Iverson shook his head. "I regret to say, ma'am, that the trustees are not allowed to spend money on such an agenda. But I understand that Mr. Stone is not destitute, that he has made a small fortune under his own auspices in America. If he feels he needs guarding, he is perfectly capable of hiring some trustworthy men to look out for him."

She sighed. "I suppose you are right and there's no need for me to worry. Forgive me for wasting your time, sir." It was clear that the solicitor would not prevail upon the trustees for an expenditure of that nature, and therefore any possibility of Merrileigh persuading the emissary to do a little extra work on her behalf was out of the question. She rose and gathered her reticule and fan.

Iverson jumped up. "Not at all, ma'am. I'm sure Mr. Stone would appreciate your concern."

"Hmm. It will be a relief to us all when he's home and officially instated."

"Then we agree." Iverson smiled and guided her to the door.

Merrileigh bid him good day and went out to her hackney. She wished she hadn't come. It was worse than a wasted half hour—she'd put a hint in Iverson's mind that she opposed David's claiming his title. And Iverson had neither confirmed nor denied her mention of New York as David's port of embarkation. She'd have done better to keep quiet. And now she had to pay for the time the cabby had waited for her—Peregrin wasn't here to play the gallant for his sister this time. She felt very sour indeed when she descended from the carriage in front of her house and handed over several coins to the driver. Where would she find a man to carry out the task she wanted done for the pittance she would be able to offer?

# CHAPTER 11

Ｄavid purchased two tickets the next morning, relieved that he was able to book passage through to Independence. Millie was prompt, meeting him outside the stage stop. She carried the same battered valise she'd left The Dalles with. David made sure no one was watching them when he handed over her ticket. He then strolled over to watch the tenders hitch up the team, thus avoiding conversation with her.

"We'll be meeting a wagon train on the first stage," the driver told him. "A couple of troopers from their escort rode in last night. Said they're camped six miles east of here."

"Will that delay us?" David asked.

"Naw, we'll go around 'em."

Two men joined them in the coach—bearded men dressed as farmers. They seemed to know each other but said little. David let Millie and the others board first and wound up sitting beside her. He kept to his corner, and she stayed in hers.

They met the wagon train head-on a few miles out. The wagons were strung out in four or five columns to lessen the dust, but even so, it choked the coach passengers. They kept the windows shut, but it drifted in through cracks and settled on their clothing. David's eyes began to water. Millie, he noted, was still using the linen handkerchief he'd given her in Idaho Territory. No matter—he still had half a dozen, and had found a laundry on one of his delays. By this time he knew well enough to carry two at all times.

Hers looked clean when she took it out. That meant she'd washed it at least once, maybe several times. Millie somehow kept a clean, neat appearance under the abominable travel conditions. He did wonder about her scanty wardrobe. Perhaps she'd never had many clothes, only given the illusion of bounty as part of her confidence game.

He wished he could chat with the wagon master or his scouts and pick up some news, but probably what he'd heard at the fort was as fresh as any these travelers would have.

Nebraska seemed endless. David reminded himself countless times that crossing it had taken much longer when he'd done it with three freight wagons. Ten or fifteen miles a day was all they'd done on that trip, at the pace of oxen. The stagecoach was doing ten times that, easily.

Whenever possible, he avoided sitting next to Millie or directly across from her. Still, she looked and smelled better than a lot of people they wound up sharing their cramped space with. Looking at her was preferable to gazing at some grizzled old prospector or a glittery card sharp.

David kept his mind from dwelling on Millie by thinking about England. If all went well, he'd be at Stoneford in a couple of months. He looked forward to spending autumn at the country estate. He hoped the letter he had sent via ship before leaving Oregon had reached the family's solicitor by now.

Of course, he'd communicated to the solicitor earlier. David's niece, Anne, had insisted he do so shortly after she'd found him in Oregon and broken the news of her father's death to him. Even if David never claimed the estate and the title that went with it, she had prevailed on him to let Conrad know he was alive and eligible to do so. That would put many minds to rest in England, she had said.

Now David wondered if that had been the wisest course. After all, an assassin had tried to kill him eighteen months ago. His right shoulder still ached every time it rained, and probably would for the rest of his life. Who had paid Peterson? They'd never found out.

If only the experimental telegraph cable under the Atlantic was completed. He could get a message to Conrad in minutes, if that succeeded. At least when he reached St. Louis, he'd be able to send a telegram to New York and have it forwarded to England on the next steamship.

At a way station came a welcome break from his reverie. The passengers all got out to use the necessary, then boarded again. The other two men lingered, and for a few minutes, David and Millie were the only two in the coach. The silence between them stretched into awkwardness. A real gentleman would make polite conversation. Most women would have spoken unbidden. David suspected Millie didn't dare utter a word for fear of offending him.

At last he could stand it no longer. "You seem to bear the rigors of the journey well, ma'am."

"Thank you. I cannot complain—but if I did, it would do no good."

He smiled. "Indeed. I give thanks often that we're moving forward. I ask no more."

She nodded, then said hesitantly, "Might I inquire after your niece's health, Mr. Stone?"

"Anne? She's fine. Married and happily settled."

"Oh? I'm pleased to hear that. Has she gone back to England then?"

"No, she married an American. Daniel Adams. He was with her in Scottsburg."

Millie's cheeks pinked up, the highest color he'd seen in them since the day of Sam's interment. He realized that Millie had met Anne and Daniel at the time when Sam had impersonated him. Perhaps she was thinking now of the gown she had stolen from Anne's trunk. But David could never mention that. Only a churl would overtly remind her of her past. And she said she'd changed. Had she really? None of the other passengers had complained of missing wallets or trinkets. Perhaps she really had given up stealing.

Her choice not to attach herself to one of the cavalry officers at Fort Laramie still stymied him. Wasn't that one of her old tricks? Playing up to a man with means? Perhaps none of the unmarried men at the fort had enough income to suit her. And of course she'd rather get back East, where the standard of living was higher. The Millie—or rather, the Charlotte—he knew wanted a much higher standard than a career army man or a farmer in some soddy could give her.

He found it ironic that Anne had married a farmer-turned-stagecoach-agent, and her lovely personal maid, Elise Finster, had settled for a rancher who'd been the scout on their wagon train. And here was Millie, born into poverty, yet apparently too good to marry an American pioneer. With her looks and domestic skills, she could have had her pick of men in Eugene. But it seemed she needed a man of a higher class. Well, if David had anything to say about it, she would never know that he was born to the aristocracy. So far as he knew, she'd never learned about the earldom waiting for him across the Atlantic. If she found out about that, he feared she would try again to sink her claws in.

"Now was that the gentleman who. . ."

The door to the coach opened, and Millie let her sentence trail off unfinished. David was just as glad. Too close an examination of their mutual acquaintances could only lead to further embarrassment.

The two hayseeds got in, followed by a man dressed in somewhat dandyish clothing—though if David thought about it, they probably considered him a bit overdressed himself. This man he judged to be in business of some sort, and it wasn't long before he found out.

The dandy sat directly across from David, and he introduced himself to all and sundry with a booming voice that bounced painfully off the ceiling. "Kendall's the name. I'm with the Northern Pacific Railroad."

"Oh, scouting out some new routes?" one of the other men asked.

"Something like that."

Kendall proceeded to fill them in on his travels and complain about the necessity of depending on stagecoaches.

"It won't be many years before you can travel from one ocean to the other by rail," he declared. "And you can rest assured that journey will be more comfortable than this one."

He moved on to describing the short lines being built in California. "We'll be pushing up to Oregon soon and then who knows where."

David stopped listening. It would be awhile before they took rail service to Eugene, where his stage company was based. By then,

Dan and Anne ought to have a nice nest egg. Dan could go back to farming if he wanted. Or if he preferred, he could take Anne to England. David would find a place for him at Stoneford. Maybe he should hold the position of land steward open until he knew what Dan wanted to do.

"And you, sir," Kendall said heartily, fixing his gaze on David. "Where are you bound?"

"Oh, I'm just a traveler headed home." Immediately David wished he'd worded his reply differently. The three men plied him with inquiries about where "home" was and what he'd been up to.

David smiled as blandly as he could. Americans just didn't seem to understand the concept of ennui, however, and he felt he had to answer.

"Yes, I'm from England. Haven't been there in many years."

"And you're going there now?" Kendall asked. "Tell me, how are the railroads there?"

David laughed. "I'm afraid there were none when I left, sir. I was but a youth, and things have changed greatly."

"Ah. I expect you'll find everything modernized. Will you be going to London?"

"Perhaps. But I plan to go directly to my family home, in the country."

He glanced over at Millie. Her green eyes watched him, and he thought he detected a great deal of speculation and scheming.

Merrileigh hurried to the hall when she heard her brother's voice. As the footman took his hat, she beckoned to him and then retreated into the morning room. If Randolph had the chance, he would spirit Peregrin off for an hour to talk about horses and tailors and who knew what.

"Good day, Merry." The tall young man stooped and kissed her cheek. He was smiling, which made her curious.

"Good morning, darling. I've rung for fresh tea. Do sit down."

Peregrin took a chair nearby. "So. Anything new on the matter we discussed a few days ago?"

"Well yes, I have a great many thoughts on the subject." Merrileigh picked up her fan and fluttered it languidly. "It appears that Mr. Iverson and associates are firmly attached to David."

"As they should be," Peregrin said.

"Yes. Alas, they've served all of the Stones since Randolph's grandfather's day or earlier, so they are our solicitors as well. But that becomes a conflict of interest in this matter, I'm afraid."

"So, you're going to consult a different solicitor?" Peregrin frowned at her. "That will take money."

"I daresay. But there's something you need to know." She leaned toward him and studied his face. Her brother might not be as shrewd as she would like, but he had common sense and a bit of pluck. She hoped he would fall in with her newly formed plans to bring home the title. "Perry, I'm determined that my son shall one day own Stoneford and the title that goes with it. And I'm ready to move toward that end."

Peregrin frowned. "You indicated that this is not the first time you've made an attempt to—shall we say—swing the pendulum of fate in your direction."

"It's not. I hired a man who came highly recommended to me. An American known for his efficiency and discretion."

"And yet he failed."

"Yes." Merrileigh sighed. If only Peterson had succeeded in carrying out her plan. But the scanty information she'd been able to gather since that disaster told her only that her distant employee—whom she had never met—had reached his demise in Oregon. She wasn't certain, but it seemed likely that David Stone had killed Peterson in some sort of altercation. David had certainly been badly injured and taken some time to recover.

She would never reveal any of that sordid business to anyone—not even her brother. And the person who'd recommended the emissary—a sharp old friend of her father's who had spent time in America—was gone now. Took a tumble off his hunter last spring and broke his neck. She didn't know anyone else to turn to if she wanted to hire another emissary willing to carry out her scheme.

No, if she was going to do anything, it had to be on her own, and with only one other person—someone she could trust implicitly. She'd decided Peregrin was that person. Perry, if he thought he stood to gain by it, would do a great deal for her.

She leaned toward him and lowered her voice. "I have a new plan, and I'm ready to put it in motion."

Peregrin's eyes flickered. "Indeed? I take it Randolph doesn't know?"

Merrileigh smiled ruefully and shook her head. "No idea at all."

# CHAPTER 12

## Missouri

Millie had nearly reached her limits of overland travel—but she had also nearly reached the end of the stage line. At Independence, they could take a local railroad line to St. Louis, cross the river on a steamer, and from there it would be smooth going to Philadelphia by train. She could hardly wait to leave the crowded, smelly stagecoaches behind.

The station agents had packed in as many passengers as possible for the last six or eight stages, and wedged mail sacks between them. Sleep was nearly impossible, though Millie's eyelids drooped constantly. She made some attempt at each stop to freshen her appearance and always tried to be one of the first back inside the coach, so that she could claim a corner. Even so, discomfort reached new levels.

Nine people squeezed inside, and three or four rode the roof. Extra bags were tied on top with them. Millie didn't know how the six-horse teams could pull the weight.

David largely ignored her these days, though he did ask her once—quietly, at a nighttime way stop—if she needed more money for food. He seemed to have an endless supply of cash. Fortunately for both of them, Lucky's gang hadn't made it down the line to David when they were collecting donations.

Beside Millie sat a man who had obviously never ridden a stagecoach before. Not only were his clothes too clean and nice for the rough traveling conditions, he had also made no effort to hide his prosperity—something discreet gentlemen like David Stone did not flaunt in public, knowing it would make him the target of pickpockets and outlaws.

The newcomer wore a snowy-white shirt with a winged collar bearing points so crisp and sharp that Millie smiled and endeavored not to look at them. The collar was of the "patricide" fashion, so called because of a story in which a young man went home after a long absence and embraced his father. His collar points were so sharp that they cut his father's throat. It was all Millie could do to hold back a chortle.

The man's black frock coat was perfectly respectable, but again a bit overdone for travel, with a velvet collar. His outfit was completed with a woolen vest and black trousers. His watch chain draped conspicuously across his middle, from pocket to button hole, and his pristine cuffs were held in place with monogrammed gold studs. He balanced a top hat on his lap. The odor of the pomade that kept his hair in formation was not unpleasant at the outset, but as time passed, Millie found it annoying in the closed space.

Several of the men seemed inclined to converse. One, a Mr. Nelson, had journeyed a couple of stops westward to investigate the possibility of opening a dry goods store.

"My stores in Independence and St. Joseph have been quite successful," he said with a satisfied smile. "I envision expanding westward as the rail lines grow."

"Sounds like a good idea," said a man wearing rough trousers and an unmatched sack jacket.

"And you sell ready-made clothing?" the dandy asked.

"Yes sir, but we have a tailor employed at each store, to make alterations as needed. In Independence, we have enough business to keep a seamstress employed full time as well. She does dressmaking in addition to the alterations, and we have a large yard-goods section."

"It sounds like a store I should like to patronize," said the woman who sat with her husband opposite Millie.

The merchant turned and smiled at her. "Oh yes, ma'am. If you are in Independence any length of time, you must visit Nelson's Dry Goods and Sundries."

The woman fluttered her eyelashes at her husband. "Well, Mr. Brackett, perhaps we shall have opportunity to do that."

"Perhaps."

Her husband seemed to feel no need to elaborate, but Mrs. Brackett beamed on the merchant. "We are visiting his family for a few weeks."

"By all means, then," Mr. Nelson said, "I do hope you will stop by." He glanced at Millie. "And you, ma'am. I'm sure you'd find our merchandise to your liking."

"Thank you," Millie said. "I am going on to St. Louis, so I doubt I'll have time."

"Oh, I am going to St. Louis as well," said the dandy.

Millie gave him a polite nod.

He fingered the knot of his Windsor tie. "Perhaps we shall ride the train together."

She mimicked Mr. Brackett and said only, "Perhaps." She hoped her tone and brevity would send the dandy a message that he could clearly read—that she didn't wish to divulge her personal plans to him or the rest of the company.

"My name is George Andrews," the dandy said.

Millie nodded. Several of the other passengers were watching her, and she knew she would be insufferably rude not to divulge her name.

"Mrs. Evans."

"Pleased to make your acquaintance," Andrews said with just a hint of triumph in his tone.

"Evans," said Mrs. Brackett. "Are you related to the Cleveland Evanses?"

Millie puzzled over that. "I don't think so, ma'am. I've never been to Cleveland, and so far as I know, Mr. Evans had not either."

"Was that thunder?" one of the men on the middle seat asked.

Millie perked up and listened. They were less than a day from Independence, and she didn't want anything to slow them down now.

Sure enough, an ominous rumbling sounded above the rattling of the wheels and drumming of hoofbeats.

"I do hope we shan't run into a bad storm," Andrews said, leaning toward Millie to look out her window—or perhaps that was a pretext to lean closer. She pulled back and tried to flatten herself against the seat cushions. His well-oiled hair came within two inches of her nose.

"Really, sir," she gasped.

"Oh. Pardon." He resumed his former position, and Millie grabbed a deep breath.

A flash of lightning illuminated the inside of the coach. Mrs. Brackett was clinging to her husband's arm. The seven men's faces glared stark white for an instant. All seemed to be frowning, except David. Millie caught only the merest glimpse of his expression, but he looked rather amused.

A moment later, rain pummeled the stage, and someone on top gave a shout. Scuffling and thumping on the roof brought Millie a mental image of the hapless "outside" passengers pulling their coats over their heads and burrowing down amidst the luggage to make less-tempting targets for the lightning.

"Has a stage ever been struck by a thunderbolt?" She wished she hadn't spoken aloud, as Mrs. Brackett began to simper and fuss to her husband, and several of the male passengers began telling horrific tales of stagecoach disasters, whether involving lightning or not.

Since leaving Oregon, Millie had driven through several storms, some of them severe, but this one seemed more determined than the others. Wind rocked the coach, and the horses began to snort and whinny, pulling unevenly with jerks and sudden starts.

One of the men swore—in the darkness, Millie couldn't tell who the offender was, except that it wasn't David or the dandy. The horses settled into a pounding gallop, and the coach hurtled along. The driver's even-toned calls to the team were interspersed with thumps on the roof and muffled shouts from the men riding there. How on earth did they stay on? Millie had heard a man saying he'd tied himself to the roof the night before, so he could sleep without fear of falling off. Perhaps they were all anchored to the top of the stage like hog-tied calves waiting for a branding iron. She shuddered and clung to the edge of her seat, bracing with her feet so she wouldn't slide into Mr. Andrews.

After two or three minutes, the horses slowed somewhat, and she unclenched her fists. The coach settled into a steady, swaying pace as the thunder abated.

The next flash of lightning showed seven faces much relieved—and David Stone, apparently asleep, with his hat tilted downward so that the brim hid his eyes.

"And so, you see, it's time to hire someone else to go across the Atlantic," Mereleigh said in a matter-of-fact tone as she poured out the tea. "I had thought at first that perhaps Conrad's associates would send a man and we might persuade their fellow to take our part."

"Pay him off, you mean," Peregrin said.

Merrileigh glanced toward the doorway. "Please, dear, you never know when one of the servants will appear, or when Randolph will pop in."

"Of course. Forgive me."

She nodded and passed him his cup. "They do have an agent who conducts business on the continent for them, but they're not inclined to send anyone to America. In fact, Iverson seemed to consider me a bit of a mother hen to think David couldn't get himself home without assistance."

"So, what do you intend to do? Hire someone in America again?"

"I don't think there is time, even if we knew whom to contact."

"Whom did you contact before?"

"Someone Colonel Waterston had met. I simply told him I needed a person who could do any sort of job and not be too scrupulous about it."

Peregrin blinked at her in surprise. "Didn't the old boy want an explanation?"

"Oh, I made one up. Something about Father having invested in the States and been bilked. I said I wanted someone who could put things right for me. The colonel never batted an eye."

"Really?"

"Yes, but of course he is dead now, and I don't want to leave any sort of a trail leading back to me—correspondence or bank drafts, any of that."

Peregrin nodded. "So, what will you do?"

"I thought I'd send someone from England."

"Is there time?"

"I think so. There's a steamship leaving Liverpool on Monday for New York."

"So quickly?" Her brother sipped his tea, frowning. "Have you the funds to pay someone and buy his passage? And how will you hire him? Cast about Soho for a footpad or some such person? Really, Merry, it's too dark. And too dangerous for a lady to get involved in."

"That is why I need your help."

"My help?" Peregrin laughed. "You want me to hire an"—he looked cautiously toward the doorway and whispered—"an assassin?"

"Heavens, no. I just want you to help me get the money. Then we'll worry about finding someone who can...who can keep David from returning to Stoneford. That's all."

Peregrin was silent for a long moment. Did he not understand? Or maybe he understood every word and was too appalled to speak.

If her brother decided to call a halt to her scheming, Merrileigh would be at his mercy. Any time she stepped astray, he might tell her husband and his cousin what she had attempted to do—and what she had already done. Her heart lay like a stone in her breast while she waited for a clue to Peregrin's thinking.

"I know you haven't much money of your own, Merry."

"No, and I daren't ask for any from Randolph. He'd demand to know why I needed such a sum."

Peregrin swallowed hard. "How much are we talking about?"

She tried to give a casual shrug, but it turned out more of a nervous jerk. "The last attempt cost me several thousand."

"Really?" Peregrin's eyes flared, and his mouth crinkled into a jagged line. "And here I've just cleared my debts and thought perhaps I could be of assistance."

"You've cleared your debts?" Merrileigh pounced on it with glee.

"Oh Perry, I've always had faith in you."

He sat back, grinning. "I had a very good night on Saturday last. I kept winning and winning. It seemed like a dream. And the last round, I thought, 'Am I an imbecile? What if I lose it all now?' But I won again! And I pushed back my chair and left the game."

"I'm so proud of you!" She eyed him severely. "Now don't you go thinking how much you might have won if you hadn't quit."

He shook his head. "No. Instead I was thinking of you, Merry, and how much it would mean to you that I'd paid off my own gambling chits and caught up on my bills, instead of dunning you or old Randolph to tide me over."

"Oh, it does, truly."

Peregrin smiled. "There's not much left over, but—"

"How much is 'not much'?"

"Forty quid, but it's got to last until my next allowance—"

Merrileigh leaped up and paced to the window. Could they pull this off? It would cost her dearly—and more so if Randolph got wind of it. But the possible reward was so alluring. Lady Stoneford. A countess. Mistress of the estate. No more wrangling over expenses. She could have an allowance ten times what she got now, without causing Randolph a twinge of apprehension.

She clenched her teeth. When she'd learned that her first attempt at stopping David had failed—after months of careful planning and thousands of pounds sunk into the endeavor—she'd felt she would never recover. But Randolph never learned how much she'd lost, nor where she'd spent the money.

She'd borrowed from friends and taken an advance on her small yearly income. Though it had pierced her deeply, she'd sold a diamond necklace she'd inherited from her aunt and replaced it with paste. If Randolph had any idea! But he wasn't all that observant, and she didn't wear the necklace very often. When he'd insisted she wear it this spring to a gala event, she took out the replacement, which looked generally similar to the original, and he hadn't noticed the difference.

"If only we had a way to increase what little we have," she murmured.

"Yes. Believe me, Merry, if I had a bundle, I'd loan it to you. You've helped me so many times." Peregrin set down his teacup and stood. "Well, I suppose I'll toddle across the hall and say good day to Randolph before I go."

"Oh, must you leave so soon?" Merrileigh fluttered her fan. "I hoped you could stay to dinner."

"Afraid not." He grinned at her. "My mates have been so good about springing me a loan when I needed it that I thought I should treat them tonight."

She frowned. "But darling, you'll go through your forty pounds quickly if you start that sort of thing."

He shrugged. "Can't be helped. I've touched both the fellows more than once, and it's my turn to show a little generosity. And after we eat, there's a pastiche at the Golden Door this evening—"

"Pastiche!" Merrileigh nearly shrieked the word.

Peregrin halted and eyed her cautiously. "Yes, that's what I said. We're going to the theater. Hedgely's cried off to take Miss Linden to an assembly, but—"

"It's a horse." Merrileigh hastened to his side. "Do you know of a horse called Pastiche?"

"What? A horse? Hmm, well yes, now that you mention it. Old Cardigan's got one."

"Lord Cardigan? Good heavens!"

"No, not him. His uncle. Or are they cousins? Doesn't matter. It's Edmund I'm speaking of."

"Of course." Merrileigh nodded. "I saw him at Conrad's two days past—the day I spoke to Mr. Iverson."

"Oh?" Peregrin shrugged. "Bit of a stiff shirt, if you ask me."

"But he owns racehorses."

"Yes, he's part owner in an Irish stud, I'm told. Brought over a couple of three-year-olds for the season. That Pastiche you mentioned is one of them."

Merrileigh touched her closed fan to her lips and smiled. "Yes. How fortuitous."

"How do you mean?"

101

"I think this is the opportunity we need."

"Opportunity for what?" he asked.

"Why, to increase our funds."

"*Our* funds?"

"Cardigan seemed certain his horse will win on Saturday."

"Well. . .doesn't every owner think his horse will win?"

"I suppose so," she said doubtfully. "No, darling, I think this is a sign."

Her brother grimaced. "I'm not so sure, Merry. You know I can't get down to nothing again so soon. It would be horribly bad form."

She turned to him eagerly, excitement building in her chest. "But you'll win. I know you will."

He smiled indulgently. "I'll give it a try."

"And if we win, you'll go?"

"Go where?" Peregrin's eyes clouded. "You mean me go to America? Good heavens, Merry! I'm not sure I could. . .well, do anything permanent. I never knew David Stone before he went away, but his brother was a good chap."

"You can't think about that." Merrileigh seized his wrist. "Think of the good that will come to us if he never returns. If he met with an accident, I'd be in a position to favor you."

"With what? Invitations? I mean, a good time is nice, but really, Merry—"

"I'd pay you two thousand after Randolph came into his title. I might not be able to get it right away, but I promise you, over time, I'll give it to you."

Peregrin's eyes narrowed, and he inhaled slowly. "I will consider it. And now I must pay my respects to Randolph." He winked at her. "Or should I say, the future earl?"

# CHAPTER 13

"Wouldn't you know it?" the dandy asked. "It's the last river we have to ferry, and it's flooded."

"That shouldn't matter," said one of the men who'd been riding on the roof of the stagecoach in the rain. "What's a little more water?"

"The current is unpredictable," the station agent said. "We dasn't take the horses over until things look calmer."

David sighed. Farther east, they would leave the horses behind and get a fresh team on the other side. They were still far enough into the frontier that the horses had to ford or ferry with them.

But another day wouldn't really matter to him. Besides, it would be good to sleep in a bed for a change, instead of propped up on the stage seat. Now that they were closer to civilization, they had a full quota of passengers on every leg of the journey, which meant they had no room to stretch out to sleep as they rode.

He made a trip out back to wash. When he came inside, the odors of stew and cinnamon struck him and set his mouth watering. Millie was off to one side with the station agent, speaking to him earnestly. At least a dozen people sat around two tables in the dining room, and he realized another coach had also halted here. The station agent's wife was plying them with chicken stew, cornbread, and pie.

David decided he'd better speak for a bed quickly, given the number of passengers needing accommodations. He stepped up behind Millie, hoping to be next in line.

She cast him a glance over her shoulder and immediately her anxious wrinkles smoothed out. "Oh Mr. Stone. I'm told there is only one room left, and—"

"Your wife says two dollars is too much, but I could put six men in there for fifty cents apiece," Mr. McLeary, the station agent, said, as though daring David to refute his logic.

"Well, first of all, we aren't married."

"Oh. Sorry. My mistake. Well, I certainly can't give a whole room over to one woman."

David looked around the room. He spotted only one other woman among the passengers, sitting at the far end of the room, deep in conversation with the man seated next to her.

"And what is that woman doing?"

"Why, she and her husband hired a room before your stage even got here. Their two sons are with them, so they took a full room for the family."

David frowned. "I don't suppose that lady would go in with Mrs. Evans and let another man take her place?"

"I highly doubt it," McLeary said primly.

"Well, what are the other gents doing?" David tried to remain calm and sent Millie a glance he hoped she would take as reassurance.

"I told the last three they'd have to sleep in the barn. I'm only charging a dime out there."

"Then I suppose that's where I'll be tonight. But you certainly can't send Mrs. Evans out there." David took his wallet from his inside pocket and took out two one-dollar bills. "Here. Mrs. Evans shall have the room you spoke of. And don't you think for one instant of putting anyone else in there with her."

Millie grasped his sleeve, but not before the station agent had seized the money.

"Oh, you mustn't. It's too much."

"I know it's too much, but it's the way it is." David fished in his pocket for a dime and handed it to McLeary. "That's for me." He pulled Millie aside. "Do you have enough left for supper?"

"Yes." She looked down at the floor, her face coloring. "Thank you."

"Good. Have a pleasant evening." He walked away in search of his own meal, knowing McLeary and his family would speculate mightily over this friendship. He wished he'd been more alert and taken care of the lodgings first thing.

He wasn't surprised when Millie approached him later. Outside, the rain continued to fall and the wind howled. The passengers who had rooms retired early. The men who'd been relegated to sleep in the barn sat around the dining room stove, telling yarns and drinking coffee or whiskey, as their preferences fell. David kept quiet but listened with half an ear.

About eight o'clock, Millie came down the stairs and asked the agent's wife if she might get a cup of tea. While she waited, she looked David's way. He made himself turn his gaze away quickly, but most of the other men were ogling her. Millie was wearing the lovely gown she'd worn in Scottsburg. He wondered why she had put it on in this rustic place. Was she out to snare a man this evening?

"My, don't we look fine?" Andrews murmured.

David shifted in his chair and took a swallow of coffee.

A moment later, Millie was at his elbow.

"Excuse me, Mr. Stone. If you don't wish to speak to me, I understand, but I thought perhaps we could have a word."

As David rose, Andrews winked at him, but David ignored him.

He followed Millie to the far end of the room, near the kitchen door, carrying his coffee mug with him. He pulled out a chair for her at the end of one of the tables and sat down kitty-corner from her.

"You're looking very elegant this evening," he said.

"Thank you. I didn't like to wear this dress, but my traveling clothes needed washing so badly, I felt I should take advantage of the stop. This is the only thing I had available that wasn't in dire need of laundering."

"Aha." What she said made perfect sense—his own stock of shirts was getting quite soiled, but he'd had no opportunity to have them laundered lately, and he was sure he smelled no worse than the other men they traveled with. At least Millie had a washbowl in her room where she could rinse out a few items.

"I hope you won't think I put it on to taunt you." Her lovely green eyes studied him anxiously.

"Because you were wearing that frock the last time I saw you? In Scottsburg, I mean?"

"Yes. That and. . .well, your niece must have told you it was her dress."

"I seem to recall her saying as much. But she didn't know how you could have come by it."

Millie's cheeks went scarlet, and she looked down at her hands. "I took it from her luggage in Eugene. Her friends were taking her trunks to their house to keep for her, and I—I took it from their wagon."

David nodded. Rob and Dulcie Whistler, who had escorted Anne to Eugene in her search for him, had surmised as much.

"I regret the action deeply," Millie said, "but I haven't the means of making restitution just now."

David wished she hadn't brought it up. Or had he been the one to steer the conversation? No matter—they were both thoroughly embarrassed now. But that was progress, wasn't it? He doubted Millie had known how to be ashamed when she'd first worn the dress. Here she was, talking of restitution.

He cleared his throat. "I'm sure Anne doesn't expect anything of the sort."

"No, but it was wicked of me. I see that now. Perhaps you could give me her address, and later on I could send her the cost of the gown."

"No need." Hearing from the thief who stole her belongings was probably the last thing Anne wanted now. And Millie would no doubt be staggered to learn the cost of that gown. Anne had probably had it sewn by a skilled modiste in London or Paris.

"But I would feel better, sir."

"Perhaps she would feel worse."

"Oh." Millie eyed him pensively. "I hadn't thought of it that way. You're saying it is kinder not to remind her?"

David shrugged. "Let the past go, Mrs. Evans. That is my advice."

"I've sought to do that, but it's been difficult."

"Yes, I can see that." He took a sip of his cooling coffee.

The mistress of the house bustled in from the kitchen with a tray and set it down beside Millie.

"There you go. Sorry it took so long, ma'am."

"It's quite all right," Millie said. "Thank you."

"Ten cents, please," said Mrs. McLeary.

"Oh." Millie's eyes went wide, and a panicky look drew her mouth in a pucker.

David reached automatically for another coin. "I'd like more coffee as well, please."

"Certainly, sir." Mrs. McLeary accepted his money with alacrity and headed into the kitchen again.

"I'm sorry," Millie said. "I didn't think she would charge me for a cup of tea, after I'd paid full price for supper."

"Ah, but that was more than an hour ago." David smiled. "These folks have us over a barrel, as the saying goes, and they seem eager to take advantage of that."

"Well, thank you for your courtesy and generosity." Millie looked anxiously toward the window. "This storm! What if it doesn't let up?"

"Then we may be here awhile."

She winced, and David could almost read her thoughts.

"Don't fret, Mrs. Evans. I have enough to see us both through."

Tears stood in her eyes when she turned to face him. "But I shall owe you such an awful lot."

"There now, don't weep on me. I'm running out of handkerchiefs."

Her startled look made him chuckle. The hostess returned with the coffeepot and topped off his mug. David lifted it and winked at Millie. "To good weather."

Her smile was only a bit watery as she lifted her teacup. "And a swift journey." He noted that her hand trembled as she took a sip.

Merrileigh Stone could scarcely wait to see her brother again. She'd persuaded Randolph to take her to a large, noisy party thrown by a woman her husband detested. Mrs. Simwell held a rout once each season and invited far too many people. Her father had made his vast fortune in coal, and many of the aristocrats snubbed the couple. But Chester Simwell was a likable man, the younger son of the younger son of a knight. Barely in the upper class. Yet he was so much fun that the men of the ton embraced Chester and tolerated his wife when they couldn't get around it.

Randolph took a few turns about the dance floor but tended to slink off into a corner with a few of his cronies to chat with a glass of punch in his hand. Merrileigh danced a couple of times, but mostly she worked her way around the room, conversing with dowagers and watching the door for her brother. Peregrin had promised her by way of a note that he would see her at the Simwells' tonight.

Midnight was nearing before he arrived. As soon as he'd greeted the hostess, Merrileigh pounced. She knew his habits. If she didn't corner him quickly, Peregrin would slide off into the card room, and she wouldn't see him again before dawn. She seriously doubted Randolph would last that long.

"Perry! Come here." She plucked at the sleeve of his rather flamboyant blue velvet tail coat and practically dragged him into the adjoining room. It held a pianoforte and a few chairs, and Mrs. Simwell referred to it as the music room.

"What's got you in a dither, Merry?" her brother asked. "Don't tell me. It's about David Stone."

"Shh. Yes." Merrileigh closed the door and unclipped her reticule from her sash. "I've got thirty pounds more for you."

"Really?" His eyes lit. "How did you get it?"

"I told Randolph I needed a new corset and shoes for tonight. Of course, my old corset doesn't show—it will last for some time yet—and he was good enough not to pay any mind to my shoes this evening. He never noticed they are the same pair I bought last fall with new buckles." She hiked her skirt a few inches and smiled down at her kid slippers.

"A most accommodating man, your husband," Peregrin said with a saucy grin.

"I think so sometimes. I'll tell you, I was very surprised he came across for me. I think he's happy because Albert is doing so well at school."

"Ah. So we have your son to thank for this piece of good fortune as well."

"Indeed." Merrileigh took out the cash Randolph had given her the day before and handed it over. "I was afraid he would say no or tell me to have the bill sent to him. So I told him I wanted to be sure I didn't start incurring debts for him, and he seemed to think me a considerate and frugal housewife."

Peregrin guffawed and then looked quickly over his shoulder toward the closed door. "Sorry. Now, I take it you want me to put this with my bit for tonight?"

"Only if you feel lucky."

"All right. I'll see how things are going."

"Perry, if you're losing, you'll walk away from the table, won't you?"

"Yes, darling. Don't worry. And whatever I win, I'll put it all on Pastiche tomorrow?"

"Yes. Everything. If we win tomorrow, we'll have enough to send a man to New York and intercept David."

"But if we lose? Merry, can you stand that?"

"I. . .don't know. Just don't tell me how much you have tonight unless you've kept even or worse. If you come out ahead. . ."

"Oh, I see. You won't miss it if you don't know how much it is?"

"Something like that. And you mustn't breathe a word to Randolph. He's not above betting now and then himself, but he'd kick up an awful fuss if he knew what I am up to."

"No fear." Peregrin leaned down and kissed her cheek just as Merrileigh's friend, Lady Eleanor Fitzhugh, opened the door of the music room.

"Oh, excuse me—dear me, Merrileigh! It's you and your *brother*. I thought I'd interrupted a tryst."

Merrileigh laughed. "Nothing so exciting, my dear. Just catching up on things with Perry. We don't see enough of each other these days."

"That's right," Peregrin said, edging toward the door. "I'll drop by and see the kiddies one day this week, Merry. Oh, and do tell Randolph I want to see his new shotgun." He nodded with a dazzling smile toward Eleanor and ducked out.

Eleanor frowned. "Dash it, I wanted to make him promise to

dance with my Cornelia. She thinks he's ever so handsome."

Merrileigh grinned. "Well, he is." For the moment, she was inordinately pleased with her brother, and with herself. "I suppose Randolph is looking for me. He'll want to go home as soon as supper is over."

"I thought this party was a little better than the usual Simwell standard, didn't you?" Lady Eleanor asked as they glided toward the door.

"Oh, I don't know. . . ." Merrileigh realized she'd been too focused on her scheme with Peregrin to pay much attention to the decorations, the music, or the other guests' evening wear.

"Did you see the flowers in the little drawing room?" Eleanor took her arm and led her back toward the crowd.

# CHAPTER 14

**D**avid lay wrapped in a blanket in the hayloft in the barn. Below him, the extra horses from the stage line's stalled coach teams snorted and stamped. Four other men had staked out spots in the mounds of loose hay and burrowed in for the night. The rain drummed on the roof for the first hour, but then it let up.

Maybe they'd be able to cross the river in the morning. David sent up a quick prayer to that effect. The delay in Idaho, where they'd buried Sam Hastings, had been less depressing than this place. And less expensive.

Thinking of money made him think of Millie. He wished she'd leave him alone. Yet he anticipated seeing her again in the morning. Would she wear the drab traveling dress, or would she enter the stagecoach in Anne's gown? The men in their party had thronged her as soon as she and David had ended their conversation. The dandy—Andrews—was bolder than the others. He'd tried to draw her into conversation and had even offered to buy her a drink. Millie had brushed him off with the rest by giving a cheerful *goodnight* and escaping to her room. That had made David feel perversely contented.

Now he pondered the things she'd said to him over tea. Since they'd left The Dalles, she'd told him several times that she was truly sorry for what she had done in Scottsburg. To all appearances, her penitence was real. Why couldn't he accept that? He supposed it was his male pride that still stung.

She'd said tonight that she prayed for him—that all would go well for him. That bothered him perhaps more than his attraction to her green eyes and appealing face. How could he think she and God were on speaking terms? That seemed a little farfetched to him, knowing she'd lived for some time by stealing and deceit. Shouldn't he be the one praying for her?

He'd watched her on the stagecoach, and honestly, he hadn't seen any behavior on her part that he could criticize—other than asking him for money. He hated it when acquaintances approached him for loans. In the old days, he would have given her a set-down.

The only thing was, now he knew the cruelty of the West. There was a sort of unwritten code of chivalry out here. Not all the men he met were gentlemen, but very few would leave a woman stranded in the wilderness when they had the means to help.

David rolled over in the hay, comforting himself with that knowledge. He hadn't helped her because she was Millie. He'd have done the same for anyone.

But she *was* Millie. And this Millie held up well under strain and hardship. She exhibited great patience and discretion. And her green eyes danced through his mind whenever he tried to sleep.

He just wished he could know for sure that she was telling the truth and that she had really repented. She'd mentioned reading his Bible. Was that true, or had she said it to gain his sympathy? He pressed his lips together in a firm line. A bewitching smile wouldn't fool him again. Still—if he knew she'd truly settled things with the Almighty, would he feel differently about her? He told himself he would not, but he couldn't be certain he believed that.

One of the other men coughed and rustled about in the hay. David wondered what these rustics would say if he told them they were sharing their hay mow with an earl. He smiled in the darkness. They wouldn't believe him, not a man of them.

Millie rose early. The stage station was packed to the rafters with stranded travelers waiting to cross the river. The agent and his wife had their hands full, and this might be the one time during her journey when she stood a chance of earning some money. Her brown traveling dress was still damp around the hem, but she put it on anyway.

She tiptoed down the stairs and through the dining room. Two men had spread their bedrolls on the floor near the stove, and she didn't want to awaken them. She pushed open the kitchen door. Sure enough, Mrs. McLeary was coaxing the coals in her cookstove into life. Her eyes were rimmed below with dark circles, and her shoulders had a weary stoop to them. Millie eased into the room and shut the door softly.

"Good morning."

Mrs. McLeary jumped and dropped her poker with a clatter loud enough to wake everyone in the house.

"I'm sorry." Millie hurried forward to pick it up for her.

"What do you want?" Mrs. McLeary eyed her suspiciously. "Breakfast won't be served for another hour."

"I thought perhaps I could help you this morning." Millie smiled. "You have so many guests, surely you could use a bit of help setting the table or serving coffee—anything that will ease your load, ma'am."

"Well. . ." The hostess's eyes narrowed. "Can you make biscuits?"

"Oh yes. How many do you want?"

"Ten dozen."

Millie smiled. "Give me an apron, and point me to the lard and flour, ma'am. The first batch will be ready by the time you have the oven hot."

Mrs. McLeary opened a cupboard and tossed an apron to her. "Good, because I'll be hard-pressed to fill those men up. My hens only gave eight eggs this morning. Maybe I should charge extra for the eggs."

Appalled, Millie tried to stay calm as she tied the apron strings. "You seem to have plenty of side meat. Perhaps you could scramble the eggs and give them each a small portion. Or if you have plenty of potatoes, I know a recipe for an egg and potato dish that goes well in the morning. Oh, a bit of cheese helps it."

"Yes, I've got spuds and some cheese," Mrs. McLeary said grudgingly. "I guess that would be all right."

"Marvelous. And have you any dried apples?"

When the men started filtering to the dining tables an hour later, the women were ready with mounds of biscuits, a large crockery bowl of applesauce, fried bacon, and a large pan of what Mrs. McLeary told them was "my special breakfast ramekin." It gave off such a tempting odor that all of the diners accepted a portion.

Mrs. McLeary scurried into the kitchen with an armful of empty dishes. "Is the new coffee ready? My, they like your egg-potato dish, Mrs. Evans."

Millie, who was elbow deep in a pan of dishwater, smiled. "Oh, I'm glad. And yes, I think that pot of coffee should be just about drinkable by now."

"Would you care to serve it?" Mrs. McLeary asked doubtfully.

Millie took that as praise—the hostess was willing to let her appear in the dining room and perhaps acknowledge her part in the success of the meal, rather than keeping her hidden in the kitchen. But Millie felt she'd gain more by working hard and letting someone else take the glory.

"No, you go ahead, ma'am. I'm making fine progress on these dishes."

Mrs. McLeary cast a glance over the sideboard, where Millie had set the clean cooking pans to drip dry.

"I must say, you're a regular plow horse when it comes to kitchen work."

"I'll accept that as a compliment."

The hostess picked up the coffeepot. "It was intended for one, to be sure. I don't suppose you'd consider stopping here for a while? As a cook?"

"No, but thank you. I hope to press onward as soon as the river permits it." Millie couldn't imagine the station agent paying her much, and when the flood season was past, they might not want her at all. Best to move on. She hummed as she plunged a stack of dirty plates into the water.

"Oh, and be sure you eat, too," Mrs. McLeary said. "Heaven knows you've earned it."

"Thank you, I shall."

That was two bits she'd saved David, Millie reflected as the hostess left the room.

The dining room door flew open, and Mr. McLeary lumbered in. His gaze settled on Millie. "Ah, Mrs. Evans. How nice of you to help my wife this morning."

"You're welcome, sir." Millie kept scrubbing away at the cheese baked on to a tin pan.

"I knew someone other than my wife made those biscuits—she hasn't the touch for them."

Millie smiled.

"And that potato ramekin, as she calls it, was mighty tasty."

"I'm glad you enjoyed it, sir."

Mr. McLeary nodded. "If you're interested in finding work, ma'am, I'll pay you a dollar a day, and you can have Sundays and Thursdays off. We don't generally get any stagecoach passengers for meals on those days."

A dollar a day was a decent wage for most jobs, especially for those a woman might find, but it was much less than Millie had earned when cooking in a restaurant that catered to miners. Beside, this stage stop was fairly isolated. There wouldn't be any social life to speak of. Where would the cook sleep? In one of the rooms they now rented out for guests? Or would they stick her in a tiny cupboard with a cot? Though she wasn't afraid of hard work, a life of drudgery and fending off men's advances didn't appeal to Millie. Philadelphia, with her connections there, was her best chance at finding a new and pleasant life.

"I do thank you for the offer, sir, but I must go on with the stage."

"Hmm." McLeary frowned. "Well, the river's still too high for you to go today. Too dangerous."

"Oh?" She looked up at him as she squeezed out her dishrag. "Do you think we shall be able to cross tomorrow?"

"Perhaps. And if you want to keep helping my wife today, I'll pay you that dollar, and you can have your meals besides."

"Thank you. I'll accept, if you don't charge for my room tonight either."

He opened his mouth as if to protest then grimaced. "You drive a hard bargain, Mrs. Evans, but my wife gets quite harried when we're filled up with guests. It's a deal."

David reached for a third biscuit. For once, a stage stop provided ample food for the travelers. Perhaps it was because they were stranded and the owners wanted to keep them from complaining overmuch. This breakfast seemed vastly better than last night's supper. Though not ill-tasting, the stew had been a bit watery and bland. That and the cornbread had been served in stingy portions. But these biscuits—David had never tasted better.

The driver who'd brought them to McLeary's the day before reached past David for the butter.

"They must have a new cook. I've never knowed Miz McLeary to make such fine biscuits before. Even the coffee's good."

"Oh?" David looked down the table, where their hostess was refilling some of the other men's cups.

The one woman dining with them said loudly, "This potato and egg dish is delicious. Would you share your receipt?"

Mrs. McLeary hesitated, then laughed. "You've caught me out, ma'am. 'Tis not mine at all. The other lady what's staying here made it from scratch, and not having a receipt book or anything."

Other lady? David glanced quickly about for Millie, but she was nowhere to be seen. He'd assumed the noise of the overly full house had kept her wakeful last night and she had slept late. Had she really risen early to cook for them?

When Mrs. McLeary came down the table with the coffeepot, he held out his mug. As she poured, he said softly, "Pardon me, ma'am, but did I understand you to say that Mrs. Evans cooked this meal?"

"She gave me a bit of assistance this morning." Mrs. McLeary didn't seem happy with the accolades the others were giving the food. "That's not to say she did it all, by any means, but I was telling Mrs. Willard that Mrs. Evans did volunteer her way of making the egg dish. We were short on eggs this morning, you see, being as we have so many guests."

David nodded. "And where is Mrs. Evans now?"

"Oh, she's about," Mrs. McLeary said vaguely.

David said no more but finished his breakfast. Afterward, he went outside and strolled toward the river. The water roiled among the trees, which rose from it like pilings. It lapped at the doors of a barnlike structure, and two men stood next to the building, mournfully watching the swollen river.

David ambled toward them and called, "Are you the ferryman?"

Both men turned toward him, and the older one nodded. "I am, sir."

"What's the forecast? Shall we get across soon?"

The gray-haired man shook his head. "She's crested, but you see the ferry." He pointed, and David saw the flat boat then, tied to a tree several yards out from shore.

"The dock's clear under water," the ferryman said. "Wish I'd put a longer rope on the ferry. We may lose it yet."

"If you're lucky, you might get over tomorrow," the other man said. "Or the next day."

David thanked them and walked back to the house. On impulse, he walked around to the back. The kitchen door on the back porch stood open, and he looked inside.

Millie was wrist deep in a large pan of dishwater. The plates and cups flew through her hands, into the suds. Scrub, turn, swish, and she dropped one in the big kettle beside her, which David assumed was clean water. Scrub, turn, swish, plunk. After repeating the motions half a dozen times, she shook the drops from her hands and picked up a pair of tongs, then proceeded to pluck the clean dishes from the rinse and place them to drip dry in a rack.

Mrs. McLeary came back from the dining room with a tray of dirty coffee cups and silverware. She set it on the sideboard near the dishpan, and Millie went back to her routine of scrub, turn, swish, plunk.

David almost stepped into the kitchen, but he thought better of it and backed away, slipping down the steps and around the corner of the house in silence.

He went to the barn and rummaged through his luggage. His leather-bound Bible met his fingers, and he pulled it out. Near the barn door, he found a keg of horseshoes. Placing a short board across the top, he made a stool. For the next half hour, he read undisturbed and closed his eyes to reflect and pray.

*Lord, I don't know what to ask for. My instinct is to plead with You to get me away from this place, but You know better than I do. Bring us along in our journey in Your own time.*

At the sound of men approaching, he opened his eyes. Two of the tenders came into the barn.

"Mr. Stone." One of them nodded to him as they passed and went on to care for the idle teams.

David rose with the vague feeling that there was something important he should have prayed about, but whatever it was had slipped his mind now. He climbed the mow ladder and put his Bible back in his valise. Too bad he hadn't brought another book along. He hadn't seen any reading material in the station house, but perhaps the McLearys had some books in their private quarters.

He ambled across the yard. The ground there was still muddy, though the grass around the house had dried in the sunshine.

The station agent was inside, sorting mail from the sacks the stages had brought in. It occurred to David that the longer they remained stranded, the more people would collect at the stage stop. The hay mow might be as full as the house by tonight.

"Mr. McLeary," he called, walking over to the agent's sorting table. "I wondered if you had any books about the place."

"Well now, we used to have an old volume of Edmund Burke's essays that a lawyer left here, but it disappeared last spring. I suspect the division agent swiped it, but he won't admit it. And there was a copy of *King Lear* kicking about. I'll ask the wife."

"Oh, don't bother, sir," David said. The shotgun messengers for the two stalled eastbound stages had a card game going in one corner, and a couple of passengers off the second coach were seated with mugs before them. David headed toward them, but Millie came out of the kitchen carrying a pitcher of water, and he found himself smiling at her.

"Mrs. Evans, I am told you had a hand in preparing our sumptuous breakfast this morning."

"Well, yes."

"That was a proper meal, if you'll allow me to say it. Very tasty."

"Thank you." Her long lashes swept upward, revealing her captivating green eyes, but she quickly veiled them again. "I trust you had a restful night, sir."

"Perhaps not as restful as some, but more so than others," David said, thinking of the stamping horses beneath the hay mow and the rustling noises and snoring that wakened him repeatedly in the darkness.

She nodded and gave him the ghost of a smile. "I expect that's right. And if you'll excuse me, I shall rest myself. The house seems to be quieter now than during the night."

He inclined his head in a bow and watched her go up the stairs. Millie really was a charming woman. Quite personable, and that auburn hair. . . Though she must be at least thirty, she'd kept her youthful grace and winsomeness, not to mention her figure, which of course, a gentleman never would comment on. If she'd been born to different circumstances, she could have fit easily into his social circle in England. David couldn't think of another woman besides his niece or Elise Bentley that he'd rather make small talk with at a party.

He turned away with a sigh. What was he thinking of—social circles indeed! This was America, where such things didn't matter. Perhaps he could get a cup of coffee and join the other men. Their conversations started up again, and David became aware that they'd stopped talking while Millie was in the room. It seemed every man's eye was drawn to her, and they'd all postponed their business until she'd left.

# CHAPTER 15

A commotion in the hall disturbed Merrileigh. She and her husband were just having tea with the children, and then she would dress for a card party at the Fitzhughs' home. She did hope this interruption wouldn't force them to change their plans.

The maid entered with a perturbed look on her face.

"What is it, Mary?" Merrileigh asked. "Did someone come in? I heard voices."

"It's Mr. Walmore, mum. He insists on seeing you."

Randolph frowned. "Tell him to come on in."

The maid looked doubtfully toward Merrileigh.

"I'll go and see what he wants," Merrileigh said quickly. Pastiche's race must have been over two hours ago, and she dearly wanted to hear the outcome, but not in front of her husband.

"Father, do you think I'll be able to go shooting with you in the fall?" asked Albert.

*That's it,* Merrileigh thought. *Distract your father for a few minutes. That's all I need.* She smiled as she crossed the hall to the morning room. What good children she had!

"Perry, what's to do?"

He turned toward her, and she caught her breath. His hair stood on end, as though he'd run his hands through it many times. His cravat was undone and hanging loose about his neck, and his complexion was pale as ice.

"What's happened?" She strode to him and took his hands. "You lost, didn't you?"

He frowned and shook his head rapidly. "No. No, I won. You were right about Pastiche."

"Then—what's the matter?"

"Merry, you'll hate me so!"

"Just tell me."

"Hedge and I went round to the club after the race, and Lord Brampton was there. He wanted to get up a game of faro."

"Faro?" Things fell rapidly into place in Merrileigh's mind. "You didn't. Tell me you didn't lose the whole bundle."

"No, but. . ." His breath came in shallow gulps. "Merry, he accused me of cheating."

"What?" She stared at him. "Are you mad?"

"No, but he was. Stark, raving insane. He claimed there was no way I could be so lucky."

"Lucky? You mean you won again?"

"Bless you, dear." He reached a trembling hand into his coat pocket and pulled out a fistful of notes. "Five thousand pounds I came away with."

Merrileigh's jaw dropped. "You. . .you won that much?"

He nodded. "Last night after the game at Tattersall's, I had six hundred. After the race, I had two thousand and a half. And Brampton and the others—Merry, I clipped their wings but proper, I'll tell you."

She laughed. "But that's wonderful!"

Peregrin sobered and shook his head. "No. No, it's not. He accused me of cheating, and. . ." He stared at her, his face stricken. "I must bolt, Merry."

"Bolt? What are you talking about?"

"The old curmudgeon wanted satisfaction."

"You mean he wants to duel you?"

"Worse. He pulled a pistol then and there."

"But. . .what happened?" Obviously her brother was still in one piece. Merrileigh wanted to shake him and make him blurt out the story faster.

"Hedgely put a gun in my hand."

"What? You're joking! He's your friend."

"Yes. Said he would stand as my second."

"But. . .there are rules."

"Yes, and laws, too. We broke every one of 'em. Brampton refused to wait until dawn. He was going to blow my head off."

Merrileigh drew in as deep a breath as her corset would allow. "What did you do?"

"Blew his, of course." Peregrin hung his head. "What on earth am I to do? Hedge told me to run out the back. The club had to call the coppers in, you see."

"Naturally." Meredith swallowed hard. "You'll have to leave England."

"That's what I said. They'll have me in irons if I don't. Merry, they might hang me. I mean—he was a lord."

"But you kept your winnings."

"Yes. Hedge and Rutherford scooped the bills off the table and stuffed my pockets and told me to run for it. Said they'd handle the police, and no one would dispute the money was mine. But I don't dare to go home for my things."

"Let me think." Merrileigh pressed her hands to her temples. "We can't stop the scandal now. We must tell Randolph." She raised her hands. "Oh, not everything, just the part about the club and Brampton. That ship that's leaving Liverpool—you can make it if you have a good horse."

"You still want me to go to New York?" Peregrin stared at his sister with a silly twist to his lips and his eyebrows nearly meeting his hairline.

"More than ever now. Only we won't tell where you've gone. Not even Randolph will know." Merrileigh said. "Your winnings will keep you for a long while, especially if you're careful and don't gamble." She nodded slowly. "You stay here. I'll bring Randolph in so you can tell him. I'll suggest we send our footman around to get your clothes. Just don't tell Randolph that you have a destination in mind. Say that you'll run for it and hop on the first ship you find that's ready to sail. He won't know that I am aware of where you're going."

"And I hoof it to New York and try to find David?"

"Yes. If we can fix it so that Randolph comes into the title, he might be able to fix it for you later, so that you can come back. Do you understand?"

Peregrin nodded. "Merry, I'm scared."

"Don't be." She gave him a quick hug. "Buck up, little brother. And my previous offer stands. Two thousand."

"Half my winnings are yours." His brow furrowed, and the rest of his face tightened.

"Take the two thousand out of that. You have plenty to live on in America for a long time."

The door opened, and Randolph came in.

"Hullo, Perry. You look awful."

The fact that her brother didn't laugh showed Merrileigh how shaken he was.

"I'm afraid I've pulled a stunner, Randolph. Don't hate me. I was only defending myself."

"What?" Randolph stared at him, then swiveled his head to look at Merrileigh. "What's going on?"

"Sit down, my dear," Merrileigh said. "Peregrin has a tale to tell, and then he must flee. Meanwhile, I propose we send Thomas to pack a bag for Perry and bring it here."

Randolph eyed his brother-in-law severely. "What? You've got in so deeply you're ruined?"

"Worse than that, I'm afraid."

"Sit, dear." Merrileigh practically pushed her husband into a chair.

Peregrin walked shakily to a chair opposite Randolph and sat down. "I've shot a man. A lord."

"What on earth?"

Merrileigh gave a quick account, which Randolph punctuated with questions. At last he took out his handkerchief and wiped his brow.

"I suppose you're right. There's nothing for it but to skip until things blow over." He looked up and scowled at the miscreant. "Perry, how could you?"

"It wasn't his fault," Merrileigh said.

"Couldn't you at least have shot him in the arm?" Randolph asked.

Peregrin lowered his head into his hands. "He was going to kill me. That's all I knew. It was him or me. And now I can't show my face in London."

"More like the whole empire." Randolph stood with a sigh. "I shall ask Thomas to go round to your lodgings and pack your things. But you can't stay here long. Most likely the police will come here when they don't find you at home or at your club."

"Thank you," Peregrin choked out. When Randolph had left the room, he looked bleakly at his sister. "I'm not sure I'll be able to carry it out."

"What? New York?"

"You know."

She gritted her teeth. "This is for more than just money and position now, Perry. If you ever want to come back to this country again, you need someone in a high place to watch out for you and smooth the way."

He nodded, raking a hand through his wild hair. "Yes. I see that. But I had no idea at first that you wanted *me* to carry it out. Perhaps I could hire someone there."

"Discretion is of the utmost."

"There was so much blood."

Merrileigh swallowed. "Well, the first thing is to get you off English soil. You've never been to New York, dearest. You'll find it exciting. And there's absolutely no one else we can trust in this matter."

Peregrin frowned. "I say, it's hard when I've just lined my pockets. I was looking forward to living large for a short time at least."

"Well then, go and live large in New York. But do not let David Stone set foot on the deck of a ship. You can cut all the capers you want, so long as you see that through. And keep me informed. When Randolph thinks it's safe, we'll tell you, and you can come home."

"But my friends! Hedge wanted me to go to Ascot with him,

and Rutherford is getting up a house party in a couple of weeks."

"Hedgely has done enough for you, don't you think?" Merrileigh couldn't keep the bitterness from creeping into her voice. "Besides, they have horses in America."

Peregrin fingered his cravat, which usually hung in a beautiful waterfall. "Lord Raglan's nephew is in New York, I believe. Might be one to show me about, with no questions asked."

Merrileigh reached for the fan she'd left on a side table and opened it to cloak her expression. "Yes, that's right. Make all the friends you can. It may help you later. Didn't Lady DeGraves marry an American plantation owner?"

"He's in the Carolinas, dear. Not close to New York at all."

She shrugged. "Just put on a good face. And never talk about this to anyone. Ever. If it comes up, tell the truth—it was self-defense. If the man were a commoner, you'd be in the clear. Most people will understand that."

He nodded. "What if David has already boarded a steamer?"

"I think it's too early, but if you miss him, we'll have to deal with the consequences."

"And what if I miss the steamer in Liverpool?"

Merrileigh pursed her lips. She had researched the available berths well during the past few days. "There's another leaving from Dover on Tuesday next, but you must do all you can to make the one in Liverpool. And Perry, these steamers are so efficient. You'll be there in two weeks, and you'll miss some of the hot, muggy weather while you are at sea."

Peregrin smiled wryly. "How delightful. Can't argue with a good sea breeze, can you? Hmm. Always thought that if I got too deeply in debt, I could skip to America or Australia."

"You'll be fine," Merrileigh whispered eagerly. "When you return in a year or two, your name will be clear. Your friends will want to hear every detail. You'll be in demand for parties. People might whisper behind your back a bit, but the young ladies will find you mysterious and dangerous." She fluttered her fan.

"You make it sound like a good thing."

"Men who weather a good scandal are the most fascinating, you know. They're said to make good husbands, too."

"If you say so." Peregrin's face scrunched up in puzzlement. "America's huge, you know. How could I be certain whether or not he'd left port already?"

"I'll ask Randolph to contact the solicitor—not Conrad. The young one, Iverson. I'll send you a letter as soon as we learn anything."

"Where?"

"Hmm. I believe there's a hotel called the Metropolitan. Lord and Lady Wingford stayed there. I'll write to you there unless I hear first from you, with a more complete address."

He nodded his consent. "I suppose I shall have to travel without a valet."

"You goose!" Merrileigh spanked his hand with her fan. "It's not as if you have a private valet now. You three fellows share one footman, and you know it."

Her brother squared his shoulders and pursed his lips. "Hogg's not a footman. He's our houseman, thank you very much. And I was thinking of hiring my own valet. If I didn't have to spend all my winnings on a voyage, that is."

Merrileigh eyed him narrowly. "Hogg? You could at least call him something more dignified."

"That is his name."

She scowled, wondering what sort of name that was. She called all her parlor maids Mary, no matter what their real names were. "Well, if you do hire a valet, make sure you get one with a dignified name. If you're careful, you can hire one."

Randolph entered. "I've dispatched Thomas. Merrileigh, if we're going to the Fitzhughs' tonight, you'll have to get dressed."

"Oh. Yes." She looked uncertainly at Peregrin. "I hate to leave you, but if we don't show up, Eleanor will be very cross at me."

"I suppose the story's already all over town," Peregrin said.

Randolph frowned. "Then we must go out and stand up for you. Do you have funds?"

Peregrin nodded. "Yes, thank you."

Randolph looked distinctly relieved. "If what you've told us is true, then it *was* self-defense. Get us an address as soon as you can, and we'll let you know if the coast is clear. But if Brampton's people want to prosecute, I suppose you'll have to stay away."

"Do you think it will go worse for him if he flees?" Merrileigh asked.

"I don't know. But if he stays, they might hang him quickly to satisfy the screaming aristocrats."

Perry's complexion took on a greenish tinge. "I'll go. And thanks." He extended his hand.

Randolph shook it. "I'm sorry this happened, Perry. Rent a horse, now. Don't mess about with a coach or anything like that. Too easy to trace. And if you have a choice, the farther away you land, the better. Canada, the Indies. . ."

"Right. I'll just stop here until your man returns with my bag."

Merrileigh stepped up to him and kissed his cheek. "This will all turn out, Perry." Would he have the nerve to carry out her request? She turned away, aware that she might never see her brother again.

# CHAPTER 16

Millie laid aside her Bible—David's Bible—when someone rapped on her door.

"Who is it?" she called.

"It's McLeary. Can I talk to you?"

Millie frowned and rose from the bed, where she'd lain down and napped for an hour before reaching for the book that now meant so much to her. She supposed it was time to go back to the kitchen and help Mrs. McLeary.

She brushed her skirt smooth and quickly patted the impression of her body from the quilt. A glance in the looking glass showed that her hair was passable, and she opened the door six inches.

"May I help you, sir?"

"I'm hoping so, Mrs. Evans. See, the missus don't feel so chipper. She wondered if you was up to fixin' the midday meal by yourself. She started beans and put bread to rise, but now she's feelin' all-overish."

"Oh, she must lie down," Millie said. "I shall come down directly, sir. Just leave all to me. Oh—" She paused with her hand on the edge of the door. "How many are we for dinner?"

McLeary ran his meaty fingers into his beard. "Hmm. Seems to me about twenty. No, if you count the drivers and shotgun riders, I suppose nearer twenty-six."

"Has another coach come in, then?"

"Yes ma'am. The ferrymen want to put the nosebag on here this noon as well."

She grimaced. "I'll plan on thirty then. How does the river look?"

"I think she's startin' to ebb. But no one will cross today."

"What about dishes? Do you have enough?"

"I'm thinkin' two sittings."

Millie nodded soberly. "And could you get someone to wash them, please? I'll have my hands full."

"Mm. I'll put one of the tenders to work. They got nothin' to do today, since the stages ain't runnin'."

He left her, and Millie quickly washed her face and hands, ran a comb through her hair, and took an apron from her satchel. Mrs. McLeary's aprons could wrap around her twice, and she'd rather wear her own.

She retrieved the Bible and laid it reverently on the upended crate beside the bed. "Lord, give me strength, and thank You for this opportunity," she said aloud.

David ignored the temptation to join his fellow travelers in raising a glass of beer. A couple of them couldn't seem to quit after one or two, or even three, though it was still an hour shy of noon. He stuck to his coffee.

Listening to their stories passed the time. One of the shotgun riders tried to coax him into a card game that now had five participants, but David waved him off with a smile.

"I'm not much of a gambler, sir. But enjoy yourselves."

"Well now, I recollect back in '41, when I first saw the Rockies," one of the passengers said. His full beard and worn buckskin jacket led David to believe the man, who was about his age, had a history with the mountains. He seemed about to draw the longbow, as the old-timers said when one set out to tell a story, and he had an appealing manner of speech. David took a deep swallow of coffee and settled back to hear the tale.

Despite the overcrowded inn, the travelers spent a quiet day. The sun shone gloriously throughout the afternoon, lending a touch of unreality to the scene. With such favorable weather, they ought to be moving toward their destinations, yet here they were, becalmed at McLeary's way station, listening to a rough man regale them with an account of his early trapping adventures.

The meals constituted the highlights of the day. The dishes at dinner, though plain fare, hit the gustatory spot. David thought the beans were especially well seasoned, and the cornbread melted in his mouth—not the dry, crumbling version they'd eaten their first evening here. Pudding and cookies followed, fit for a king, or at least the ruler of a small duchy.

Millie was again absent from their table, and David wondered if she was behind the toothsome menu. Mr. McLeary served their main course, but when it was time to refill the coffee cups and pass the desserts, Millie emerged with the host. She wore a colorful, pieced pinafore apron over her plain traveling dress. From across the room, she might have passed for a twenty-five-year-old farmer's wife. A very pretty farmer's wife.

David tried not to follow her with his eyes. When she came near, he smiled and thanked her but said no more. The other men all got a word in, teasing and trying to flirt with her.

"Capital food, Mrs. Evans," called Andrews, the dandy from their stagecoach.

She cast a charming smile his way. "Thank you, sir." She moved on to the next diner, and Andrews stared after her with a silly, vacant look on his face.

"This your cookin'?" one of the drivers asked her.

"Some," she said briskly. "Mrs. McLeary had things started."

"Whyn't you take a stroll with me after dinner?" the driver said. "I'll show you round the barn and all the corrals."

Millie laughed and moved away with her tray. "I think not, but thank you, sir."

Supper turned off even better. David had heard in the interval that Mrs. McLeary kept to her bed all day. He couldn't wait to see what Millie produced for them, and he was not disappointed.

Yet another stagecoach arrived from the west, and Mr. McLeary apparently felt it was time to sacrifice a few chickens. What Millie did to those birds he would never know, but the fried chicken surpassed anything David had ever had the privilege to taste. Mashed potatoes would have been the perfect complement, but it was too early in the season for those, and it seemed the McLearys' supply from last fall was exhausted. When he tasted Millie's rice dish, he forgot about potatoes. This was even better.

Where had that minx learned to cook like this? Was she born knowing about herbs and sauces and how to cut lard into pastry dough? He doubted it, but she certainly had a gift. Even the greens went down well. The only part of the meal he would criticize if asked—which, of course, he wasn't—would be the bread. It was disappointing after the feather-light biscuits they'd had at breakfast.

Of course, David thought as he sipped his perfect coffee. Mrs. McLeary had started the bread before she succumbed to her illness. The jelly and pickles of course, were hers. The rest was Millie's. The smooth, flavorful gravy, the tart lemon pie with toasty-browned meringue topping and flaky piecrust.

With so many guests crowding the tables in shifts, he couldn't hope for a second slice, so he left the dining room satisfied yet slightly wistful.

He considered going around to the back kitchen door and offering his compliments to the cook but thought better of it. After all, he wouldn't want Millie to think he was going soft on her again—though many a man would marry a woman on the spot if he knew she cooked like an angel.

No, he wouldn't think about that. He'd escaped her clutches once. Nothing could induce him to get close to her again. Beneath that appealing exterior lay a hardened, unscrupulous soul, whether she admitted it or not.

The odd thing was, other than her appeal to him at Fort Laramie, he hadn't seen her grasping for anything on this journey or chumming up to a man, though she'd had plenty of opportunities. She was as pretty as ever—nay, beautiful, if you replaced the apron and threadbare dress with a proper wardrobe and loaned her a hairdresser for an hour. Millie Evans would stand out in any company.

But for some reason, she no longer sought to stand out. Rather, she tried to avoid notice. Very strange.

The next morning, Mr. McLeary announced at breakfast that they would cross the river on the ferry as soon as they had eaten. Millie hurried to put out the food and an extra pot of coffee, then dashed up to her room to gather her things. The passengers from her coach would be in the first group crossing.

As they walked toward the river carrying their luggage, she could see the brown expanse before them. It still overflowed its banks and spread wider than it should, but the ferryman seemed confident they could cross safely.

The swirling water frightened Millie. She'd crossed many a stream in her day, but not at flood stage. Still, the ferry appeared to be sturdy. The ferryman said it would take two trips to get them all across. She considered holding back and seeing how the first group did, but all of the others from her coach were taking the initial trip. It she waited for the next, she would delay them. Or perhaps they would go on without her. Tales ran rampant of drivers leaving without passengers who were late.

Their coach and team had to cross with them, though the other stages would stay on the west side of the river. What if the horses panicked in midstream? She wished the stage line could just have another coach and team waiting for them on the other side.

The animals were loaded first and securely hitched to iron rings in the ferry's deck. Since the dock had been damaged in the flooding, the ferry was brought close to shore, and a sturdy plank ramp was constructed for animals and people to use in boarding.

Once the coach and team were secure, Millie and her fellow passengers, along with the travelers from the second coach, were permitted to board.

The family that had shared the inn with them went first, and the wife seemed surefooted when she embarked, though she did hold fast to her husband's arm as they ventured onto the ramp.

Millie had no one to help her. She gathered handfuls of her skirt and set foot on the end of the gangplank. The boards quivered just a bit. The ferry was tied fore and aft to pilings, so the boat would not move during this process, but still it swayed a little. Millie gulped and stepped forward.

"May I assist you?"

It was Andrews who had spoken. Millie had avoided him as much as possible during their stay at the McLearys', and when he'd attempted to engage her in conversation, she'd made sure others were included. Treat them all alike, she'd told herself. That was the key. Don't let any one man think you're singling him out for special treatment.

Only one man in the party stood a chance of snaring her heart—indeed, it was half caught already. But David Stone remained aloof so far as Millie was concerned. He had praised her cooking, but not overmuch, and for the last two days he had greeted her pleasantly if they happened to meet in a doorway. Other than that, he'd barely spoken to her during their delay at the stage stop.

Since adolescence, Millie had instinctively allowed men to help her. She had come to expect it, and it was one of her tools in working toward success. Most men would offer to help a woman, especially if she was neat and ladylike in her appearance. If she was pretty to boot, she could choose whose arm she wished to hold. In this case, Andrews was first in line. Glancing about, she saw at least three other men fall back with disappointed frowns. Perhaps if she had paid them more attention at breakfast this morning, they would have been bolder in offering their protection and aid.

At once she felt a pang of remorse. Since she'd turned to the Lord, she'd begun to learn that God looked upon men—and women—differently than mortals did. And using another human being for one's own gain and comfort was not acceptable in God's view. Millie strove to attain humility and selflessness in her new life, but those lessons went down very hard. She was still trying to fathom their meaning and what good could come from self-effacement.

Now she felt she should accept the gentleman's offer, but with reservation. She gave Andrews what she hoped was a modest and thankful smile, but one that did not promise anything beyond her gratitude.

He responded with a generous grin and patted her gloved hand reassuringly. "We shall be fine, you'll see. Why, in thirty minutes we'll be over and ready to move on."

"I do hope you're correct, sir," Millie murmured.

Andrews's expression deepened into caring concern. "My dear Mrs. Evans, I've longed to converse with you. Perhaps we shall have the opportunity now, and I shall be allowed to distract you from the disagreeable manner of our voyage."

"Indeed." Millie supposed she could stand a half hour's conversation with him in exchange for having a robust young man standing solidly beside her during the crossing. As they stepped off the gangplank onto the ferry, he steadied her and then drew her toward the center, where the ferryman was tying down the luggage to keep the weight low in the craft. Once the coach was on solid ground again, the baggage would be reloaded in the boot and on the roof.

"Does the water frighten you?" Andrews asked.

She opened her mouth to lie and stopped short. Even in polite conversation, she was sure the Almighty would expect the truth. Still, she didn't want this man's overbearing sympathy. "A bit," she managed. "But not overmuch."

"Then let us stand in the center, near the stage. If you wish, you can hold on to the door handle for support."

"Thank you."

Two other gentlemen soon joined them. They held back a bit, seeming bashful in her presence, yet drawn to her. One in particular—a shopkeeper from St. Joseph, she'd learned—seemed especially determined to further his acquaintance with her.

David, on the other hand, flicked a glance her way as he boarded and turned at once toward the bow, where he stood with a couple of other men, partially concealed from Millie's view by the lead horses' heads.

The ferryman closed the gate on the landward side of the craft, and they started across. The current pulled at the boat, and Millie leaned a little, trying to remain steady.

Something struck the side of the ferry, and the craft lurched. The horses whinnied and shifted, and Andrews shot out his other arm to steady Millie. Behind her, the shopkeeper also reached to keep her from stumbling. Caught between them, Millie began to feel like a piece of cheese between the two halves of a biscuit.

Her cheeks heated as she pushed slowly away from them. "Thank you, gentlemen, but if you'll excuse me, I'll stand by the rail."

The ferry still swayed, and she staggered between the other passengers to grasp the peeled log that formed the railing around the sides. The muddy water was only inches below her feet, and the movement of the craft prompted her to cling to the log. Her stomach heaved, and she raised her gaze quickly to the shore. The distance to the far shore was not great now. Trees swayed in the breeze, and a cluster of people awaited their arrival. No dock stood in place, just a landing where the ferryman would run one end of the craft aground. They wouldn't need to use a gangplank, and Millie was grateful.

"I hope you're well, ma'am."

She gasped and looked up into David's blue eyes.

"Quite."

He gave her a half smile, nodded, and edged away.

So. He wasn't totally ignoring her. Millie took some consolation from that. She squared her shoulders and resolved to keep her wits and maintain her balance.

Millie held her own, David had to give her that. She didn't let any of the men take liberties, and she didn't look to them for favors. She could take care of herself, and she seemed to want to do that, so he let her.

Something about the entire situation went against the grain with him. He'd been reared to be a gentleman and to make the way easier for ladies whenever it was within his power. But he kept telling himself he'd done more than his share for Millie already. Besides, he wasn't 100 percent convinced yet that she was a lady.

The ferry bumped the landing hard, and everyone struggled to keep their feet. The horses scrambled for purchase on the deck. Millie flew to her knees on the rough planking.

David stepped quickly to her side. "Are you all right?"

"Oh, I..."

He held out a hand. "May I help you?" At least three other gentlemen eyed them with disappointment and turned away.

Millie grasped his hand and rose slowly. "Thank you."

"Are you certain you're not injured?" He wanted to ask if she'd hurt her knees, but that would be most improper. One never insinuated that a lady had limbs beneath her skirt.

"I shall be fine, thank you."

He nodded. "Let me see you ashore."

"Oh—my bag." She glanced toward the pile of luggage.

"I'll see to it."

He turned and located the ferryman's helper and gave him four bits. "Please take my bags and Mrs. Evans's to shore, would you?"

"Glad to, sir." The man pocketed the coins and grabbed the bags David indicated. The passengers disembarked first and gathered to one side of the landing to watch the ferrymen unload their coach and team.

Millie gazed at the tenders while they hitched up the horses, and David gazed at Millie. He didn't sidle up to her like three or four other fellows tried to. He imagined that if he stepped back, she'd have plenty of gallants to hand her into the coach.

Two passengers left them immediately for destinations in the town, and another went off in the second coach, which was bound for a local train depot. David had weighed the options and decided to ride the stage to the railroad station in Independence, where he and Millie could catch a train to St. Louis. Once they were across the Mississippi, he intended to buy her a ticket to Philadelphia and be quit of her. He saw no reason whatsoever to stay in her proximity once he was sure she had the means to reach her friends.

He turned to make sure their bags were loaded and allowed Andrews to offer Millie his assistance in boarding. To David's surprise, when he entered, he landed next to her and was a little confused as to how it had come about. Had she somehow shuffled and arranged it? Andrews was sitting on her other side.

For some reason, the other men felt they were now well enough acquainted with Mrs. Evans to chatter away at her all the way into town. David said little, though Andrews made repeated attempts to lure him into the conversation.

"Won't you tell us a bit about England?" the dandy asked after a while. "I misdoubt any of us has been there."

David shrugged. "Parts of it look like western Oregon Territory."

"Have you ever been to London?" another man asked.

"Yes, I have. It's quite a place."

"Have you seen the Queen?" The dandy leaned toward him.

"No. When I left England, she was not the Queen. Her uncle William was on the throne then."

"Ah, William IV," Andrews said sagely. "I don't expect you ran in his circles."

"Uh. . .no."

The other passengers laughed, and one of the men on the middle seat winked at David. "Not one of them lords, eh, Stone?"

David smiled but considered it wise to remain silent. The alternatives were to lie or to spill his lineage, so he let them think the other man had made a clever jest. Millie, however, eyed him in silence from beneath her long lashes.

They rode along for some time in amiable conversation, and he thought they must be drawing close to Independence. The horses topped a long hill and started down the other side. The stage lurched forward suddenly, and the driver yelled, "Whoa, you! Slow down, boys."

They plunged downhill at an imprudent pace, and the men on the middle and rear seats braced themselves. Loose articles hurtled to the floor, and Millie grabbed David's arm. The coach continued on, bumping and jolting, and the driver's yells turned to curses.

A sharp drop on one side signified that the wheels had gone off the edge of the road. They slipped across the seats and slammed against the folks on the far side of the stage.

"We shall overset," Millie cried. Her green eyes filled with terror, and she clung tightly to his arm.

"Cover your head!"

It was all David had time to say before the coach tumbled on its side and the horses screamed. In the midst of a fierce clattering and cracking, Millie flew into David's lap, and they both rolled with the stage. He yanked her to his chest and held her close for a second, but the coach crashed into something and jolted her away from him.

# CHAPTER 17

Millie moaned and stirred. Someone was yelling, and a horse shrieked piteously. The whole side of her face smarted, and she put her hand to it. It hurt to open her eyes, but she tried to get her bearings. She lay atop a tangle of bodies—all male but hers. She cringed away and winced at the pain in her wrist.

"Anyone alive in there?"

It was the shotgun rider's voice. His head appeared above Millie, poking in through the window, which was now part of the ceiling.

"Y–yes," she managed to say and reached a hand toward him.

"Easy, ma'am. We'll get you out."

She wondered how he and the driver had escaped injury, but they both seemed to be in one piece. Probably they jumped off the box when they saw that the stage was going over.

The driver appeared on the far side of the damaged vehicle, and she realized then that the bottom of the coach was ripped half away. The driver squeezed in between a broken floorboard and the end of one of the seats.

"Come on out this way, ma'am. Looks like you're the topmost one and the easiest to get out."

It took both of them to pull her through the opening, and her skirt snagged on a splintered board. Before she could tell the men to stop pulling, a rent a foot long ventilated her brown bombazine skirt.

She stood shakily and looked around. The screaming horse lay on his side. The other three were unhitched from the wreckage, but still in their harness, standing off a ways and huffing out deep breaths.

"Is he going to be all right?" Millie asked, indicating the injured animal.

"Not sure." The shotgun messenger grunted. "We'll check him over once we get all the passengers out."

"Of course." Millie stepped away from the shattered coach.

"Whyn't you see to Stone?" the driver said as he dove toward the hole in the floorboards once more.

"Stone?" Millie whipped her head around, looking for David.

"He's yonder," the shotgun rider said glumly, pointing up the hillside down which they'd evidently plummeted.

A figure in dark clothing lay halfway up, sprawled near a large rock. Millie gasped. He must have been thrown out through the gaping hole in the floor as they rolled.

She hiked up her skirt and staggered up the slope. At least her limbs worked. How many of her fellow travelers were severely wounded?

She reached David's side and fell, panting, to her knees.

"Mr. Stone!"

He lay face down, and she grasped his shoulder to turn him toward her but stopped. One of his pant legs was saturated with blood, and his leg's crooked attitude made her heart sink. If nothing else, his leg was broken. She'd heard people could bleed to death if the large blood vessel in the leg was severed.

She didn't want to cause him more harm, but she couldn't let him lie there bleeding. She wondered if she could find the source and put pressure on it. That was the way to stop it, wasn't it? She touched his leg gingerly, but he didn't react. Her cotton glove came away red with his blood.

The terrible thought seized her that he might be already dead. She tore off her gloves and scooted around to his other side. She peered down at his pale face. Reaching out hesitantly, she put her fingertips to his neck. She couldn't feel his pulse, but at that moment he took in a shuddering breath.

Her relief was so great that she felt lightheaded. Surely they should loosen his necktie and collar. What else could she do to make him comfortable without causing more hurt? At the bottom of the hill, the driver and shotgun rider pulled a man from the debris. They laid him on the grass and turned back to get another. Millie counted three passengers down there—one sitting up and rubbing his arm, and the other two prone and still. It would be a while before anyone came to help her.

Frantically, she tugged at David's coat. If she could get her hands in his pockets, she would surely find something useful. David Stone never went anywhere without a clean handkerchief.

David awoke to a loud noise. At first he thought he was in the middle of a gun battle again. He opened his eyes to blue sky, green grass, and pain.

A handsome woman with auburn hair glinting in the sun leaned over him.

"Charlotte." It came out a whisper, but she heard, and she smiled.

"It's Millie, but yes."

He tried to sit up and fell back at once with a groan. The stabbing pain in his leg ran all through him and left him breathless, with a tight, sick feeling below his breastbone.

"Am I shot?"

"No, but you're hurt bad. Relax, Mr. Stone: I've got a farmer bringing some blankets to carry you on. We'll get you to Independence and a doctor."

He tried to sort that out while taking a few careful breaths and looking up at the high branches of a tree that waved gently overhead. A cool breeze lifted a few strands of his hair.

"Was there a shot? I thought I heard. . ."

She grimaced. "That was Gip. He had to put down one of the horses."

"Gip?" David blinked up at her, feeling as though they'd shared a long history, but he couldn't remember the half of it.

"He's our shotgun rider. The driver couldn't do it, so Gip did. It's very sad, but better a horse than a man."

"Yes, indeed." David gritted his teeth. "If I may ask, what happened?"

"The stage went off the edge of the road and tumbled down this hill. Gip said the horses bolted, and the driver couldn't stop them. The stage is now a heap of kindling. I think you fell out when the floorboards ripped open."

David couldn't think of a response. This tale was so bizarre, no one would believe it. It might make for good drawing room talk, though—if he survived.

The pain swept over him again, and he gasped.

Millie touched his brow gently. "Try to relax, Mr. Stone. We'll get you to a doctor as quickly as we can. Your leg is bleeding a lot, but I've tied a cloth around it, and I don't think you'll die of it."

She sounded dubious, and he didn't ask for particulars.

"Does anything else hurt?" she asked.

"My head aches. And my side." He patted his ribcage and winced.

"Hmm. Your breathing is all right though."

"Seems so." He squinted up at her. When she moved her head, the rays of sunlight made vagrant wisps of her hair gleam like firebrands.

"Ah, here's the farmer."

Millie stood, and David tried to see the man she had mentioned, but that involved moving more than his head, and it wasn't worth the stabbing pain.

"This 'un?" a man said.

"Yes, take him first."

"Looks like there's a lot of people hurt down yonder."

"You take this man *now*," Millie said firmly. "I'll help you, if you and your son can't do it."

"Maybe one of them other fellas—"

"They are busy with the other passengers. You said you can't get your wagon any closer."

"No'm."

"Then let us get Mr. Stone into it, and you can take us as quickly as you can to a doctor and send others back to help the stage-coach men."

"Awright."

They shuffled about him, and he lay panting and trying to assess his wounds. His leg. How bad was it really? Were his ribs broken? How would they ever get him to the wagon? He was at Millie's mercy.

"Hey!"

At the shout, David rolled his head slightly and gazed down the slope. The driver was climbing the hill toward them.

"You!" he yelled. "Help us get those men up to the road."

Millie stepped around to where her skirts blocked David's view of the driver. "Mr. Stone is likely to bleed to death if we don't take him straight to a doctor. We'll send help back to you."

"I got four men down there in about as bad condition," the driver said testily.

"But Mr. Stone is up here, and we can have him in the wagon in five minutes. If we wait while you cart those men up here, he may die."

David let the air out of his lungs in a *whoosh*. Was he really that bad off, or was she just being bossy, exaggerating his injuries to get her way? He did feel lightheaded, and he had barely stirred.

"How far is it?" the driver shouted.

The farmer was closer than David had realized, on his other side.

"Nary a mile and a half."

After a pause the driver said, "All right, but you hurry back here. We'll get those others up if we can. We need help right away though. If a doctor can come out here, it would be good."

"Let's go," Millie said grimly. "Sir, you and your son lift him. Be careful. I'll move his leg over onto the blanket while you get the rest of him."

The farmer hesitated, and Millie cried, "Now!"

She was barking orders like an enraged fishwife, which David found oddly comforting and reassuring—it confirmed his assumption that she wasn't a real lady at all, though she could don a cloak of gentility when it served her purposes. Right now, he didn't need a lady. He needed a tough, determined advocate. It seemed

Millie fit the bill.

The farmer snarled and grabbed him roughly under his shoulders. His strapping son bent on David's other side. David braced himself for their rough touch, but when his leg jostled, he tensed and then surrendered to the swirling blackness.

Peregrin Walmore leaned out the window of the hack, gazing at the buildings that lined the street. He was here, on the infamous thoroughfare known as Broadway, in New York City. Though nothing here was more than two hundred years old, he couldn't help being impressed. While not London, the city had a busyness, a vitality about it that warmed his blood.

The cabbie stopped before a row of fashionable shops whose windows displayed clothing, home furnishings, and exotic foods. The door opened, and Peregrin blinked at the driver.

"Are we there?"

"We are, sir."

Peregrin hopped out on the sidewalk, and then he saw the sign, high on the side of the four-story brownstone edifice: Metropolitan. This was the hotel, all right.

"Where do I go in?"

The cabbie nodded toward a door topped by an awning. "Yonder, sir. Your hotel takes up an entire city block. The bottom is all shops and such."

"Very impressive." Peregrin stroked his new mustache as he deciphered the man's words. The accent was going to be a challenge; he could see that.

"Well said, sir. I'll give your luggage to the boy."

"Oh, yes." Peregrin swiveled and saw a young man in a smart uniform approaching. He took out his purse and paid the driver, adding an extra coin.

"I say, how would I go about finding out whether an acquaintance has sailed for England yet?"

The cabbie frowned. "Hmm. Not sure. P'raps you could ask at

the desk. Some of these desk clerks can work wonders."

Peregrin approached the door gingerly. A man in a long livery coat smiled at him.

"Good day, sir. Welcome to the Metropolitan."

"Er, thank you," Peregrin said. "Do I just. . ."

The uniformed man opened the glass-paneled door for him. "Right up the stairs to the lobby, sir."

"Thank you." The carpeted stairs muffled his footsteps. The curved mahogany railing was a wonder, smooth as glass. On the walls along the stairway were paintings of harbor scenes and the city skyline. Peregrin emerged into a chamber as large as a ballroom and as elegantly furnished. The settees, chairs, and side tables appeared to be European-made. Paintings hung in ornate gilt frames, and a magnificent chandelier illuminated the cavernous room.

In a daze, he glided toward the counter that must be the check-in desk. He'd never imagined Americans could build such a lovely hostelry. It was as good as anything in London—more ostentatious than most. He could understand why traveling aristocrats made this their temporary home.

"May I help you, sir?"

"Oh yes, thank you. I should like apartments, please. A bed-sitter if you've one available."

"Certainly, sir." The clerk went on to list several options.

Peregrin ventured uncertainly, "And what is the price of the three-room suite, as opposed to the bed-sitter?"

The clerk smiled as though the British accent amused him. At any rate, Peregrin was a bit put off by the prices. He wasn't bad at mathematics—he fancied that was what made him a moderately successful gambler—and he was fairly certain he'd done the mental conversion correctly. He hadn't expected to pay so much for a room. If he paid full price, his funds would run low within a few months, and he might be on this side of the ocean for years.

Perhaps he could stay here for a few days while he got his bearings, and then move to a less-expensive establishment. That was it. He felt better just working that out.

"Thank you. I'll take the bed-sitting room, please."

"And how long will you be with us, sir?"

"Oh, well, what's today?" He flushed at having shown his ignorance, but after all, he'd just stepped off a steamship.

"It's Tuesday, sir. June second."

"I expect I'll stay until Friday, then."

The bellboy arrived with his luggage, and the desk clerk gave the boy Peregrin's room number. Before turning away, Peregrin put forth his question on how to locate someone in as vast a city as New York.

"Did he stay at this hotel, sir?" the clerk asked.

"I'm not sure. A lot of our friends do, but I expect there are a great many hotels in New York."

"Hundreds. Do you know the name of his ship?"

Peregrin winced. "No, afraid not. Only that he planned to come overland from Oregon this spring and sail from New York."

"Oh, if he's coming that far, I doubt he's reached the city yet," the clerk said. "If you like, I can check our registry for the last month and our upcoming reservations and send word up to your room."

"Thank you." Peregrin slipped him a quarter-dollar and hoped it was enough.

"Oh, and you might inquire with the steamship companies," the clerk added. "I can't do that myself—haven't time—but you might hire someone to do it for you."

Peregrin mulled that over as he followed the bellboy up another flight of stairs and down a hallway that seemed longer than the carriage drive to Stoneford—the place his sister hoped one day to rule over as mistress. Lady Stoneford. He hoped he wouldn't disappoint her. He hated to let Merry down, and she had ways of making one uncomfortable if that happened. Though he loved her, they were very much alike in that way. He had no doubt she'd manage to punish him somehow if he failed, even from across the Atlantic.

# CHAPTER 18

"Gently, gently," Millie called, her distress jacking her voice higher than its normal alto timbre. They'd torn over the road to town, with her urging the driver to make all speed possible, though it jostled her uncomfortably in the wagon bed. She was glad David wasn't conscious during that mad ride.

She looked away as the men lifted David's inert form from the back of the wagon onto a wheeled cot. But she had to look back to make sure they were handling his leg carefully, so as not to cause any further injury. If she had anything to say about it, David would get the best care available.

The fellow helping the farmer and his son looked to be in his late twenties. He moved swiftly but seemed to know what he was doing.

"Are you the doctor?" she asked.

"Yes ma'am. Are you the wife?"

"No. I'm a fellow passenger, but I was previously acquainted with this gentleman. Please give him your best care."

The doctor straightened and glanced at her. "From what your driver tells me, I should hurry out to the scene of the stage accident."

Millie glanced uneasily at the farmer and back to the physician. "I understand. But if you can just take a quick look at Mr. Stone's leg and make sure the bleeding's stopped. His pulse is faint—you must have seen that yourself when you examined him a moment ago. You wouldn't want him to bleed to death while you drive to the crash."

"I've got to be going," the farmer said.

"Help me get him inside," the doctor told him. "I'll send my wife to get someone to go with me, but I can't move this fellow to my examining table alone."

As she followed them into the house, Millie spotted a modest signboard hanging on the wall beside the front door: MARTIN LEE, M.D. A pretty young woman stood in a doorway, watching anxiously as they wheeled the cot past her.

"Jane, hop over to Billy Croft's and see if he can help me. There's been a stagecoach accident on the river road, and this man is the first of several casualties. And if his boy can go round to Dr. Nelson's, I'd appreciate it. We need all the medical help we can get."

Millie noted how quickly the woman moved to obey, without questioning her husband about the situation. Apparently Mrs. Lee was used to taking her husband's orders.

Millie didn't wait for an invitation but trailed the men into a room set up for patient care. The farmer helped transfer David to the table and then left, but within five minutes the man called Billy appeared.

"Want I should ride out there, Doc?" he asked from the doorway.

Dr. Lee glanced at Millie. "Mrs. Evans, was it?"

"Yes sir."

"What do you think? Should we send many men to the accident?"

"I think they'll need help. There were nine of us in the coach when it overset. I saw the driver and shotgun rider moving about afterward—they pulled me from the wreckage. But most of the others are injured, I fear."

"They're off the road then?" Dr. Lee asked.

"Yes. Down a steep hill—it will take some labor to bring them up."

"I'll get my wagon and a couple other fellows if I can," Billy said.

Dr. Lee opened a cupboard and stuffed a bag with rolled bandages and some short sticks. "Take these. If Mr. Stone can wait, I'll ride out in a few minutes."

Billy left, and the doctor turned back to David. "You done any nursing?" he asked Millie as he unbuttoned David's waistcoat.

"Some," Millie said.

"Wash your hands yonder." The doctor nodded toward a wash-basin on a stand in the corner and took a pair of scissors from a drawer. He began cutting David's pant leg open without another word.

Millie looked down at her hands. Blood and dirt caked her fingers. She poured water into the basin and used the bar of soap in a dish next to it. After pouring water over each hand, rinsing thoroughly, she dried them on a towel that hung at the side of the stand.

"All right, what can I do for you?" she asked.

"Go to the kitchen and see if my wife has a kettle of hot water on the stove. She usually keeps one going for me."

It took Millie only seconds to find the kitchen and lift the steaming kettle from the stove. She carried it back to the treatment room. Dr. Lee had David's lower leg exposed and was swabbing at it with cloth. He nodded toward the chest of drawers that held his instruments.

"Take one of those pans on top and pour hot water into it. Get a clean cloth from the second drawer and soak it for me."

Millie obeyed and watched him clean the blood from David's leg, revealing a jagged gash with blood still oozing from it and a stark bit of white bone poking out.

"This is pretty mean looking. There's wood in the wound—at least one long sliver, maybe more. I'll have to take it out. I won't put the cast on his leg until the swelling's down, but I need to close this wound."

"It's broken," Millie said, feeling rather stupid.

"Yes, and badly so." Dr. Lee glanced up at her. "Can you hold his leg for me? Rotate it like this?" He showed her how she would need to hold it so that he could work on the wound with both hands.

Millie stepped closer and reached out to help. A wave of embarrassment washed over her. She was touching a man's. . . limb. . .with her bare hands. She glanced at Dr. Lee, but he was intent on preparing his instruments. He picked up a needle and some sort of thread or fine cord.

"I'm not bad at threading needles," she said.

He kept on with his task. "I'm not bad at it either." He poked the end of the thread through the eye of the needle. "But thank you."

He didn't seem to notice her flushed face but bent over his work.

Hurried steps came through the house, and Millie looked toward the doorway.

"Hold still," Dr. Lee said sternly.

She turned back to the job, but she'd gotten a glimpse of Mrs. Lee, entering briskly.

"Can I help?"

The doctor didn't look his wife's way but asked, "Do I need to go out to the stagecoach?"

"Dr. Nelson is going now. Billy and two other men saddled up to ride with him and assist."

Dr. Lee grunted. "Well, we'll probably have more patients coming in soon. I might do better to stay here and be ready when they arrive. Prepare the bed in the isolation room for this man."

Mrs. Lee whirled and left the room.

"Steady now," said the doctor. "I think I've got the bleeding stopped, but I need to set that leg." A moment later he clipped his thread and straightened. "All right, you can let go."

Millie released her hold on David's leg and arched her aching back.

"I don't think he'll wake when I shift his leg, but I want you to hold on to him anyway, just in case. I had a man sock me in the kidney once when I thought he was out cold."

Millie looked down at her hands, found a finger that wasn't too bloody, and brushed back a lock of her hair. "Just tell me what to do, Doctor."

When he roused, David was lying on a bed, or at least something more comfortable than the ground. The pain in his leg was unbearable. He ground his teeth together and sucked in a breath. The movement caused a sharp pain in his side, and his head felt as big as a bushel basket, but all of that was dwarfed by the agony of his leg.

He peered through slits between his eyelids. A lantern cast harsh light over the room. When he moved his head, a rustling sound warned him that he wasn't alone. Millie appeared at the bedside. Her hair was disheveled, escaping from the knot on the back of her head, and dark circles rimmed her eyes, but if possible, that only made her prettier.

"Mr. Stone."

He blinked, but she still looked a bit hazy. "Where are we?"

"In a doctor's house on the outskirts of Independence."

"We crossed a river. Not the Missouri."

"One of its tributaries."

He started to nod but winced and kept his head still. "I was injured."

"It was after the river crossing. The horses were skittish, and they ran away." She pushed back a lock of auburn hair, and he watched, fascinated, as it fell forward again.

"I remember." He wanted her to talk some more. Her voice was gentle, musical, familiar. "What's the damage?"

"Your left leg is badly broken. Dr. Lee fears you have at least one broken rib as well, and you may be concussed. But you still came out better than the stagecoach."

"Oh?"

She nodded. "It's matchwood. Two of the passengers died."

That knowledge landed on him like a rock on his chest. "Not Andrews?" For some reason, he hoped the dandy had survived. Maybe it was because the fellow was likable—and they both admired Millie in their own way.

"No, he's stove up some, but he'll be all right. I didn't see the worst of it. Once Gip and the driver hauled me out, I went up where you were."

David vaguely recalled her telling him about Gip on the hillside.

"The gentleman from Illinois was one of the deceased. I'm not sure of the other. I think he was one of those in the center when we crashed." She pulled a chair close to the bedside and sat down.

"Well. At least you came through all right."

Her face went sober. "Yes. I'm very thankful."

"How long have I been here?"

"Since yesterday afternoon."

He stared at her until his headache made him close his eyes for relief. "Yesterday? We've been here a night already?"

"Yes."

"Where did you stay?"

"After I'd done what I could to help Dr. Lee, his wife took me to an inn about a mile away. I spoke for a room for you, for when you can be moved."

Just the thought of being moved again clamped David's teeth shut tightly.

"Dr. Lee wanted to keep you here a few days," Millie said matter-of-factly. "But a couple of men were worse off than you, so he said to find a place where I can tend to you, and he'll call on you daily until you're better."

"Where you. . ." David broke off, startled. Did the doctor think Millie was his wife? It seemed he'd be plagued with that assumption until they parted company. And when *would* they part company, anyway? "You mustn't delay your journey for my sake."

She smiled indulgently. "And who would care for you? I don't mind. Really." Her face flushed, and he thought she was quite beautiful.

He closed his eyes to shut out the sight of her. He didn't *want* her hovering over him and blushing like a schoolgirl. And he certainly couldn't let her take on his personal care. Surely he could hire an experienced manservant. . . .

Nonsense, he told himself. A valet in the rambunctious young town of Independence? Only a deluded man would think that.

The truth hit him squarely between the eyes. Millie couldn't go on without him, short of lifting the price of a ticket from his wallet. She was stuck here until he gave her the means to leave. He looked beyond her, seeking a bedside table or a dresser.

"What is it?" she asked.

"I just. . .wondered where my things are." He shifted enough to look down at his own body, covered by a sheet and light blanket. Unless he was mistaken, he wore nothing but his underclothing.

Now it was his turn to blush.

"Your trousers were beyond repair," Millie said bluntly. "The rest of your things are over there." She pointed over his prone form, toward the other side of the room, but David hadn't the energy to roll over. Even if he had the strength, whatever entrapped his injured leg would probably prevent that.

She bent closer and smoothed the edge of the blanket. "Don't worry, Mr. Stone. All of your belongings are safe. When you're ready to get up again, I can go to a haberdashery and find some suitable trousers to replace the ones you had on in the crash. Or perhaps you have others in your luggage. Gip brought it here last night, but no one has opened it."

David could think of nothing to say but "Thank you."

After all, she was not the only one in need. Yes, she was dependent on him now. But even more desperately, he needed Millie.

# CHAPTER 19

Millie's eyelids drifted down, and she jerked suddenly awake. She shifted in her chair and straightened her shoulders. She supposed it was foolish to sit here at David's bedside all night. She ought to go across the hall to her own hotel room and sleep for a few hours.

But she couldn't stand the thought of him awakening alone in the strange room and trying to move about. Dr. Lee had not yet put the cast on his leg, and David might do further damage if he thrashed around.

No, she would stay here until morning, and then perhaps she could pay Billy, the young man who carried bags and did other chores and errands for the hotel owners, to sit with him while she got a nap. Uncomfortable as she was, she would rather stay in case David needed her.

Dr. Lee had dosed him heavily with laudanum before they moved him here. David had protested at first, but the doctor assured him that he wouldn't give him too much of the drug, and that he would regret it if he refused. The trip was apt to be excruciating if he wasn't medicated in advance.

Millie had heard stories about people who were given too much of the concoction. It could stop your heart, some said. She didn't blame David for being wary. Not only was there a danger of overdose, but he was also the type of man who liked his wits about him. Knowing he hadn't been in control of his faculties for hours at a time was probably a great frustration to him in his lucid moments.

At last he had given in, but he'd looked almost fearful. Millie was sure the pain and the uncertainty about his recovery had much to do with that. He looked like a frightened little boy as he lay waiting for the doctor to mix his tonic. Out of empathy so sharp that it hurt, Millie had reached for his hand and held it until Dr. Lee had the dose ready, and then she'd helped prop David up so that he could drink it without spilling.

She'd sat beside him afterward, while Dr. Lee repeatedly checked his pulse and respiration rate. David didn't seem to mind when she reached out and patted his hand. When he slipped gently into slumber, the doctor summoned another man to help him get David into the wagon.

That was nearly twenty hours ago. Millie didn't have a clock, but she consulted David's watch occasionally, to reassure herself that the night was not really endless.

David hadn't stirred for the first eight hours after they put him to bed in the hotel room. It was only as night came on that he began to move slightly now and then, and sometimes he let out a sound that might have been a garbled word or a moan. Millie felt his brow frequently, but he didn't seem to have any fever. She used it as an excuse to brush the blond hair back from his forehead. He really was a striking man.

While the light lasted, she read off and on from her Bible. To save lamp oil—which guests must pay to replenish—she used a candle once true darkness had fallen. Candles cost less and gave enough light for her to get about the room, but the single taper's illumination was too dim for her to read by without sitting very close to it and squinting. She'd put the volume aside hours ago and sat quietly, thinking about David and Sam, and even James, whom she rarely contemplated anymore.

She was growing very fond of David—again, she realized. She liked him even more than she had when she first knew him. He was smart and discreet, though his personality was not the warmest. He seemed to reserve the easy camaraderie she knew he was capable of for those he knew well and trusted.

Even the fact that he now eschewed her fueled Millie's admiration for the handsome Englishman. After all, a true gentleman should avoid women like her—or such as she had once been. She didn't take it as snobbery. Rather, she thought he might be quite devout, though he didn't broadcast it. She'd had his Bible for some time now and had seen how well-worn it had become. She'd found dozens of passages underlined within the book, and her heart sang when she read them, because they often spoke to her own spirit, and she felt she shared something with him.

Dawn had turned the room gray when she startled awake again. A sharp pain hitched between her shoulder blades. She'd slumped in the chair, and she'd probably have a crick all day from it.

She arched her back and stretched her arms and legs. She glanced toward the pillow and froze. David's eyes were open.

She jumped from the chair and bent over him. "You're awake. Can I get you some water?"

He nodded, and she poured some from the pitcher on the washstand into a tumbler.

"It's time for your medicine, too. Past time. I should have given it to you an hour ago, but I'm afraid I fell asleep."

He blinked and said in a low, raspy voice, "Where are we?"

"At a hotel. Remember, Dr. Lee got some men to help move you?"

David shook his head.

"Well, we're settled in here, and you must tell me if there's anything I can do to make you more comfortable. I need to mix your laudanum, but take a sip of water first. You'll feel better."

She helped him raise his head enough to take a small swallow from the glass.

"There. Now just lie still—"

"I need to get up."

"Oh dear." She'd feared this. "You can't. You see, your leg is badly fractured. I'll have to help you."

He stared up at her. She'd never seen a man look so terrified.

"Or perhaps I can rout the boy out, though I hate to wake him."

"Boy?"

"The one who carries the bags in for people."

"Get him."

Millie decided it was best to do as he wished. She set down the medicine bottle and scooted for the back stairs. If Billy wasn't about yet, perhaps Mr. Simmons, the hotel's owner, was. She'd try the kitchen first. Surely the cook would be there and could advise her.

Fifteen minutes later, David wished he hadn't sent Millie away so fast. The boy might be able to help him tend to his personal needs, but he wouldn't trust the lad to mix the opium tincture, and he hadn't allowed Millie time to fix it. Consequently, the screaming pain in his leg got worse and worse.

He hated to take the laudanum. When he didn't, he could think without it clouding his mind. But the pain! He supposed he'd have to give in to the opiate for a while longer.

At last he was settled in the bed again, though he wouldn't say he was comfortable, and the boy stood back.

"Anything else I can do for you, sir?"

David said between clenched teeth, "Send Mrs. Evans in."

"Right."

A moment later Millie was at his side.

"I'm so sorry," she began, but David raised his hand to cut her off.

"Laudanum."

"Of course."

She went to the washstand and began to measure and stir.

"Here you go, sir."

David shuddered as he swallowed it. The vile stuff would put him into darkness for several hours, but by now it was obvious he needed the dose.

"There!" Millie smiled down at him and took the tumbler away.

"I'll need to send a letter right away," he managed.

"Of course. I'll get paper and take it down for you."

He nodded, saving his breath. She left the room, and he let his head sink into the pillow. He wasn't sure he could stay awake until she got back. At least he had someone looking out for him, and for that he was thankful. Before he could form a coherent prayer of thanks, she was back.

"I have a scrap here. If you'd like to tell me what you want in the letter, I'll take it down. Later I'll get some good paper and an envelope and write it over nice."

He blinked up at her, trying to make sense of her rapid speech.

"Mr. Stone?" she asked doubtfully, a stub of a pencil poised over her bit of paper.

"Yes. To my solicitor, Jonathan Conrad. His address is in my valise. Tell him I will be delayed. And whatever the doctor said about recovery time." David couldn't recall anything Dr. Lee had told him, but a month was batting about in the recesses of his mind. He would lose a full month. At least. "Millie?" He looked up at her suddenly, a fearful thought seizing him.

"Yes?" She leaned close.

"I will get better, won't I?"

"Of course!"

He exhaled. "My leg?"

"Once the swelling is down, Dr. Lee will put a plaster cast on it. Later today, I expect, or perhaps tomorrow. Now, I shall write this out for you and have it ready for you to look over whenever you feel up to it."

"Thank you."

"Would you like anything to eat?" she asked.

"No, I. . ." He closed his eyes and let go of the worries and the pain, drifting into misty dreams.

"New York? What is your brother doing in New York?" Randolph Stone waved a sheet of paper over his head as he entered the morning room.

Merrileigh flicked her fan open and fluttered it before her face. "Goodness, Husband! What is all this to-do?"

"Here's a letter come from Peregrin, and he's in New York, at one of the finest hotels. I thought he'd cut and run to Australia, or at least to Canada. How can he afford to gad about in the best circles in New York? He says he met up with Freddie Wallace's cousin and went with him to a card game. What on earth is that lad thinking?"

Merrileigh stood and plucked the letter from his hand. "Come now, dear. What's the harm in his enjoying a little company with a fellow Britisher? And Perry left here with enough money to keep him in style for a bit."

"But he's likely to be in exile for years. And a card game is what put him in this fix to begin with." Randolph sighed and strode to the bell pull. "Your brother never did have any common sense. When he's flush, he lives high, and when he's broke, he cadges on us. Well, I don't intend to be sending him an allowance to keep him at the Metropolitan, I'll tell you that."

Merrileigh skimmed the letter quickly. "Relax, Mr. Stone. He says right here he walked out of the game ten dollars to the good. So long as he's winning, you won't have to support him."

"Oh wonderful. My brother-in-law is now supporting himself as a professional gambler. That is so much better." Randolph rolled his eyes and yanked the bell pull.

A moment later Thomas appeared in the doorway.

"Yes sir?"

"Sherry," Randolph said.

"Yes sir." Thomas went to the sideboard and poured his master a glass of wine.

Merrileigh turned the sheet over and caught her breath. Apparently Randolph hadn't read this far, to where Peregrin mentioned that he'd put out some feelers but hadn't caught word of David yet. The foolish boy! He hadn't bargained on Randolph opening the mail before she did. Usually she had first look at the post, but not today. At least he'd worded it so that she could make a plausible explanation if need be.

"Oh, Conrad's man was here earlier," Randolph said.

"Was he?" Merrileigh jerked her head toward him. She'd gone out for two hours after lunch to make a few courtesy calls and leave her card at a few of her acquaintances' homes. Nothing ever happened when she was on the premises, but set foot outside, and the fireworks began.

"Yes. They'd had a letter from David."

"Indeed?" Merrileigh tucked Peregrin's letter into her sleeve. She would peruse it again later in private. "What did he say? Is he coming soon?"

"Apparently not. He's stalled in the middle of the country."

"St. Louis?"

"No, but somewhere out there." Randolph frowned and sipped his sherry. "Said he'd had an accident and would be delayed several weeks." Randolph grinned at her, obviously delighted with himself. "Independence, that's it. The name of the town, I mean."

Merrileigh shelved that bit of information for later contemplation as well. "Did he say when he expects to arrive?"

"Iverson thought it would be at least a month."

"Oh."

Randolph chuckled. "Maybe he'll run into your brother. Wouldn't that be a corker?"

"Yes," Merrileigh said thoughtfully. "Wouldn't it just?"

# CHAPTER 20

"I'll need to send another letter." David's voice held authority that Millie hadn't heard in more than two weeks. She turned from where she'd been arranging his clean linen in the dresser and stepped over to the bedside, glad he was feeling better. His will to do something showed her that the pain no longer overpowered him. "Of course. I'll get you some paper and ink."

She went downstairs and stopped at the desk in the front hall, where Mr. Simmons was bent over a ledger.

"I'm in need of stationery, sir. I don't suppose—"

"Oh yes, Mrs. Evans. I took your suggestion and laid in a supply."

Millie smiled. "That was good of you, sir. I'm sure other guests will be pleased, too. I'd like two sheets, please, and an envelope."

The first time she'd written a letter for David, she'd had to go out to find a mercantile for the supplies. She'd purchased a small bottle of ink and a pen at the time. She was grateful she wouldn't have to do that again.

She got the stationery she needed from the landlord and thanked him, then went back up to David's room. He was still awake, scowling at the ceiling.

"There, I think we're ready," she said cheerfully. "I only got one envelope."

"That's enough—unless you need to send a letter as well."

"No, I've no need, but thank you." She hesitated.

He raised his head suddenly, fixing her with an inquisitive stare. "Did you pay for it yourself?"

"This time, yes. But earlier, I. . .there were some coins in the pocket of the trousers you wore at the time of the accident. Dr. Lee cut the trousers off you, and. . .well, I salvaged the contents of your pockets for you." Her cheeks flushed, and she couldn't look him in the eye.

"Did you pay the doctor?"

"Yes, and the man who carted us here. I'm sorry, Mr. Stone, but I had to take the money for them from your wallet. I didn't ask you then. You were indisposed." Unconscious, actually, but she didn't like to remind him of his weakness too vividly.

"Bring it here." He stirred and gasped, sinking back onto the pillow, his face ashen.

Millie grabbed the wallet from the dresser and hurried to his side. "Are you all right?"

"No."

"What can I do?"

He said nothing but stared upward with clenched teeth.

She wanted to give him another dose of the painkiller, but Dr. Lee had told her yesterday to lengthen the intervals between doses, lest David become addicted to the stuff. "It will be time for more laudanum in an hour."

"Yes." It was barely a whisper, and she thought that an hour must seem very long to a man in pain.

She put his wallet in his hand, and he held it up where he could see it. He inspected the contents.

"What do I owe you for the stationery—and anything else you've paid for yourself?"

"Nothing." Need she remind him that every cent she had came from him to begin with?

He withdrew a dollar and handed it to her. "You must have used up most of what I gave you before."

"Well. . .yes. Thank you." She pocketed the dollar. "Would you like to dictate your letter now?"

"Yes. Do you mind? It pains me to sit up, and I don't think I'm ready to undertake it myself."

"I'd be happy to."

He dictated slowly, so that she could write nicely as he talked. The message was destined for his niece. Millie's color heightened as she wrote the name, but neither she nor David said anything about Millie's past connection to Anne.

"My dear niece," David said. "I regret to inform you that I have been delayed in my travels. The stagecoach on which I was bound for Independence met with an accident, and it seems my leg is broken. I've been sequestered two weeks in a hotel on the outskirts of town. The doctor assures me I shall have full use of the limb again within a month or so. Meanwhile, I submit to the kind ministrations of others. You probably will not recognize this hand, for the letter is penned by one who has been of assistance to me.

"Do not worry, dear Anne. Your uncle may be nearly twice your age, but I assure you that I will mend. Please tell Daniel I am confident leaving all in his hands so far as the line is concerned. I trust the arrangements we made earlier are working smoothly. I expect that I shall be gone from here by the time you read this, as the overland mail is so slow. I am now at the Frontier Hotel in Independence, but if you have urgent news, a missive might catch me at Astor House in New York before I sail. With great affection, your uncle."

Millie wrote it as neatly as she could and blew on it to dry the ink before handing it over to him to sign.

"I expect she'll be relieved to hear from you," she said.

"Yes, though this news may unsettle her. I almost hate to tell her. There's nothing she can do, and I don't like to worry her. Still, if I don't tell her and she learns of my mishap later, she'll be upset that I didn't say anything."

"She can pray for your speedy recovery, sir."

"Yes, there is that." He gritted his teeth. "I shall have to sit up a bit if I'm to sign that."

"Are you sure you want to?" Millie asked.

"Yes. I want her to see by my signature that I'm well enough to write it."

She put an extra pillow behind his shoulders, and he let out a groan as he shifted.

"I'm sorry," Millie said.

"No matter. Hand me the pen, please."

His face had gone white, but he managed to write his name with a confident flourish. Then he thrust the pen into her hand and sank back with his eyes closed, his mouth in a tight line.

Millie set aside the letter and pen. "I think we can give you the laudanum now, Mr. Stone."

"Good. I think I'm ready for it, thank you."

Sweat trickled from his temple down his cheek as she held him up to drink the dose, and Millie fetched his towel to wipe it away.

"I'm sorry you feel so bad."

"Ah well, the doctor assures me I'm healing. I daresay it's not as bad now as it was at first, but we forget, don't we?"

"Yes, mercifully, we do. Would you like to rest now?"

"I would. Oh, Anne's address. . ."

"She's Mrs. Adams, is she not? Of Corvallis?"

"Yes. Mrs. Daniel Adams. . ."

"That's all I need then."

She removed the extra pillow and arranged the bedclothes neatly. David was already asleep when she turned away.

She folded the letter and put it into the envelope. *Mrs. Daniel Adams, Corvallis, Oregon,* she wrote across the front. She decided to take it directly to the post office, rather than relying on Mr. Simmons to get it there swiftly.

The owner of the Frontier Hotel was greeting a new customer when she passed through the lobby, but when she returned, he was in the dining room, drinking coffee.

Millie hesitated, but she wondered if David had enough money left to get them both to the East Coast. She'd counted his money the first time she opened the wallet, and she'd felt seven shades of guilty ever since. There was plenty for the journey, for both of them. But David hadn't planned on stopping six weeks or more in Independence, and he probably had not yet paid his passage to England.

She couldn't leave him now. If she did go her own way, he would save money by not having to pay for her food and lodging. But he was completely helpless. For at least three or four more weeks, he would need someone to do everything for him. The hotel owner wouldn't do it. The bellboy could do only so much. The doctor had no nurse to spare. Millie couldn't see any way around it. She couldn't let David spend all his money to keep her near him, but she couldn't leave him alone either.

She would have to get a job.

As she approached Mr. Simmons's table in the corner of the otherwise-deserted dining room, she worked up her courage.

"Sir," she ventured, not quite looking into his eyes, "I'm known to be a good cook, dressmaker, and housekeeper. Would you happen to know of any employment openings a lady could fill?"

Peregrin was delighted to have a letter delivered to his room. Mail from England—imagine that! His sister's flowery hand greeted him. Of course—who else would write to him here? He held the envelope to his nose for a moment. Did it smell faintly of English roses, or was that his imagination?

He'd been in New York near a month, and so far he'd accomplished little but deplete his funds. He'd lost a few hundred pounds at the last couple of poker games he'd indulged in—and heaven knew his lodgings cost enough. He'd hoped they'd let him run up a tab indefinitely, but the management insisted, politely but coldly, that he pay on a weekly basis.

If he didn't start winning again soon, he'd have to move to a cheaper establishment. He'd hate to do that and give up all the amenities here, but realistically, he had to plan on an extended stay in America. And that meant frugality. Unless of course, he wanted to seek employment, but he shuddered at the thought. What was he good for, anyway? Not manual labor. He supposed he might get on as a bartender or some such occupation. He certainly knew how to pour a drink.

He carried Merry's letter to the desk and slit it open with his ivory-handled letter opener. He'd bought that at a shop on Fifth

Avenue, along with a silver pen and some paper and ink. Probably should have saved the money, but one needed basic supplies if one was going to carry on correspondence.

*Dearest Brother,*
    *How delightful to receive a missive in your own hand.*

Really. Who else's hand did she think he'd write in?

*I'm so pleased that you've found a comfortable, if temporary, place to stay, and that you've run into some acquaintances.*
    *You'll be pleased to know that Randolph caught wind of his cousin's situation today. It seems David has been delayed for several weeks in the town of Independence. I am not sure how far that is from New York—perhaps you could investigate. It might behoove you to go there.*

Peregrin scowled at the words. Independence! Wasn't that the place where folks gathered to form emigrant trains before going into the vast wilderness that comprised the West? He read on.

*I don't know what's keeping him there—I believe Randolph said something about a mishap. Anyway, if he sent the message two or three weeks ago, he's likely still there. Perhaps Nigel Wallace can enlighten you—or someone at the post office or railway station.*
    *At any rate, after going over your missive again, I was pleased with the information you'd gathered on steamships, but I must warn you. Randolph opened your letter while I was out. He did it in all innocence. I'm thankful he didn't read as far as the second page, however. When I returned home, he was sputtering about the fact that you'd gone to New York instead of Canada or New South Wales. Be very careful, dear brother, what you say in your future letters.*
    *Perhaps we should work out a code, so that if Randolph*

*reads another letter, he won't realize that you are interested in his cousin. Perhaps we could use another name. Instead of David Stone, you could say "Donald Steppington" or some such thing. Just make up a name with the same initials, and I will understand. And don't mention Independence. You might say Freedom instead. You see, it's all very simple. Your friend Donald has left Freedom and hopes to return home soon. Something like that. Or you might say—if it were warranted—that poor Donald met with an untimely demise. Oh dear, you can work it out, I'm sure. We simply need to practice discretion.*

*With that in mind, I urge you to destroy this letter after you've absorbed its contents. We wouldn't want your friend Donald to stumble upon it, now would we?*

*Your affectionate sister,*
*Merry*

Peregrin stood for a long moment, staring at the signature. He'd hoped, as he settled into his new life, that Merry had given up the ridiculous scheme. It appeared not. She wanted him to go through with it. It was up to him to stop David Stone from boarding a ship for England—ever.

He sighed heavily. It was too bad. He might have made a good life for himself here if he had a run of luck. And Nigel Wallace had promised to introduce him to some people in the higher set of New York society. Now it appeared he'd have to move on to some frontier backwater.

Well, he might as well enjoy himself tonight. There was a game on at Nigel's lodgings. He could spend the afternoon learning all he could about Independence and how to get there and then pass the evening singeing the other fellows' tail feathers. Maybe he'd leave the Metropolitan with more swag than he'd brought.

# CHAPTER 21

David sat up on the edge of the bed, determined to get dressed without help. It was high time he was up and about. Dr. Lee had left him a pair of crutches, saying that, as it had been nearly four weeks since the accident, he could begin hobbling about the room. He mustn't attempt the stairs yet, but even a foray down the corridor would be a relief. David had never in his life grown so sick of a room.

Millie had been a tremendous help, he had to admit. She'd done everything from seeing that his clothes were laundered to reading aloud when he was bored—which was often. And who knew what she'd done during the times when he'd been unconscious or in a drugged sleep?

But he wasn't about to let her help him put his trousers on. Now that he was fully aware of what was going on, he deserved to have his dignity preserved. If need be, he'd summon the innkeeper or the bellboy. They'd been pressed into service several times to help David bathe. But this time he resolved that he didn't really need either of them. With a bit of patience and determination, he could do it himself.

The pants were of coarse whipcord, not something he would have chosen himself, especially in this stifling July heat. But Millie had of necessity purchased what the storekeeper had shown her for a man his size. His only other pair was of fine quality and matched his tailcoat. Millie didn't think the cast would fit through the trouser leg, so she'd gone shopping for him and found these.

She'd offered several times to help him try them on, but he'd put her off repeatedly. The fact that she'd been married didn't matter one whit. Even the thought was unseemly.

But today he'd been granted permission to stump about with the crutches, and he couldn't wait another moment. He'd asked early on for a wheeled sick-chair, but Dr. Lee hadn't been able to come up with one, and anyway, the formidable stairs would have curtailed its usefulness. For the last week or so, he'd gotten as far as the armchair a few feet away, but getting to it had been a trial. He looked on the crutches with great optimism—but he'd need the trousers on before he could appear outside the confines of his room.

He made an attempt to work the garment over his cast and nearly fell off the bed in the effort. His dismal conclusion daunted him—this pant leg would not fit over the cast either, though it was cut much looser than his formalwear. He would certainly have to replenish his wardrobe when he reached New York. He couldn't arrive in England so poorly outfitted.

Disgusted, he reached for the dressing gown Millie had left looped over the bedpost at the foot of the bed. He donned it whenever he had to leave his bed of necessity, but so far that had only been for brief and painful moments. He would suffer agony gladly, rather than have Millie or some stranger tend his basic needs with a bedpan.

But today he wanted freedom. And he would not give up.

He knotted the belt of the dressing gown, seized the crutches, and fitted them under his armpits. The doctor had assured him they were the right length for a tall man. David tested his weight on them and hopped experimentally to the window, keeping the foot of his injured leg a hair's breadth off the floor.

At last he stood before the casement. Millie had kept the window clean—he'd seen her wash it at least twice since they'd been here. He looked out on the street three stories below. The thoroughfare was rutted and muddy, and across the way were a saloon, a laundry, and a disreputable-looking ironmonger's. That accounted for a lot of the noise that annoyed him during the day. But it was a different scene than he could glimpse from his bed or even from the chair, and he drank it in. By leaning on the crutches, he was able to shove the sash up a few inches, but the air outside seemed no cooler than what he had in his room. He shut the window so dust and bugs wouldn't come in.

His thoughts flew beyond Independence, all the way to England.

His letter to Jonathan Conrad must have reached its destination long ago. He'd asked to have that one sent to St. Louis, and then across the Mississippi, and on by express train to New York, where it would be put on a steamship. Steamers made the voyage in less than two weeks. He might get a return message any day.

He turned and swung his way toward the dresser. Hadn't the doctor said he might try a little weight on his foot now? He rested the bottom of the cast on the floor and stepped gingerly on it. His leg ached, but the pain was not unbearable. He kept the greater part of his weight on the crutches, but used his damaged leg for gentle support.

Immense satisfaction filled him when he reached the oak dresser. He balanced with the crutches and picked up his wallet. He still seemed to have most of the money he'd had before the accident. Of course, more bills were secured in his boot top, but that was money to be used only when the unforeseen occurred.

At that thought, he grimaced. If this wasn't unforeseen, what was? He might well need to delve into the hidden trove to pay for his ship's berth to England.

He stumped to the wall where his coat, vest, and a shirt hung from pegs and checked his pockets. His documents and letters from Conrad were also intact, and he let out a sigh of relief. Apparently Millie had kept her paws off his belongings. Hard to believe, but he couldn't think of anything that was missing. Even the little box with the onyx cuff links was in the side pocket, but he'd fully expected to find that. After all, it would be a bit blatant for her to steal them again.

As he thought it over, it seemed odd that he had so much cash left. He hobbled to the chair and sank into it, suddenly weary. His leg ached, stretched out before him, and he clenched his teeth. The angle of the rigid cast caused him quite a bit of pain. He shifted in the chair, wondering if he could get up again unassisted, but that seemed unlikely. He hoped someone would come along before it became too unbearable.

At a tap on the door, he called, "Come in," almost joyfully.

Millie entered, her eyes sweeping over him in surprise.

"Well now, look at you! Are you all right?"

"It hurts a bit to have my foot resting on the floor like this, but I really hate to get back in bed."

"A pillow under your heel, perhaps?" Millie laid a book on the bedside table and picked up one of the two pillows he'd been using. She fluffed up the feathers inside and knelt. "There, now, I'll just lift your foot and slide it under."

He grimaced as she moved his leg, but as soon as the feather pillow was under his foot, the pain lessened.

"Ah, that's what I needed. Thank you." He refused to think about how much of his person she was viewing.

"Would you like the other one as well?" she asked.

"No, I think not."

She rose and brushed her skirt with her hands. "This might be a good time for me to change your bed linen, if you're comfortable there for ten minutes."

"As you wish." It felt odd, sitting there and watching her work like a chambermaid. David wondered if he ought to look into hiring someone to come in and clean. Or would the hotel pay someone to do that?

"Millie. . ." He'd taken to calling her that—when, he couldn't say. Somewhere between seeing her bully the men on the hillside and the tenth time he watched her straighten his bedclothes.

"Yes?" She turned with her arms full of cotton sheets. Her face made a rosy contrast to their whiteness, and her fiery hair caught a ray of sun from the window, topping off the image like the flame of a burning candle.

"You oughtn't to do all this for me."

"Nonsense. We've had this conversation before. You did much for me, and I'm happy to return the favor." She stepped toward the door, but when he spoke again, she stopped.

"Millie, how are you paying for our rooms? Have you told the innkeeper I'll pay him, and he trusted us, or what?"

She turned, her green eyes wide. "Oh, he expects you to pay for your own room, sir. I gave him five dollars the first week we were here, out of your wallet. I expect he'll tot up your bill any time you want it."

"And yours? Did you give him something down on your own as well?"

"Only for the first week. I've been able to keep my account current since then."

"You have? But how?"

"I. . .I've been cleaning other people's rooms and doing laundry for the hotel while you slept." Her cheeks had gone pinker, and her eyes flashed a bit, as though she dared him to tell her she was behaving in a vulgar manner.

"I see."

She nodded and went out the door with his sheets.

David struggled with the conflicting thoughts teeming in his mind. A lady wouldn't do such a thing. But would a real lady let a gentleman—even if he were a friend—pay for her lodgings? And was he her friend, when it came to that? Another part of him raised a defiant chin and asked whether it mattered if she was a "real" lady or not. Millie, it seemed, could cook like a fine chef, work like a deckhand, and take charge of a situation like a gunnery sergeant. In the face of such evidence, what did gentle birth and impeccable manners matter? Yet something buried deep in his psyche raised a stubborn hand and cried, "She would not be received at Almack's."

Millie returned a few minutes later with an armful of clean, folded sheets.

"There, this will just take a minute." She laid the stack on the dresser and shook out the bottom sheet, sending it in a glorious, white pouf, like the filling sail of a schooner, half the width of the room.

She hummed as she spread the sheet and tucked it in all around. David watched her quick, deft hands.

"It's a magnificent day outside." She smiled at him across the featherbed. "Not too hot. Perhaps I can open the window."

"That would be nice." He didn't mention dust or bugs. Odd how much more beauty she saw in the day than he had, and he was the one who'd been confined.

She crossed to the casement and pushed the sash up, securing it in place with a wooden block. This time a breeze fluttered through, setting a stray tendril of her hair dancing.

"There!" Millie stepped back from the window. "I read in the scripture that 'This is the day which the Lord hath made.' It struck me that every day is His day. Some of them we like more than others, but still, the Almighty gives us what He deems best. And today He gave us a stunner." She went back to the dresser, snatched a pillowcase from the pile, and worried the extra pillow into it.

*A stunner,* David thought. *Yes, and there's one right here in my room.*

Appalled at the thought, he looked toward the window, where the breeze flirted with the muslin curtain. How little he had thought about God this past month, and how much about David Stone and his comfort or lack of it. Perhaps he could take a lesson from this common woman who seemed to have undergone a massive change of heart.

Unless this was all a show, for his benefit. Was she still trying to lure him in? He didn't feel as though she was. For several weeks she'd been friendly, helpful, and almost unfailingly cheerful. She had assured him countless times that he was healing and would soon have his strength back. But she had never once cast sheep eyes at him. Was it possible that she was no longer interested in him as a man?

Millie spread the top sheet and laid the quilt over the whole.

"That's it, but for the pillow under your foot," she said. "When you're tired of sitting, I'll help you back to bed and put a new slip on that one."

"Millie, do you suppose there's a minister nearby who might visit me?"

Her eyebrows shot up, and he thought how delicate and well-shaped they were.

"Why yes. I've met one, as a matter of fact."

"You have?"

She nodded. "I've been going to a church a couple of blocks away.

The pastor and his wife have treated me very kindly. In fact, they've been praying for you, sir. I hope you don't mind. I didn't give a lot of details, just told them an acquaintance of mine was badly injured."

David blinked at her. She hadn't mentioned going to church nor making new friends. But then, he hadn't known she was working in the hotel either. Millie, it seemed, was a woman of discretion, and also a woman of mystery.

"Would you like me to invite him here?" she asked.

"Yes, thank you. I do wish I could get downstairs."

Millie shook her head. "Two flights. It would never do at this stage. You must be patient."

David sighed. Not for the first time, he wished she'd been able to secure rooms on the ground floor. "I suppose you're right. Could you help me back into bed now? My leg is beginning to ache."

"Of course." Millie paused to look at his pocket watch, which had made its home on the bedside table since they moved in. "Look at that! It's an hour past the time when you can have more laudanum. I do believe you're getting better, sir, but I'll fix you a dose after you're in bed if you want it."

"I think not. Is that a new book?"

She glanced at the volume she'd brought earlier. "Oh yes, it is. A Mrs. Fleming, in 201, had it. She finished it this morning, and she offered to lend it to me. She says it's prodigious exciting. Alexandre Dumas."

He smiled. "Would you—oh, I don't suppose you have time."

"To read to you?"

He ought to just read to himself. He was turning into rather a lazy fellow. But the truth was, he liked the way she read aloud. She brought the characters right into the room.

"I think I could stay half an hour," she said.

"Thank you," he said meekly.

Millie knocked on the door of David's room. She'd left him twenty minutes ago, clean shaven, washed, and brushed. On her way out of the hotel, she'd sent the bellboy up to help him put on the trousers she'd modified by slitting one leg to allow the cast to go through. She hoped the venture had been successful.

"Come in," came his voice, and she pushed open the door.

Her gaze flew to his armchair, positioned beside the window. David sat in it, fully clothed. The trouser leg was pinned together so that one hardly noticed the cast—well, not much. And he wore his exquisitely made shirt, tie, and jacket.

She smiled at him. "Mr. Stone. Glad to see you looking so well. I've brought the Reverend Mr. Harden."

The pastor stepped past her and extended his hand to David. "I'm pleased to meet you, sir."

"Mutual," David said, stretching to shake hands. The two were about the same age. Mr. Harden was several inches shorter than David, and his complexion and hair darker. David's features relaxed as he looked him over. "Won't you sit down, sir?"

Mr. Harden sat opposite him, and Millie was suddenly loath to quit the room. But she knew she ought to, so she cleared her throat and gave a little curtsey.

"I'll leave you gentlemen alone. May I bring a tea tray up?"

"That would be nice," David said. "Thank you."

She bowed her head slightly. *Why am I acting so servile with him? Just because he's rich doesn't mean he has to treat everyone like servants.*

If the truth were told, he had not treated her like a domestic. Instead, he'd been generous to her and grateful for her ministrations— as a friend would be, not a master. And he'd never asked her to scrape and curtsey.

"Thank you, Mrs. Evans," Mr. Harden said.

Millie managed a little smile and swept out of the room. She closed the door behind her and stood for a moment in the hallway to catch her breath.

What would David say to him? Would he tell the minister how she'd tried to cheat him once and had nearly gotten him killed?

She bit her lip. Why should she fear that? David was a gentleman. Besides, she had already told Mr. and Mrs. Harden much of the tale herself. But how differently would the situation appear from David's viewpoint? And had she colored her account to show herself in a more favorable light than she deserved?

There was no sense fretting over it. Today was washday at the hotel, and she'd be busy all afternoon.

*Dear Lord, it's up to You. If You want Mr. Stone to sully my reputation—well, I suppose I deserve it. Teach me not to be so proud. I've really no reason to think highly of myself. No reason at all.*

Resolved to complete her day's work well, she gathered her skirt and flew down the stairs.

# CHAPTER 22

**D**avid spent the most enjoyable hour he'd had since he left Oregon. Millie brought a tea tray fifteen minutes after the minister's arrival and retreated again with a cheerful wave, though she looked a bit tired. Now that he thought about it, Millie often had an air of fatigue. The innkeeper was probably demanding too much of her. He turned his attention back to his visitor, making a mental note to ask her about it later.

Joseph Harden was a most amiable man. He didn't swing every topic round to theology, but once they got into it, he turned out to have a most practical view of Christianity. He also knew the minister who had held the pulpit at the church David had attended many years ago, when he lived in Independence, but informed him that a different man now preached in that church.

David liked Harden and soon found himself revealing his situation in a general way—no specifics.

"Of course I never expected to inherit from my brother Richard. I thought he'd have a dozen progeny, and if anything should happen to prevent that, why then, our brother John would step up."

"So very tragic that you are the last brother," Mr. Harden said.

"Yes. Of course, I would gladly have given Richard's daughter a home, but an odd thing happened when she came to Oregon to find me."

"Oh? What was that?"

"She fell in love with a plain but honest man." David smiled, remembering how Anne would flush whenever Dan Adams came around. "He's a capital fellow, and he's making her a good husband."

"At least that part of the tale ends happily."

"Yes." David frowned as he recalled other moments in Oregon.

"What is your overall impression of Mrs. Evans?"

"Oh, she is most amiable, Mr. Stone, and she has a tender heart." David considered that.

"You seem troubled by this assessment, sir," said Mr. Harden.

"Oh no, not at all," David said. "This past month, I've found her to be as you say." However, he kept thinking about the minister's words.

"Come now," Harden said. "You have known her longer than I have, haven't you?"

"Yes, I first met her more than eighteen months ago, out in western Oregon. But she was...considerably different then."

Mr. Harden's features sobered. "Yes. She has told my wife and me some about her past. I must say, we admire her. With God's help, she has made some commendable changes in her life, both inward and outward."

David eyed him in surprise. "She is now penniless and dependent upon the kindness of a slight acquaintance. How is that a better outward situation than when I first met her? She was staying then in a hotel a bit better than this one and dining well each day. She owned a horse, at least, and seemed to have no shortage of money."

"Ah, it is not up to me to divulge the things she told us, Mr. Stone. I assumed you knew her fairly well and what her life has been like since her husband died."

"I know she was not completely honest, if that is what you mean."

Mr. Harden smiled ruefully. "Shall we let it rest there, then? Let the cloak of charity cover her past transgressions. Millie Evans is now a sister in Christ. For all I can tell, she is sincere in her new faith, and she has given up her old habits. While she may not be affluent now, she has nothing to hide, and I assure you, your wallet is safe in her presence."

David froze for a moment. It sounded as though Millie had confessed her sins rather particularly to the pastor. If she were still in the fraud business, would she have done that? Or was this all part of an even larger, more sweeping scheme? He'd begun to trust her, but was that wise? One thing was certain—until he was 100 percent confident of her honesty, Millie must not learn about Stoneford.

He'd been extremely careful since their unexpected reunion not to let a word of his expectations pass his lips—to Millie, or to anyone else he met on the journey. He believed she remained ignorant of the title and fortune awaiting him in England. He intended that it should stay that way. Therefore, he would not now discuss the matter further, not even with a man of the cloth. He'd told Joseph Harden he must settle his brother's estate, but no more, and so it would remain.

"Mr. Harden, I do hope you won't take me amiss when I ask you not to reveal anything I've told you about my purpose in returning to England."

"Rest assured, it shall not leave my lips, sir. And how does the doctor say you are progressing?"

"Quite well, though from where I sit, it seems to be rather a slow process. He's letting me put a little weight on my leg now. I hope within a couple more weeks to cast aside the crutches and resume my journey."

"And Mrs. Evans will travel with you?"

David blinked at him. "We haven't discussed it recently. I had told her before our accident that I would give her enough for her ticket to Philadelphia, where she has friends. Now that I'm getting about a little, perhaps I should ask if she'd like to go on now. She need not wait for me."

"Indeed?"

"I'm sure I can tend my own needs now," David said uncertainly, glancing about the room. At the moment it was clean, but only because Millie had kept it so. Without her, when would his bed be changed again, or his shirts washed, or the floor swept? He supposed there were other hotel employees who did such tasks for other guests, but thanks to Millie, he hadn't had occasion to meet them.

When the minister took his leave, he smiled and extended his hand to David. "May I call upon you again, sir?"

"I should like that excessively. I'm afraid I suffer great boredom within these walls."

"Then I promise to return before too long."

"Thank you. I shall look forward to it." David smiled until his visitor was out the door, and then let out a low moan. His leg ached horribly, and he wanted only to get back to bed. But who would help him?

He struggled to rise but fell back into the chair with a painful thud.

A moment later there was a tap on the door.

"Come in!"

Millie peeked round the edge of the door. "I saw Mr. Harden leaving. Would you like some assistance?"

David gritted his teeth. "Yes, if it's not too much trouble."

She hurried into the room, her lovely face lined with worry. "Are you all right, sir?" She stooped and let him drape an arm over her shoulders. "There now, one—two—three."

David pushed himself upward. He couldn't help but notice how gentle she was, and yet she had the strength of a woman who knew hard work. He realized he was looking at her lovely hair and thinking how soft it must be. He looked away.

"Steady now." She stood still for a moment, letting him collect himself. "Ready?"

"Yes."

"It's only three steps."

He wanted to tell her he could make it just fine if she'd hand him the crutches, but the truth was he felt weak as a newborn colt. He let her support him as he hobbled the short distance. He tried not to lean too heavily on her, but he liked the way her shoulders were at just the right height for her to fit beneath his arm. They reached the bed, and he sat on the edge quite precipitously. She lifted his injured leg gently, swinging it onto the mattress.

"I should have laid back the covers," she said.

"Leave it," David gasped.

"Yes, I shall. Let me take off your shoe, and then I'll get you a blanket and some laudanum. Next time, perhaps you shouldn't sit up so long."

"I'll be fine." He spoke rather crossly, though he didn't intend to. It was her femininity that flummoxed him, he thought, and the fact that he liked her more and more without wanting to.

Millie only smiled. "Of course you will."

Peregrin lingered in New York three more days after he received his sister's letter. He hated to leave his nest at the Metropolitan, but on Friday night it became clear that he must waste no more time. That was the night Nigel Wallace's friend, Lionel Baxter, took him for every cent he had on him and a thousand dollars more in IOUs.

Appalled at his losses, as each hand played out, Peregrin insisted on going one more. Finally Nigel would hear no more and insisted it was time they cleared out. Peregrin was nine-tenths drunk, and Nigel dropped him off at the hotel and bribed the doorman to see him safely up to his room. It was a good thing Nigel was feeling generous, or Peregrin might have spent the night huddled on the sidewalk.

He awoke Saturday morning with a splitting headache. He put on his dressing gown and rang for breakfast. When the bellboy delivered it, Peregrin remembered he had no more cash. He would have to get to the bank Monday morning. He told the bellboy he'd tip him double when he got the ready, but the young man was not pleased.

He would surely spend a dull weekend, since he was short of funds. Why had he put so much in the bank, anyway? That was a mistake. He swallowed down the herb tea that was brewed to help dispel hangovers.

When his headache receded, Peregrin admitted to himself that he'd banked the larger part of his funds—two thousand dollars—as a safeguard against the very thing he'd done last night. And now he owed half of that to Lionel Baxter. He'd better pay Lionel off and hop a train to Independence. If he put off Merrileigh's business much longer, he might end up flat broke and unable to carry it out.

On the other hand, if he stayed in New York, Merry might send him some money.

He decided against asking, as it would probably take close to a month to receive her reply. She'd said nothing about sending more money in her letter, and he'd better not count on it. He'd left London with enough to keep any man in good shape for a year—he'd have been the first to say so. He'd gone through two-thirds of it in a couple of months. It was up to him to use the rest wisely.

He frowned at himself in the large, gilt-framed mirror. How could he have lost so much in one game? If he went back to Baxter's tonight. . .

No, that would never do. Baxter had said he wouldn't play with him again unless he put the money on the table. No more IOUs.

Wearily, Peregrin began to lather his shaving soap. He sorely missed his houseman, even though he'd had to share Hogg with his housemates in London.

Somewhere between the first nick on his chin and knocking the water pitcher over as he grabbed for a towel, it occurred to Peregrin that he could get his money from the bank on Monday and leave for Independence without paying a visit to Lionel Baxter. The fellows would have no idea where he'd gone to. He hadn't told even Nigel Wallace that he planned to go there, for fear of exposing his scheme with Merrileigh.

He liked the idea. He could disappear. With his two thousand dollars intact. He doubted Baxter would pursue him all the way across the Mississippi, even if he did get wind of his flight. Would he? A man might chase him across England for less, but England was such a small country, compared to this one.

Peregrin was just unbuttoning his shirt—he'd done it up wrong and came out with a button too many—when someone knocked on his door.

He stepped closer. "Who is it?"

"A friend of Lionel Baxter's."

Cautiously, Peregrin unlocked the door and opened it a crack.

A man the size of a plow horse shoved it open, throwing Peregrin back. The giant entered, with a companion close behind.

"I say," Peregrin stammered.

The giant tapped his palm with a stick about a foot and a half long. "Mr. Baxter says good morning. And don't forget to visit the bank first thing on Monday."

"Er. . .right." Peregrin looked from the man to his smaller but more sinister chum. The second man had a jagged scar running from one cheekbone to his chin. He stared ominously at Peregrin.

"Give him my best, won't you?" Peregrin tried to affect a carefree smile.

It slipped a little when the big man said, "Don't fail him, or you'll wish you'd never set foot in New York."

# CHAPTER 23

When Dr. Lee paid his next call on David, Millie waited in the lobby until he came down the stairs, and then she followed him outside.

"How is Mr. Stone doing?" she asked.

"Ah, Mrs. Evans. I hoped I would see you. The patient was in a restless mood today. Apparently he overdid a bit yesterday."

"I'm afraid so. I shouldn't have let him sit up so long with his visitor. I didn't realize he was in pain the entire time."

The doctor nodded. "Give him the regular doses of laudanum today. Tomorrow he might slack off again, if he feels better. Now, you mustn't let him do too much too soon. And whatever he tells you, I think it would be unwise for him to travel for several more weeks."

Millie swallowed hard. "That long?"

"Yes. Perhaps another month. He's not healing as fast as a child would. But he is healing. That itching he complains of is part of it. But I won't remove the plaster for at least two weeks more. And even then, it will take him a little while to regain strength in those muscles."

"I see."

Dr. Lee nodded and untied his horse from the hitching rail. "Mr. Stone seemed to think you might be traveling on soon without him."

"I have no such intentions," Millie said.

"Good. I fear he'd injure himself again if you—or someone else capable—were not here to keep him from doing so."

"I shall stay as long as he'll put up with me," Millie said. "I hope that will be until he's ready to travel again."

"Excellent." Dr. Lee laughed. "I take it you have some history with him. He told me today that every time he's around you, he winds up injured."

Millie stared at him. "I should hope he didn't imply that I had anything to do with causing the stagecoach accident."

"Oh no, he said it in jest. I saw the scar on his shoulder and asked him about it. He said he'd suffered a gunshot wound not long after he'd met you. He didn't say the two events were connected—in fact, I got the feeling he made it sound that way just to get a laugh from me."

"Oh, I see. Actually, I hadn't seen him after he received that wound until we met again on a stagecoach this spring."

"Ah. Then it's as I thought—I shouldn't take seriously his allegation that you are a dangerous woman." The doctor winked at her and climbed into his buggy.

Millie stood for a long moment staring after him, her hands on her hips. Of all the disgraceful nerve.

David had found it hard to concentrate since the minister discussed Millie with him and told him that he believed her faith was genuine.

"Trust her, and let God handle the rest," Mr. Harden had said.

It appeared that Millie was now trustworthy, so far as money and trinkets were concerned. But what of his heart? That was a different matter, and David had no intention of entrusting it to her again. Not that he had been so foolish on their first acquaintance—but if the truth were told, it was a near thing.

Instead of the languid lady he'd met in Scottsburg, Oregon, or the shameless fraud, she was now a capable nursemaid and housekeeper. When he remembered her conduct after the stagecoach accident, David felt she should be made a brevet general for her valor in combat.

But that did not mean he wanted to form a permanent attachment with her. In fact, he intended to send her off soon. Very soon. If only Dr. Lee weren't so pessimistic. Surely he'd be able to fend for himself within a couple of weeks. He had made a joke of Millie's ministrations when the doctor asked about their relationship. The physician only wanted reassurance that David had a competent attendant, he was sure, but the topic was a delicate one. Sooner or later, he had to face it head-on.

The morning after Dr. Lee's visit, after much thought, David summoned the innkeeper, Mr. Simmons.

"How may I help you, Mr. Stone?" Simmons asked, approaching his bed with a smile that promised to meet any need—for a price.

"I should like to know how much I owe you, sir."

Simmons told him the total. "Will you be leaving us soon, sir?"

"No, not for at least two weeks, perhaps longer, but I'd like to keep my account short. Oh, and Mrs. Evans said she's been paying for her own board and lodging?"

"That's right, sir."

"Well, she's been a great help to me, and I'd like to give you enough to bring my bill and hers up to date and pay for the next fortnight in advance. Is that amenable?"

"Very much so."

David paid the man from his wallet, and a few minutes later Simmons left well content with his long-term guests.

Millie, however, seemed far from pleased when she brought up his supper that evening.

"Mr. Stone!"

"Ah, Millie." He'd loafed about all day and was tiring of his bed again. He nodded at the tray she carried. "Is that my supper?"

"It is."

"I should like to sit in the chair to eat it, if you don't mind."

She frowned but set the tray on top of the dresser. "I suppose you can, but when I say it's time to retire, you must obey."

He laughed. "And now you're my governess, it seems."

"Not I. Those are Doctor Lee's orders. You must be cautious."

She brought his robe and crutches, and after a bit of exertion and fussing about his dressing gown, he made it into the chair.

"Now, what is this about you paying my bill?" she asked.

"It's nothing. Bring the tray, please."

"Not until I hear a satisfactory answer. I am able to pay for my own expenses now, and you know it."

"How do I know it?" David asked.

"Because I told you so."

"But you might have need of your earnings when you travel on to Philadelphia."

"Then I shall have to earn some more."

David sighed. "Don't be difficult, Millie. Come now, I'm hungry. What's on the menu tonight?"

"A nice beefsteak, potatoes, squash, and some rather dry cornbread." She made no move to retrieve the tray.

"All right, going to be stubborn, are you?"

"Difficult times call for extreme measures."

David threw his hands up in exasperation. "Difficult times? You think a disagreement with me is a dire situation?"

"Indeed, sir." She regarded him with steady green eyes. "Through all our acquaintance, I think we've managed to be civil to one another."

"That's neither here nor there. You're wearing yourself out, and I won't have it."

"Oho."

"What?" he asked.

"Telling me what you will and won't have, so far as my behavior is concerned."

He clenched his teeth, seeing that he must take a new tack. "Millie."

"Yes sir?"

"It's only that I don't want you working day and night to earn your keep. You've been tending to me, and I'm happy to recompense you for your time and labor. You don't need to take on these other exhausting jobs."

"But you are feeling better now, sir. You've said so yourself. And so you will be needing less care, am I right?"

"Well, I hope that is true. I don't need dosing so often, and I think I shall soon be dressing myself without assistance."

"So I shall be getting more rest," Millie said. "I don't mind earning an honest living."

"I didn't say you should, madam." Really, she was impossible. He'd tried to smooth her way, and she was taking offense.

"Mr. Stone, I think we both agree that I should maintain my independence if I am able. You must admit that it was never your intention to support me."

He felt the blood rush to his face. "Well, no. Hardly."

"I rest my case, sir. And I shall be paying my own way from here on. I hope to earn enough by the time you've recovered to buy my own ticket to Philadelphia." She picked up the tray and brought it to him.

"I suppose everything is cold by now." He picked up the napkin and spread it over his front.

"Oh, and you're going to get crotchety again?" She placed her hands on her hips and glared at him. "Mr. Stone—"

"Now, Millie, I don't know what's gotten into you, but you've 'Mr. Stoned' me too many times. You told me recently to call you by your given name, and I believe I once asked you to use mine. So why can't we be on equal footing?"

She lowered her gaze, and her cheeks went pink. "That was a long time ago, sir."

"Yes, I suppose it was. But you don't mind my calling you Millie."

"I thought it would be easier for you. More natural."

He thought about that, and he didn't like the implications.

"Oh. So you think I'm used to ordering servants about, is that it? You suppose I look on you as I would a scullery maid or an undercook?"

"Well. . ." She turned away and spread up the covers on his bed.

"I do not see you in that way, and if you insist on calling me 'Mr. Stone,' then I shall go back to 'Mrs. Evans.'"

"Whatever you wish. Now eat your supper, or it really will be cold."

"I don't suppose. . ." He glanced toward the dresser.

"What, you want me to read? We've finished *The Black Tulip*. I hoped to find a volume of Dickens at the ordinary, but the only one they had was *David Copperfield*, and you told me you've read that."

"Well, perhaps you could read me a chapter or two from the Psalms."

She froze for a moment, then nodded. "I shall be happy to."

She fetched his new Bible from the dresser—the one he'd bought in Oregon after she made off with the other—and drew a chair close.

"Any special chapter?"

"I've always been fond of the thirty-seventh."

She turned to it and read it with great spirit, as though giving a dramatic recitation. When she lowered the book, she sighed. "I don't think I've ever read that before. It's lovely."

"Millie."

"Yes?"

"Why did you take my Bible?"

For a long moment, she was silent.

"I don't really know. I thought you were dead when I took it, and I was feeling horribly guilty. I saw it lying there in the hotel room, and I was curious about you. When I opened it, I saw that you'd marked some of the verses, and I thought perhaps I could learn more about you if I read what you'd thought was important. I never knew anyone who wrote in a Bible before—well, except births and deaths. But I thought you'd been a very special man, and I'd gotten you killed. And I—well, I just took it."

He felt as though he'd missed something important—something crucial to Millie's story. He also knew that when he returned to England, he would never look at servants in quite the same way.

Peregrin waited until eleven o'clock Monday morning before going to the bank. For one thing, he'd slept late. For another, he didn't want to run into Lionel Baxter's "friends."

He kept a sharp eye out as he left the Metropolitan and hurried down the street. He wished he could afford a cab, but thanks to the two ruffians, he hadn't a cent until he made his withdrawal from the bank.

Instead of just getting out Baxter's thousand, or that much plus a bit more for his ordinary expenses, Peregrin closed his account.

"Leaving us, are you, sir?" the teller asked.

"Yes, I'm—" Peregrin caught himself and avoided blurting out his destination. One never knew who was listening. "I'm headed for Boston."

"Boston? Ah, well have a good journey." The teller counted out his money and smiled at him.

"Thank you." Peregrin put half the bills in his wallet and split the rest between a couple of pockets. If he were held up—as he'd learned New Yorkers were apt to be—he didn't want to lose all of his cash.

He hurried back to his hotel room and began to pack. What he wouldn't give to have Hogg there to do it for him! He supposed he could ring for the bellboy, but then he'd have to tip him.

He threw his clothes and toilet articles, along with his stationery, into his valise. He decided to leave the bottle of ink, though he hadn't used a quarter of it. Such a mess it would make if it leaked on his limited wardrobe.

On second thought, he ought to send a note to Merrileigh. With a sigh, he unpacked his silver pen and stationery case. After a moment's thought he scrawled,

> *Yr letter rec'd. I am going to Freedom to visit my friend, Donald*

Peregrin scratched his head, trying to recall the name Merrileigh had invented. It started with *S*. That was all he could remember. After a couple of minutes he gave up and wrote "Smith."

> *...Donald Smith. I am told the Sanders is a good hostelry there. You may direct any correspondence to me there.*

He considered what he'd written and wondered what sort of chaos that would cause. Would Randolph or somebody else send him mail at the nonexistent town of Freedom? Or maybe there was a town by that name. Oh well, Merrileigh would have to figure it out.

Now to get to the train station undetected. He briefly considered leaving without paying the hotel bill, but that seemed counter-productive. Lionel Baxter wouldn't alert the police to his transgressions at the card table, but the hotel manager would call them in a second if he realized a guest had left without paying up. No way around it.

He carried his bags down and stopped at the front desk.

"Checking out."

The desk clerk looked at him in surprise and said, rather loudly, "What? Leaving us, Mr. Walmore?"

Peregrin looked over his shoulder then leaned toward the man. "I'd like to keep it quiet. You see, my—my friend is always after me to borrow money, and I'd prefer he didn't know where I've gone—or even that I've gone, if you take my meaning—at least for a while." He slipped a dollar bill across the counter.

"Oh yes, I see, sir. Just a moment, and I'll total your account. You just paid on Friday, so it won't be much. Would you like the doorman to call a hansom for you while you wait?"

"Er, yes, that would be fine. And could I leave this letter here for the post?"

At last he was able to get away. He paid his bill, paid for the letter to England, tipped the doorman, paid the driver when they got to the station, and gave him an extra dime for a tip. Peregrin went inside, bought a ticket, and tipped a porter for carrying his valise to the platform. All the while he felt his life's blood was trickling away with the coins. The large amounts he'd lost at the gaming table weren't the half of it. It was this daily drain on his funds that had brought him to this pass.

He boarded one of the passenger cars and huddled in a seat near the back of the carriage, watching the doors with apprehension until they closed. At last the train set off westward, and he was reasonably sure the thugs hadn't followed him.

# CHAPTER 24

**I** don't see why you can't go down to the dining room for dinner tonight." Dr. Lee eyed David's leg in its plaster cast critically. "Take it easy, and have a stout fellow to lean on, and if you need it, get two to help get you back up again."

"I'll be fine," David said.

"I know you think that, but it's been six weeks since you took a flight of stairs, let alone two. It will be a big exertion, and you may need to rest awhile before you come back up to your room."

"Don't you worry about me."

The doctor shook his head. "I won't waste time worrying, but I shall have a word with Mrs. Evans before I leave. One thing about her—I know that if she's on duty, you'll mind."

David's jaw dropped, but he quickly closed his mouth. He did have a point. Millie bossed him around like she did everyone else, now that he was getting better. "Time to practice walking in the hall," she would say, with no room for protest, and "Don't toss your laundry on the floor, sir," and "Surely you can do that for yourself now."

"Remember," the doctor said, closing his bag, "you have a compound fracture that is still healing. I know it seems like it's been a long while, but it would be easy to overdo now. Go slowly, and build up your activity gradually. Keep using the crutches for a few days at least, until you feel steady. I'll bring you a cane next time I come."

"So, when can I travel?"

Dr. Lee hesitated. "Not for a while yet. I'd like to take the cast off next week, and I would like to see you at least one more time after that. We'll see if you get your strength up. Then we'll talk about travel."

When the doctor had left, David got up and walked slowly to the window, stepping gingerly on his left foot. His leg ached a little, but that would pass in time—Dr. Lee had said so.

About fifteen minutes later, Millie arrived with his clean laundry.

"I'm going downstairs for supper tonight," David said eagerly. "The doctor said I may."

She smiled indulgently. "I saw him, and he told me. That's wonderful." She opened a drawer and tucked a few clean garments into the dresser. "I asked Billy to come up at five o'clock and help you downstairs."

"Who is Billy?"

She frowned at him. "He's the young man who carries luggage for people. He's been in this room at least a hundred times since we've been here. Don't you know his name?"

"He told me it was Wilfred."

"So it is, but his friends call him Billy."

That struck David as odd—foremost because Millie was implying that she was Billy's friend. It also seemed to him that a boy named Wilfred ought to be called Willie or Fred.

"So he'll still answer to Wilfred?"

"I should think so, especially if you give him a half dime for his trouble."

"Ah." David peered at Millie, but her green eyes were inscrutable. Did she think he was treating Wilfred in that "servant" way? Perhaps he was, but he didn't think it would be proper to treat the young man like a chum. "I suppose I should put on a clean shirt and a tie if I'm going into the dining room."

"Trust me, the dining room here is very informal. However, I'd be happy to lay those things out for you if you wish." Millie stepped toward the armoire.

"Thank—" David stopped short. He ought to be doing things for himself now. After all, he was able. And Millie wouldn't be with him forever. "I can do it," he said.

"All right. And are you content with those trousers?" She looked his pants up and down.

David squelched his natural embarrassment. He was too old to blush when a woman looked him over. "Well, I guess I'll have to be, since they're the only pair I own that fits, at least until I'm rid of this cast."

"Yes, that's true." She walked over and stooped, then twitched the material at the level of his knee. "Stand up and let me adjust that. I think I can do it a little better, so the pins don't show." She held up his crutches while he positioned himself.

"Hmm." Millie tugged and fussed with the fabric. "I suppose I could baste you into them."

"Is that necessary?"

"No, I don't think so." Finally she stood. "There. You'll pass. Now, is there anything else I can do for you, or shall I see you in the dining room?"

"Meet me there," he said. "It will be like old times."

An odd look crossed her face, and he wished his comment hadn't slipped out. The less they thought about Scottsburg, the better.

Peregrin arrived in Independence at dusk on a Sunday. He'd waited out two days of rain in St. Louis, at a dismal hotel with bland food and sluggish room service. The train he'd ridden from there to Independence had nearly deafened him, and he had several small holes in his suit, where cinders had fallen. But he was here at last.

He had several ideas on how he would find David Stone. The town was not very large, and there couldn't be many hotels a gentleman would patronize. More to the point, how would he stop David from going on to England?

He'd half expected to find the town buttoned down for the Sabbath, especially at this hour of the day. To his surprise, he found that the West was apparently as rowdy as it was rumored to be. Taverns and saloons esteemed all days alike and kept their doors open. Some of them, in fact, had no proper doors, but only hinged panels that reached neither the threshold nor the lintel. Men were entering and emerging from these watering holes in steady streams.

Peregrin decided to stop at one first thing and get rid of the smell of the locomotive.

The hotel he'd heard about, to which he was duly directed by two somewhat inebriated loafers and a bartender, turned out to be not a tenth as good as the one he'd left in New York, and Peregrin mourned his losses, especially when he learned that this one charged nearly as much as the Metropolitan had.

"I say," he sputtered to the desk clerk, who hadn't a proper desk at all, but a wobbly table in the entry hall. "How can you charge so much for such a small, shabby room?"

"Think of all the trouble we must take to bring in supplies, mister." The clerk looked him testily in the eye. "Everything in this place was floated up the river. It takes a lot of muscle to freight in amenities."

"Hmpf." Peregrin looked him up and down. "Well, I'd like a bath in my room, and when I'm done, I'll have you send up my supper by room service; there's a good chap."

The clerk stared at him for a moment. A smile spread slowly over his face.

"Ain'tchu somethin'? We don't do no room service, mister, and the closest place you can get a hot bath is down the street. The laundry on the corner will give you one if you treat 'em nice and show your silver." He looked down at Peregrin's baggage, which he'd dropped on the floor while signing the register. "Oh, and you'll have to haul your own truck upstairs tonight. Jojo's sick."

Peregrin shook his head and stooped to pick up his bags. There had to be a better hotel in this town. There just had to be. He couldn't imagine Anne Stone staying in this monstrosity, but he was sure he'd heard she'd gone overland to Oregon, and chances were pretty good she had passed through this place.

The room was tiny and none too clean. He put his bags next to the bed, freshened up, and went out again in search of supper. Apparently this hotel served only breakfast to its patrons. On the street, he met a pair of rudely dressed men. If the filthy state of their clothing was any indication, they came straight from a farm into town without cleaning up first.

"Say, gents, is there a good place to put on the feed bag near here?" he asked, smiling brightly.

They stared at him.

"What did you say?" one asked.

"Is there an eatery close by?"

"Oh. Surely." The rustic turned and pointed. "Up yonder to the corner and turn left. Casey's."

"Thank you," Peregrin said.

The other man elbowed his companion. "Of course, if it's drink you be wantin'. . ."

"Oh? And where might a man find a glass or two and a card game?" Peregrin asked. He'd learned in New York that Americans played more poker than anything else, so he didn't ask for a game of whist or faro.

"You oughta come with us if you've a mind to sit in on a game," the first man said.

"Can I get something to eat there?" Peregrin asked, torn between his empty stomach's needs and his love of gambling.

"Sure—well, maybe. Or you can go eat at Casey's and come on down to the Bear Paw afterwards."

It was a difficult decision, but Peregrin decided to get a meal under his belt first thing. He knew his head would stay clearer for the game if he put something solid down first. His two new friends told him how to get to the Bear Paw, slapped him on the back, and sent him on his way.

Millie asked Mrs. Simmons, who held sway over the dining room, to hold a small table in reserve. She went back to her room and freshened up and then waited near the bottom of the stairs as Billy went up to help David.

Getting him down the two flights of stairs took its toll, as Dr. Lee had predicted. David had apparently insisted on leaving his crutches behind. Millie frowned, but perhaps that was wise—they might be too cumbersome on the stairs. The satisfaction on David's face when he reached the bottom testified that he felt it was worth the trouble.

"Mr. Stone, you're looking very chipper." She stepped forward and took his arm. "Thank you so much, Billy." David didn't reach for a coin—he seemed preoccupied with maintaining his balance—so she took a half dime from her pocket and passed it to Billy.

"Thanks, Miz Evans," he said, pulling at his forelock.

"Oh," David said, blinking at her. "I should have—"

"Forget it. Let's get you to a chair. I asked Mrs. Simmons to let us have one of the smaller tables, over to the side, so we won't be right in the middle of the traffic."

In the doorway, David paused, looking around a bit anxiously at the roomful of townspeople, farmers, and adventurers. "Is it always this busy?"

"Supper is very popular here. You know Mrs. Simmons is an excellent cook—you've been eating her meals for some time now."

"Yes." David walked slowly with her along one side of the crowded room to their table.

If Mrs. Simmons weren't such an accomplished cook, Millie reflected, she might have had a chance of getting a job in the kitchen here instead of doing laundry and cleaning. She would have much preferred cooking—but Mrs. Simmons also had a sharp tongue and was very jealous of her territory. Keeping out of the kitchen was no doubt less stressful than the job of cook's helper, even if the work Millie did now was harder physically.

Once they were seated, a homely girl whom she had learned was the Simmonses' niece came to stand beside the table.

"What can I get you folks?" she asked.

David stared up into her abundantly freckled face for a moment, then looked across at Millie.

"You like the fried chicken," Millie said. "Today they also have corn chowder, beef stew, and pork cutlets."

"Ah." David looked less lost. "I'll try the chowder, and then I'll have some chicken. What about you?"

"I'll have the beef stew, please, and biscuits."

"Put Mrs. Evans's meal on my bill, won't you?" David said cordially.

"No, don't do that." Millie frowned at him and leaned across the table. "Mr. Simmons allows me my meals as part of my wages."

"I see." David raised his eyebrows and smiled at the waitress. "Cancel that last request."

"Yes sir. Would you like coffee?"

"Gallons of it."

When the girl had gone to give their order, Millie smiled at him. "Does it feel good to be out in company again?"

"Very good. In fact, I feel so well that I think I'll be able to fend for myself soon."

She nodded and spread the calico napkin in her lap. "Now that you're getting about more, perhaps we could ask Mr. Simmons if he can give you a room on the first floor—or at least the second."

"That would make things easier," David said, "though I do hate the bother of moving."

She smiled at that but said nothing. David resisted any sort of change in his routine when it was first proposed. She'd found it surprising in such an energetic man, but she'd decided it was his way of trying to retain some control in his helpless condition.

"Dr. Lee says I'm not quite ready to resume my journey," David continued, "but I see no reason for you to remain here."

"I. . .beg your pardon." She hadn't supposed he wished her gone just yet, though Dr. Lee had said David mentioned the possibility. She looked across the table into his blue eyes. "I'm not displeased to stay a bit longer."

"Surely you'd rather get on to Philadelphia and get settled. I know you've been anxious to get to your friends and find a permanent situation."

His smile made her heart flutter. How could he be so charming while pushing her away?

Her cheeks grew warm, and she looked down at the tablecloth. "Do you wish me to leave?"

"I wish you to be happy and secure, Millie. You've been very kind and generous with your time and attention, but I can manage now, if you want to go."

The freckled girl, Sarah, came with her tray and put a plate of biscuits on the table between them. Carefully, she eased a bowl of stew off and set it before Millie, then presented David with his corn chowder.

"Butter, jam, and salt is yonder," she said, nodding toward a sideboard where the guests were expected to help themselves. "Anything else?"

"Just the coffee," David said with a smile. Indeed, he seemed to have regained his pleasant demeanor and left the crotchety complaining up in the third-story room.

"Oops. I'll bring it straightaway." The girl whirled about, her skirts billowing.

Millie couldn't help smiling. This *was* like Scottsburg, in some ways, though she no longer tried to beguile him into buying her meals. But she'd enjoyed his company immensely then—as she did now, when he wasn't talking of getting rid of her.

"Now, Millie—"

She stifled her laugh with her napkin. He'd sworn not to call her that anymore unless she used his first name.

He eyed her suspiciously. "What?"

She shook her head and waved one hand. If she told him what amused her, he'd make sure he stuck to his hasty proclamation, and she didn't want him to go back to formalities with her. But if she called him "David," would he think she was trying to coax him into friendship as she had once before? She didn't want to summon back his distrust.

He frowned but went on, "I was only going to say that you should go on as soon as you can. It's August already, and you'll want to get to Phila—"

"Would you please stop talking about that?" she asked, more sharply than was necessary. She lowered her gaze. So much for convincing him she was no longer a woman of the rough frontier.

"I beg your pardon."

David was staring at her. She could feel it. After several seconds, she looked up at him.

"You aren't eating."

"I'm wondering if I've made you cross," he said.

"No, I—" She sighed. "Mr. Stone, if it's all the same to you, I'd rather stay."

"Stay? In Independence? Do you mean. . .you want to settle here, instead of going on to Philadelphia? I realize you've made some friends here. The Hardens—"

Millie shook her head vigorously. "That's not what I mean. I'd like to stay with you until you're certain that you're well. If you don't mind, that is. Mr. Stone, I have no desire to surfeit you with my company. If you truly wish for me to leave. . ."

Now he was smiling, almost gleefully. Millie's cheeks flushed. Was she making a complete fool of herself?

"As a friend," she said hastily. "I feel a certain responsibility to you now, since you were so kind to me, and I wish to stay as long as I can be of help to you."

David said nothing for a long moment. Finally he nodded. "All right. I don't mind, but there are two things we must address."

What on earth? She shot him a keen gaze, but his eyes still held a hint of amusement, and she looked down at her plate. She really was hungry, and the beef stew smelled delicious. She reached for her spoon.

"What two things?"

"First of all, *Mrs. Evans*—"

She winced involuntarily.

David, on the other hand, grinned. "I knew it. You hate for me to call you that."

She shrugged and said carelessly, "It's my name."

"Yes, but I'd rather call you Millie."

She said nothing, knowing what was coming next.

"Or Charlotte, or whatever you desire," David said softly, almost caressingly.

Her cheeks now felt as if they were on fire. "Please. You know that 'Charlotte' was a ruse. In short, I lied to you back then. I don't lie anymore. My real name is Mildred."

"A lovely name. May I use it instead of Millie?"

She nearly strangled to get out, "As you wish."

"Ah. Thank you. And I also wish you would call me David."

"For old times' sake?" she asked cynically.

"No. Not at all. I should like to mark this as the beginning of a new phase in our acquaintance."

"What is the second matter?" she asked uneasily, not willing to commit to anything yet, even something so small as how to address him.

"The second matter—"

"Here you are, Mr. Stone."

Sarah arrived with the coffeepot so precipitously that she bumped into the table, and Millie feared she would slop hot coffee all over David. She opened her mouth to issue a sharp rebuke but clamped it shut. The new Mildred would hold her peace and let the gentleman deal with it.

"Oh, I'm so sorry." A few drops of coffee had sloshed on the table.

"Think nothing of it," David said. He set his cup closer to Sarah so that she could fill it more easily.

"Is there anything else I can bring you?"

"No, thank you."

When she was gone again, David inhaled deeply and looked over at Millie.

"Now, where were we?"

"Your dinner is getting cold." Millie took a bite of her stew.

"So it is. But I'd like to put this traveling matter to rest."

"Oh? Then perhaps we shouldn't discuss it any further."

David frowned and shook his head. "No, I want to settle it. I still need help, Mildred. I admit that. If you leave, I'll probably have to hire someone for the next couple of weeks. If you truly wish to stay, I'd be happy to have you continue as my—shall we say, my aide?"

Millie took a sip of water but had trouble swallowing around the lump in her throat. She blotted her lips and finally met his gaze.

"Yes, David. I accept."

He smiled. "Good." Then he frowned. He looked as though he would speak again, but instead he began to eat his chowder.

# CHAPTER 25

Y ou win again, Cy," crowed the fellow called Jim. He grinned around at the others, showing his brownish teeth. "We'uns are goin' to lose our shirts if this keeps up."

Peregrin lifted his glass and took a swig of his beer. Most of the players at the table were locals, but a couple were men just passing through town. Cy, Jim, and the shaggy man known as Beater, which Peregrin optimistically assumed was his surname—though it seemed many a man jettisoned his real name when he crossed the Mississippi—gathered at the Bear Paw nearly every night to play poker. They must win a good portion of the time, or they wouldn't be able to sustain the regular game.

They probably viewed Peregrin as one of the well-feathered strangers, ready to be plucked. Well, he'd have to teach them a thing or two. They had no idea what sort of card player they were up against.

Last night, they'd jollied him along and played the game almost carelessly. Peregrin had listened to their stories of the frontier and stood them all a couple of drinks. But tonight they were joined by two strangers, and the three locals seemed more serious, more intent, and more ruthless. Peregrin had come out three dollars to the good last night, and they'd parted with a general feeling of camaraderie. But tonight—tonight he got the feeling the boys were out for blood.

Beater proved it when he raised the ante by a hundred dollars, not the customary dollar or two. Surprised the man could lay claim to that much, Peregrin eyed his hand dubiously. Did he want to lose that much, along with the easterner whom Beater seemed eager to trounce? His beer hadn't yet clouded his judgment too much. He didn't stand a chance of winning this round.

He looked over at Cy. Peregrin had learned last night that the scruffy farmer had sixty acres outside of town. Cy and his two buddies had seemed to like the Englishman, and they'd treated him like a long-lost chum. Did they still feel that way? Or had he been bumped into the same class with the other newcomers tonight?

Cy winked at him. Peregrin felt suddenly wiser—and smarter than the travelers who'd dared to take on these fellows.

"I'm out." Peregrin folded his cards. Let Beater take this one. He'd jump back in on the next hand.

Cy nodded. "How about you fetch us another drink, Perry?"

"Glad to." Peregrin rose and walked to the bar just a little less steadily than usual.

Merrileigh would be proud of him for keeping his head.

"Listen to this," David said eagerly. He stood leaning on his crutches while Millie adjusted his clothing, and in his hand was a letter from his niece.

"Hold still, please. I'm trying to fasten these hooks." Millie tried not to let the impatience she felt show in her attitude. She'd spent three hours yesterday shopping for the right trousers and a piece of material that would match—or near enough that no one would notice. It had taken her half of today to alter the pants to her satisfaction.

"Are you sure this will look all right in church?" David asked.

"Yes, I'm sure." Millie had slit the inside seam on the left pant leg and inserted a gusset of the extra black cloth. Then she'd sewn a row of tiny hooks and eyes beneath the flap of material. If her painstaking work didn't pay off, she would be sorely disappointed.

"Well, you must hear Anne's news. I'm delighted that she and Daniel have added a little Adams to the family."

"What?" Millie blinked up at him. "I had no idea."

"No, well. . . Anyway, they have."

"That's wonderful." Of course he, being a gentleman, would never have mentioned that Anne was in a delicate condition. Still, it felt odd, having been so close to David these past four months and not having known anything about it.

"They've named him Richard, after Anne's father."

"Oh, how nice." Millie could barely see the dark little hooks against the black fabric, but at last she managed to fasten the last one. "There!" She sat back on her heels. "I think no one will have an inkling that you're wearing a cast."

"Won't my left. . .limb. . .look fatter than my right?"

"Well of course, but who will notice? If you wear your nice frock coat, and with the crutches—"

"I shan't use the crutches."

She looked up into his stubborn gaze. "I see."

"I shall be fine with the cane." David flicked a glance toward the stick lying on the bed.

"Well, your one leg is a bit out of proportion, but the black cloth helps hide that. I really think this is the best we can do."

"Hmpf."

What was he thinking? When he got that faraway look in his eyes, she couldn't follow him.

"Do you have a better idea?" She almost hoped he didn't, as it would negate all her labor.

"If I were in London, I'd wear a caped greatcoat."

"Ah. Well, we're not, and I don't think I could find one of those in Independence, especially not in August. You'd look more peculiar wearing a heavy woolen coat in this heat than you do with an odd leg."

He winced, and she supposed he felt she was being indelicate. Of course she wouldn't chatter on about a gentleman's legs in public. She wouldn't so much as glance at them. But he didn't know how discreet she could be.

She stood and reached for the cane. "Take a turn down the hallway, and see what you think."

He did so, holding himself almost straight. She could tell he attempted to limp as little as possible. When he came back into the room, she tilted the mirror on top of the dresser.

"Look in here. Tell me if you don't see a fine gentleman."

David looked grudgingly. "I suppose it will have to do."

"Yes. If you wish to go to church this week, it will."

"And there's no way Dr. Lee would consent to remove the cast tomorrow?"

"No way on this green earth."

He sighed. "All right then. And you've spoken for a buggy?"

"I have. A driver will bring it here Sunday morning in plenty of time. I shall return it after our outing."

She could tell he wasn't entirely satisfied with that arrangement, but she wasn't about to change it now. She gathered up her sewing things and put them in the small bag where she stored them.

"Now, if you'll excuse me, I need to put in a few hours working for the Simmonses this afternoon. I shall see you at supper."

David's expression fell even more. "Of course. And thank you."

She wished she hadn't mentioned her work, but she'd taken the equivalent of nearly a full day off, unpaid, to see him decently clothed for church. Mrs. Simmons had a long list of chores she'd wanted completed this morning. Millie would do well to finish it by evening. If only David had been content to wear the pinned trousers to church! But no. She could understand his feeling on that. She didn't think he was an especially vain man, but who could feel confident with pins and a streak of plaster showing? It would be worse than a lady allowing her petticoats to show.

After four days of gambling and wending home to his cramped hotel room half drunk in the early morning, Peregrin came to a decision. It came about when he woke past noon with a violent headache and five hundred dollars less than he'd had the day before.

He examined himself distrustfully in the mirror. His eyes were bloodshot, his hair matted, his face covered in an unbecoming stubble—and his hands shook so badly he didn't dare shave.

Turning away in disgust, he cursed the shabby hotel. In New York he'd have rung for a houseman and asked for a drink and a moderate breakfast. He could even get someone to shave him there.

Here, he was on his own.

Sinking down on the edge of the narrow bed, he considered what to do. First, he decided, he would dress and go downstairs to partake of breakfast. A look at his watch disabused him of that notion. It was closer to dinnertime, and he couldn't get a midday meal here. He would seek out a restaurant and then look for a better hotel. His pitcher held water, and he poured some in a cup. A swig of the lukewarm liquid took away some of the stale dryness in his mouth. With trembling hands, he dressed and added another task to his mental list: find that laundry where he could get a bath. Both his clothes and his person badly needed cleansing.

Finally he brushed his hair almost flat and made a fair attempt at shaving. It took him awhile to staunch the bleeding from the three nicks he made, but at last he felt he was ready to venture into the daylight world of Independence.

Once more he faced his reflection.

"Buck up, old boy."

He scowled at himself. He couldn't keep on like this. Freedom from responsibility was nice to a point, and he enjoyed not having anyone looking over his shoulder and scolding him when he behaved badly. But he knew he must change his ways, or he'd wind up penniless. His luck had turned sour since he'd come to America, and he had enough sense left to know that this wasn't the time to push it.

He needed to stop both drinking to excess and losing money. Immediately. If he went on the way he was, he'd be penniless within a week.

And he needed to do two positive things, also at once: find better lodgings and start looking for David Stone.

Millie considered it a triumph when she got David to church on Sunday. Not that he resisted—in fact, he was eager to go. The Hardens had invited them to take dinner at the parsonage after the service.

Getting David dressed and groomed for church was her first

challenge in the morning. She got ready early, putting on her brown traveling dress and her best hat. She sent Billy to set out David's shaving things and help him into his clean smallclothes and a shirt she'd starched and ironed to perfection, along with the modified trousers. When she came upon the scene, David was tying his necktie, and Billy was hovering with the cane. Apparently Billy had managed all the hooks, as she couldn't discern from two yards distant where the gusset met the seam.

David looked so handsome, she caught her breath and studied his reflection in the looking glass. His face seemed to have dropped ten years. She realized that she had grown accustomed to the lines and pallor the pain had brought to his face since the accident. Now he seemed more like the dashing gentleman she'd first met in Oregon. Not young, but certainly not old. A man in his prime.

She noted that he was also looking at her in the mirror. His hands had stilled with the ribbon half tied, and his blue eyes searched her face for—what?

Smiling, she stepped forward. "Don't you look fine? Billy, thank you for helping Mr. Stone this morning."

"Yes'm." Billy ducked his head in acknowledgment and sneaked a glance at David.

"Give him two bits, will you, Mildred?"

She went to the bedside table, where David's latest reading material and a few coins lay near the lamp. Twenty-five cents was an awfully large tip for the boy, but she didn't argue. David was in a sunny mood this morning, and who was she to dispute his largesse?

"Thank you," Billy muttered. He turned to observe David, who had finished with his necktie and now reached for his frock coat. "Help you, sir?"

Billy held the coat and handed David his cane as he turned.

"Thank you, Wilfred," David said. "Will you be able to help me down the stairs now?"

"Surely can, sir."

"Good. Let me just get my wallet."

"Shall I bring your Bible?" Millie asked.

"Thank you."

She picked it up from the dresser and placed her own smaller brown one on top. These and her handbag she carried down in the wake of the two men. David really was doing better these days, though he still had to pause on each step and make sure he was balanced before venturing to the next.

The buggy was waiting, with the driver's saddle horse tied behind it. When David was seated and Millie had taken the reins, the driver tipped his hat and rode off on the horse.

"Let me drive," David said.

Millie eyed him askance. "Do you think you're ready?"

"Of course I'm ready. It's my leg that was injured this time."

She flinched at the "this time," a flagrant reminder that she'd as good as caused his earlier shoulder wound. Well, it wasn't her fault that the stage had overturned.

"I'm in the driver's seat," she pointed out.

"So what? I'm sure the horse won't mind, so long as I adjust the reins."

She wanted to dig her heels in, but it struck her suddenly that the mood for the day lay in her lap. Did she want a peevish, out-of-sorts man with an acerbic tongue to accompany her today, or a charming gentleman who'd had his first opportunity in months to drive? She suspected that men of David's social caliber looked upon their right to drive the same way some women regarded their right to pour tea.

She said no more but handed over the reins and whip.

They reached the church in good time, as David didn't allow the horse to slack. She helped him to the ground and then unhitched the horse, led him into the shed beside the church, and covered him with a blanket the owner had provided. During this interval, David stood waiting and frowning. Did he think he was in danger of being perceived as a lesser man because the woman accompanying him tended the horse? Such notions bordered on the ridiculous, but Millie could see this wasn't the time to say so.

"Didn't you used to live in Independence?" she asked as she

removed the horse's bridle.

"Yes. Five years. I kept a mercantile."

"Do you want to visit any of your old acquaintances, now that you're feeling better?"

"Don't think so."

Millie was not too surprised at this—more than a decade had passed since David's move to Oregon. A lot of the people he'd known in Independence had probably moved on, too. Apparently he hadn't formed close friendships here in the past, which made for fewer complications now—though the distraction of a larger social circle might have been welcome during the healing phase.

When she was ready, she took their Bibles and her purse from the buggy. David offered his left arm and carried the cane in his right hand. He halted only a little as they walked to the church door.

When they reached the heavy portal, he pulled on the handle and staggered a bit, catching himself with his cane. Millie grabbed the edge of the door and put her strength into the pull. Together they got it open, and David leaned against it.

He caught his breath and nodded. "After you, madam."

He was treating her like a lady. Not that he'd ever disdained her, but when they'd embarked on the stagecoach journey, he'd held himself aloof and made it plain that he wanted nothing to do with her. Now he was going as far as his health would allow to be courteous—beyond that, to pay small but welcome attention to her.

Millie smiled at him. "Thank you."

The church pews were about half-filled, and Mr. Harden was just taking his place on the platform at the front.

"I see a place there." Millie pointed as discreetly as she could to a half-empty bench near the back.

David nodded, waited until she laced her hand once more through the crook of his arm, and then led her toward it.

"She's a hard worker," David said, watching Millie from a distance. He and Pastor Harden sat in the parsonage garden, talking and drinking coffee in the shade while Millie and Mrs. Harden strolled about looking at the hostess's flowerbeds. Apparently Mrs. Harden loved to garden and used her blooms in decorating the sanctuary.

"Does that surprise you?" Joseph Harden asked.

"Some. When I first met Millie, I saw her more as a lady of leisure. A woman of means."

"But you've told me that was a false impression."

"Yes." It still troubled David. "She's always working now. She says that I don't need her, so she can spend all day cleaning and doing laundry for other people."

"She wants to support herself. To prove she's not helpless—or dependent on you."

David nodded. "I suppose you're right. One thing she was then and is still—she's independent. I think she hated having to rely on me. But I didn't mind helping her." After a moment, his conscience prompted him to add, "Well, maybe at first. I was afraid she saw me as easy pickings—again."

"But you don't think that now?" Harden said.

"No. I've watched her long enough to know this new attitude of hers is genuine. A lazy person wouldn't keep up the drudgery so long. And most thieves are lazy."

"Mildred has told my wife and me quite a bit about her early life." The minister eyed him thoughtfully. "It's not my place to reveal any of that to you, but I believe we know her well enough to assure you that she has truly changed her ways. She wants to please God now, and she's contrite about some of the things she did in the past—including the plot she became involved in that nearly killed you."

"She's told me she didn't know that fellow wanted me dead."

"And we believe her." Mr. Harden sipped his coffee.

"Did she tell you how she got her Bible?"

The minister smiled. "Yes, she did. And she said she had some cockeyed notion at first that if she read from it, she'd atone somehow for what she'd done. But the message touched her heart, Mr. Stone. I firmly believe Millie is a true sister in Christ now."

David watched the two women and mulled that over. Would

this have mattered to him ten years ago? It did now, but for most of his life, faith had not been the prime criterion he considered in a woman. Instead, if he were looking for a wife, he would look at her family's pedigree, her appearance, her manners, and her fortune or lack of one.

Millie had no family to be proud of. The only one of her relatives David had met died while committing a robbery. She was pretty, in an earthy way, with her glossy auburn hair and green eyes. Her complexion was quite good, and when she was able, she dressed well. But today she wore a simple brown dress that had neither style nor allure. He studied her posture and her manner as she conversed with Mrs. Harden, and he found nothing to criticize. Of course she didn't have two dimes to rub together. But was fortune really that important?

"You have long thoughts, Mr. Stone."

"Yes." He turned his attention back to Mr. Harden. "Did she really think she could redeem herself with good deeds?"

"She had some idea along those lines, I believe. That if she did more and more good, and if she turned aside when tempted to do evil, this might save her, and eventually she could become a good Christian through her own efforts."

"I trust you and your wife were able to set her on the right path."

"She'd discovered her error by the time she came to us. She realized what she'd believed didn't fit with what Christ said. That she had to trust Him in order to be relieved of her transgressions."

David inhaled carefully. He'd had many long hours in his bed at the hotel to consider this very thing. "I'm afraid I was a rather proud and vain young man and did not improve much with age."

"Oh?" Mr. Harden smiled. "Is that still your outlook, sir?"

David shook his head. "Twice in the past two years, God has laid me low. The first time, I made a slow recovery, but I renewed my fellowship with the Almighty."

"Praise be."

"Yes. This time, the Lord is showing me other lessons."

# CHAPTER 26

Peregrin entered the doctor's office and looked around. Two men and a woman holding a baby sat in the waiting room. He took a seat. About ten minutes later, a pretty, round young woman came from deeper in the house.

"You can go in, Mrs. Jackson."

The baby's mother rose and shuffled through the doorway. The woman who'd directed her looked at Peregrin.

"May I help you, sir?"

"Yes, I hope so." Peregrin stood and walked over to her.

For several days, he'd inquired for David Stone at various hotels, but without success. He was beginning to think he'd missed his quarry after all. David must have gone on eastward. Peregrin feared he'd have to give up.

His search had brought one good result—he'd found a couple of hotels that offered better rooms than his own and promptly changed his lodgings. He'd taken his time settling in and getting used to his new environment. And he'd found a higher class of poker game in one of the other hotel guests' sitting room. But he hadn't allowed himself to get in too deep again. Right now he had nearly as much cash as he'd arrived with, and he intended not to lose it all.

He was determined to catch wind of David. That took precedence over everything else. A newcomer at the poker game last night had mentioned that he'd taken an English gentleman from a stagecoach wreck a couple of months previously. Peregrin had perked up at that news. It was the first clue he'd gotten, and on inquiry, the man had told him that he'd delivered the gentleman to a local doctor's house. Peregrin had gotten the address, and this morning he'd found the office and was feeling hopeful.

"I'm looking for a British man," he said with a smile that he hoped was winsome.

"Oh, an acquaintance of yours, sir?" Her face lit up, and she smiled back. His accent seemed to have that effect on American women.

"Yes ma'am. And I heard that Dr. Lee treated such a man several weeks ago. I'm trying to find him. Uh. . ." He glanced about. The other two men were listening, but he couldn't see any way out of letting them hear. "His name's Stone."

"Oh yes," the woman said. "The doctor tells me Mr. Stone is on the mend. He'll probably leave town soon. He's very fortunate to have made a good recovery."

Peregrin nodded, smiling. "I'm so glad to hear it. Could you tell me where he's lodging, please?"

"Well, I don't see any harm in that. Are you a relation of his, sir?"

"No. Well, yes, in a spotty sort of way. My sister is married to his cousin, don't you see?"

She laughed. "Yes, I do see. Well, you might try the Frontier Hotel." She gave him directions and assured him it wasn't far.

Peregrin thanked her heartily and departed, avoiding the other men's direct gazes. People would remember him, but there was no help for it. He'd have to leave town as soon as he'd finished his business, that was all. Even better, he could wait until David left Independence. Perhaps he could follow him and make sure David's next mishap took place a good distance from here. Then people wouldn't connect it to his inquiries. Maybe he could even travel with David.

Peregrin liked that idea. Why shouldn't he march right up to Stone and introduce himself? They did have a social connection, and he could use that to gain the man's confidence. Of course, he'd have to make up a story explaining his presence in the middle of North America, but that shouldn't be too difficult.

If they traveled eastward together, Peregrin could watch for an opportunity to complete Merrileigh's commission unobtrusively. Maybe David would fall off a moving train in some isolated part of the wilderness. And who would know if he hit his head as he fell—or before?

"Does this mean he can travel?" Millie stood in the doorway of David's hotel room, after having been summoned by Dr. Lee.

"Yes," the doctor said, "I think he's ready. You'll take the train to St. Louis, not a boat?"

"We thought we would," David said.

Millie said hesitantly, "There's been talk of disease spreading on the steamboats."

"Yes, and I thought it would be simpler to take the railroad. Of course, we'll have to cross the Mississippi by steamer, but that shouldn't be so bad. Mrs. Evans will make sure I'm comfortable, won't you?" David smiled at her across the room.

"Of course." Millie entered and stood at the foot of the bed. It was so good to see David looking happy and eager to get on with life.

"I am going to remove the cast now," Dr. Lee said. "Mrs. Evans, would you be able to get me a large basin or box to put the plaster in? I don't want to make too big a mess. You might want to bring a broom as well."

"I'd be delighted." Millie dashed down the back stairs to the kitchen and found a large enameled wash pan. In it she placed a dustpan and a couple of rags.

Mrs. Simmons was chopping onions at her work table, and she eyed Millie testily. "What are you up to?"

"The doctor's taking the cast off Mr. Stone's leg."

"Ah. I suppose that means the two of you will be leaving us soon."

Millie wanted to say, "I hope so," but that would be rude, so she said only, "Perhaps." She grabbed a broom and scooted back into the stairway with her unwieldy load.

Was she really eager to leave Independence? David, she knew, could hardly wait to depart from this hotel. When they left here, they would also separate, if not immediately, then surely after they crossed the Mississippi. She'd come to dread the day.

Lately he'd grown more solicitous of her, taking pains not to cause her extra work. She'd praised him for taking on his own care and becoming self-sufficient once more. But the truth was, she missed spending time with him. More than two weeks had passed since the last time she'd read aloud to him. David had gone up and down the stairs slowly, but unassisted, the past two days. Without the cast, he'd be chafing to resume his travels.

When she got back to his room, Dr. Lee had already begun to cut through the plaster and had removed several large chunks, which he had placed on a newspaper.

"Ah, there you are. Thank you, Mrs. Evans." He dropped the next section into the wash pan.

Millie dumped the debris he'd already created into the pan and concentrated on not looking at David's limb while the doctor exposed it. She felt her cheeks flush anyway and decided sweeping the floor would give her a good reason to look elsewhere.

"It would be wise to take a few extra days here to exercise a little more," Dr. Lee said to David. "In moderation of course. Walk down the street tomorrow morning and get a glimpse of the town. Perhaps buy your train tickets for a few days hence."

"I suppose we could do that," David said, a little of his old stubbornness creeping into his tone. "I should rather leave tomorrow."

"I know," Dr. Lee replied, "but you want to make sure your leg will support you before you set out. Your muscles have grown quite weak from lack of use during the last two months. Take Mrs. Evans or someone else with you when you walk. And take the cane along, too. You might suddenly get a cramp or lose your balance—you just never know. Give it a few days, and then, if you're feeling well, go ahead and make your journey."

All of this made perfect sense to Millie, and she hoped David would see the wisdom of it and take the doctor's advice. She would hate to see him have a setback, even though his recovery meant they would soon be parting.

"It's getting late," she said. "Probably it will be suppertime when

Dr. Lee finishes. But in the morning, we could take a stroll, as he suggested, and see how you do. I really think going to the dining room and perhaps a walk around the hotel grounds would be plenty for this evening. Don't you?"

David frowned but raised one hand in defeat. "You may be right. Let's see how it goes."

She nodded, and something in her heart contracted. Her job now was to make sure David was capable of leaving her behind.

Peregrin entered the Frontier Hotel. He decided that he wouldn't get far if he tried to conceal his purpose. He would use the direct approach, as he had at the doctor's office. He reached for his wallet and walked to the desk.

"Are you wanting a room, mister?" the innkeeper asked.

"Well no, actually I'm here to visit one of your guests. Mr. Stone."

The man smiled, and Peregrin decided he might not need to bribe him after all.

"Mr. Stone? Sure, we've got 'im."

Peregrin was almost surprised that he'd at last found the man he'd sought so long. He let out a quick laugh. "Honestly? He's here?"

"Tall English gent with a broken leg?"

"Yes, I suppose so. I'd heard he was injured. Didn't know his leg was fractured."

"Oh yes. Been staying here nigh on two months now."

Peregrin smiled. "My good man, I see that you serve meals here. Tell me, do you also take a bathtub to a guest's room when he wants one?"

"Nope, but we've got a bath shed out back. You can get your hot bath out there when you've a mind to. You're English, too, ain'tcha?"

"Well yes." Peregrin frowned, wondering if he should admit it, but he supposed it wasn't any use to try to hide the fact. But should he risk taking a room here? The scents of chocolate cake and frying chicken, wafting from the kitchen, swayed him. "Would you have a room free?"

"Yup. You want ter be next to Mr. Stone?"

"Oh no," Peregrin said quickly. "In fact, a different floor is fine."

"Awright. Got a room on the second-floor landing." He passed Peregrin a key. "Sign here. You'll want to catch Mr. Stone today or tomorrow though."

"Oh?" Peregrin eyed him keenly. "Why is that?"

"The sawbones came 'round and took the plaster off his leg this afternoon. Mr. Stone says he'll likely leave in a day or two. Mrs. Evans is trying to talk him into staying out the week, but I doubt he'll be here that long."

"Mrs. Evans?" Peregrin asked.

"The woman what came here with him. Millie, her name is. Millie Evans."

"Indeed." Peregrin would have a juicy morsel to tell Merrileigh in his next letter. David Stone had a woman traveling with him. Very interesting.

Simmons shook his head. "We sure will miss her when she's gone."

"Why is that, sir?"

"H'ain't nobody cleans as well or gets the sheets as white as Mrs. Evans. I'll have to send the linen out to be laundered again. Well, nothing good stays, does it?"

"If you say so."

Simmons shrugged. "Anyway, Mr. Stone's in 302. You talk just like 'im. It beats all."

Peregrin pondered Mr. Simmons's words as he climbed the stairs to the second-floor landing. He'd best send a note to Merrileigh right away. He hoped he could wire the message to New York, but even if he could, it would still take ten days or so for it to reach England from there by ship. Perhaps he'd send a short message for now, and save the news about David's female companion until he knew more. But he needed to tell Merry he'd found David—alive, but injured, and, most importantly, unmarried.

# CHAPTER 27

Millie insisted that David sit and rest while she packed his valise, though he would much rather have handed things to her or even done the packing himself. She'd taken away all his shirts and linen but what he was wearing that morning to launder them, and now she had a big stack of clean clothing to fold and stow in his two traveling bags.

"I put a new button on this shirt," she said, folding the one that was now his second best. "And I mended the tear in the sleeve of the plaid one."

"That old thing." He'd worn the plaid shirt while puttering about his farm in Oregon and had brought it along mostly in case he needed to do something that would get him dirty. "I suppose I shall have to buy an entire new wardrobe when I get to England, or decent folks won't receive me."

She paused and frowned at him. "Is that so? And here I was thinking how splendid it is that you have so many shirts and such a fine frock suit, not to mention the tailcoat and trousers, besides your everyday."

"Oh." He'd never thought of it quite that way. Even when he'd divested himself of most of his worldly goods, he was still much better off than many of the people around him.

"Do you want to keep these?" She held up the two pairs of trousers she had modified to fit over the cast.

"I hardly think so."

Millie shrugged. "I shall take them to Mrs. Lee then. They might keep them for another patient, I suppose—or someone could put them back to rights for a person without a plaster cast. The black pair is quite good quality, and I hate to see it wasted."

"Do whatever you wish," David said.

Millie folded them carefully. "Perhaps Rev. Harden could use the black pair if his wife gives them some attention and removes the gusset."

"Fine."

"I'll leave out the things you'll need tomorrow," Millie said.

"I still don't see why we can't board the train tomorrow morning." David winced at the sound of his own voice. "Sorry. That's childish of me, isn't it?"

"Getting a bit anxious now?" She smiled at him. "One more day. Dr. Lee insists."

"Yes, yes." He huffed out a breath. Part of him wanted to bound down the two flights of stairs and stride off to the railroad station this minute. He'd been stalled far too long on this trip. The sooner he got to England the better.

But another voice within him cautioned that all too soon he'd be pining for America—the rough beauty of the West and the gentler exuberance of the East Coast. And beyond all of that, he would miss a certain lady.

Yes, she was a lady. He'd settled that in his heart. Millie had some unpolished facets, but she had more substance than most Englishwomen could imagine. Oh, he knew the British were supposed to be staunch to the bone, but nowadays he felt a lot of the upper class in England were too soft by far.

Millie could outride, out-cook, out-scrub, and out-sew most of the women he'd known in his homeland, and on top of all that, she could shoot and drive and do business as well as most men. She might not play the harpsichord or speak Italian, but what did those things matter?

She shook out one of his under-vests, and David looked away, embarrassed that she was handling his personal things. She did it matter-of-factly, almost the way a servant would. But he'd long ago determined he wouldn't treat her like a servant or think of her as one. Whether a woman became a duchess or a maid was in most cases an accident of birth. Look at Elise Finster, his niece's lady's maid. She'd begun life as a lowly servant girl. Now she was the wife of a well-respected, independent rancher in Oregon.

Why couldn't Millie cross the line in the other direction? An American woman of questionable birth and rearing, to be sure. But she had the stuff that would let her hold her head high in the finest of company.

"There. That's the lot. I'll put your bags in the armoire. Anything else I can do for you now?"

"No, I don't think so. Thank you."

"Well, then, I'll be off. Mrs. Simmons wants me to wash dishes tonight, which will probably last until bedtime."

"You shouldn't have to do such mean work."

She laughed. "Why not? Somebody has to do it. And they're paying me."

"Not nearly enough, I'll wager."

He looked at her again. Her thick auburn hair was pulled up on the back of her head, and she wore a plain calico dress, one she'd bought a few weeks ago to wear while cleaning, in order to save her traveling costume and her one "good" dress. An urge came over him to see her again in a well-cut gown of fine material, this time with jewels at her throat and her ears, and an ivory-cased fan at her waist, with her beautiful hair cascading about her shoulders. It could happen, if he weren't so set in his ways.

It was not the first time David had contemplated the matter. He pictured Millie—no, Mildred—on his arm at a ball. Suitably gowned and coiffed, she could stand next to any Englishwoman and compare favorably. And if she had the fortune to allow her to stop working so hard, her roughened hands would soften. Yes, Millie with the advantages of, say, his niece, Anne, could hold her own in any social circle. Because she knew how to charm people. She listened and learned. She studied and mimicked. She could be more polite than the Queen herself.

And she would do everything necessary to avoid embarrassing a man who treated her well. He knew this somehow without being told—without being shown beyond what he had seen of her already.

With a little training, he was sure she could pass for a countess. Could even *be* a countess. Almost, David felt a man could marry her and take her into the highest of English society and not be shamed.

But more importantly, in Millie's company, a man would never be bored.

Peregrin lingered on the third-story landing, watching the door of room 302. He also kept a sharp eye out to make sure nobody else came along and found him loitering. He was still undecided on how to go about Merrileigh's commission. Should he introduce himself to David or remain in the shadows? The woman accompanying David was an unknown quantity. Perhaps he should learn more about her before he made himself known. She might be an obstacle.

A door at the end of the hallway opened, and a woman emerged. Peregrin had previously scouted this doorway and found that it gave on a dim, narrow stairway that he assumed led down to the kitchen. The woman now walking toward him wore a dress his peers would call dowdy, topped by a large apron. One of the hotel staff, no doubt, though she was quite pretty. Fiery highlights shone in her dark hair as she passed beneath a wall lamp, and she carried herself well. In better clothes, she might dazzle him.

All of this Peregrin learned in a quick glance as he moved toward the head of the main stairs. He started down and darted another look over his shoulder. She paid him no attention but was opening a door across the hall from Stone's. Peregrin descended a couple more steps, paused, and turned to go back up, as if he'd forgotten something.

When he reached the landing again, the woman had disappeared. Softly, he walked past her door. It was numbered 303. Could this be the woman that Mr. Simmons had described—David's companion of the laundry talents?

This bore looking into. It seemed odd that David would allow a woman traveling with him to do laundry for the hotel. Had the next earl lost all his money? Peregrin could hardly believe she was working to pay for their lodgings. What gentleman would ask his lady friend to support them? Such an attractive woman must have some options other than drudgery. Surely she would have little trouble finding herself a husband.

It was a regular bumblebroth. Peregrin decided to take supper elsewhere—not in the hotel's dining room—and give it some more thought.

David was in pain. Millie could tell as soon as she saw his face. The fact that he hadn't dressed, but sat in the armchair wearing his dressing gown, confirmed her impression.

"Your leg hurts." She crossed to his bedside table and picked up the laudanum bottle. "Let me fix you a dose."

"No," David said sharply.

She turned and frowned at him. He'd been so polite the last few days!

"I'm sorry," he said. "I only mean that I don't want to take the stuff. It makes me groggy, and I can't think clearly."

"But if you are in pain. . ."

"Pain is not the worst thing in the world."

"Ah." She stood with the bottle in her hand, waiting for a cue from him as to what to do. He had overtaxed himself yesterday, but she wouldn't say that. He could figure it out for himself, and if she stated the fact, it would only irritate him.

"I believe we were going to the train station to buy our tickets," he said.

"Yes, but it's too far for you to walk, especially if your leg is bothering you."

"I daresay you're right. Can we get a carriage? Or even a farm wagon?"

Millie considered that. "It would be much simpler if I go. I can walk it in half an hour, while you rest."

"I hate resting. It's all I ever do."

"But if you do too much now, you'll have a setback. Then where will you be come time to travel?"

He looked away and rested his chin on his hand. "I suppose you're right—but I don't like it."

She laughed. David never liked it when someone else was right. "Just tell me what you want, and I'll get it. I suppose you want a through ticket to New York if they have such a thing."

"No doubt we'll have to go to St. Louis first. Get across the Mississippi, and then deal with the ticket question again."

"You're probably right. Shall I get two train tickets to the ferry, then, and we'll cross together?"

"Why not?"

"Would you like me to help you back into bed before I go? I could ask Billy to bring you a breakfast tray."

"I think I'll sit here, but I would like the tray, thank you." David's blue eyes seemed melancholy today.

"Perhaps some willow bark tea would ease the pain, though it's not nearly so strong as laudanum. I'm sure Mrs. Simmons keeps some in the pantry."

"All right." He looked up at her suddenly. "Mildred, there's something else."

Something about his tone softened her heart, and she stepped closer. "What is it?"

"I think I'd like to travel with you as far as Philadelphia. I can surely get a ship from there for England."

This unexpected news set her pulse off in a jagged path. "I expect you could, but why?"

He shrugged and looked out the window. "I should worry about you if you went off alone."

She wanted to laugh. She'd been fending for herself for years, and she didn't need an escort. But the simple fact that someone cared about her welfare touched her heart. And this wasn't just anyone. It was David.

She closed the distance between them and bent to touch his hand. "Thank you. You don't need to, but that—that means a good deal to me. I'll see about the tickets."

"All right. Take the money from my wallet." He turned his hand and clutched her fingers for a moment, then let them slide from his grasp. "I shall see you later, then."

"Yes, I'll be back before dinnertime."

She'd gone to his room prepared to take breakfast with him and then set out for the train station, so after she got the money for the tickets, she went right down to the dining room. This morning she would eat alone, as she had for many weeks.

Last night she'd given Mr. Simmons her notice, so she'd have to pay for the rest of the meals she ate here, but that was all right. She needed the next couple of days to tie up the loose ends for their travel. She'd saved enough to purchase her own fare to Philadelphia, with several dollars besides. With care, she could keep herself until she found work in the city.

In the dining room, she ordered David's tray, but only coffee and biscuits for herself—the cheapest thing she could get and still fill her stomach. She was eating a bit later than her normal hour, and only a few guests were still in the room. In the far corner sat a gentleman she didn't remember seeing before. A new guest, no doubt. He looked to be about her own age, and handsome in an ornate sort of way. She decided it was his well-cut coat and the necktie at breakfast that gave her this impression—that and the way he'd combed his hair. She doubted most men in Independence had more than a nodding acquaintance with a looking glass. This one had obviously spent some time gazing into one. He seemed more intent on his newspaper than his meal, however.

As she ate, she mulled over what David had said. Her heart was tearing in two. On the one hand, she was glad he wanted to stay with her a little longer. But he showed no regrets about their imminent parting. In fact, from what he'd said this morning, it appeared he wanted to see her safely to her destination, and then be rid of her once and for all. These last few days, he'd seemed to truly enjoy her company, but that was coming to an end. It still seemed to Millie that he couldn't wait to be rid of her, although his conscience bade him to make sure she was safe.

A steady ache formed in her chest, and she feared she might begin to weep. That would never do! Just because she'd developed feelings for a man was no reason to fall to pieces. She wouldn't call David an uncaring man. Indeed, lately he'd shown himself quite compassionate. But he didn't love her, and in spite of her efforts to resist the longing, that was what she truly desired.

What would he say if she bought her ticket for a different day than his and refused to travel with him? That seemed a bit crass, in light of his past kindnesses. Furthermore, she knew she could never bring herself to do it.

Millie finished her coffee and resolved to make the most of her limited time with David. Inside, she might be mourning as they rode the rails eastward, but she would show him her charming, lighthearted demeanor. Once she'd fancied marrying him—for his fortune, nothing else. Now she couldn't care less about that. She loved him with all her heart. But she would never let him know.

Peregrin watched the auburn-haired woman over the top of his newspaper. This was the mysterious Mrs. Evans who was traveling with Randolph Stone's cousin. She was pretty enough, even in the stark morning light of the dining room. She wasn't wearing an apron today, but a practical, coarse calico dress. She wore a hat as well, and that looked to be of better quality than the dress. So...she was going out.

Peregrin had hoped David would come down to breakfast so he could get a look at him. But it seemed he was keeping to his room this morning. Just how ill was he?

Should he wait for this Mrs. Evans to leave and then run up to David's room? Peregrin decided against that. He wasn't ready to carry out Merrileigh's ultimate wishes yet—not here, in the hotel. And it might be best if David remained unaware of his presence a little longer.

Mrs. Evans rose, and Peregrin made a quick decision. He cast aside his newspaper, laid a few coins on the table, and followed her out. She was already striding rapidly up the street. He'd have to dash to keep up, and Peregrin wasn't the sort of man who liked to hurry. But if he hired a hack, he'd have to instruct the driver to hover behind her—a distasteful position. Besides, there didn't seem to be any hackneys lingering about the hotel this morning.

Shank's mare it was. He set out briskly, telling himself she wouldn't go far. What woman would set out on foot to walk more than a few blocks?

The streets were crowded with wagons, saddle horses, and pedestrians. The emigrant trains going west this year had all left, his poker-playing friends had told him. For the next couple of months, people headed the other way would come through. The town was growing ever larger, and thousands more would pass through next spring, headed west.

Peregrin couldn't see what the attraction was. More land like this to break with a plow and till? He supposed that for the lower classes, the prospect of a few acres was alluring. Personally, he'd rather have stayed in the more settled and civilized East.

Mrs. Evans turned out to be a difficult person to follow. She moved quickly through the morning crowds, apparently focused on her destination. Peregrin dashed after her, trying to keep an eye on her bonnet.

About twenty minutes later, he pulled up, wheezing and clutching his chest, before the railroad station. She must have gone in here. He hadn't actually seen her enter, but she'd headed up this street with a purposeful stride, and the station was the largest building in the vicinity. He stood on the corner, catching his breath and waiting. Surely she'd come out again. Unless she took a train. But no—she hadn't carried any luggage.

He congratulated himself on this keen deduction. He was really getting rather good at this cloak-and-dagger business. Mrs. Evans must have come to buy tickets. That meant she and David planned to leave Independence soon, perhaps today or tomorrow. He'd come just in time.

He pulled in several steadying breaths. His pulse began to slack off. At that moment, the woman in question emerged from the station. She didn't dawdle but headed immediately back the way she had come. As she reached the corner where Peregrin stood observing her, she glanced at him.

"Good morning," he said cheerfully, lifting his hat.

She nodded and started to pass, then stopped dead in her tracks. She whirled around. "Didn't I see you at the Frontier Hotel this morning?"

# CHAPTER 28

**D**avid lay on his bed, rubbing his thigh and wishing the pain away. He ought to have listened to Millie and taken the laudanum this morning. At this rate, he wouldn't be fit to take dinner with her, let alone travel tomorrow.

He glanced about the room. Where were those crutches? Millie must have put them away in the wardrobe, since he hadn't used them for a day or two. Oh well, he could reach the cane. Perhaps if he hobbled out into the hallway, he could summon Wilfred to come and give him some laudanum.

What was he thinking? That boy couldn't mix the dose. Millie always did it. He supposed he could mix it himself. He seemed to recall that half a teaspoon made the usual dose, in a glass of water. Maybe he'd use only half that. He truly didn't want to lose consciousness for hours, just to stop feeling as though his leg were being crushed under a boulder—or a stagecoach. The willow bark tea probably helped some—everyone swore by its curative powers—but a strong cup of it hadn't seemed to take more than the sharpest edge off his pain.

Perhaps he could lessen the discomfort if he put his mind to something else. Or someone else?

Millie.

There, he might as well face the facts and stop trying to trick himself. He wanted Millie for his bride. How sharply would his friends in England cut him if he arrived with Mildred as his legal wife? Of even more concern, how badly would they treat Millie? Could she stand up to disdain and scorn? He wasn't sure he could abide with that. If people were going to treat her abominably—or just ignore her, which in London was even worse—he might lose his good nature. But so much in English society depended on having the good will of the upper crust.

"What am I thinking?" he said aloud. "Millie can pull it off. Why, with two weeks in New York, I can outfit her like the countess she'll be and teach her how to address the nobility." She could probably dance already, and he had no doubt she could handle the staff at Stoneford. She had a commanding manner when she needed it and could give orders that other people sprang to obey.

And she was lovely. Not a sugary-sweet debutante, but a handsome young widow who knew her way around the lamppost. She picked up on nuances quickly. Yes, he could give her sufficient training in the time it would take to cross the Atlantic. Millie would be accepted—and loved—as his treasured bride. As Lady Stoneford.

"Oh. . .well. . .uh. . .yes, I believe you might have." Peregrin whipped off his hat and bowed at the waist. "I did take my breakfast there. Came out for a constitutional afterward."

"Indeed?" Millie surveyed the man in the smartly tailored suit with some misgiving. It seemed very odd that a man had set out for a stroll and gone in the same direction as she had and kept pace with her as well. "It's not been thirty minutes since I left the hotel."

The man didn't quite meet her eyes. "Oh yes. I like a brisk walk after breakfast, don't you know."

"You're English, aren't you?" He was about thirty years old and had a pleasant face, but what had really caught her attention was his accent. In those few words, she knew he was not only British but also of gentle birth. And how did she know this, she asked herself. Because he talked like David of course.

"Why yes. I've only been in this half of the world a few weeks. Liking it, rather, though it's a bit rustic."

"I suppose so," she said, though to Millie, Independence was as big as any town she'd seen in the last twenty years. Philadelphia would probably shock her when she saw it again. "Excuse me, I must be going." She turned away.

"Might I not accompany you back to the hotel?" He hopped along to catch up and fell into stride with her.

She shot him a sideways glance. He was a bit forward and overeager, but really, he behaved no worse than scores of other men she'd encountered. And the poor fellow probably knew no one in the area. He looked like a gentleman. Could she assume he would behave like one? And his presence would keep other men from accosting her. Really, what was the harm?

"I suppose you might," she said demurely.

"Oh, thank you, madam. I shall be honored."

He didn't offer his arm, and Millie was glad. That would be spooning it on a bit thick.

"I do hope your visit to the depot doesn't foreshadow a journey in the near future," he said.

"Why yes. I shall be traveling soon."

"What? Not leaving us? But I've only just made your acquaintance." He touched her sleeve and stopped walking, peering down at her in consternation.

"Really, sir," Millie said, a bit more severely, "you haven't made my acquaintance at all."

For a moment he gazed at her in assessment, and Millie fancied his eyes took on a bit of a gleam, as though he was accepting a challenge. He bowed slightly.

"You're absolutely right. Since we have no one to perform the ceremonies, allow me to introduce myself. The name is Peregrin Walmore."

She wanted to repeat the strange name, just to hear the cadence on her tongue, but she managed to get by with only a slight twitch of the lip as she thought about it.

"That's a very odd name, sir. I've never heard one like it."

"Oh, it was quite the fashion in England some years back, which I suppose is why my mother chose it."

"I see."

"And your name, if I may be so bold?"

She hesitated but could see no reason not to divulge it. All of the hotel staff knew her and would probably not scruple to give another guest her name.

"Mrs. Evans."

"Ah."

Millie began walking again, and Walmore hurried to keep up.

"May I inquire how Mr. Evans is doing? Is he traveling with you?"

"No, Mr. Evans has left this mortal life."

"My condolences." His smile belied his words. "So you might say your husband has journeyed on before you."

Millie said nothing. She strongly doubted James had passed through the pearly gates, and she certainly didn't want to follow him in his otherworldly travels.

"Might I invite you to take dinner with me this noon?" Walmore asked.

He did have a charming smile, and that delightful accent that was so like David's. It occurred to Millie that having another English gentleman approach her in the frontier town amounted to a coincidence so large as to be unwieldy.

"May I inquire what you do for a living, sir?"

"What I do?" Mr. Walmore blinked down at her. "Well, I've a couple of thousand a year, if you must know, but that's a bit brash, isn't it?"

"I don't understand you." Millie stopped walking again. "I didn't ask your income, sir. I asked your profession."

"Ah, I see. As a matter of fact, I am of the class that has a living but does not need to *make* one."

"Oh. A gentleman, as they say."

"Well yes."

She nodded and walked on. She decided to ask David if he knew anything about the Walmore family. "And where in England do you reside, if I may ask?"

"You may. My father's house is in Reading, and I myself am lately of London. And where are you from?"

"I was born in Pennsylvania, but my mother married a man with a restless foot." A wandering eye, too, but that was none of his business. "We eventually moved to San Francisco, and later to Oregon Territory. I have recently come from there."

"I see. A westerner."

"Yes." She doubted he knew where the places she'd mentioned were located, or had any idea of the vast distance she'd covered in the last few months. She opened her mouth to ask if he knew the Stone family in England, but something held her back. Perhaps it was the memory of Peterson in Scottsburg—the man who had persuaded her to deliver an innocent man into his hands. It might be wiser to ask David first whether he knew a family in England named Walmore.

This man would have been only a boy when David left his homeland, but he spoke as though his father still lived. She walked onward, mulling this over.

"So, will you dine with me?"

She glanced at him and shook her head. "I'm afraid not."

"Oh, you wound me." He put on a smile that was winsome indeed. Under other circumstances, Millie would have gladly accepted this handsome young man's invitation. "Dare I hope I might prevail upon you to join me at supper?"

"I. . .I don't think so, Mr. Walmore. I am assisting a person who has been ill, you see, and I may be needed. I'm often required to help at mealtimes."

"Ah." He eyed her thoughtfully.

"Watch out." Millie thrust out a hand to stop him. Walmore was so engrossed in the conversation, he'd almost stepped off the walk at a corner, into the path of a mule team.

"Oh. Quite." He pulled back and waited with her until the big freight wagon had passed. "Allow me." He seized her hand, tucked it through his arm, and hurried her across the street.

"Thank you." Millie removed her hand from his elbow as soon as they were safely on the boardwalk beyond the intersection.

"So. . .no supper either?" he asked genially.

"I do thank you for your offer, sir, but I shall be otherwise occupied." They were within sight of the hotel, and she gave him an impersonal smile. "Excuse me, won't you? I'll go around to the back and speak to Mrs. Simmons about my friend's meal."

She bustled away before he could say anything about her friend or dinner or any other topic. She'd skip through the kitchen and up the back stairs. There was no point in forming a new acquaintance, since she and David would leave tomorrow. The young man was probably all right—but she'd grown wary. And she wasn't looking about to replace James.

Peregrin stood on the sidewalk in front of the hotel, gazing after Mrs. Evans. From behind, she looked like an ordinary woman dressed in attire suitable for the working class. Only the carriage of her shoulders and her more elegant hat, with a faint glint of reddish hair peeping from under it at the nape of her neck, bespoke her quality. Their short acquaintance had convinced him that she was a woman of substance. Not wealth, perhaps, but she had an innate savoir faire he hadn't expected. Perhaps that was what attracted David to her.

Now that he thought about it, most women in her situation would have remarked on the other Englishman she knew. Mrs. Evans was cautious, which was not to say secretive, but she was protecting David. Or perhaps it was more a matter of safeguarding her own reputation. That was probably it—she didn't want other people to know she was traveling with a man. He should have guessed it at once.

With no inkling of how to proceed, Peregrin decided a trip to the Bear Paw wouldn't be amiss. A pint of beer might help him sort through his options. If only he could get some good British ale in this desolate place!

He entered the saloon a few minutes later and looked around. Seeing none of his new friends, he strolled to the bar and ordered a beer. As he waited, he was startled by a heavy hand laid on his shoulder.

He whirled and found himself staring at the chest of a huge man. Craning his neck back, he looked upward into the face of the giant who had accosted him at the Metropolitan Hotel in New York.

"Well now, Walmore, we meet again. Ain't that sumthin'?"

# CHAPTER 29

Millie tapped on David's door and received a hearty "Come in." She opened it and peeked inside. Pastor Harden was sitting with David near the window.

"Oh, I'm sorry to interrupt," she said. "I just wanted to tell you that I have our train tickets in hand."

"Well done," David said.

Mr. Harden stood. "We'll be sorry to see you go, Mrs. Evans, but I'm glad you'll be able to get on with what you want to do."

"Thank you." Millie wasn't exactly sure what it was she wanted to do—that seemed to have changed since she arrived in Independence. But now was not the time to discuss it. "Our journey has been enriched by meeting you and Mrs. Harden."

"Indeed it has," David said. "I say, Mildred, would you be able to ask the kitchen to send up coffee for Mr. Harden and me?"

Millie smiled. "I'll fetch it myself, as soon as I drop my things in my room."

"I hate to see you go to the trouble," Mr. Harden said.

"I don't mind."

"Join us, if you'd like," David said, smiling at her across the room.

While the prospect was tempting, Millie felt he would be better off to have a last private conversation with the minister. "I have my packing to do, but I'm happy to bring a tray for you."

She hurried across to her own chamber and left her shawl, hat, and purse on the bed. After smoothing down her hair, she went out again, locked her door, and went along to the back stairs. While she could have gone down the front stairs, this way was more direct, and she'd have no chance of running into that other Englishman on this route.

She puzzled over him again. What was he doing out here? He'd admitted he had no business interests, and he'd mentioned no friends or acquaintances or a further destination. Perhaps she should have accepted his dinner invitation so that she could learn more about him. It really did seem odd that a young, well-to-do Englishman should come to Independence, Missouri. If he wanted to go to the gold fields, wouldn't a man of means sail to Panama and take the railroad across the isthmus?

Perhaps it would be a good idea to speak to him again and pump him for more information. If David wanted to go down for dinner, they might meet him in the dining room. Or maybe that was what Walmore hoped would happen. She shivered. David had better stay in his room until she learned more about the young man.

As she stepped into the busy kitchen, Mrs. Simmons fixed her with a disapproving frown.

"Millie? Thought you weren't going to work today."

"I'm not, but Mr. Stone is entertaining the reverend and would like coffee for him and his guest. I thought I'd save you some trouble and fix it myself."

"Fine, but you can be sure it will go on his bill."

"I wouldn't expect anything else, ma'am." Millie went about preparing the tray, avoiding Mrs. Simmons's sour gaze. She knew David would prefer tea but had no doubt requested coffee for the minister's sake. She fixed a pot of tea and a mug of coffee and added a small pitcher of cream and some loaf sugar to the tray.

"I see you have a few muffins left from breakfast. May I add a couple?" she asked the innkeeper's wife.

"Just leave my Charles one of the apple ones."

"Certainly." Millie added two spoons and napkins to the tray and lifted it. The burden would be tricky to carry up the winding back stairs, but she could do it.

A few minutes later, she emerged in the third-floor hallway, puffing a little. She rested the tray on the windowsill at the end of the hall for a minute and caught her breath. She didn't want to bother David, but perhaps it would be best to put in a casual inquiry now.

She hefted the tray again and went along to his room. At her knock, Mr. Harden opened the door.

"Ah, let me take that for you," he said.

"Thanks, but I'm fine." She passed him, walked to the small table beside David's chair, and lowered the tray, setting the edge on the surface.

David reached over to help her set the dishes off the tray.

"Oh, you fixed me a pot of tea. That was very kind of you, Mildred."

She smiled. "I thought you might prefer it. And Mrs. Simmons had some muffins left from this morning."

"Very nice."

She straightened and set the tray over on his dresser. "I'll leave you gentlemen, but I wanted to ask you a question first, Mr. Stone." She still used his surname in front of other people. She wouldn't want anyone to assume their relationship had become more personal than was seemly.

"Oh? What is it?" David asked as he poured tea into his cup.

"I met a man this morning. He's a new guest here. And it seemed a bit odd to me—he was at breakfast when I ate, and then he followed me to the train station."

"What?" David set the teapot down with a clunk. "A man is following you?"

She felt her cheeks warm. "Well, he said he was only out for a walk, but I was moving quite quickly. He asked me to have dinner with him at noon. I turned him down, but—well, I thought—in light of—" She threw a glance Mr. Harden's way in apology. She didn't think he knew everything about her past with David, though she'd given him an abbreviated account. "Well, the thing is, he's English, like you."

"That does seem odd," David said thoughtfully. "Did he mention me?"

"No, which I found even odder. Wouldn't that be the first thing Mr. Simmons would tell another Englishman when he checked in here—that one of his countrymen was staying in the hotel?"

"Perhaps." David sipped his tea absently, then seemed to recall what he was doing and set it down to add cream. "I don't suppose he gave his name?"

"Yes, he did. It's Walmore."

"Walmore. . ."

"Do you know anyone by that name?" Mr. Harden asked.

"I don't think so," David said. "No, wait. It almost seems that Anne told me something. . . . Ah yes, that's it. She said my cousin married a Walmore. Mary, I think. Something like that."

"Your cousin?" Millie stared at him.

"Might bear looking into," David said pensively. "Yes, I believe she said my cousin Randolph's wife was a Walmore. There was a family. . . ." He shook his head. "Not in the top tier of society, but respectable, I'm sure."

Millie watched him, fascinated. It was as though he'd become a different man, in a different time and place. The type of man who would know in an instant whether or not someone belonged to the highest circles of English society.

He smiled at her. "Perhaps I should make this gentleman's acquaintance."

"Or perhaps you should not," Millie said.

"You're not thinking—" He paused, eyeing her with speculation. "You are, aren't you?"

Mr. Harden watched them with obvious interest but said nothing.

"Well, one can't be too careful," Millie said.

"Yes, especially if one is prone to accidents." David nodded, and she was sure he'd reached a decision. "If you're game, Mildred, you shall go down to dinner without me in an hour. And if this gentleman is about, perhaps you could further your acquaintance with him."

"What?" Peregrin stared up at the big man, whose leathery face was set in a gruesome sneer. "I—oh—please—"

During his stammering the giant and another fellow pushed him down the boardwalk and into a secluded alley between a haberdashery and a carriage house.

"Please," Peregrin said. "Whatever do you want? This is highly irregular."

"Is it, now?" the giant asked. "Hear that, Teddy? We're irregulars."

"Right," his partner said.

The bigger man grabbed the front of Peregrin's shirt and twisted it with his fist. "You know what we want, Walmore."

"Er...do I?" Peregrin blinked and turned his face, owl-like, from one to the other, terrified that they would beat him and unable to think of a reason why they shouldn't.

The giant shoved him against the wall. "You do. The same thing we wanted in New York. Baxter's money."

"Oh." Peregrin gulped. "I thought you looked familiar, but since we've not been introduced—"

"Idiot," said Teddy.

The giant hit Peregrin, landing a wallop just south of his left eye. He gasped and sagged back against the rough boards behind him.

"I'm Wilkes," the giant said. "Sorry, but I ain't got no calling card. So fork over the blunt."

"The. . .uh. . .I'm sorry, but I don't believe I have what you're looking for. That's why I left New York."

"That warn't smart," Teddy said.

Wilkes continued to hold Peregrin by his shirtfront. "You told Baxter you'd get it for him. Now, you give it over, or we'll have to make you regret it."

"I already regret it," Peregrin said, "but I can't pay the thousand I owe him."

"It's twelve hunnerd now," Teddy growled.

"That's right," Wilkes said. "Baxter had to send us out here after you, and that's expensive. You need to pay up, or it'll be even more." He clamped one massive hand around Peregrin's throat and pushed his head back against the wall.

"I can't, I tell you," Peregrin gasped.

"Why not?"

"Lost it."

"That's bad."

"Ask 'im how much he's got," Teddy said, elbowing the giant.

"Yeah," Wilkes said. "How much you got, Walmore?"

Peregrin was finding it hard to breathe with the man's huge hand compressing his throat. "Let me go," he squeaked.

Wilkes released his hold, and Peregrin sucked in a big breath, doubling over and grasping his thighs.

"Don't get sick on me," Wilkes growled. "How much you got on you?"

"On me? About thirty dollars."

"What?" Wilkes grabbed his arm, jerked him upward, and punched him in the stomach. "You better say you got more in the bank, pal."

When the swirling kaleidoscope faded, Peregrin held his abdomen and tried to think fast. If they knew he had eight hundred in cash, they'd take it all, and he'd have nothing left to work with. "I've only got five hundred," he gasped.

"Awright, let's go get it," Wilkes said.

# CHAPTER 30

"**B**egging your pardon," Mr. Harden said. "I don't want to intrude, but it seems you are suspicious of this Walmore fellow. If I'm able to be of assistance, I'd be happy to serve you."

Millie eyed him thoughtfully. "What could you do, Pastor?"

"I thought perhaps, since David is going to keep to his room, I could go down to dinner with you."

"He might not want to talk to me if I've another gentleman with me." Millie looked to David. "What do you think?"

"That's true," David said. "Perhaps I should just go and seek him out. Find out if he means to meet me or not."

"You must safeguard your health," Millie said, "if only for the journey."

Mr. Harden's eyebrows shot up. "You don't think this man would harm Mr. Stone, do you? Is this a matter for the constabulary?"

"Oh, I doubt it," David said. "It's just a case of once bit, twice shy where I'm concerned."

"But still, it might be good to have another person at hand who knows the lay of the land," Millie said.

"How about this?" The pastor seemed eager to take part in the drama, and Millie listened with growing approval. "I could go home and get my Isabelle to come and eat dinner with me here at the hotel."

"It might be helpful," Millie said. "If Mr. Walmore became obnoxious, I could appeal to the Hardens as an excuse to leave his company."

"Isabelle would love a chance to eat out," Mr. Harden said, smiling at David.

"All right, but only if you do it at my expense."

"Oh no, you mustn't." The minister flushed.

"Yes, I must. This is purely for my welfare, and I insist on seeing to it. Mildred, would you bring my wallet, please?"

Millie fetched it with alacrity and handed it to David, who took out a dollar bill and held it out to Mr. Harden.

"Please, sir. I will consider it money well spent. Not only will I be sure Mildred has a friend nearby, but also you and your wife, who have been so kind to us both, will have—I hope—a pleasant meal."

"If you insist," Mr. Harden said, tucking the money into his waistcoat pocket. "But I must hurry home and inform Isabelle, so that she knows before she has dinner on the table for me."

"If it's any inconvenience, do not bother to come back," Millie said. She didn't think Isabelle, who was of a sunny temperament, would object, but some women would want to be told in advance of such a venture.

"No fear," Mr. Harden said. "We shall be in the dining room by a quarter till noon."

"Excellent," Millie told him. "I shall go down a little after that. I was hoping to avoid Mr. Walmore for the rest of the day, but now I hope very much that he turns up for dinner."

Peregrin staggered up the stairs to his room with Wilkes and Teddy right behind him. The only way to get rid of these two was to pay them something. He'd have to be careful and not let them know that he was holding out on them, or they might kill him.

He unlocked his door with shaky hands. The two thugs followed him in, and Teddy shut the door.

"Where is it?" Wilkes asked.

"I'll get it."

"No, tell me. I'll get it."

Peregrin swallowed. His Adam's apple hurt, where the giant had squeezed it. He had some cash hidden in the dresser drawer, as well as some in his luggage, besides the bit they'd already taken from his wallet. He hoped he could satisfy them with one stash and keep them from tossing the room looking for more.

"It's in my valise. There's a purse under my clothes."

Teddy pawed through the bag, not seeming to notice how few clothes were in it. Most of them were now in the dresser, but Peregrin studiously avoided looking in the direction of that article of furniture.

"This is only four-fifty," Teddy whined.

"You said you had five hunnert." Wilkes came toward him menacingly.

"I thought I did. You got some out of my wallet."

"Thirty-two dollars and change."

"Well, that's it then." Peregrin tried to smile, but he felt sick to his stomach, and his throat and face hurt.

"You better get the rest," Wilkes said, towering over him.

"How am I supposed to do that? You're not leaving me any capital to work with. I can't even go out and join a poker game tonight."

"You got friends?"

"Not here."

"There must be somebody you know."

"Uh, well. . ." Peregrin thought of David Stone, but he couldn't drag him into this. That would alert David to his presence and put the wind up so far as Peregrin's integrity went. And he couldn't borrow seven hundred dollars from a man and then do him in, could he? Of course, if the one he borrowed from was dead, he'd be less apt to ask for a repayment of the loan.

Peregrin shook his head. It was all so confusing and gruesome. Bad enough to plan an accident for an upstanding gentleman, but to use him to repay a gambling debt. . . That was beyond dishonor. Peregrin knew that he could never again respect himself if he followed through with this.

No, he wouldn't breathe a word about David if he could possibly get by without. If he could just make these fellows go away, maybe he could escape them and flee. He had no idea where he would go, and they'd taken the bulk of his remaining funds. But he couldn't stay here.

"I'll see what I can do." Peregrin attempted to brush his shirt into smoothness, but it was grimy and creased now. "Why don't you gentlemen come back tomorrow, and we'll see if I've been successful, what?"

Wilkes looked at his chum questioningly. "What say, Teddy? Shall we give him a few hours to come across?"

"No more'n that. I'm sick of this place. I wanna get back to New York."

"All right." Wilkes fixed Peregrin with a malevolent scowl. "You've got until three o'clock. We'll be watching the hotel. Meet us out front with the dough."

"Dough?" Peregrin frowned. "I say—"

"The money, you numbskull," Wilkes said.

"Oh. Right. But what if I can't get it by then?"

"Then we'll take it out of your hide."

Teddy smirked. "That's right, chum. Baxter told us if we couldn't squeeze the twelve hunnerd out of ya, to do whatever we wanted. So think hard about getting every cent."

"And don't even think about running," Wilkes said, giving his shoulder a little shove. "We'll be watching you."

"Right." In spite of his roiling stomach and throbbing face, Peregrin straightened his coat and tie. He walked to the door and held it open.

As the two men passed him, Wilkes turned back and pointed a finger so close Peregrin could have bitten it. "Three o'clock. Don't be late."

Millie went down to the dining room, wearing her best dress. She didn't like to draw attention to herself, but past experience had shown her that this outfit would impress an English gentleman. Of course, the gown was somewhat the worse for wear now, but she'd kept it mended and fairly stainless. Before donning it, she'd carefully pressed all the wrinkles out of the wide skirt.

Every eye was upon her as she entered the dining room. Simmons's niece turned her way and gaped at her. Millie hid her smile. The waitress probably wondered if she'd spent all her earnings on clothing.

Millie didn't see Mr. Walmore, but the pastor and his wife were seated at one of the center tables and already had soup and biscuits before them. Millie smiled at them but didn't stop to speak. She didn't want Walmore to see her with them if he should walk in behind her.

A man who'd been staying at the hotel for several days jumped up and stood in her path.

"Good day, ma'am. Care to join me?"

"Oh, no thank you," Millie said, and she brushed past him.

She was afraid some of the other guests would come and sit with her—people usually shared tables when the dining room was busy. She took a seat at the end of one of the long tables, with two seats between her and the nearest diner. She avoided looking around at people, so as to discourage them from engaging her in conversation.

When Sarah came to her side, Millie gave her order for soup and corn pone. She laid a hand on the girl's arm and leaned toward her.

"Do you know Mr. Walmore? He's a guest here."

"That new fellow?" she asked. "Funny accent?"

"He's the one," Millie said. "Has he been in for dinner yet?"

"Don't think so. I'd have seen him."

Millie nodded. "Thank you. Oh, and I'd like a pot of tea, please."

The freckle-faced girl arched her eyebrows. "A whole pot?"

"Yes, please." Millie smiled at her. She could see that Sarah was trying to work this out in her mind. Millie usually had a cup of coffee with her meal. Few people asked for tea, and even fewer for an entire pot. But then, Millie had never appeared wearing such a fine dress either.

"Is Mr. Stone coming down to join you?"

"I don't think so."

"Oh." The waitress turned away, frowning.

Millie smiled to herself and then glanced about surreptitiously. Mrs. Harden caught her eye and gave a slight nod, then looked back at her husband. The door from the front entrance opened, and in came Mr. Walmore. He kept his head down and shuffled between the tables, hardly looking at other people, but taking tiny glances ahead as he searched for an empty seat. When he noticed Millie he started to smile, then winced.

Millie caught her breath. A red and purple bruise spread over Walmore's left cheekbone, and the flesh around his eye was swollen and discolored. She'd seen quite a few black eyes in her day—mostly on Sam—but this one was a prizewinner.

She pushed back her chair and half stood.

"Mr. Walmore! Won't you join me?"

"Oh, uh. . .Mrs. . . .uh. . .Evans, isn't it? Are you certain you—"

"Yes. Please, sit down, sir. Are you all right?" She hoped her concern for his injury was enough to atone for her earlier refusal to dine with him.

His rueful smile was somewhat of a grimace. "I shan't say it's not painful."

"Dear me, what happened?"

"Oh, I. . .I misjudged which way a horse was going to move."

"I see." Millie shook her head. "I don't suppose you want to see a doctor?"

"No, it will be all right in a couple of days."

She doubted the bruises would fade in a fortnight, but the swelling would probably be gone in less time. The waitress was approaching with a brown teapot on a tray.

"Well please, go ahead and order your dinner," Millie said. "And feel free to share my pot of tea. I'm sure I won't be able to drink it all."

"Most kind of you," Mr. Walmore murmured.

Sarah set down the teapot and turned to him with a smile. "Help you, sir?" Her smile skewed. "Oh my! That's a beaut."

Mr. Walmore chuckled. "I expect it looks worse than it feels. I'd like some roast beef, if you have it."

"Not until suppertime, sir. This noon we have soup and lamb chops and chicken and dumplings."

"The chicken, then. Thank you."

"Oh, and we'd like an extra cup for Mr. Walmore," Millie said.

The waitress flicked her a glance. "There's cups and things yonder, with the butter and jam."

"Right," Mr. Walmore said, rising. "I'll get it."

He didn't seem to worry about the fact that Millie had reversed her position by welcoming him at her table. Perhaps he thought she was just being flirtatious earlier when she turned him down. Millie wondered how to bring him around to talking about David without mentioning the gentleman's name. She decided to pry a little into Walmore's history first.

When he returned with his cup and saucer, she smiled across the table at him. "I'm afraid they don't bring milk for the tea unless you ask them, and I forgot."

"Well, when the girl comes back, we'll put in a request, hey?" If his face wasn't so colorful and puffy, he would no doubt look very charming.

"So, Mr. Walmore, what brings you to Independence?" Millie asked.

"Oh, business. You know. How about yourself?"

This seemed to contradict what he had told her earlier, when he'd implied that he was a gentleman of means who needed no business. It certainly bore further investigation. "I'm just traveling through. Returning from the West. Uh. . .what sort of business?"

He hesitated. "Just looking over some property for a friend. Are you traveling alone? I believe you told me you've been helping an invalid?"

"Not an invalid precisely. One of my fellow travelers was injured in a stagecoach accident, and I stayed here to help."

"Oh, I see. That was most compassionate of you."

"I don't know. . . . It seemed the proper thing to do."

The waitress brought Mr. Walmore's plate of chicken and dumplings. While she set his dish down, Millie dipped a piece of corn pone in her soup and ate it. She wondered if that was considered proper etiquette and shot a glance at her dinner companion, but he wasn't looking at her. Even so, Millie picked up her spoon and determined to eat as aristocratically as she could.

"I wonder if we could get a little milk?" Walmore asked the waitress.

"Milk?" Sarah shrugged. "I suppose so." She flounced away, clearly baffled that a grown man would wish to drink milk with his dinner.

As they ate, Millie continued to ply him with questions. Before long she had him telling her about London. None of his stories had to do with industry or business, but rather he told her about parties he'd attended, and his club—which, it seemed, was like a private restaurant for gentlemen—and his friends' horses and equipages and their impromptu races down Jermyn Street.

"Your friends must be men of means," she said, picking up her cup. Over the rim, she glanced toward the Hardens. The waitress was serving them pie.

"Oh yes, they're good chaps."

"I'm surprised you wanted to leave them and come out here."

"Oh." Walmore sobered and speared a dumpling with his fork. "Well, business. You know."

Millie decided she wasn't going to get anything pertinent from him, and at last she declined dessert and gathered her things. "I must go upstairs and pack. I expect to travel tomorrow. It was pleasant eating with you, Mr. Walmore."

"Oh, indeed. Thank you for allowing me to join you."

He stood and bowed. Millie gave him a smile and walked away.

Peregrin ate two pieces of pie and emptied the teapot. He supposed he'd have to go down to the saloon to get a real drink to top off his meal—but would the two thugs let him?

Sitting through dinner with Mrs. Evans had been an ordeal. What was she scheming at? She'd flat out rejected his invitation this morning, and then she practically forced him to sit with her. If he hadn't feared that Wilkes and Teddy would thwart him, he would have gone elsewhere for his dinner just to avoid meeting her again. And then she turned all charming.

No matter. Now he needed to formulate a plan. Her chatter had kept him from thinking things through. If he wasn't going to try to borrow from David, what *was* he going to do? He needed money, and quickly.

He couldn't up and kill the man here, or he'd be found out. On the other hand, if he did, he might be able to lift some funds from David's person or luggage. And he needed cash if he was going to flee from Baxter's thugs.

Carefully he weighed the options. He really disliked the idea of harming Randolph's cousin, on a purely physical level. However, if he didn't somehow stop David, Randolph and Merry would never own Stoneford. And he might need their goodwill in the future, not to mention a loan now and then. So he *had* to do something to keep David from returning to England...permanently.

But if he hung about Independence too long in order to do that, Wilkes and Teddy would hound him, in which case his own life would be worth less than David's. That giant, Wilkes, could crush him like a gnat.

Peregrin touched his cheek gingerly and winced at the pain. He did not want to deal with Wilkes again, but if he lingered until three o'clock, he would have no alternative. The scant three hundred dollars he had left would take him back East. Perhaps that was best. He couldn't return to New York, where Baxter was, but some other city, perhaps.

On consideration, it appeared that he had two possible courses of action. He could either flee from his adversaries immediately or stay to carry out Merrileigh's business. His fear of Wilkes loomed larger and more immediate than his desire to please Merry— tempered as it was with his distaste for completing her charge. He drained his teacup and mustered his courage.

Millie passed the Hardens' table and gave a little nod. They appeared to be finished as well. She went into the lobby, if one could call the dim entrance hall that, and waited near the stairs. A moment later, the couple emerged from the dining room.

"Do you have time to come up to Mr. Stone's room?" Millie asked.

"Should we?" Mr. Harden glanced at his wife and back to Millie. "Did you learn something?"

"No, not really. He never mentioned David or the Stone family. He seems a rather vacuous, lazy fellow who likes to go about with his chums and watch horseraces."

"Ah," said Isabelle Harden. "Perhaps you'll have to be more direct."

"Yes," Mr. Harden said. "You might have to ask him flat out if he knows Mr. Stone."

"I guess it comes down to that if we want to know what he's about," Millie said.

"Speaking of his rather nebulous activities," Mrs. Harden said, "did he explain to you why his face is so disfigured?"

"And was it that way the first time you met him?" the reverend asked. "You didn't mention it."

"No, he looked fine this morning. He said something about running into a horse."

Isabelle frowned and shook her head, as though she'd never heard anything sillier.

Millie looked back toward the dining room. "Do you think I should—"

The door opened, and Mr. Walmore, glorious in his multi-hued bruises, emerged.

"Mr. Walmore," Millie called without benefit of further deliberation, "come and meet my friends."

He looked at her, startled, and approached, uneasily eyeing the couple with her. "Hullo."

Millie put on her brightest smile. "I was just telling Mr. and Mrs. Harden about you." She smiled at the couple. "This is Mr. Walmore, a guest here."

"How do you do," said Isabelle.

Mr. Harden shook Walmore's hand. "Pleased to meet you, sir."

"Likewise," Walmore said.

"When Mrs. Evans told us about you, we of course thought of our other acquaintance here at the hotel," Mr. Harden said. "Pray tell us, are you acquainted with Mr. David Stone?"

"I—" Walmore blinked at him, then shot a glance at Millie. "Uh, Stone, you say? Here in this hotel? I don't believe—"

"He's from England," Millie said quickly. "We thought perhaps you knew him."

"Oh. Well, there are lots of people in England."

"True."

He hesitated. "There was a family. . .hmm. . .country estate. . . well, I wouldn't say I'm chummy with them, but if that's the family you mean. . ."

"It may well be," Millie said. "I'm sure Mr. Stone would be happy to make your acquaintance."

"Oh well!" Unless she was mistaken, Walmore's face flushed, but it wasn't easy to tell because of his injuries. "Er. . .not sure I know the chap personally. Perhaps. . ."

"May we look for you in the dining room this evening?" Millie asked. "Say, six o'clock? You could meet him then."

He chuckled, but it sounded a bit nervous. "You Americans eat so awfully early, what?"

"I suppose we do," Millie said. "Would seven be better?"

"Oh no, six is fine. And now, if you'll excuse me. . ."

"Of course," Millie said.

The Hardens bade him farewell, and Walmore strode to the front door. He opened it and stood for a moment, looking out. To Millie's surprise, he backed away from the door and turned about. He kept his head down and didn't meet her gaze as he walked quickly to the main staircase.

"Well!" Isabelle said when he'd disappeared above.

"Well indeed," her husband mused. "Didn't want to come out and say he knew the Stones, did he?"

"No, he certainly didn't," Millie said. "What shall I do?"

"I suppose you should tell Mr. Stone and let him decide whether

251

he thinks it would be a risk to come down to supper.

"Yes. I can't think of anything else."

"Well, we really ought to go home," Isabelle said. "I left the girls alone, and they're good girls, but I don't like to be gone too long."

"Yes, and I must work on my sermon this afternoon," her husband said. "Please thank Mr. Stone. I'm sorry you didn't learn something useful."

Millie shook his hand and gave Isabelle a brief hug. "Thank you both for your kindness."

"You're welcome, dear," Isabelle said. "Have a safe journey. Joseph and I shall be praying for you."

Millie hurried up the stairs. She had a feeling David wouldn't be pleased, but there wasn't much she could do about that.

# CHAPTER 31

Peregrin hurried to his room and hastily threw all his things into his bags. He could leave word for Millie Evans that he'd been called away suddenly. He had to leave quickly. If he stayed around for a couple more hours, Wilkes and Teddy would pay him another visit and thrash him—or worse. They were lurking directly across the street, in plain view. When he'd looked out, Wilkes had leered at him, while Teddy calmly whittled away at a stick with a lethal-looking knife. Peregrin shuddered and pocketed the stash of money from the dresser drawer.

Fleeing now would mean he wouldn't meet David Stone tonight. But if he came face to face with Stone, he doubted he'd have the nerve to go ahead with Merrileigh's request. No, it would be better to leave before the thugs' deadline expired.

He flirted with the idea of going up to David's room now and introducing himself. But what then? He'd already convinced himself that he couldn't kill the man in his hotel room and get away with it. He doubted he could steal from him either, without being caught. And one could hardly barge into a fellow's chamber and say, "Hello, I'm a social connection of your family's. Would you give me a loan?"

On top of all that, Merrileigh would be furious if he borrowed from David for his own purposes. And she'd still expect him to turn around and kill the poor man. Why had he ever told her he'd do it? Peregrin clutched his head with both hands. Was he insane?

Best to make a run for it. If all else failed, he would appeal to Stone, but it seemed horribly bad form to cadge from a fellow you planned to kill later.

He couldn't walk out the front door, or they'd see him immediately. Besides, his luggage was too heavy to carry all the way to the train station, and it would make him conspicuous. After some thought, Peregrin went downstairs and found the boy, Wilfred, and paid him to go and hire a rig at the nearest livery stable.

"And tell the driver to be sure and come to the back door," he said sternly.

It was almost too easy. He gave Wilfred enough money to cover his hotel bill and a tip. With the rest of the three hundred dollars he'd salvaged divided among his pockets and a five-dollar bill in his shoe, he urged the driver to head out the lane behind the inn and take a back street for the first few blocks.

He hoped a train would be ready to leave when he arrived, so that he could board it at once, with no waiting about on the platform. He didn't particularly care where the first train was headed.

Over and over he played out his conversations with Millie Evans. How close were she and David? If he *had* gone up to Stone's room, would she have been there? Maybe he should have stayed and tried to set up David's "accident" at once. Or if he could have hidden from the thugs long enough, maybe he could have gotten into Stone's room while he was at dinner. Other scenarios appeared, now that he was out of striking distance. Could he have killed him and taken all his money, so that it looked like a stranger had robbed him?

The driver pulled up before the depot and climbed down to set his bags out. Peregrin paid him, though it hurt to part with more of his funds. Now to buy a ticket and board a train. He wouldn't feel safe until the wheels were rolling over the rails.

He didn't even make it to the ticket window. Wilkes stepped out from the shadows at the depot entrance and yanked him aside.

"Going someplace, Walmore?"

"Uh. . ." Peregrin swiveled his head and took in Wilkes's sneer and Teddy's grim face. "Just seeing off a friend."

"Oh, and taking his luggage in for him, were you?" Teddy asked brightly.

Peregrin's stomach dropped. He should have taken a steamboat instead of the train. But they probably would have followed him there as well. He let go of the bags, and they thudded to the ground.

"Come on." Wilkes steered Peregrin toward the street. "Get his baggage, Ted."

"Listen, this isn't what you think," Peregrin said.

"And what do we think?" Teddy asked as he bent to pick up Peregrin's fine-grained leather valises.

He had no answer, and Wilkes pulled him along roughly until they came to a gap between a saloon and a wheelwright's shop. The giant shoved Peregrin into the alley and pulled him up behind the saloon.

"All right, give up everything you've got, right now. Then we'll talk about the balance."

"But I. . .I haven't anything," Peregrin said.

"Oh, and how were you going to buy a ticket, then?"

"Besides," Teddy said drily from behind him, "we saw you pay off the liveryman. You've got *somethin'* in your pocket, man."

"I should have gone down with you." David tapped the floor hard with his cane. He shouldn't let Millie run this fox to earth for him.

"If all goes well, you'll see him tonight. Then maybe we'll get to the bottom of it." Millie shook her head ruefully as she gathered the dishes from David's dinner and stacked them on the tray. "I'm sorry I didn't find out more for you."

"Well, it's clear he had no intention of making himself known to me."

Millie clamped her teeth together and puzzled over Walmore's behavior. "You don't suppose he could be telling the truth, do you, and he barely remembers your family?"

"I don't see how. I mean, if his sister is married to Randolph, every member of the Stone family in England was probably at the wedding."

"Maybe he's just slow-witted."

David shook his head. "I don't know. But I can't see how he can have helped knowing who I am." He laughed and gave a little shrug. "There. Perhaps I think too much of myself. I suppose it's possible no one in England remembers me."

"Oh, I doubt that," Millie said.

Yes, David reflected. The Earl of Stoneford was known throughout British society. Not that Richard had carried himself with pomp or self-importance. He'd been a regular fellow, whom everyone liked. But he was conspicuous in his position. If Walmore hadn't lived under a rock near the Scottish border, he *had* to know who the Stones were. Especially if he was related to Randolph's wife.

"Well, I'm through being helpless. I'm going to meet this fellow, one way or another."

"Fine," Millie said. "We'll go down at six and watch for him."

"No. I want you to ask Simmons for his room number. I intend to pay a call on Mr. Walmore. At once."

Wilkes held Peregrin pinned against the saloon wall, and Teddy moved in. He drew back his fist.

"Wait! Don't hit me. Please."

"Why not?" Teddy asked. "I been wantin' to pound you all day."

"There is something I could do."

Wilkes let go of him with one hand and waved Teddy back. "Spill it."

"There's a fellow at the hotel. I don't know him really, but I believe we have some mutual acquaintances. I don't know if he has any money or not, but perhaps I could ask him to help me."

Wilkes scowled. "We're not talking about borrowing a buck here."

"I know," Peregrin said hastily. "This fellow—well, he seems pretty well set up. He may not be able to give me anything, but it might be worth a try."

Wilkes looked at his pal. "What do you think, Teddy?"

Teddy scratched his head. "How well do you know this gent?"

"Uh, well. . ." Peregrin gulped. "He's connected to my family."

"What do you mean, connected?" Wilkes asked. "Like he's hitched to their mule team?"

"No." The more Peregrin thought about it, the better this idea seemed. He forgot all his previous objections. Surely if David knew it was a matter of life or death, he would come through. "He's actually...well, my sister's married to his cousin, but he doesn't really know me."

The two thugs frowned at each other.

"You're both staying in the same hotel, and he's married to your sister, and he doesn't know you?" Teddy asked.

"That's not what I said. His *cousin* is married to my sister."

"Oh." Teddy looked doubtfully to Wilkes.

The giant shrugged. "Has he got the ready?"

"I don't know. Maybe. His family's swimming in it. But he hasn't seen me since I've been here."

"Do tell." Wilkes relaxed his grasp on Peregrin's shirt. "So you're going to renew your acquaintance with this sort-of kin of yours and see how much you can get from him. You got that?"

"Yes."

"First, give us every red cent you have on you or in your things," Teddy said. "No holding back."

"Yeah." Wilkes grinned. "And Teddy, you can hit him once if you want, for holding out on us this morning. But just once."

"Is that really necess—" Peregrin gasped as Teddy's fist rammed his stomach. He doubled over, fighting dizziness and nausea.

After a few seconds, his spinning world began to slow down. Wilkes took hold of his coat collar and pulled him erect.

"All right, now. Give it up. All of it."

Peregrin fumbled for his wallet. Before he could open it, Teddy plucked it from his hands. He riffled through it and handed it back to Peregrin empty.

"Now the rest," he growled.

"The rest?"

Wilkes hit him hard, a little higher than Teddy's blow, and Peregrin saw colorful flashes of light. He couldn't haul in a breath. He sank to the ground and felt himself sinking into darkness. When he could register that he was still alive, Wilkes was rifling his pockets. Maybe if he feigned continued unconsciousness, they'd take his cash and leave him alone.

"Well, that's another two hunnert," Wilkes muttered.

"Here's another wad." Teddy pulled more money from Peregrin's trouser pocket.

"Come on, Walmore, on your feet." The giant lifted him bodily, and Peregrin couldn't see any sense in flopping back down in the dirt.

He opened his eyes slowly and hung on Wilkes's meaty arm. "Wha—"

"You're going back to the hotel," Teddy said.

Wilkes nodded, grinning. "That's right. You find this friend of yours and put the squeeze on him. We'll be waiting outside—and watching both doors. You hear me?" He shook Peregrin as though trying to make his instructions settle quicker.

"Yes!" The shaking stopped. Peregrin stood still for a long moment as he caught his breath and rubbed his abdomen.

"What's the matter?" Teddy asked sweetly. "You look like you got a bellyache."

Peregrin grimaced and set out for the hotel without looking at them. He could hear their footsteps behind him as he staggered from the alley. Once he got out on the street, passersby stared at him, but he kept his head down and trudged for the Frontier Hotel.

David rapped smartly on the door of 201. He waited, but no sound came from within. He looked at Millie, who stood beside him.

"Try again, just in case," she said.

He lifted his cane and used the handle to knock—a loud, authoritative sound.

After a few seconds, he turned away. "All right, he's not in."

"I guess we'll have to wait until supper and see if he shows up," Millie said. "Come, let's get you back upstairs."

David huffed out a breath. "I'll be glad when we put this place behind us."

"And that will be at first light," Millie said cheerfully. "Come. Just one more night here and we're off."

Peregrin entered the hotel at half past four. He ought to go right up to 302 and accost Stone, but he didn't like the idea. Better to keep his supper engagement and approach the matter like a gentleman. Perhaps he could get some money out of David without telling him everything.

A mirror graced the wall in the entry, above a horsehair-covered settee. Peregrin caught a glimpse of his battered face in it as he passed through the lobby. What would Stone think of his appearance? Had that gentleman ever been attacked in the street? Mrs. Evans had shown sympathy, but Stone might just peg him for a fool.

He stopped at the desk and got his key back. Mr. Simmons welcomed him back and assured him his room was as he'd left it. Resigned, Peregrin dragged himself up the stairs. He ached all over, and his stomach and breastbone were tender and sore. His cheek still smarted some, too, and his head throbbed unbearably. He might as well have thrown himself in front of a battering ram as to face those two thugs.

His hand shook as he unlocked the door. He would lie down and try to rest for an hour. What else could he do?

If he lingered in his room, would Wilkes and Teddy storm the establishment and come after him, as they had before? He hoped not. If they did, he would tell them David was out and he hoped to see him at supper. That ought to work, or it would with any reasonable man.

Of course, Wilkes and Teddy were not always reasonable.

Peregrin wished he had a bottle of whiskey, but there was no way he could get past the bloodhounds to buy one, and Mr. Simmons had already informed him that he didn't serve liquor. Besides, if he spent part of his last five dollars on drink, he would be truly destitute.

Always before, he'd had his friends to fall back on until his next allowance came through, or else he could go join a friendly card game with the hope of winning a few pounds. In a tight pinch, there was Merrileigh and her husband, slightly better off than middle class. His sister could be counted on for short-term small loans, so long as he didn't ask too often.

But now he was left to his own devices, and it felt horrid.

# CHAPTER 32

Millie and David entered the dining room at quarter to six. A strong odor of cooking grease wafted out from the kitchen. Millie surveyed the patrons.

"He's not here. Let us find a table with an extra seat and watch for him."

They claimed one that would allow them to observe the door and ordered tea.

"We expect Mr. Walmore to join us," Millie told Sarah. When the waitress had left them, she appraised David. He was a bit pale, but that was understandable. He looked fit, and his tailored clothing and impeccable grooming set him off as what he was—a fine English gentleman. She had no doubt that within a few weeks he would regain his strength and agility.

"What are you smirking at?" David asked.

"Was I smirking? I suppose, if you want the truth, I was thinking how different you look from the first time I saw you."

He frowned for a moment. "Oh yes, in the lobby of the hotel in Scottsburg. I believe I'd just come in from my mining claim and was sadly in need of a bath."

She laughed, glad they could mention it without either of them prickling. "You were a handsome man then. It was obvious to all that you didn't avoid hard work."

"As opposed to my appearance now?"

She shrugged. "Those who know you realize you are a complex man, Mr. Stone. But yes, those who've never made your acquaintance might, on first glance, assume you are a man of leisure."

"And those who met you for the first time tonight would find you a fascinating woman—one whose acquaintance they longed to cultivate."

She felt her cheeks flush. "Thank you, sir." He'd never spoken to her in such a manner, not even in Scottsburg. His words confused her. She would like to think he'd changed his opinion of her, but still he intended to leave her in Philadelphia and sail out of her life. That much they both understood. The rest was still murky, and a change of subject might be in order.

"How is your leg?"

"Better. In fact, I felt hardly a twinge as we came down the stairs."

Sarah brought their tea and set out the pot and three cups. "Do you want to order now?"

Millie looked to David, quirking her eyebrows.

"We might as well," he said.

"All right, it's roast beef or fried fish tonight."

They told Sarah their wishes from the limited menu. A few minutes later, Millie glimpsed Walmore, peering in at the doorway.

"He's here," she whispered to David.

When Walmore's gaze landed on her, she smiled and beckoned discreetly. His face was still hideously discolored, and he moved slowly. As he approached their table, David rose.

"Mr. Walmore, may I present Mr. Stone?" Millie said.

"Good evening, sir." Walmore extended his hand tentatively, and David shook it.

"Have a seat." David resumed his place, and Walmore sat down opposite him, with Millie between them. "That's quite a badge you're wearing on your face, sir. May I ask how you got it?"

Walmore put his fingertips up to his swollen cheek. "I hate to admit it, but I ran afoul of some rather obnoxious thugs."

Millie arched her eyebrows. "That's not quite what you told me this morning, sir."

"Well, no." He gave her a deprecating smile. "One doesn't like to admit to a lady that he's been bested at fisticuffs and robbed."

"Robbed?" Millie said.

"Really, sir! Have you spoken to the constabulary?" David asked.

"No. No, I haven't."

"Why ever not?" Millie asked.

"It's not a happy tale." Walmore looked at David. "I hoped perhaps I could have a private word with you later, Mr. Stone."

David's eyes narrowed, but he said affably, "Of course." He looked up as Sarah approached the table. "Oh, here's the waitress. Why don't you order your dinner, Mr. Walmore, and we'll talk of more pleasant things for now."

When he had ordered, the newcomer fixed his tea and smiled at Millie. "So, you are both leaving Independence tomorrow—is that correct?"

"Yes," she said.

"I'm thinking I may leave, too," Walmore said. "I've not had the best of fortune here."

"Are you going back to England?" David asked.

"Not just yet, but I shall head back to the East Coast."

"Ah." David waited until the waitress placed his and Millie's plates before them and took Walmore's order before changing the subject. Millie just sipped her tea, unfolded her napkin, and smiled.

"Now, tell me, sir," David said, "is your family not connected with mine by marriage? It seems to me that my niece said my cousin Randolph married a Walmore."

"That's correct. My sister. Merrileigh, her name is. They have a townhouse in London."

"Yes, and Randolph's father had a small country house as well...."

"I believe that's gone out of the family since you left England," Walmore said. He took a quick gulp of his tea.

"I see. Well, it's quite a coincidence us meeting up on the frontier like this." David smiled at him, but his tone clearly asked for information.

"I came out here to see a bit of the West," Walmore said. "Oh, and a friend asked me to look over some land. But since I'm now nearly penniless, I think I'd best head back to civilization and see if I can't recoup my losses."

"Perhaps your bank could send you some money here," David suggested.

Walmore frowned. "Unfortunately, I closed my bank account in New York when I left there. I'm afraid I'll have to rely on the charity of friends until I can get a bank draft from England." His eyes flickered, and Millie wondered if he really thought he could do that. Maybe he was just saying it so they wouldn't think he was a complete derelict. But from her experience, she felt it was more likely he was sizing David up as a potential "friend."

"I wish you the best," David said and turned back to his meal.

They continued eating, and the two men discussed a few mutual acquaintances. Mr. Walmore described some recent happenings in London and occasionally shot a remark or a question Millie's way, but he seemed intent on winning David over.

Sarah had just delivered three slices of apple pie and a fresh pot of tea when Walmore smiled ingratiatingly at David and said, "I suppose your first order of business on British soil will be to claim your late brother's title."

Millie caught her breath. She didn't mean to stare at David, but she couldn't help it. Why hadn't she known about this? It made sense, starting with the day Anne arrived at the farm in Oregon, telling her and Sam that David had inherited something from his brother. Did no one in America know that he was a true aristocrat? He must have kept it a secret. All the way from Oregon to Independence, he'd certainly been reticent about his background. He had mentioned a country home once or twice, and lately he'd let fall a few tidbits that led Millie to believe his family traveled high in London society. But she'd never dreamed he held a title. Or would, it appeared, when he returned to England.

David was looking at her. She reached for her teacup as a way to camouflage her dismay. How could she have allowed herself to hope he was warming toward her? A lord would never marry someone like her. And he'd done all in his power to make sure she knew nothing of his true situation.

"Mr. Walmore," David said evenly, "I'd appreciate it if you didn't speak of this matter. It's not settled yet, and I don't wish people to hear rumors and speculate."

"Of course not, sir. Forgive my thoughtlessness. But I wish you the best."

David nodded and took a bite of his pie.

Millie could scarcely keep her cup steady enough to take a sip. Would David be willing to talk to her about this later? Or would he deposit her in Philadelphia without explanation and go off to live in his castle?

"Won't you come up to my room, Mr. Walmore?" David said when they all had finished their dessert. "I believe we can talk privately there."

"That's most kind of you," Walmore murmured.

David rose, but his stiffness slowed him, and Walmore jumped to pull out Millie's chair before he could.

Her features were impassive, but her cheeks bore spots of high color that David didn't think were caused by rouge. He'd have to tell her everything now. She probably deserved to know. He almost wished he'd told her earlier, but he couldn't change that. She would be discreet about it—he was sure of that now. Keeping Walmore quiet might be more difficult.

When they reached the stairs, Walmore said, "Lean on me, if you will, sir. I see that your injury is not completely healed."

"I'm fine," David said, slightly annoyed. "I shall come along a little slowly, but I'll get there." Using his cane and the railing, he mounted the first few steps as vigorously as he could. The pain in his bones was still there, but much less than it had been previously, and he was able to put up a good front for the first flight. Walmore himself seemed to limp a bit, and David wondered how badly he'd been beaten.

They reached the landing, and Millie gazed at him anxiously.

"One minute," David said, leaning heavily on the railing. He tried not to pant, but to breathe slowly and normally.

"I say, my room is right here," Walmore said. "You could come in there for our chat if you wish. I could help you up to your own room afterward."

David hesitated. Millie looked alarmed. Was she worried about leaving him alone with Walmore? He supposed he would feel a little less vulnerable if they met in his own room. He had a sitting area there, and Millie would be just across the hall. He could leave his door open to reassure her. After the attacks on him last year, he supposed it made sense, though this fellow seemed rather a vacuous young whip, one of the useless, idle society lads he disdained. He'd refused to become like Walmore—that was part of coming to America in the first place. He'd never wanted it said that he was the lazy third son of an earl who never got his hands dirty.

"I think perhaps I'll be more comfortable in my own chamber," he said. "My leg still pains me some, and Mrs. Evans can help me get settled before she leaves us." Millie gave a tiny nod. David wished he could speak to her without Walmore overhearing. He smiled and set his cane on the first step of the next flight. "Shall we?"

A few minutes later, they had reached the sanctuary of his room. With a sigh, he sank into the chair by the window. Millie set the straight chair in place for Walmore.

"Shall I get your medicine, Mr. Stone?" she asked.

"Oh, no thank you," David said. "I think I'm all right for now."

They both knew she'd dosed him shortly before their trip to the dining room. Millie must be giving him an opening to keep her there a little longer.

"It's warm in here, however," David said. "I'd appreciate it if you'd crack this window open and leave the door ajar when you leave."

"Certainly." Millie opened the window a few inches, as he'd requested. It did let in a soothing breeze, and it also gave credence to his ruse about leaving the door open.

"Well, gentlemen, if there's nothing else. . ." She gazed expectantly at David.

"I shall call out if I need you."

She nodded and left the room. David had no doubt she would also leave her door open and be ready to return at an instant. This, he hoped, would serve as notice to Walmore that any funny business would come home to rest squarely on him.

And now, he thought, how long before he asks for money?

Peregrin sat facing David Stone, completely at a loss for words.

"Tell me what happened when you were robbed," Stone said. "Did it take place here in the hotel?"

"No, out on the street. A couple of fellows accosted me. One was a huge brute. I tried to put up a fight, but that was a mistake."

"It usually is," Stone replied. "So, I suppose your pockets are to let now."

Peregrin winced. "I'm afraid so, sir. They took everything I owned but five dollars, which I had hidden away. If not for that— well, let us just say that by the time I settle my bill here, I shall be strapped. I doubt I can get passage back to New York."

Stone sighed and eyed him thoughtfully—disapprovingly, Peregrin felt. "I don't like to see a countryman in need. But neither do I like to give out large sums of money, especially to people I don't know."

"Perfectly understandable," Peregrin said quickly. "In fact, I feel the same way, sir, and it pains me greatly to ask you to come to my aid."

"Well, I shan't leave you here in dire straits. After all, you are connected somewhat to the family." Stone reached inside his coat— for his wallet, Peregrin hoped. Of course, his plan to ask David to cover his entire debt to Baxter and his flunkies could hardly come to fruition now. He'd look awfully shabby if he touched David for more than the minimum to get him to New York.

Instead of a wallet, however, Stone brought out a pair of railway tickets and squinted at them.

"Let's see, our train goes at 7:20 in the morning. Can you meet us at the station by seven? Or ride with us if you like. I'll purchase your ticket then, and you can go with us as far as Philadelphia. I'm going to escort Mrs. Evans to her friends there, before I go on to New York."

"That's very good of you."

Inside, Peregrin fumed. He wasn't going to hand over a cent.

Not one penny. How was that supposed to help him with Wilkes and Teddy? Should he tell Stone everything and throw himself on his mercy?

"Well then," Stone said cordially, "we shall see you in the morning."

Peregrin caught his breath. He hadn't expected to be dismissed quite so summarily. But if he showed displeasure, Stone might back out on his offer to buy his train ticket. Peregrin rose.

"Yes, indeed. Thank you very much." At the doorway, he dared to turn back. "I don't suppose. . ." He appraised David's impassive face. What plausible excuse could he give to elicit a few more dollars? "Well, I don't like to mention it, but I had hoped to see a medical man before I leave here. I'm afraid those thugs cracked a rib or something." He rubbed his abdomen, which truthfully was very sore.

"I doubt any doctor would come out tonight unless it was an emergency. But go around to Doctor Lee this evening if you want. Tell him to add it to my bill." David rattled off the address.

Peregrin blinked. Best to just accept that graciously, he supposed.

"Thank you, sir." Recognizing defeat, he bowed himself out of the room. The door across the hall stood a bit ajar, but he could see no sign of Mrs. Evans in his brief glance. He strolled to the landing and down to his room below. Now what? He certainly couldn't go out to consult the doctor, much as he would like to. His head ached terribly, and his ribcage pained every time he moved. But he'd hurt a lot worse if he tried to leave the hotel again without paying Wilkes and Teddy.

For the next hour, Peregrin paced his room. What could he do? Maybe if he sneaked up to David's room in the night, he could take his wallet and. . . No, as much as Merrileigh would like to see the job done, he wasn't going to raise a hand against David Stone in this hotel. He would be the first suspect. But if he met Stone and Mrs. Evans in the morning and got on the train with them. . .

He fetched up by his window and peered out around the edge of the curtain. Teddy stood across the street whittling, as seemed to be his hobby. No doubt Wilkes was nearby. Or perhaps they spelled each other so they could eat dinner in turns and not lose sight of him.

As he watched, Wilkes joined Teddy. Peregrin drew back a little. The two talked for a minute. Teddy shook his head and whittled. Wilkes crossed his arms and leaned against the building, watching the hotel.

Millie hustled to get their bags out to the landing in the morning. She'd suggested that David shave the evening before, to save time. Yawning, Billy answered her summons and carried their bags down. The driver she'd engaged was on time, but there was no sign of Walmore. She tipped Billy and ran upstairs to see that David got down in one piece.

They met on the second-floor landing. David was moving fairly confidently, using the cane more as an accessory than a crutch.

"Where's Walmore?" he asked first thing.

"Haven't seen him," Millie replied.

David nodded to the door marked 201. "That's his room. I'll see if I can raise him."

"All right. I'm going down and make sure the bags are all loaded. If Mrs. Simmons is up, I'll see if she has hot water. Maybe you can get a cup of tea."

"No time." David strode to Walmore's door and rapped on it with his cane.

Millie bustled on down the stairs. Let David handle this. The young paragon of British indolence was probably sound asleep. Would David wait for him? She strongly doubted that. David was a good traveler and never missed a departure unless he meant to. Rather wise of him not to give Walmore any money, nor purchase the man's ticket until they reached the station. He was a shrewd businessman, and she liked that in him.

The driver lounged on the seat of his wagon but straightened when she came out of the hotel, wrapping her shawl snugly about her shoulders.

"All ready now?" he asked.

"Almost. Mr. Stone is checking on the third member of our party."

"Got plenty of time, have you?" the man asked.

"I should think so." The sun was barely over the horizon, and that meant they had about an hour before train time. Even so, Millie looked anxiously back toward the door. As of yet, there was no sign of David or Walmore. Across the street, a large man rose from behind a rain barrel, stretching. Had he slept there? Maybe he fell into a drunken stupor in the shadow of the building last night. Millie looked hastily away. Had she seen that big fellow before?

"You can climb up if you want to, ma'am."

She glanced at the driver, then the wagon seat, and decided to wait until David was present. Besides, what kind of gentleman told a woman to climb up without getting down to offer his assistance?

At last the door of the hotel opened. Billy ambled out carrying two leather bags.

"Where is Mr. Stone?" Millie asked when he reached the wagon.

"He's dressing the other gent."

Millie sighed. "All right. After you put those in the wagon, could you give me a hand up, Billy?"

He smiled at her. "Sure can, Miz Evans."

He'd been so helpful over the past two months, and so good-natured, that on impulse Millie dug out an extra half dime for him.

At last David came out, followed by a rumpled and scruffy-looking Walmore. The young man hadn't shaved, and he wore his hat pulled low over his face, shadowing his black eye.

"Jump in," David said, indicating the wagon bed. He climbed up beside Millie. When Walmore had dragged himself up over the wheel and thumped into the back with the luggage, the driver cracked his whip smartly, and they moved off up the street toward the train station.

Millie looked back and saw the large man by the rain barrel staring after them.

Peregrin shuddered and hunkered down in the wagon bed. Wilkes was on watch across the street, and he'd seen him. He could only hope that the two thugs would not confront them. If he stuck close to Stone and Mrs. Evans, perhaps he could get away with this, but those two were persistent.

The early morning streets were all but empty, and the horse trotted right along. Next thing Peregrin knew, they were pulling the baggage out of the wagon, and David paid off the driver. Peregrin grabbed his own luggage and flung a glance over his shoulder. So far, so good. Wilkes would have had to hoof it mighty fast to get here by now, and Peregrin was banking on the giant's having to go round up his friend first. With any luck, they'd lost the pair. Of course they'd seen all the bags loaded, but they just might head for the steamboat docks first.

Inside the station, he waited impatiently for the others. Of course, being a gentleman, Stone was pampering Mrs. Evans. Peregrin supposed he oughtn't to have dashed inside so quickly, but he wanted to get off the street and out of sight. A minute later, they entered with the remaining luggage. Stone was limping but couldn't use his cane because both his hands were full of baggage.

"I say, let me help you," Peregrin dropped one of his own valises and stepped forward. "Forgive me, I should have thought."

"I hoped the driver would carry our things in," David said, "but he wanted to go. I'll see about a porter once we've purchased your ticket."

Peregrin broke out in a sweat while he waited. He couldn't stop staring at the main entrance to the depot. Mrs. Evans stood serenely beside the pile of luggage while Stone completed the transaction at the ticket window. Finally Peregrin had the ticket in his hand.

"I can't tell you how much I appreciate this." He glanced once more toward the door, hoping he would never need to explain the exact depth of his gratitude.

"Don't mention it." Stone waved a porter over and showed him his ticket.

"You want to go right out there, sir," said the porter. "Your train is just pulling in. I'll take your luggage to the baggage car."

"Thank you." Stone put some money in the man's hand and

took Mrs. Evans's arm. "Come, Mildred." He threw a glance over his shoulder.

Peregrin pasted on a smile and hastened after them, leaving his bags with theirs. The train chuffed in, and they all stopped on the platform and clapped their hands to their ears. Once it had stopped, they had to wait for disembarking passengers to climb down. Peregrin thought he might die of apoplexy if they didn't get aboard soon.

At last they were seated in the passenger car. He deliberately avoided a window seat, not wanting a chance of Wilkes and Teddy spotting him from outside. The wait for the wheels to start rolling seemed interminable, but Stone and Mrs. Evans chatted amiably.

Peregrin noted Stone's attentions to the lady—nothing excessive, yet when he inquired whether she was warm enough and had sufficient room for her sundries, Stone sounded as solicitous as a new husband might on his honeymoon. All his addresses lacked were *my dear*s and *darling Mildred*s. Peregrin didn't doubt for half a second that David Stone was a smitten man. Perhaps he could use that to his advantage. He only hoped that dear Mildred didn't get in his way when the time came to execute the rest of his plan.

# CHAPTER 33

The ride to St. Louis took most of the day, but David found the journey almost pleasant with Millie at his side. It would have been even more enjoyable if Peregrin Walmore had not sat opposite him.

The young man appeared to be ill—apart from his black eye. His nerves apparently jangled badly, so that he jumped every time someone came down the aisle from behind him. He perspired copiously, though the railway car was not overly warm.

At one stop, they got up to stretch their legs, and David managed to take him aside for a moment.

"Are you all right, Walmore?"

"What? Me? Oh, I'm fine, sir."

"I thought perhaps you were ill. You did say the men who robbed you roughed you up a bit."

"I'll be fine, I assure you. I just. . .travel doesn't agree with me."

"I see." David wanted to ask why on earth he'd come all the way across the ocean and halfway across the continent. But he would leave impertinence to the young.

Millie had found an urchin selling sandwiches and apple fritters on the platform, and David willingly handed her enough money to purchase a lunch for the three of them. Walmore seemed very grateful and stammered out an offer to pay for his own, but David didn't want to see him hand over his last few coins. He wasn't heartless. Assuming, of course, that Walmore was telling the truth about his funds.

Millie exhibited more courtesy and charm toward their new companion than David felt, and he was proud of her. Aside from her accent, no one would think she was any less a lady than Anne.

He wasn't the only man observing her. Walmore seemed quite taken with her, and David intercepted the gazes of several other male passengers who also found Millie pleasing to look at.

And why not? Her face and form would attract any man, and she had an alluring combination of good health, an active spirit, and a pleasant demeanor. She was also a thinking woman, and a spiritual one. In short, she had every quality one would expect in a lady. So why should she not be designated such?

By the time they reached St. Louis, David's mind was made up. There was no one else he would rather have beside him when he took his title—or when he returned to his childhood home. Mildred Evans was the perfect candidate to become the next Lady Stoneford.

Peregrin feared that, for Mrs. Evans's sake, Stone would insist they spend a night in St. Louis. They reached the city late in the day, and the lady did admit to mild fatigue, but she insisted they should push on if possible.

This greatly relieved Peregrin. He wanted to keep moving until they were far away from Independence. And he doubted he'd ride all the way to New York. That would be foolhardy in his current situation. He'd have to find another coastal city where he could set himself up comfortably and yet not run into Baxter's minions. Perhaps he could cash in part of his ticket before they reached New York and fade into another municipality.

The ferry embarked just before sunset, and they were able to get a light supper on board. Once they reached the other side, a hack took them from the ferry dock to the railway station. To Peregrin's dismay, they had a two-hour wait. Their train would travel through the night, and Stone tried to engage a compartment, where they could sit in privacy, but none were available on this train. They would have to sit in a car with rows of seats, among the other travelers.

They escorted Mrs. Evans to the door of a ladies' waiting room in the depot, where she could rest in safety. Stone was of a mind to wander about the station and perhaps buy a newspaper. Peregrin would have preferred to stay out of sight, but there was no gentlemen's waiting room. He reasoned that he'd eluded his pursuers and had nothing to fear. Still, he couldn't help looking about for Wilkes, who would stand out in any crowd.

After a short while, Stone invited him to walk a couple of blocks to stretch his legs and buy something for them to eat on the train. Peregrin decided it was better than lolling about the depot, where he could be easily spotted. They found a general store still open, and Stone purchased a basket and filled it with crackers, dried fruit, peppermints, cheese, and jerky. After they returned to the station, they kicked about for another hour until their train was ready, and at last they were able to retrieve Mrs. Evans and board.

Rather than discuss his own activities or draw suspicion by inquiring about Stone's affairs in England, Peregrin asked him about his life in the West. Mrs. Evans seemed interested, too, though Peregrin had been under the impression that the two had known each other in Oregon. Stone grew more talkative than he had been to date and told about the stagecoach line he'd started with his niece's husband. Mrs. Evans asked him many questions about the line and how he had gone about establishing the stations and promoting its services. Peregrin observed them with interest. He still wasn't sure exactly the nature of their relationship.

"I'm surprised you wanted to take such an active part in the business, sir," he said. "An investment, yes, but it sounds as though you did most of the buying and organizing."

"Yes, I did." Stone fixed him with a keen eye. "I've been a working man the past twenty years, Walmore. And I don't intend to stop once I reach Stoneford."

"Ah, then you have plans for the estate."

"Indeed I do. I have no idea what has happened since Richard died, but Anne has given me a fair idea of the way things were before his death. I intend to keep the farms going and perhaps add a couple of other ventures."

"What sort of ventures?"

Stone lowered his gaze and shrugged. "I'd rather not discuss it until I see how things are at Stoneford, but if things go well, I shall institute some modern methods there."

Walmore nodded, more curious than ever. "I wish you success, sir." It was too bad the man wouldn't live long enough to carry out his plans.

The train rattled on through the night, making several brief stops to take on and discharge passengers and replenish their water and coal. A gas lamp flickered low at each end of the car, and the uncurtained windows let in moonlight. When it was too dark to read, they talked as quietly as the noise of their journey would allow.

"I'm sorry that we have to sit up all night," Stone said to Mrs. Evans. "The conductor tells me that we'll change to a different train in Illinois tomorrow, and we'll be able to get berths on that one."

"Well, it is only the two nights," Mrs. Evans said. "I'm sure we'll survive it."

Peregrin couldn't help thinking what a fuss Merrileigh would make if Randolph informed her that she would have to sit up all night in a common railroad carriage.

The conductor put out all but two gas lamps, one at each end of the car. After a while, most of the passengers sank down in their seats. Peregrin drifted in and out of sleep, using his wadded jacket as a pillow.

They stopped at a small town in Illinois just after dawn.

"This is where we change trains," Stone said.

The conductor assured them that their baggage would be transferred, and they climbed down to the platform. Walmore was beginning to feel secure, but he still looked sharply about as they strolled toward the depot.

They soon learned that they must wait three hours until the Philadelphia train was ready, and the station agent suggested a boardinghouse that would serve breakfast to early travelers.

"What do you say, Mildred?" Stone asked. "Shall we sit down to a hot breakfast?"

"It sounds lovely," she replied.

"Ah, excuse me for a minute." Stone eyed a sign on the wall. "They have a telegraph office, and I believe I'll send a wire, if you don't mind."

"Of course," Mrs. Evans told him. "Mr. Walmore and I shall ramble on to the end of the platform and back." She smiled at Peregrin. "Shall we?"

"Delighted." He offered his arm as Stone strode off to the telegraph operator's window, and she placed her gloved hand inside the crook of his elbow. Was the telegram going to David's banker in New York? Or perhaps he was sending a message to be forwarded to England.

Peregrin straightened his shoulders a bit. It felt good to be perambulating with a lady on his arm. He had neglected the fair sex too long on this journey. In fact, he hadn't come into the company of any women he'd call "ladies" since a party Nigel Wallace had thrown in New York. But Mrs. Evans definitely qualified. He'd decided that much since they'd boarded the train in Independence. She lacked a certain polish that British women of the upper class possessed, but she was gracious and kind. She also had discretion, and she managed to look lovely on a sooty train journey, which was saying a lot.

Stone returned as they ambled back toward the telegraph booth. "There, that's taken care of. Oh, and I spoke for sleeping compartments for us all tonight. We shan't have to worry about a thing until tomorrow evening, when we'll approach Philadelphia."

"Excellent," Mrs. Evans said.

"That's very good of you," Peregrin added.

They took their time over breakfast, savoring fresh fruit, good coffee, and perfectly cooked eggs. Still, they returned to the depot with time to spare. At last they settled in on the new train. The seats were better padded than those on the last train, and the car looked generally cleaner and better maintained. They passed the time in pleasant conversation, and at noon picnicked out of the basket, adding hot muffins and a jug of milk that Stone purchased from a vendor at one of the stops.

The day wore on, and Peregrin grew restless. He learned from the porter that the last carriage before the baggage car was open to gentlemen who wanted to smoke. His interest piqued immediately. Surely a card game would be found there. This train was definitely a cut about the last.

Around eight o'clock in the evening, Mrs. Evans confessed she was tired and rose.

"If you gentlemen will forgive me, I'd like to retire."

"Of course," Stone said. "Let me get the porter and ask him to get your berth ready."

"Have a good night," Peregrin said. When David had gone off down the aisle with Mrs. Evans, he headed in the opposite direction, for the smoking car. He had hardly any money on him, but he'd found that Americans sometimes played for very low stakes. He hadn't so much as mentioned it earlier—one didn't discuss gambling in the presence of a lady, and he was sure Stone wouldn't like to think he would borrow from him and then risk the small amount he had left.

But Stone didn't seem to be a smoker—or a drinker either, now that Peregrin thought about it. While that was odd, the gentleman wasn't likely to make his way to the smoking car. Unless, of course, he'd been waiting for Mrs. Evans to leave them to indulge. The poor chap had been cooped up in a hotel room for weeks, after all. It was just possible he might kick up his heels now. If Peregrin got into a game, he'd have to sit where he wouldn't easily be noticed if Stone glanced in.

He had to walk through two other carriages to reach the smoking car. Porters were beginning to lower the sleeping berths that hung above the seats, and passengers were moving about, rearranging their belongings and preparing to retire.

On the open platforms between cars, the wind tore at Peregrin. The night had turned quite chilly, and he hurried to get inside again.

The atmosphere was hazy blue in the smoking car, and the occupants looked quieter than he'd imagined. Several men sat chatting amiably with glasses in their hands. Peregrin smiled. They had a small bar back here, at the far end of the car. Apparently ladies were excluded, or perhaps they weren't told about it. And there was indeed a poker game going on in a corner. Four men sat around a small table that folded down from the wall, fanning out their cards.

Peregrin was just about to step forward and ask to be dealt in when he noticed a large man getting a drink at the bar.

A very large man.

Peregrin caught his breath and glanced quickly about. Sure enough, sitting with his back to the door of the car was a smaller man whose ears and worn jacket looked suspiciously like Teddy's. Peregrin ducked back, bumping into another passenger who'd just entered.

"Oh, excuse me."

He shoved past the man, wishing he hadn't opened his mouth. His accent would draw attention. He bustled out onto the little platform between cars and stood gasping for a moment. He didn't want to go inside the next car appearing discomposed, but he couldn't stay here. If Wilkes or Teddy came out, they'd have him at their mercy in a dangerous spot. He hurried into the next carriage, not daring to look back.

How had they caught up? They would kill him; he was sure of it—unless he somehow came up with the full amount he owed them. But Peregrin hadn't the means to win it back, even if he dared waltz in there and join the poker game. No, he could never do that with Wilkes and Teddy relaxing and wetting their whistles. He'd be too nervous to concentrate on a game, assuming they let him sit down and play. With his limited funds for a stake, the best he could hope for was to come away with pocket money for the trip, and that would never make the two toughs happy.

He mustn't let them know he'd seen them. Maybe he could leave the train at the next stop and disappear into the night.

But could he survive with only a few cents in his pocket? He hadn't enough for the meanest hotel room.

The only thing he could think of that would give him a remote chance of living through this horrible journey was to do what Merrileigh had sent him to do—and to pick David's pockets before he threw him off the train. He could pay the thugs from David's plump wallet and keep whatever was left.

The thought made him feel ill, and he slumped down into the

nearest empty seat. It was the only way, he told himself. He couldn't rob David Stone and leave him alive, or he'd be arrested before he had time to count his plunder.

His short-lived notion that he could bypass his sister's plan and continue supporting himself in America had gone by the wayside. He'd failed to make good on his first attempts at bringing in more money and had in fact lost most of what he began with. When he reached New York, or whatever destination he settled on, he would need money. And if he wanted Merrileigh to help him in the future, he had to get rid of David. No other way presented itself for him to satisfy his debt to Lionel Baxter and cut loose from the savage hounds nipping at his heels.

David made his way down the aisle from the tiny washroom toward his berth. Millie had settled in for the night in hers, and he supposed he may as well get as much sleep as he could. He paused halfway down the aisle. The porters had lowered most of the berths along the length of the car, but at the one he was sure was his, a man stood with his head poked inside the curtains. A man not in uniform. David was quite certain from his clothing that it was Peregrin Walmore.

He stepped as briskly down the aisle as possible, dodging other passengers. Now the fellow had his arms inside the berth, too. David checked the numbers, just to be sure. It was his, just beyond Millie's compartment.

"May I help you?" He tapped the man on the shoulder.

Peregrin Walmore pulled his head quickly from the curtains and blinked at him, his cheeks flushing pink amid his purple and yellow bruises. "Oh, I say. Stone. Uh. . .sorry, I thought this was my berth. But I see now that it's your bag in there."

"Yes," David said coldly. "Yours is across the way."

"Pardon," Walmore said.

David didn't like it one bit. Something was fishy about this fellow's behavior and had been from the start. He glanced around. Several other passengers were within earshot, and Millie, if she wasn't sleeping already, must be able to hear them as well. He frowned at Walmore. "I'd like to speak to you privately, please."

"Well. . .uh. . ." Walmore glanced over his shoulder. "I suppose we'll have to go outside. No privacy in here."

"True enough. Shall we?"

Walmore hesitated. "If you insist."

"I do."

David followed him to the end of the car and out onto the platform. The cool night air rushed by. He paused for a moment to observe the dark countryside zooming past. They must be making thirty miles an hour. He didn't know as he'd ever gone this fast except for when he was riding a good horse at a full gallop. He thought fondly of Captain, the faithful mount he'd turned over to Anne before he left Oregon. Maybe he could build up the stable in Stoneford after he'd got his feet under him.

Hands pushed against his back—hard. David fell forward, doubling over the low iron railing. He grabbed it and held himself fast. If he'd missed his hold, he'd have tumbled right off the train.

He regained his balance and whipped around as Walmore lunged at him. David caught his wrists as the younger man dove for his throat. Squeezing with all his might, David stared into Walmore's eyes.

"What are you doing?"

Walmore grimaced. "N–nothing. I—you slipped. I was trying to help you. Gave me a fright, you did."

David shoved him, slamming him against the door of the next car. Pinning him against the door wasn't all that difficult, which surprised David, considering what little exercise he'd had lately. He was breathing a bit hard, but not nearly so desperately as Walmore, who gasped for air. The young whelp might be a gentleman of sorts, but he had no manners, and he was sadly out of shape.

"Look, we both know you attempted to kill me," David said grimly. "I think I know why."

"You do?" Walmore gulped, still staring at him, bug-eyed.

The door behind Walmore opened, and the young man almost

fell into the car. Behind him, the conductor said, "Everything all right out here?"

"Yes, thank you," David said.

The conductor shot Walmore a suspicious glance but nodded and said, "Very good, Mr. Stone. We're approaching Terra Haute." The train's doleful whistle accentuated his words. "Let me know if you need anything, sir."

"I will," David said.

The conductor closed the door, and David faced Walmore. He loosened his grip somewhat, but didn't let go altogether. "Tell me now who put you up to this. Was it Randolph?"

"N–no," Walmore said. "I wasn't—oh, please, you mustn't think me so vile."

"But I do."

"It's—it's—"

"It's what? Tell me!" David grabbed his lapels and shook him. Walmore raised a hand in supplication, and David let go of him.

"I owe some money. I know, it was stupid of me, but I thought—"

"You thought what? That I'd pay off your debt? You were disappointed, weren't you? I bought you a train ticket instead, and some meals and sundries. But you needed more. Is that what you were doing in my sleeping berth? Going through my things, looking for cash?"

The sky was quite dark, but David fancied Walmore's face went scarlet, and he didn't readily deny the accusation. The train lurched as the brake went on, and they both reached for the railing.

In the moment when they struggled to keep their balance, David considered telling the bounder to keep clear of him and Millie for the rest of the journey. But it might be wiser to keep an eye on him.

He eyed the young man sternly as they shifted their weight and the train slowed further, with the wheels squealing against the rails. "I'm warning you, Walmore. Anything short of impeccable behavior from you, and I shall have you arrested. Do you understand?"

"I—well, yes, but—"

"I mean it. If there's any more of this nonsense, I shall turn you over to the authorities."

The train had slid into the next station, where the platform was brilliantly lighted and crowded with people. David turned his back on Walmore and entered their carriage. Best to get out of the way before new passengers came on. He didn't like the idea of going to sleep with Walmore close at hand, but at least he had put the fellow on notice. Perhaps he could catch the conductor after things settled down and ask him to keep an eye on his fellow traveler.

He was about to climb into his berth when Millie poked her head out between the curtains next door.

"Is everything all right?" she asked. "I thought I heard you and Mr. Walmore having words."

David glanced about. New passengers were boarding, with porters carrying their overnight bags into the car. "Everything's fine. We'll speak in the morning."

She nodded.

"We're at Terre Haute," he added, "wherever that is."

"Indiana, I expect."

"Ah. Sleep if you can. I shall stay here now. Call out if you need anything."

She gazed at him for a moment, her green eyes full of questions. He hated to leave her wondering, but they really couldn't discuss the matter with all these people about.

"Good night then." She gave him a wan smile and withdrew her head.

David looked toward the end of the car where he'd had the altercation with Walmore, but there was no sign of the young man. He climbed onto the sleeping platform and pulled the curtains closed. One latch was unfastened on his small valise. He shoved it aside and removed his shoes.

"Now I lay me down to sleep," he muttered as his fatigue overtook him. "I pray thee, Lord. . . Up to You, really."

To Millie's surprise, David was already up when she left her sleeping compartment in the morning, and the porter was folding up his hanging berth so he could sit down. She had thought she was rising early, but there he was, looking splendid. She suspected he had given his shoes to the porter to polish last night, and perhaps had his jacket pressed as well.

David caught sight of her as she stood admiring him, and she flushed.

"Good morning, Mildred," he said with a smile. "I'm told we're nearing Cincinnati. We're stopping soon at a town on the outskirts."

"Can we get breakfast there?"

"There'll be vendors coming on with coffee and food. The train will only stop for twenty minutes, so they don't recommend that we leave it."

"That's fine," Millie said. "Did you sleep?"

"Fitfully."

She nodded. She'd slept in her brown traveling dress, and it was now rumpled and decidedly in need of a laundering, but she had managed to sleep. David had a stubble of beard shadowing his chin, and dark shadows lay beneath his eyes.

"Shall I make up your berth, ma'am?" the porter asked.

"I still have a few things in it." She turned to David. "Excuse me just a few minutes, won't you?"

"Certainly. I shall be sitting here, where we sat yesterday. Please join me at your convenience."

A short time later, when she made her way carefully back to their seats, the train had stopped. She found David perusing a newspaper. Nearly all of the sleeping compartments had been folded up out of the way.

"Where is Mr. Walmore this morning?" she asked as she seated herself. She glanced at Peregrin's sleeping berth, which was in its storage position.

"I expect he's about somewhere."

"I see his berth is made up."

"Yes. And the vendor came through a minute ago. I got us some coffee and biscuits with bacon in them, and a couple of apples."

"That sounds delightful," Millie said.

"We shall be in Philadelphia by evening." David smiled, and she wondered if he was eager to put the United States behind him and get home. He must be growing more excited as he grew nearer to his destination.

Millie, on the other hand, was headed into the unknown. She would have to try to rekindle old acquaintances and meet new people who could help her. She'd need new living quarters, a paying position, a new church. . .so much to think about. She wanted to follow David's example and anticipate these changes with optimism. But she wasn't like him—she had no estate waiting, and no counselors, and most of all, no seemingly limitless bank account.

"So soon?" She managed a smile—who couldn't smile, after all, when gazing into those stunning blue eyes?

He had set the two tin cups of coffee on the floor while he waited, and he picked one up and handed it to her.

"There you are. I'm sorry it's not tea."

"That's all right. I don't suppose I mind as much as you do. Just think—you'll soon be able to get all the tea you want."

"Yes." His eyes went sober. "It's coming right up on us, isn't it?"

She knew he meant the separation, and suddenly the morning turned gray. By evening they would part. She hated to think of a life without David. Apparently it gave him pause as well, and she took a small consolation from that.

The conductor came by. "All set, Mr. Stone? Ma'am?"

"Yes, thank you," David said.

Millie nodded, and the conductor moved on. She had noted that all the railroad employees knew David by name and showed him the utmost respect. They treated all the passengers politely but seemed to have a special preference for David and a willingness to do extra favors for him. She supposed it was because he acted like a proper gentleman and showed them respect as well.

Her thoughts turned again to her prospects in Philadelphia. She did hope she could find a paying situation quickly. She had a little money left, but not enough to keep her more than a couple of weeks at the high prices she expected in the city.

"I suppose I might find a position as a cook," she said as she took a biscuit from the packet.

"A cook." David's face fell. "Well, yes, I suppose you might."

"I was thinking at a hotel, perhaps, or a restaurant in the city. It generally pays better than housework or sewing."

"I see. But really, Mildred, do you think—"

"What?" She smiled. "You're thinking it wouldn't be proper?"

"No. Well, actually. . ." He squared his shoulders. "There's a matter I'd like to discuss with you, but this is perhaps not the place for it. Maybe when we stop again, we can take a short stroll together, if—" He looked over his shoulder.

"Yes, it is difficult to get privacy when you have a traveling companion, is it not?" she said.

"Very difficult. But—about our traveling companion." He leaned toward her and lowered his voice. "I don't trust him by half." His charming smile sent all her blue thoughts scattering, yet he seemed a bit guarded—almost worried.

"You intrigue me." Something must have happened last night, as she'd suspected. David's tone when she'd heard him speak to Walmore, close outside her sleeping berth, sounded stern—almost accusing.

He frowned for a moment, then went on in low tones, "It's distasteful for me to tell you this, but I feel I must warn you. Walmore attacked me physically last night."

"What?" She drew back to study his face. David seemed perfectly sincere, and she leaned toward him again. "Tell me more, please."

"He said afterward that he didn't mean it, but I know he did. And he was rummaging in my luggage before that—when I came back from the washroom."

"That must be when I heard you confront him."

"Yes. I didn't realize it at the time, but my cuff links are missing."

"Not the onyx ones?"

"Yes."

Neither of them mentioned Millie's own theft of the same cuff links, but it hung between them. Millie hadn't supposed they were particularly valuable. She had taken them more out of sentiment. But would Walmore take them if they were mere trinkets?

"When we went out onto the platform," David continued, "he tried to push me over the railing."

Millie tried to picture that, but Walmore seemed so unpretentious and even awkward that she found it hard to accept. "Do you really think he wanted to do that?"

"It wasn't accidental. Perhaps he wanted my wallet, but I got the impression he wanted something more. . .permanent."

Millie swallowed hard. "You think he is acting for your cousin?"

"I don't know. It's the most logical explanation."

Millie inhaled slowly. What if Walmore had succeeded last night? She wouldn't have known until now that David was missing. If the man truly wanted to kill David—or even if he merely hoped to steal his valuables, it seemed to her that they should turn him over to the police.

"Do you think he's left the train now?" she asked.

"I doubt it, since he's penniless. But maybe." David glanced back at the travelers behind them. "I say."

"Yes?"

"There's a fellow just sitting down—don't gawk, but when you think it's appropriate, take a look. I swear I saw him from my hotel window in Independence."

"Doing what?" Millie asked.

"Nothing. Just hanging about and watching the hotel."

She frowned. That didn't sound good.

"Brown jacket," David said, "in the aisle seat about four rows behind us and on the other side of the aisle. Big man—very big."

Millie eyed David for a moment. She let her gaze flicker for a moment toward the rear of the car. She saw the man he referred to and puzzled in her mind over whether she'd seen him before or not. He was too big to ignore. Her heart skipped, but she turned forward impassively.

She touched David's sleeve and, when he leaned toward her, said in his ear, "I think you are right."

"Come outside for a moment."

They rose and left the car, reaching the little platform in between cars. Millie clung to the railing with one hand and her hat with the other as she turned to face David.

"I've seen him, too," she said. "That large man was across the street from our hotel the morning we left. I saw him stand up from behind the rain barrel over there, and I wondered if he'd slept there all night. A vagrant, I supposed. He watched us as we left for the train station."

"Interesting," David said.

"But the other one, the one he's sitting with—"

"Yes?"

Millie frowned. "He looks awfully like a man who stood across the street, whittling, on more than one occasion."

David turned and peered into the carriage for a moment. "Ah, you're right. I almost overlooked him. I saw the indolent whittler myself, and I believe that is the man."

Millie grasped his sleeve. "What does it mean?"

David covered her hand with his warm one and gazed down into her eyes. "I'm not sure."

"I'm frightened." All she could think of was Scottsburg and the assassin who had stalked him. She tried to remain calm, but David looked concerned, too. She wouldn't sit by and let someone try to kill him again.

David spent the next hour deep in thought. Walmore had returned just before the train started, but he was quiet after the initial greetings and sat across from them, eating the biscuit David had saved for him.

"Sorry I didn't get you anything to drink," David said. "I couldn't handle three cups, and I wasn't sure when you wanted to eat."

Walmore waved a hand as though it was nothing, but he must wish he had something to help the biscuit go down.

David noted that while he brushed the crumbs off his clothing,

Walmore snatched repeated glances toward the suspicious men he and Millie had noted earlier.

At last a plan formed in his mind. It wasn't ideal, but David believed that the longer he stayed on the train, the more danger he was in.

"Excuse me a moment, won't you?" He got up and spoke to the porter. He wished he could discuss it with Millie first. She'd been very patient with him, considering how inconsiderately quiet he'd been. Finally, another hour into the trip, Walmore rose and excused himself, heading toward the washroom. David noted that the two suspicious men watched Walmore's every move. After he passed their seats, the larger man got up and lurched down the aisle and out the far end of the car.

"My dear," David said, leaning close to Millie's ear, "I wonder if you might be able to leave this train with me at the next stop. The conductor will see that our luggage is put off for us, and we can collect it after the train has gone on."

She arched her pretty auburn eyebrows. "Of course, if you think it is prudent. I trust your instincts."

"Well, my instincts aren't sure what to think, but they don't like this latest turn of events, if you catch my meaning. That whittler is even now sitting in the last row of this carriage, no doubt keeping an eye on us and anticipating Walmore's movements. Where his partner has got to, I have no idea."

Millie nodded gravely. "I have been wondering. . ."

"Yes?" David asked.

"Whether they are watching us or Mr. Walmore."

"A not unreasonable question. I supposed they were shadowing me, but since we took note of them this morning, I've been studying them. They may have an interest in us, but they seem to be shadowing Walmore, and I wonder if we are merely unwitting intruders in their little scheme."

"As opposed to being the objects of it?"

David nodded, though he didn't like either alternative.

"In any event," Millie said, "I am of the same mind as you, sir.

I do not like it."

"We shall get off, then? If they are following Walmore, they'll stay with him. And if they're after us, perhaps we can lose them if we move quickly. We can catch another train later in the day, I'm sure. If you don't mind a few hours' delay, that is."

"Why should I? Delay will only give me more time in your company."

Her cheeks flushed adoringly, and David could not resist reaching for her hand. She had not chastised him for calling her "my dear," and now her words were tantamount to a confession that she dreaded parting from him. He dared to think her feelings mirrored his own—a pleasant thought.

They were traveling across Ohio, and after further discussion with the conductor, David chose Pittsburgh as the city in which they would disembark. He had hoped to give Millie the particulars, but when he returned to his seat beside her, he saw Walmore approaching from the opposite end of the carriage.

The erstwhile whittler had disappeared, but his companion, the big man, sat toward the rear of the car with a newspaper open before him. When Walmore walked past him, the hulk of a man watched him openly.

David considered asking Walmore if he knew the pair but decided against it. If the three were in league against him, he didn't want any of them to dream that he was about to escape their clutches.

Millie attempted a placid conversation about the lush farm country they passed through, but David's mind wandered. Was he mad to think his cousin's brother-in-law could be plotting against him? After careful consideration, he thought madness was out of the question. He might be overly suspicious, but after all, he had nearly lost his life to an assassin in Oregon. He'd thought at the time that Randolph was behind the attempt, but his solicitor sent word that his cousin swore he had nothing to do with it and was shocked and saddened at the tidings. Mr. Conrad had tried to assure David that his family had no ill will toward him and only wished to see him take his rightful place at Stoneford.

Well, David wasn't so sure. For one thing, Conrad was a doddering old man now. Anne had told him that the man was in his eighties, which confirmed David's assumption that the solicitor was well past his prime. Randolph was sly enough to put one over on the old man. And wouldn't any guilty man deny his actions when accused? Who would admit he'd hired an assassin to kill a relative for him?

They reached the outskirts of Pittsburgh late in the afternoon, and the train began to slow. "Mildred, would you like to get off here for some air?" he asked. "I understand the train is stopping for about twenty minutes."

"Let us go," she said and began to put on her gloves.

David looked at Walmore. The man eyed him uncertainly. David wanted to simply ignore him, but he could hardly do that. He'd restrained himself from confronting him about the cuff links, supposing he was more likely to get clean away if he didn't admit he knew of the theft or show his contempt toward Walmore. It would be best if he and Millie left the train casually, as though they intended to return in a few minutes.

"Let's see if we can get a cup of tea in the few minutes we have," he said aloud, and more than one passenger heard him, he was sure. "Walmore, can we bring you something?"

The young man had started to rise, and he blinked at David uncertainly. "Uh, no, that's all right. I may get a breath myself."

David had hoped he'd stay on the train, but he couldn't say so without arousing suspicion. He took Millie's arm and pulled her along quickly. Several other people soon separated them from Walmore in the aisle.

Outside the car, he turned Millie along the platform away from the windows through which Walmore and the others might watch them. Two cars down, they found the conductor helping an elderly man onto the train. David waited for him to finish and then spoke to him confidentially.

"This is the place of our departure. You will have our bags set out without any fanfare?"

"Certainly, sir," the conductor said. "And if you turn your ticket in at the window, they'll refund part of your fare."

As they turned away, David spotted Walmore leaving their car farther down the platform. He seized Millie's hand and was about to draw her away when Walmore spotted him.

"I think we need to give Walmore an errand," David said to Millie, and walked with her toward the young man.

When they drew near, Walmore eyed him with surprise. He tipped his hat to Millie.

"Mrs. Evans wants to look over the peddlers' wares yonder." David nodded toward where several vendors had set up business on the edge of the platform. He took out his wallet. "Would you mind seeing if you can change this for me at the ticket office? I might not have time, and I'd like to have a few coins later for tips and so forth."

"Of course." Walmore took the dollar bill, folded it, and tucked it in his coat pocket.

"Thank you," David said with a smile. Walmore being a gentleman would understand that his company was not welcome at present.

Walmore set off at once for the ticket window to change the bill, and David steered Millie in the opposite direction.

"What is our plan?" she murmured as they strode past the peddlers.

"We lose ourselves until the train pulls out again. With any luck, Walmore will simply think we boarded a different car. It should take him a little while to discover that we aren't on board. The conductor has been amply paid to calm him if he gets agitated, and after no less than an hour's journey, to tell Walmore they've discovered a message I left with one of the baggage handlers—that we decided on the spur of the moment to leave them."

"Do you think he'll come back and try to find us?" Millie asked.

"He'd be foolish if he did. After all, his ticket to New York is paid for. But if he tries to change it, he'll have to pay an additional fee, and I've left him with only one dollar. Unless he was lying to us since the beginning, he hasn't much more than that at his disposal."

Millie smiled. "And then what?"

"Then we go back to retrieve our luggage and take a hackney to a hotel."

"Oh." She looked a little uncertain.

"Do not worry, my dear," David said. "I intend to see that you have a fine dinner, and perhaps we can have that conversation I alluded to earlier."

"You mean. . .this isn't it?"

"No, darling, this is not it at all. In fact this is very unlike the conversation I wish to have with you."

Her cheeks flushed prettily, and David drew her hand through his arm and squeezed it. He looked back and paused, gazing over the heads of the people thronging the platform.

"What is it?" she asked.

"As I hoped—the big man has followed Walmore. I can't see whether his friend is with him or not. He could be following us."

"Do you really think so?"

"No. I think they want Walmore. But come. Let us make ourselves scarce."

Millie could hardly believe what was happening to her. The man she'd admired so long and despaired of winning was whisking her about and calling her *my dear* and *darling*. Did he mean those endearments, or did he speak without thinking, distracted by the fear that assassins were stalking him?

A bit of calm thinking did not rule out the possibility that Walmore had come to Independence to locate David for those evil men. Now that he'd insinuated his way into David's good graces and company, the murderers could choose the time and place to carry out their wicked deeds. It wasn't so far from what Peterson had tried to do in Scottsburg, using her as the go-between.

Or was David's theory that the thugs were chasing Walmore the correct one? It would explain his black eye and nervousness.

She felt a pang of compassion for Walmore. The young man

didn't seem able to fend for himself in this inhospitable land. She hoped they weren't throwing him to the wolves.

Whatever their current situation, she couldn't give herself entirely over to fear. She was off on an adventure with the man she loved. Even if they were in danger, she somehow found herself enjoying every minute.

David stopped a well-dressed man on the street and asked him for the name of a nice restaurant. He then hailed a horse cab and instructed the driver to take them there.

Millie shrank back when they entered. She had never eaten in such a fine place, and she certainly wasn't dressed for it. But David drew her in, and they were soon seated at a secluded corner table. The china, the spotless linen tablecloth and napkins, the glassware—all might have been found on a rich man's table. Fresh flowers filled a ceramic vase, and the cutlery appeared to be fine silver plate. When she caught sight of the prices, she nearly swooned, but David caught her eye and smiled.

"Don't let that frighten you, Mildred. When I reach New York, I shall have an infusion of cash awaiting me."

"Oh, I—" She gulped, not knowing what to say, but she felt the heat in her cheeks. She leaned toward him. "I don't like to see you spend so much on me."

"It's my choice, dear. Enjoy it, and see if you think the chef here cooks better than you. Personally, I doubt it, but it will be a pleasant study."

Millie's heart fluttered. This was all so far from what she knew. In Oregon, she'd dreamed of living in this sort of atmosphere—or she would have, if she'd known what to dream. She couldn't have conjured up the particulars because she'd never come near to this standard of luxury.

But that was long ago when she aspired to marry her way out of poverty. Now she would gladly share a log cabin with this man and forego the social whirl she'd once craved.

She attempted to read the copious bill of fare, but she kept sneaking glances at David. He was being more than kind to her.

He was acting like a suitor. Dared she hope?

When the waiter—who was dressed finer than most preachers—reappeared, she had not come close to making a choice.

"Oh dear, there are so many dishes that sound exquisite."

"Shall I order for both of us?" David asked.

Relief settled on her, and she handed the menu to the waiter. David knew her now. He would order something she would like.

"Yes, please." She smiled at him a bit shyly, wondering how they could be so calm in the midst of life-threatening turmoil.

He ordered a chicken dish she had never heard of—the name of it sounded foreign. The waiter asked if they wanted a drink, and David asked for tea for both of them.

When the waiter had gone, David bent toward her and said quietly, "Mildred, it's time I spoke to you of what is on my heart."

"You mean. . .Walmore?"

"No, no. Forget that man—and the others as well. My dear, you must realize I've grown very fond of you." David took her hand and held it tenderly on the snowy-white tablecloth. "Might I believe that you also care for me?"

She gulped. Her face must be scarlet now, and she couldn't tear her gaze away from his earnest blue eyes if she'd wanted to, which she didn't. In fact, she thought she could stare into them for the rest of her life and never be bored.

"I. . .yes. Oh yes, David, you might. I hope you will. Because I do."

He smiled. "Ah, Mildred. You are such a delight."

"Really? Because I feel rather awkward just now."

"Please don't. It's not my intention to make you ill at ease."

Her mind whirled. Where could this lead? His words seemed directed toward a proposal of marriage, but if he was truly on his way to accept a title in the British peerage and ownership of a vast estate, how could he possibly consider her as a fitting wife? And if not marriage, then what? No, she wouldn't believe that he would suggest something more vulgar. He wasn't that type of man.

He sat back a bit but did not relinquish her hand.

"I see that you are confused. Perhaps I should have chosen a more private venue, but Mildred, I have come to admire you. In fact, I love you."

Millie's heart surged into a pounding gallop. She caught her breath but could not speak.

David smiled gently. "I am asking you to consider whether you might go to England with me, my dear—as my bride."

# CHAPTER 34

The waiter returned at the most inopportune moment possible. David released Millie's hand and sat decorously silent while the food was placed before them. Millie's lovely green eyes were downcast. She seemed intent on watching how the waiter placed the dishes.

"Will that be all, sir?" the man asked.

"Yes, thank you," David said.

The man went away, and Millie raised her gaze. "I. . .I hardly know what to say, David."

"You have not said no, and I take that with optimism."

"But you. . .your position. . ."

"Ah yes. The title. I hope you won't let that put you off. But if you think you could not bear it—all that it would entail, why then I would give up the title and the estate to my cousin. I find after great deliberation that I would rather stay in America with you than return to England alone. My dear, would you accept a proposal from David Stone, commoner, who is partner in a stagecoach line?"

Millie stared at him, her cheeks going even redder. "I should be proud to if that were the case. In fact, I might say it would make me extremely happy."

"Then that is settled—you *are* willing to marry me, at least under some circumstances." He couldn't help smiling, but Millie looked astonished.

"Do you mean you would make such a sacrifice?"

He chuckled. "For me it would hardly be a sacrifice. I have done without Stoneford and all it brings for many years, and I would hardly miss it—though I do love the place, and it holds dear memories for me. But I know I could be happy with the life I established in Oregon, particularly with someone as charming and pleasant as you by my side."

Her lips twitched, and he thought perhaps he'd nearly made her smile.

"Mildred." He reached once more for her hand.

She glanced about, looking adorably timid.

"I'm sorry," he said. "I should let you eat your supper. It wasn't fair of me to raise the subject just when you're served a meal."

She did smile then. "Indeed, sir. Most inconsiderate."

He laughed aloud and picked up his fork. "Let us eat, then, but I hope you will consider my proposal while we do. We can discuss it later."

David took a bite of his salad, but he did not like to admit even to himself how nervous she had made him. He wished he'd waited until they were in a private spot—one where he could sweep her into his arms and kiss away her doubts.

Millie peered at the salad for several seconds, apparently astonished. Perhaps she had never seen fresh greens in combination with halved grapes and bits of orange and walnuts. She picked up her fork and took an experimental bite. Her expression gratified David, telling him he'd chosen well. Wait until she tried the chicken. She would probably march to the kitchen and demand a recipe or two.

However, after three bites, Millie blotted her lips with her napkin. "The food is most excellent, sir, and I thank you for it, but I must speak to your earlier point."

"Please do," David said gravely.

"I also have come to care deeply for you and to admire your character. Nothing would make me happier than to be your wife. But I know you left Oregon with a purpose in mind. I would not like to see you put aside what you felt was your duty for my sake."

Peace settled over David. He could only feel that the Lord had brought this about. "We shall speak more of this," he said, "but I assure you, I shall not shirk my duty."

She nodded. "Good. It's just that things you've said in the past have made me wonder whether you could in good conscience hand the family's heritage and responsibilities over to your cousin."

"True, my dear. For now, I will only say that you have made me the happiest man alive."

"Indeed?"

"What? Are you surprised?"

"Yes." A tiny frown wrinkled her brow. "Frankly, I am, because I had no idea I could wield such power over you."

"I hope that you shall learn in the future the strength of that power."

Millie shivered slightly, but she did not look uneasy or discontent. She fell to her dinner with enthusiasm. David relaxed and enjoyed the meal as well, and when they were nearly finished, he slipped the waiter a coin and asked him to secure a cab for them.

"Where to now?" Millie asked once they were settled in the carriage.

"Back to the depot to pick up our luggage." David took her hand and held it in both of his. At last, he had her in a place where prying eyes could not reach. "It's odd how many miles we've traveled together, but I never until these last few days wished we were the only passengers."

She laughed aloud, and he drank in the sight of her, seemingly carefree. But her face soon sobered.

"David, did you mean it?"

"What, dearest?"

"All of it. Any of it."

"Of course." He lifted his arm to encircle her shoulders and drew her near.

Millie's eyes widened then closed as he leaned in to kiss her. He was glad they hadn't trifled with romance in Scottsburg. This was as it should be—the moment when a man sealed his love for a true-hearted woman with a kiss. She brought her hand up to his collar and returned his caress with what seemed a match for his ardor, yet with enough restraint that he was encouraged. His recent assessment of the new Mildred Evans was not wrong.

"I love you," he murmured, holding her against his chest. He considered asking her to remove her hat so he could stroke her hair but decided that would come later. He may have won her love, but the time for familiarity was not yet at hand. "Let me tell you what I have in mind for us."

"I should very much like to know," she whispered.

David smiled and kissed the tip of her nose. "I know I could be happy living a simple life with you, but you're correct about my temperament. I do feel it is my duty to take on the estate at Stoneford. If there were another heir whom I thought could run it well... but there is not. Will you still marry me, my darling, if I go to England? Would you go with me and live as the right honorable Countess of Stoneford?"

After a moment's silence, she whispered, "If you will help me. I confess I haven't the least idea of what that means."

Peregrin returned to his seat as the train's whistle let out a blast. The places opposite his were vacant, and he looked anxiously toward the door. Instead of Stone and Mrs. Evans, the two thugs were coming toward him. Teddy plopped beside him, and Wilkes eased his big frame down onto David's seat.

Peregrin gulped. "That's Mr. Stone's seat."

"Was," Teddy said.

"What do you mean?" Panic seized Peregrin by the throat. He tried to jump up, but Wilkes grabbed his wrist and squeezed.

"Sit down, Perry. You and me's going to have a little chat."

"I told you, I'll get the money."

"Oh yes, you told us that several times," Teddy said. "Well, your so-called friend didn't give it to you. Then you said you could get it anyhow."

"You were supposed to get it last night." Wilkes leaned his massive head toward Peregrin. "So where is it?"

"He didn't have any—" Peregrin looked around and lowered his voice a notch. "He didn't have any in his suitcase. But you can have these." He fished a small wooden box out of his pocket and held it out.

Teddy snatched it and opened the lid. "What's this?"

"His cuff links. They're valuable. Close it up—he'll be back any second."

The train lurched, and Wilkes let out a guffaw. "That's what you know, genius. Your pigeon has flown."

"That he has," Teddy said.

"What do you mean?"

"Stone's cut and run. He and the lady got off and didn't get back on."

Peregrin sat very still. "You're joking."

"Not us," Teddy said cheerfully. "Guess your friend forgot to tell you."

Peregrin looked out the window. They were gathering speed, and the countryside flew past.

"We've got to go back."

Wilkes placed a weighty hand on his sleeve. "No, chum, we ain't going back. This all you got? 'Cause it don't look like much."

Peregrin swallowed with difficulty. "Those are onyx cuff links. They're family heirlooms, and they're worth a lot. You could probably sell them for a hundred pounds."

"Pounds of what?" Teddy asked.

"Sterling. Or a few hundred dollars."

"Those little things?" Wilkes made a sour face. "I doubt that."

"So do I," Teddy said, "but we'll find out when we get to New York." He pocketed the box. "You still owe us."

"Please—I'll get the money. Really. In fact, if you boys wanted to stake me, I could probably win half of it back today in the smoking car."

"I seen you play poker," Wilkes said in disgust.

"Isn't that how you got into this fix in the first place?" Teddy asked.

Peregrin had no answer. His stomach began to hurt as he contemplated his future, and the train hurtled onward.

"Have you any reason to stop in Philadelphia now, my dear?" David asked the next day, as they breakfasted in the sitting room of the suite he'd insisted on engaging for her.

"I don't think so."

"If you wish to see some of your old friends, or if you'd like to shop there for your trousseau. . ."

"My trousseau?" Millie frowned.

"Why, yes. I thought you would want some new clothes before we set sail. . ." He paused, trying to read her expression. She seemed distressed, though in his experience, most women went into raptures at the prospect of a new wardrobe.

"Oh David." Her voice faltered.

"What is it, Mildred?"

"I. . .I wouldn't know what to buy. Don't you see? I have no inkling of what a countess should wear. Have you? You must."

"Well, it's been some time since I've moved in fashionable circles." He puzzled over that for a minute, then smiled. "New York. There are always a few Londoners in New York. I'll warrant we can scare up some connections of a finer sort than Peregrin Walmore. A little hobnobbing, a few introductions, and surely within a day or two we'll unearth some lady or other who can help you choose your wardrobe for the voyage."

"It sounds so complicated. Perhaps one new dress and. . .well, some sundries." Millie wouldn't meet his gaze.

"Yes, well, I think you'll need more than that, my dear. On shipboard, people dress for dinner, you know, and there will no doubt be dancing and entertainments in the evening."

"Really?" She blinked as though the concept was quite novel.

David cleared his throat. "There are some things that will probably surprise you, dearest. I know it's all happening rather quickly, but I must return to London as soon as possible, and I'd like to make the voyage before winter sets in."

"Winter? Oh, surely. There's plenty of time, isn't there?"

"Yes. I was thinking we might stay in New York two or three weeks for our honeymoon. During that time, perhaps you can outfit yourself."

"If I have some guidance." Millie had never looked more helpless and unsure of herself.

"Yes. But the first thing, it seems to me, is the wedding. Where would you like to be married?"

She swallowed hard. "Why don't you decide?"

"All right. If there's no one you wish to include in the festivities. . ."

"I have no one now that Sam is gone."

David reached for her hand. "Mildred, I'm so sorry about your brother. He wasn't such a bad fellow."

"Yes he was, but thank you for saying that. You gave him a chance at an honest life, and he ruined it. I guess that was partly my fault. But we did get another opportunity, and I tried to steer Sam straight. He just. . .he didn't want to work hard, I think, which I don't understand. Our mother taught me to dig right in when it was needed. But Sam. . .well, it just didn't *take* with him, I guess."

"Mm, I suppose you're right." David waited a moment before easing the conversation to a happier topic. "If you wish it, we could find a minister today, in this town, and be married now, before we continue our journey."

Her eyes lit. "Really? Because it doesn't matter to me where we say our vows. I'd like to do it soon though, if we can work it out."

"I'll have to inquire. There may be regulations that require a public announcement or some such thing. If that is the case, we could go on to New York and refurbish your wardrobe while we wait."

"Oh." Millie's face fell. "David, I don't like to mention this, since I am not yet your wife, but. . .would you want to marry me in my traveling dress? I do have the calico. . . ."

"I'd be happy to buy you a new gown for the wedding," he said quickly.

She flushed. "Oh, but that wouldn't be seemly, would it?"

He gazed at her lovely face. Her green eyes remained downcast as she pondered.

"What would you like to do, Mildred?" He stroked her hand slowly.

"I am not sure. I don't think it would look well for you to buy my wedding dress."

"What of the other gown you had in your bag? The one that belonged to Anne?"

She glanced up. "Would you really wish to marry me if I were wearing that?"

"Why not? I expect that Anne will consider it a good joke when we tell her someday."

Millie caught her breath. "Do you think we shall have that opportunity?"

"I dearly hope so. One of the first things I intend to do when we get home is to write to Anne and invite her and Daniel to visit us at Stoneford, with young Richard in tow of course. I want to see my little grand-nephew."

"That would be wonderful, if she found she could forgive me."

"I'm sure she already has, my dear, and I should tell you that I've mentioned you to her in my last couple of letters. In fact, I apprised her that I'd met up with you shortly after Sam died. I shall probably find at least one letter from her waiting for me in New York."

"I. . .I don't know what to say."

David smiled gently. "Just say you will marry me today if it's possible."

She looked up at him and smiled. "All right. That doesn't seem too difficult, since you are going to make the arrangements."

"Yes. And if we find it's impossible, we'll work out when we can—the soonest opportunity." He stood and pushed in his chair. "Shall I go out now and see what I can learn?"

"I suppose so."

She rose, and David stepped closer and stooped to kiss her. "You've made me very happy, Millie."

"I hope you still feel that way a month or two from now, when all your connections, as you call them, have met me."

"They will love you as I do. But just to give you some confidence, we'll find a tutor in New York, and you shall have a couple of weeks of lessons."

"Lessons on being a countess?"

"Well, on fashion and deportment and protocol—what to call a duchess and stuff of that nature. You know—how to curtsey to the queen when you are presented."

"Oh," she said in a small voice.

David chuckled. "My dear Mildred, you look as though you're headed for the gallows. I promise you, we shall have excessive fun together. I'll buy you a horse, and when we have guests you may join our shooting parties if you like. And you will never have to wash dishes or do laundry again, or to cook unless you wish to."

"That sounds lovely."

"Good." He had no doubt she would roll up her sleeves and show the cook at Stoneford how to make American biscuits. "And I'm sure there's much more that I haven't thought to tell you. Don't be afraid to ask questions."

"I shall badger you all across the Atlantic."

"I can hardly wait." He kissed her again and reluctantly left the sitting room.

"Do you, Mildred, take this man to be your lawfully wedded husband?"

Millie sucked in a deep breath. Standing here with David, in the hotel's sitting room, wearing Anne's gown, was incredible enough, but a minister was lining out the marriage vows for her. Two simple words, and her life would never be the same.

David squeezed her hand. She glanced up into his blue eyes and knew that she wanted to make this change. Though she might find some muddy weather ahead, she would happily leave behind the Evans name and her past associations. She turned to the minister and said gravely, "I do."

Five minutes later, she was irrevocably Mrs. David Stone, and her husband was jubilantly kissing her. Nothing was said of the title, as David had felt there was no need to tell the minister about it. The preacher's wife and a bellboy had come as witnesses. David paid the minister and gave the bellboy a large tip.

"Won't you join us for a piece of cake?" Millie asked them,

blushing. David had stopped at a bakery on his way back to the hotel on a whim, and she was glad that he did. To her surprise, he'd also asked for tea to be sent up. She'd almost expected him to buy a bottle of wine, but she was relieved he hadn't. Memories of James Evans's drunken state after her first wedding had brought on some apprehension, but she ought to have known David wouldn't do such a thing.

At last the three guests left them, and David gathered her into his arms.

"Happy?" he asked.

"Yes," she whispered. "This is the happiest moment of my life."

"I believe it is for me, too. And I trust there will be many more."

# CHAPTER 35

A week later, David saw Millie off for a day of shopping with Lady Ashton, the wife of a man his own age whom he'd known in his misty youth in England. They'd met in the Astor House's dining room two nights previously and again at the ballet, and Millie seemed to like Ashton's wife, so David had presumed on the marchioness's good nature and asked if she'd like to shop with his bride for suitable clothing for their upcoming voyage. Lady Ashton had jumped at the opportunity.

He'd supplied his bride of seven days with a fair amount of cash and a letter of credit from his bank. Poor Millie had looked a bit at sea, but Lady Ashton would know exactly what to do, and he wouldn't have the embarrassment of watching his blushing wife pick out undergarments and question every expenditure. He'd only succeeded in persuading her to buy one new dress so far, and she probably needed a dozen, but Millie had laughed when he said as much. He would have to do something extremely nice for Lady Ashton later, in exchange for this huge favor.

After the ladies had left the hotel, David got his hat and prepared to go out for a stroll. As he left the chamber, someone called to him, and he turned. One of the bellboys approached quickly from the stairway.

"Mr. Stone, I hoped I'd find you in. This was just delivered for you." He held out a folded sheet of paper.

"Thank you." David reached into his pocket for a coin and gave it to the young man. He took the message and opened it.

"Do you wish me to wait for a reply, sir?"

David frowned as he scanned the note. *A gentleman named Perry Walmore has been arrested for vagrancy and claims you are his relation and can vouch for him. Sgt. T. H. Moore, 1ˢᵗ Precinct.*

"No, thank you. I shall tend to this myself."

The bellboy nodded and left. David sighed. It seemed he would have to make a stop at the police station. But it wouldn't hurt Walmore to sit there for a while. David decided to shop for some new shirts and linen first, and to order flowers for Lady Ashton while he decided how much money to withdraw from the bank. Because he had no doubt that extricating Peregrin Walmore from the police station would require cash.

Millie tried to add up the prices of all the clothes she was buying, but her head began to spin when they topped $250.

"This is too much!"

"Nonsense," said her shopping companion, Lady Sarah Ashton, known inexplicably to her intimates as Hoppy. "Your husband said the sky was the limit, and he charged me with seeing you have clothes appropriate for everything from a gallop in Hyde Park to a palace ball."

Millie gulped. "I had no idea. I mean—forty dollars for one gown? Really?"

Hoppy laughed. "Not just any gown. An elegant one worthy of the most exclusive ball. And really, my dear, that isn't so extravagant. You'll pay much more in Europe."

Millie shook her head in disbelief, but Hoppy was already fingering the skirt of another dress. "I haven't had this much fun in years! Now, if *my* husband gave me carte blanche for an entire new wardrobe, I'd buy out the stores without blinking. But Ashton is so tight-fisted, I'm lucky to get a few new gowns for the season and a promenade dress each spring. Now go try on that lavender poplin. It would be perfect for an at-home dress, though I'm not sure it's your best color." She eyed Millie critically. "Perhaps they could do it up in green."

"Oh no," Millie cried. "I can't have them doing special dress-making for me."

"Why not? Still, with a bright-colored fichu, that dress would look sweet. Perhaps the modiste can find something."

They spent another hour in the exclusive shop. The owner was only too happy to bring out garment after garment for Millie's inspection. The newlyweds had been in New York nearly a week, but Millie was still shocked at least six times a day by the sights she saw, the extravagance David surrounded her with, and the cost of it all.

She and Hoppy moved on to a millinery shop, where Millie would have swooned if she were the swooning kind of woman. Hoppy insisted she needed at least five hats for the voyage.

"Big hats are all the rage now, especially for promenades. And the sun is unrelenting on deck. Of course, you'll need a carriage bonnet and an opera bonnet—oh my dear, how thrilling to be able to buy multiple hats without guilt!"

"But I do feel guilty." Millie eyed the array of headgear in dismay. "Do you think David realizes how much hats cost?"

"I'm sure he does," Hoppy replied with a mischievous smile. "If not, we shall educate him. Oh, and it's fine to call him 'David' to me, but when you are in polite company, you must refer to him as 'Stoneford.'"

"Stoneford? But that's not his name. That's his house."

Hoppy brushed that aside with a wave of her hand, which bore a pink kid glove with a row of pearl buttons on the cuff. "It's his title, or will be within hours of your landing in England. Such a bore. Now, come, this is serious business. And we haven't been to the cobbler yet. You'll need kid boots and dancing slippers and— oh Mildred, shopping with you is *so* entertaining! But if we don't proceed with it, our dear menfolk will be wondering where we are. And you'll need at least an hour to dress for dinner this evening."

Although Millie returned to the hotel with trepidation, David seemed pleased with the plethora of parcels that had begun to arrive in midafternoon. Millie could hardly move about the bedchamber, but one of the hotel's maids assisted with unpacking everything. At the end of an hour, Millie's booty was all properly stored.

"Would you like me to draw you a bath, ma'am?" the maid asked.

"Yes, that sounds delightful, if there's time. Thank you."

Millie still wasn't accustomed to the luxury of bathing daily if she wished, or having another person dress her hair and help her put on the complicated clothing she had acquired, but she thought, with a little practice, she could get used to it. The full crinolines that were coming into fashion were a trial, but Hoppy had given her an impromptu lesson in one of the dressmakers' shops on how to manage the full skirts and petticoats.

She followed David's practice of tipping the hotel staff generously, using the ample supply of cash he'd given her for the purpose. Her own days of poverty hung close in her memory, and she didn't scruple to reward those who served her.

At last she was ready to go down to dinner, but she felt exhausted. She stepped out into the sitting room, and David leaped to his feet from the velvet-covered armchair where he'd been reading a newspaper.

"You look lovely, my darling." He walked toward her with gleaming eyes, his hands outstretched to her, and Millie was glad she'd made the effort and not suggested they take a quiet supper in their room. He was dressed in formal clothes—or at least, the most formal attire she'd ever seen him wear. How would she ever learn all the subtleties of fashion? Even David's choice of neckties seemed critical now that they were "in society." The other guests at the Astor House seemed overly preoccupied with appearance.

"Thank you." She accepted his kiss. "Hoppy was tireless, but I confess I'm a bit fatigued."

"I'm sorry."

"Well, the scented bath helped."

"We shall not make a long night of it. Ashton wanted to go to the theater, but I declined for us—I hope you don't mind."

"Not at all." Millie had enjoyed the ballet the previous evening, but in attending she had realized that David was right about her need for new clothes.

"I told Ashton perhaps we'd go with them tomorrow evening, if you felt so inclined. Apparently there is a new musical comedy program that's the talk of the town."

"It might be fun."

He stood back and looked her up and down. "That gown suits you."

"Thank you." Millie fingered the braid that trimmed her bodice. Hoppy had instructed her to wear the apple-green dress this evening, and so she felt confident it was appropriate, but what would she do when they left New York and Hoppy? David had said she would have a personal maid in England, and she supposed she needed one to help her avoid making social mistakes. That thought brought on a new anxiety. "And am I to call Ashton 'my lord'? I think that is what you said."

"Yes, darling. I'm sorry this is so nerve-racking for you."

"I don't wish to embarrass you."

David smiled. "If you make a mistake, we shall all laugh and set you straight, but it will all be good-natured. Come."

He drew her hand through his arm, and Millie raised her chin. She would study harder than she ever had in school, and somehow, by the time they reached England, she would know at least the basics of aristocratic manners. The odd thing was that, in spite of her apprehension, she was deliriously happy. One glance at David told her that he was, too. She wished Sam could see her as Lady Stoneford—but that thought flew from her head as David led her down the grand staircase.

Merrileigh greeted the caller—Mr. Iverson, from the solicitor's office—with her husband in the drawing room and took her seat on the sofa. She hoped this visit was occasioned by dire news. If Peregrin had done his job, today's tidings should be momentous, and she could begin packing up her household for the move to Stoneford.

Iverson bowed to his host and took a chair near the fireplace, while Randolph sauntered over and sat beside her.

The solicitor smiled at them. "You'll be happy to hear that we've had a new message from David Stone. He says he'll arrive in England later next month. . .with his wife."

"Wife? What—" Merrileigh stared at him.

"Well now," Randolph said, smiling, "when did this happy event take place?"

"Recently, I gather," Iverson said. "They are honeymooning in New York and plan to embark the second week of October on a steamship. We can expect them to dock by the twenty-fifth."

Merrileigh tried not to show her dismay. The last thing she'd expected—or wanted—to hear was that David was enjoying newly wedded bliss. The second-to-last was that he was alive, but she hadn't allowed herself to totally discount the possibility.

"There's time to direct congratulatory messages to the couple at the Astor House."

"I think we'll just wait until they reach England," Randolph said. "It will be interesting to meet the bride, I'm sure."

"Is she American?" Merrileigh asked.

"I assume so. He didn't give any details."

Merrileigh sniffed, thinking of Peregrin's message stating that David had a woman he'd met in the wilderness traveling with him. No doubt this was the one he had married—a person of questionable morals. The idea sickened her—that a coarse American doxy would take her rightful place as mistress of Stoneford. It was unthinkable. She would never forgive David for this, nor her brother for not preventing it.

The carriage drive at Stoneford was illuminated on Christmas Eve by two long rows of lanterns. Though the temperature outside hovered just above freezing, David had insisted that the front gardens be lit as well. All the rooms on the ground floor and second story glowed bright, and every fireplace held a coal fire that the servants replenished often.

The extravagance awed Millie. Though David was not one to waste money, he didn't stint when he had a purpose in mind. She knew that tonight his purpose was to impress the hundred guests and to prove that the Earl of Stoneford had indeed returned. She thought a small part of his show of ostentation had to do with his cousin, Randolph Stone. Randolph and his wife had accepted the invitation, and indeed were staying two nights. Most of the guests were leaving after tonight's festivities, but a select dozen would spend Christmas with Lord and Lady Stoneford. All of those staying had arrived and were settled in their rooms, preparing for the party.

Millie was terrified that she would make her husband look bad. But in the last two months, she had received a great deal of help from her staff, especially her housekeeper, Mrs. Lane, and her lady's maid, Briley. These women had been hired by the solicitor's office before the master and mistress arrived, and Mr. Iverson had assured Millie that if she was not completely satisfied with their performance, she could let them go and hire other domestics. Millie doubted she would have the heart to do so, but happily she liked both women and was thankful for their skill and their willingness to aid an inexperienced mistress.

She was confident at least in her outfit—Briley had dressed her for the evening in an elegant moiré gown of shimmering green. Though she'd purchased a full half-dozen dresses in New York, it seemed that wasn't nearly enough. This gown had been made especially for her in London. David had suggested a quick trip to the continent so that she could visit a famous dressmaker in Paris, but Millie had gently but firmly declined, reminding him of all they needed to do at home before the holidays.

She examined her gown in the long mirror in her room. She wasn't sure about the multiple flounces that graced the skirt, but the dressmaker had assured her that this style was the height of fashion.

"Our first guests are arriving, dearest. Are you ready?"

She turned toward the doorway. David stood there, resplendent in his evening clothes.

"I think so." She took a last glance at the mirror. Her hair, in a simple upsweep, looked fine to her. She lightly touched the emerald-and-gold necklace at her throat. It was finer than anything she'd ever seen, let alone owned, and she was certain David had spent a great deal of money on it, though she would never ask. He'd brought it to her their last night in New York, along with a gold ring bearing a sizable diamond. "To make up for the engagement present I should have given you," he explained, and she couldn't make him return the jewelry. He'd have been too disappointed.

She'd let him slip it onto her finger, next to her wedding ring, and she'd seen then that he drew great joy from giving her gifts. She hoped he wasn't overspending, but she could hardly deny him this pleasure. Perhaps in the future she could gently encourage him to bring her small things that would still have great meaning.

He stepped up behind her and encircled her with his arms. He bent to kiss her temple.

"You look lovely."

"Thank you," Millie murmured.

"Nervous?"

"Yes. Our first party."

"The first of many. I hope you enjoy yourself."

"I shall try. Oh—" She turned and eyed him uneasily. "What shall I say if Mrs. Stone inquires about her brother again?"

"You can refer her to me if you like. Just tell her again that you last saw him on the train, and he was fine then. I'll speak to Randolph before they go home and tell him a little more. I don't know whether they will want to do anything for Walmore or not, but I shall happily leave the matter to them now."

"Yes," Millie said. "I'm glad you got him out of custody though. I couldn't have borne it if we'd had to see his sister and know he was in jail or in mortal danger from those thugs."

David had paid a small fine for Peregrin in New York and assured the police that he was who he said he was. Then, at Millie's pleading, he had paid the young man's debt but impressed upon him that he must never ask David for help again.

"Well, we couldn't very well leave him in the situation he'd gotten into, but I shall tell Randolph I am done with it. Walmore will never receive another penny from me. What he makes of his future is up to him."

"I agree," Millie said. "And thank you."

David shrugged. "Well, I've learned more about the affair that sent him into exile, and I think it will be cleared up soon. He'll probably be back in England before another year is up. But I know you couldn't sleep if you knew he was still in danger when we sailed, and I do want you to sleep well—especially now."

She smiled and nestled into his arms for a kiss.

A few minutes later, they walked down the staircase together. She could still hardly believe her husband owned all of this—the elegant mansion and its expansive grounds, with tenant farms, a mill, and a large stable that David had already begun to stock with fine horses.

In just two months, he had put the estate to rights. The steward that had served his brother Richard had kept things going on a modest scale, but David had great plans for the spring. He was positive he could make the estate more than self-sustaining, and his employees and tenants had caught his optimism and flung themselves into the work.

Meanwhile, he told Millie, they would get used to living here and relax during the winter. Millie knew he was letting her get her feet wet slowly. The social connections she had met already had let her know that they hoped the Stones would take an active part in "the season" in London next spring. That, it seemed, involved lots of parties and entertaining, but it would not be a problem. Her husband also owned a townhouse in London's most fashionable quarter.

Among the first guests to enter the large drawing room off the front hall were Randolph and Merrileigh Stone. Millie inhaled deeply and pasted on a smile. She had met the couple once before this visit, a week after she and David had landed in England. Randolph was all right, rather bluff and hearty, and Millie suspected he wasn't overly intellectual. Merrileigh, on the other hand, seemed much more clever than her husband, but also a bit sly. She didn't quite look down her nose at the new countess, but Millie got the impression she would love to do so, if only David weren't quite so watchful.

"What a lovely gown, milady," she said as she grasped Millie's hand.

SUSAN PAGE DAVIS

"Thank you. Yours is quite charming." Millie swept a glance over Merrileigh's gray-and-mulberry dress. She thought the colors made the wearer look older, but of course she said nothing of that. "I trust your quarters are comfortable?"

"Yes, very nice," Merrileigh said, "though I confess Randolph had hoped for the rooms overlooking the rear gardens."

David, standing beside Millie, jumped in. "I'm sorry, but I've put the Duke of Marlborough in those rooms."

Randolph, who stood before David looking very slick and over-groomed, with his hair styled a bit too foppishly and his cravat arranged in an extravagant waterfall, raised his hand in protest.

"Our rooms are fine, Cousin. Very comfortable, I assure you. I merely made a passing reference to the time we stayed in the other suite several years ago. But I'm sure every accommodation in this house is lovely. I especially like the painting over the mantel in my current chamber."

"Ah yes, the Battle of Trafalgar." David nodded. "Well, Lady Stoneford and I hope you enjoy this visit as much as you did that other, though we shall all be put in mind of Richard and Elizabeth, I'm sure, and wish they were still with us."

"Of course," Randolph murmured.

Merrileigh opened her mouth as if to speak again, but her husband steered her aside to make way for other guests. Richly dressed people were now pouring in, and the butler dutifully announced them all, but within ten minutes, Millie's head swam with names and faces. The women she tried to organize in her mind by what they wore, but soon her brain was overtaxed by the variety and sheer volume of details she'd tried to store, and she gave up.

She stuck close to David during the hour before dinner. It seemed everyone in the world—or at least in England—wanted to meet her. Most were very kind and felicitated the bride and groom with seeming sincerity. Women ogled David shamelessly, and Millie wondered how many had mourned the dashing young man when he left their circle twenty years ago.

"My dear, all the men are agog at you," he whispered in her ear midway through the hour.

"Are they?" She looked up into his eyes and smiled. "I'm afraid I've been watching the women."

"Studying their fashions? Some are rather extreme, are they not?"

"Actually, I was watching them study you."

He smiled and squeezed her gently about the waist. "I'm sure they're curious about my American bride. Let me assure you that so far you've been the perfect hostess."

She relaxed a little. It wasn't so hard when you had a score of servants keeping things flowing smoothly. At dinner, she sat between two gentlemen who seemed determined to monopolize her attention. She swiveled back and forth between them, answering their questions about life in America and how she had met David, without giving too much detail.

"We first met in the Oregon Territory," she told the duke. "But we were only in proximity for a few days then. I believe Stoneford was doing some mining business at the time. After I left the area, I didn't see him again for more than year. We were reunited on a stagecoach journey."

That was the most she gave out about their early dealings. She and David had discussed it, and both saw the wisdom of not revealing more than the bare minimum.

Later, when the ladies had retired to what was known as the music room—which was graced by a spinet—one of them invited her to a house party in Yorkshire the last week of February.

"We'll have prodigious fun," she predicted. "And I hear you like to ride. Stoneford told my husband that he's bought you a hunter."

"Well yes," Millie said, racking her brain for the lady's name and coming up empty. "I thank you very much, but I probably shan't be doing much riding by then."

"Oh?"

Every eye turned upon her, and Millie felt her face go scarlet.

"Don't tell me you're increasing, my dear," Merrileigh said in a tone that could be construed as either horrified or merely an exaggerated surprise.

"Well. . ." Had she made a terrible social blunder? "I've only just seen the physician yesterday, but he thinks it likely."

The Duchess of Marlborough smiled and reached to squeeze her hand. "That's marvelous news, my dear. I wish you the best. It's high time there was a child in this house again."

After that the ice was broken. All of the women congratulated Millie and doled out advice. One assured her that motherhood was the most noble of callings, and another decreed that David would be the dotingest father ever. Merrileigh was the only one who said nothing. She sat on a brocade-covered wing chair in a corner with a dour expression on her lips—but that might be attributed to the coffee she sipped.

When at last the gentlemen joined them, all were laughing and grinning at David. Millie knew at once that he had also broken the news of the impending heir to his friends. He made his way to her side and joined her on the velvet settee.

Leaning close, she whispered, "I see the news is out."

"Yes. I hope you don't mind awfully. They're too polite to mention it now, but be sure all their wives will know before midnight."

"Oh, they know," Millie said. "I do hope I didn't cause a scandal. I didn't mean to announce it, but it just came out."

"Don't fret, my love." He raised her hand to his lips.

One of the men laughed—the Earl of something, Millie thought. Glastonbury? Hartford? How could she possibly keep all of their names and titles straight?

"Well, now, Stoneford, I'm impressed with what you've done here in such a short time," the gentleman said. "I hope you and your lady will have a long and happy life here."

"Thank you," David said. "We hope so, too." He squeezed Millie's hand, and she echoed the sentiment in her heart.

# Discussion Questions

1. Millie has ambivalent feelings toward her half brother, Sam. Do you think she is wise to leave him and strike out on her own?

2. Why is it so important to Millie to explain her actions to David?

3. Why doesn't David want to talk to Millie?

4. David is considered a gentleman by nearly everyone, but Millie has to earn the right to be thought of as a lady. Why, and is this fair? Who finds it hardest to think of her as a lady?

5. If you were David, what would you have done to help Mrs. Caudle when her husband died? What would you have done to help Millie? Did David do enough? Too much? What limits do you make on charitable giving?

6. Peregrin has several weaknesses that lead him into trouble. His sister is a much stronger character—and yet her heart is no purer. Why do you think Merrileigh gets into less trouble than Peregrin?

7. After the accident, Millie concentrates her efforts on protecting David and seeing that he gets care. Do you think she acts selfishly? Should she have helped the other stagecoach passengers?

8. Halfway through the book, Mille takes care of David, but later on—once they begin their train journey—the roles are reversed, and David protects Millie. Has Millie sacrificed her independence by allowing this?

9. Given the conventions of the day and the perception of "propriety" in the 1850s, do you find Millie bold, conservative, or simply practical?

10. Describe David, Millie, Merrileigh, and Peregrin using only one definitive word for each character.

11. Millie's confidence slips near the end of the story, as she prepares to enter David's world. What things do each of them do to overcome this?

12. David slips back into the privileged class quite easily after his stint on the frontier, but Millie finds it harder to deal with menial workers and servants. Compare their relationships with porters, waiters, and maids to your own attitude toward people who serve you. Are you ever embarrassed to let a worker serve you?

13. Millie's spiritual transformation takes her on a perilous road, and her faith is tested often. One of the first rough spots she encounters is her separation from her brother. How would you handle the death of a loved one who was committing a crime?

---

# About the Author

Susan Page Davis is the author of more than thirty published novels. She's a Carol Award Winner and a two-time winner of the Inspirational Readers' Choice Award. In 2011, Susan was named Favorite Author of the Year in the 18th Annual Heartsong Awards. A native of Maine, she and her husband, Jim, now live in western Kentucky.